A LATIN UNSEEN

Anthea Ingham

MINERVA PRESS
MONTREUX LONDON WASHINGTON

A LATIN UNSEEN

ISBN 1 86106 297 4

First Published 1997 by
MINERVA PRESS
195 Knightsbridge
London SW7 1RE

Printed in Great Britain by
Antony Rowe Ltd, Chippenham, Wiltshire

A LATIN UNSEEN

Contents

Afterwards

"It's all covered with jam," says Nigel Box, holding up a glutinous sheet of exercise paper.

"Oh dear, oh dear," says his mother, hopelessly. It is an expression she uses frequently. Indeed her whole life is punctuated with 'oh dears'.

Nigel is sitting at the kitchen table, with his Latin books before him. They too have a sad and sticky air.

"I've got it all wrong, anyway," says Nigel. "I hate Latin."

"Oh dear, oh dear," says Mrs Box automatically. She is a plain woman, prematurely grey. She is struck by a reassuring thought.

"You used to like it, dear."

"That was in Italy," says Nigel, "when Michael explained it." He picks his nose thoughtfully. He is as unattractive as his mother. "I liked Michael. I liked Fenella too. She was nice."

"We don't talk about Fenella," says Mrs Box, quite firmly for her. She is standing at the sink, washing up. She would not dare ask Nigel to help.

"There's Fatso," says Nigel, "you'd better get the cake out."

They watch Kate Small lumbering up the garden path. Nigel thinks she approaches the house that way so she won't get stuck in the gate at the front of the house. She is a truly enormous woman.

"You mustn't call her that, Nigel," says Mrs Box. "It's very kind of her to give you all this help for your scholarship."

"Well, she's better than Dad," says Nigel, "not so boring."

"Oh dear, oh dear," says Mrs Box.

"Aren't you going to let her in?" says Nigel. His mother is so stupid.

"Oh yes," she says, wiping her hands on her brown gathered skirt. "Whatever am I thinking of?"

Kate Small doesn't waste any time. She lowers herself down onto the bench opposite Nigel, groaning quietly.

"Nice cake," she says, helping herself. "Have you done that unseen, Nigel?"

It is a signal for Mrs Box to go and leave them to the Latin, but she is not quick on the uptake and stands, dish-mop in hand, looking foolish. Many thoughts struggle through her mind and tangle themselves together: should she offer more cake, open the packet of biscuits – but her husband likes those kept for himself, has he taken his pills, and, although it's very kind of Mrs Small to help, it does bring back that awful Italy business, and...?

"Why don't you clear off, Mum?" says Nigel. "We can't get on with you standing there."

"I hope," says Kate to Nigel, "you'll learn to speak to your mother properly when you go to your new school."

"I've got to get the scholarship first," says Nigel.

"Hmm," says Kate, "read me what you've done."

"I'll go into the other room then," says Mrs Box, smiling weakly. She adds, "I shan't be going anywhere." Mrs Small, who can sometimes see into the future, thinks Pamela Box never spoke a truer word.

"Start translating, Nigel." Nigel looks up sulkily. "It doesn't make any sense in the middle," he says.

"Yes, it does," says Kate. "Read me what you've done."

Nigel picks up the jam stained paper and reads:

"'When I was sailing through Lake Larium...'"

"That's Como," says Kate, "Lake Como. Go on."

"'... a certain old man showed me a house whose bedroom jutted out...'"

"Good..."

"'... over the lake. 'From this,' he said, 'once our fellow townswoman threw herself with her husband...'"

"Good. You see you can do it." Nigel scowls, trying to read his writing,

"'To me asking why she had done this, she said, 'My husband was affected by a serious illness'..."

"*Gravissimo* is a superlative adjective," says Kate.

"All right," says Nigel crossly, "a very serious illness. 'She begged her husband...' I can't get this, it doesn't make sense..."

"'She begged,'" says Kate, "'that they might die together ...'"

"Oh, I get it. 'Therefore she bound herself to her husband and threw herself into the lake...' That's stupid."

"Why?" says Kate.

"Well," says Nigel, licking the bits of jam off his fingers, "nobody would tie themselves to another person and throw themselves into a lake."

"They might," says Kate. "The Latin says he was very ill, remember."

"Well, I think it's stupid."

"Do you?" says Kate. Her little eyes narrow and narrow and almost disappear into the folds of fat on her face, just like they had when she was being the sibyl in that cave place at Cumae.

"Carry on," she says.

"'I, although I am a townsman, have...'"

"Had, not have, it's pluperfect."

"'... had never heard about this deed before, not because the deed was not famous, but because... because...' I can't..."

"'Because she who did it was...' now let me think," says Kate, "of a good translation for *ingloria*... ordinary, self-effacing, no... Ah, I know!... modest."

"That's stupid too," says Nigel.

"Why?" says Kate, looking wistfully at the unopened packet of biscuits. "Why is it stupid?"

"Well," says Nigel, picking at the jam with his finger nail, "it spoils the story really, I mean..." extracting the red lump from his nails, "... it doesn't matter whether she's modest or not."

"Oh, but it does," says Kate. "It's the whole point." For a moment it looks as if her eyes are going to disappear again, but she can be remarkably sharp when you least expect it,

"Stop doing disgusting things with the jam, Nigel Box, and tell me why *morerentur* is in the subjunctive."

Chapter I

At Ciampino Airport

"My God," says Michael, surveying the coach party and speaking *sotto voce*. "I've seen some rum collections in my time, but these beat the lot. I feel this course is going to be the nadir of my career. I feel I have reached the lowest part of Hades, Erebus, the bodiless regions of Dis."

Fenella smiles at him.

"You always say that, darling," she says, "but do keep away from the microphone. We don't want them to hear your views, do we, Gino?" Gino, who drives the coach, smiles at Fenella. He has no English.

"I'm going to have a fag," says Michael, poised on the steps. He hands her a plastic bag bulging with bottles of scent.

"Have some splash, Fen," he says.

For a minute Fenella watches him descending the steps, this man that she has loved (through two marriages) for more than twenty years. She has not seen him for two, not since his marriage to Tabitha. And now she is filled with the overwhelming happiness that his presence always inspires in her.

Then she picks up the microphone and welcomes them in the warm, friendly way that she has developed, partly out of the sweetness of her nature and partly out of the experience that has come to her over the past twenty years.

She sees before her sixteen earnest teachers of Classics, whose desire for culture, lavatories and sex will become apparent to her over the ensuing week. She sees potential troublemakers presently concealed behind anoraks, glasses, linen hats, maps, textbooks, cameras and bulging backpacks. Sure enough, one emerges almost instantly.

"Excuse me," says a sharp voice. The voice has a face to match, thin and severe, its owner addresses Fenella peremptorily.

"I should like to put my stick at the front." Miss Aitchinson wishes people to know about the stick. Tall and thin and of unpleasingly sharp aspect, she has not found human sympathy readily coming her way. The stick has proved in recent months an invaluable adjunct. She has learned to make the statement of her infirmity at an early stage. She does not wish to be pre-empted by rival disabilities.

"I'm afraid we're rather short of space at the front," says Fenella in her reasonable way. "I'm sure you're safe popping it under your seat. Gino has quite a full house at the front here." She indicates Gino's collection of gee-gaws, statuettes of the Virgin, statuettes of girls who certainly aren't, a bunch of artificial flowers, a rosary and a number of furry animals once left behind by an English school party.

Fenella's refusal to accommodate the stick has pleased the party. As teachers themselves, they appreciate the wisdom of not acceding to the request of the attention seeker.

"We are so extremely fortunate," commences Fenella, "in having Dr Michael Thorpe-Smith to lecture to us on this tour. Michael has just had to pop out for a minute..." Why would he insist on standing out there in full view of them all, with his fag on?

Caroline, gawky and red-haired, gives a little gasp when she hears that attractive courier woman call him Michael, just as if he was an ordinary person. She can hardly believe he is actually here in the coach, well, just outside – can he be smoking a cigarette? You don't expect the author of *The Romans in Our Lives* to be indulging in such activities, but licence must be afforded to genius; and perhaps she herself would be addressing him as Michael by the end of the course. She wonders if he likes red hair.

"Michael, as you know," continues Fenella, "is the foremost authority on Imperial Rome and author of numerous books on Roman poetry..." ('Ah yes, darling, that is why you left me for Jemima; you traded me in for a father-in-law who would publish them...')

"Michael has also recently presented the controversial television series *Bread and Circuses*, concerning the brutality of Imperial Rome. Michael... ah! Here he is now."

And there he is. Quite restored by his fag. He is smiling his lovely golden-boy smile (the one that appears on the back of the paperback edition of *Horace, The Man as Lover*), a smile that is admittedly a little more difficult to achieve now he is nearing the half century, but a smile that nevertheless has undoubted potency behind it. He is gathering his notes and microphone to himself in the effortless way that is so much his hallmark, when there is movement from the back of the coach. It is the enormous bulk of the lady whose surname, by some quirk of fate is Small, and whose archaeologist husband, Roy, is an old crony of Michael's. She is propelling before her an extremely thin and lost looking man. Fenella is irresistibly reminded of a mother seal with her cub.

"Fenella," she says, "this gentleman has left his mackintosh at the airport."

Everyone cranes their neck, to see the large one and the loser of mackintoshes (everyone except Percival Jeavons, who wishes to show his total lack of interest in the doings of lesser mortals).

"Yes," says the large lady, who oddly has a small high-pitched voice, "he has left it somewhere."

Fenella looks at the thin one, takes in the sports jacket with the patches at the elbows, and the trousers that are too short and too tight, and sees how it will be. There will be many other misadventures befalling poor Gerouin Stover before the week is much older.

Gerouin himself is miserable and embarrassed; he wasn't going to say anything about the mackintosh, but she had found him out, this large lady, and exposed him.

"I'm very sorry," he says unhappily, "I don't know how it happened. I had it with me at the baggage place." He stands exposed in his sports jacket. He feels himself already marked out as an object of contempt, just as he always is at school. He had hoped that just this once, a little time might have passed before he was found out.

"Never mind," says Fenella kindly, "let's go and see if we can find it, shall we?" Gerouin looks at her, heartened. What a nice lady she is. His eyes fasten on what most men's eyes fasten on when they meet Fenella, not her pretty pale face and abundant golden hair, but her amazingly full and curvaceous breasts. He feels he will find comfort, not, obviously, in the breasts themselves (pretty women, he appreciates, are not for him), but they are nevertheless a symbol of kindliness. He will not mind telling her when he loses things.

He knows, nevertheless, that the course members will not be as tolerant. Already he can sense they have taken against him, for they will now be delayed; he will have kept them waiting. He senses irritated shuffling and angry sighs.

"And while you're waiting..." (Oh, how Gerouin feels the knife in the wound!) "... we shan't be long... please do take advantage of Gino's wonderful modern coach. He's only..." (She smiles at Gino to mollify him too, he is tapping his fingers on the steering wheel) "... He's only bought it two months ago..."

"Mafia money?" queries Michael in Fenella's ear.

"Gino's cousin, Anna..." ("*Può stare, Anna per favore...*") "...will be coming round with coffee and mineral water."

Anna emerges from a recess somewhere near the back. She has been crouching over a machine that might conceivably contain coffee. She is most definitely not Gino's cousin, as Fenella knows well, having been persuaded by Gino to find him a room with a double bed in the Hotel Vittoria. And now Anna and Gino have almost certainly had a row. Anna looks unkempt and sultry. She is wearing a very tight black dress, a crucifix and a cardigan. She carries with her a powerful aroma of sweat, garlic and sex.

Everyone cranes their neck for a second time (all sorts of untoward things seem to be occurring). Everyone, that is, except Percival Jeavons, who has no interest, he wishes people to note, in either Anna or her machine. On the whole people are puzzled by Anna: they do not understand her function in this course on the Romans in South Italy. They rather resent her...

Gino they have to accept, as the driver, but they do not want any other spurious Italians coming between them and their Roman Studies.

Fenella, shepherding Gerouin before her, does not think for a moment she will be successful in locating the mackintosh, but she can see it is important to him in the face of the unspoken hostility of the course members. This is good of her because she would dearly like to hear Michael's introductory talk. Two years have passed without him; now she longs not to miss a minute of his company.

"Let's see what we can do," says Fenella, smiling at Gerouin as they dismount the steps. "I hope I haven't forgotten all my Italian."

Michael stands up and surveys his audience. Although he has made derogatory remarks about them to Fenella, he actually cares very much that they should feel something of the fascination that he feels for the Romans. He hates people to think of the past as dead and buried; he wants to unseal it, breathe life into it and make it part of their experience, so that their lives are enriched by it. It is what he has been trying to do with his books, lectures and television series over the past twenty years. In his quest to do this he has sacrificed Fenella, not to mention his first wife and daughters.

"Ladies and gentlemen, colleagues..." He is immediately in full spate. A lock of hair (not so plentiful as once) falls across his forehead. From time to time he tosses it back as if it is troublesome to him to cope with such an unruly shock. His denim shirt is open (three buttons worth) revealing a manly chest (grey hairs nestle among the blond) upon which sits a medallion which is, in fact, a Roman coin, a rather rare one from the Early Republic which he himself has dug up on an early excavation, in those days when he had to get his hands dirty.

Lightly he brushes aside his erudition and tells them they will be travelling down the Appian Way and visiting the Lago di Nemi. There is a great rustling at this point as everyone (not Percival – does he not know all there is to know about the lake anyway?) gets out pads of paper and exercise books. Caroline is so excited (she was sure he was addressing his words directly to her) that she drops her bargain bundle of biros and has to grovel under the seat. How awful if he thinks her clumsy!

He is telling them how they will retrace the poet Horace's footsteps down the Appian Way. He has made his own translation from the Satires. Percival sighs audibly: he himself has published, admittedly at his own expense, a very erudite translation. Although it is not in the bookshops, you can obtain a copy by sending twenty-five pounds and writing directly to him. Michael's translation is light and frothy. He makes them laugh with his description of Horace having the runs at Aricia. He hopes the same fate won't befall them. (No, indeed, Penny Diver is very conscious of the twelve lavatory rolls she has packed away in her luggage.) Would they mind if he read them a little from Strabo? He wants them to feel some of the awe and mystery of the writer, so they must excuse him if the translation is a little free. Percival Jeavons sighs again.

"The temple," he says, "lies in a sacred grove and in front of it is a lake which resembles the wide open spaces of the sea." He tosses back the troublesome lock of hair. "It is encircled by high and rugged mountains which embrace the temple and the waters which are bottomless. Just imagine, bottomless water. You go down and down forever and never feel ground beneath your feet." He shudders – this is not affectation. This he can feel with horrific clarity. "You can see," he continues, "the springs which feed the lake. One of them is called Egeria... I'm sure," he continues, "you all remember from your Livy some very suspect goings on between King Numitor and the nymph Egeria. And, talking of nymphs, how are you getting on with the drinks, Anna?" Anna, who is doing nothing and looking sulky, smiles flirtatiously at him.

"*Va bene*," she says. Gino scowls.

Michael goes on to tell them about the cult of Hippolytus and Diana at the Sacred temple. As Michael reads, red-haired Caroline, who has never experienced sexual desire, feels a strange aching and yearning for she knows not what. She knows she would like him to notice her. She clears her throat and asks him if he would read the lines again. She feels very bold and people give her funny looks, particularly the pretty dark-haired girl called Miriam who is sitting next to her. Michael, however, beams at her. He loves Virgil and is delighted when others love it too. This time he reads the Virgil in the original. He reads beautifully, his tongue gliding over the hexameters mellifluously.

William Thornton, who has the text to hand, offers to share it with Percival Jeavons. He is sure he must be quite a scholar, as he sighs so irritably when Michael reads. He has been trying to pluck up enough courage to address him, and this offering of the text seems an excellent entrée into his good offices but Percival brushes the offer aside.

"I have it by heart," he says. "For the last twenty years I have learned ten lines of Virgil every morning."

"Gosh," says William. It is difficult to know what else to say.

Now Anna is offering them coffee. William thinks he will venture upon a little Italian (he has been to evening classes).

"Una pa... du zuccheri." But, as Anna does not understand, he has to forgo the sugar. Percival gestures her away. He cannot bear the sight of this sluttish woman near him.

Fenella returns with the thin man. There is no sign of a mackintosh.

Now there is a frisson of excitement running through the coach. They are about to embark on the course. Some have saved up for it, others have had it paid for them by the educational establishments for which they work. All is before them! A week of erudition.

Miriam, however, small neat and pretty, is not happy. She thinks continuously of the two small boys she has left at home with her husband. She didn't want to come on this course anyway. It was her Head who had told her that she must come if she wanted her Classics job to remain secure. It is the first time she has left Timothy (three) and Joseph (four). Joe is on antibiotics and she wonders whether her husband, John, will remember he must have the doses regularly. She wishes, too, she was sitting next to a nice man instead of this dowdy red-haired girl, but, alas, with the exception of Michael, there doesn't seem to be much on offer. It is all very depressing. Her eyes fill with tears. Penny, sitting across the aisle to her, searches methodically through her knapsack, selects one of the twelve rolls of lavatory paper, and offers it to her in silence. She is not very sorry for Miriam but she is glad to see the lavatory paper vindicated at the earliest possible opportunity.

"No, thank you," sniffs Miriam, "I have some tissues." Penny silently replaces the cylinder; the last vestiges of sympathy with Miriam have gone with the refusal of the lavatory paper. She has not wanted to come on this course very much either, but, since Patrick left with the young PE teacher two years ago, she hasn't wanted to do much anyway.

She feels, however, she ought to make an effort. Her resolve has been strengthened by the fact that the County will pay. She wonders if she will find a new husband here. Her eyes rake through the men on their own. She has unfortunately already met with one rebuff. She had tried to sit next to the rather good-looking man in the seat in front, but he had pointed to a large wooden box on the seat beside him. Apparently he could not be separated from it.

And here they are, driving along the Appian Way. How many times they have met the Appian Way in Latin unseens, and here they are actually on it. Gino has put the radio on (which is a pity) but apparently there is a football match which he needs to follow. They stare out of the windows at the flat plains and the canals. It may be called a course, but, to most, it is a holiday. Some have read Forster; these know that Italy changes the English. In Italy they lose their inhibitions. Anything can happen.

Chapter II

Lago di Nemi

Michael has generated much enthusiasm for the Lago di Nemi, the bottomless lake in the secret grove. There is magic here and mystery. Here is a glimpse of that glamour that had first led them to the subject, had led them to the daily grind of teaching it. The hardship and the tribulation would fall away; the true essence of the Ancient World would be revealed.

So, what happens when they get to Nemi, to the very shores of this magic inland sea? Well, they have been in the coach for some time now. They had to spend time at Ciampino Airport while mackintoshes were searched for. Now, in most minds, there is but one thought: the lavatory. Indeed, this is understandable, but, that done, surely then they will be exploring the Sacred Grove? No. They want to sit at tables and drink coffee.

Does this sadden Michael and Fenella? No, not at all. They are old hands; they expect all this. Indeed, Fenella is already standing outside the coach with arm upraised in a directional manner.

The Classicists themselves are more animated now than we have hitherto seen them. The thin mackless man called Gerouin is almost bursting. He wanted to go at the airport, but it seemed ungracious somehow when Fenella was making such extensive yet fruitless enquiries for the mackintosh. He is determined to get to the lavatory before the enormous lady whom he has learned to call Kate. He has worked out that, as she is the size of two ladies, she will take twice as long in the lavatory. He has, however, not taken Miss Aitchinson's stick into consideration. At this very moment she is easing herself out into the aisle with her stick held before her.

"You will have to allow me to go first," she is saying loudly. "I fear I am a sad cripple."

Jane, in the red tracksuit, who is desperate for the lavatory herself, asks if it wouldn't be wiser for her to wait till the end when people wouldn't be in her way.

"I fear I need all the help I can get," is the staunch reply. She proceeds steadily down the aisle, the stick held before her, and is helped off by Fenella. Nobody expects Michael to help; he has got off some time ago.

Gerouin does a little dance in the aisle, moving from foot to foot. Any moment now...

There is movement certainly; the coach is emptying, but here is another hiatus, a lacuna in the steady onward movement. Colin Jones has his wooden box wedged in the exit. Fenella returns wearily.

"I'll just give it a little push from this end, and if you put it back on the front seat..."

"I'm afraid..." He turns scarlet.

"It'll be quite safe here," says Fenella firmly.

"I can't..." He is red but adamant.

People exchange glances. What has he got in there?

"Let me." William Thornton, it seems, is never happier than when executing some service for someone. "I'll take this side. Whoops-a-daisy. Down she goes." Colin watches suspiciously. He trusts no one where the box is concerned.

Now they are all off, except Gino and Anna. They have made it up and Anna is sitting on Gino's lap. They are both laughing uproariously. They find the English Classics teachers a dim and sexless lot.

When Gerouin sees there are eight people in the queue to the lavatory, he thinks that the Sacred Grove will have to be defiled. He makes a run for the nearest sacred tree. He drops his biro en route. He is just undoing his flies when he sees Michael leaning against a tree with a cigarette in his mouth. He is waiting for Fenella to finish.

"Don't mind me," says Michael, "I've just been looking for the golden bough myself. Give Egeria a quick flash. What's your name?"

"Gerouin," he replies, penis in hand. "It rhymes with heroine."

"Nice name, I like it," says Michael. "I bet you feel better now," he adds as Gerouin is zipping up his trousers. "Come with me and look at the lake. Nobody else seems interested."

Michael climbs fearlessly through holly and holm oaks, through asphodel and ash with Gerouin in tow. The latter is wondering what he has done with his pen.

"Look," says Michael at last, "bloody terrifying isn't it?"

Before them lie the swirling black waters, woods rise up on all sides, blackish green and brown as mud. Michael lights another cigarette.

"That's Avernus, for my money," he says, "the entrance to Virgil's underworld. Look, here's where they bury Misenus, there's even rowan and holm oaks here. This is as Stygian as you'll get. What do you think?"

But Gerouin only teaches ten year olds. He has never read Virgil. He is also feeling rather worried about his pen. "I think I'd better go back," he says.

Michael nods absently. He has forgotten Gerouin altogether. He stares into the black water and thinks of Aeneas' descent into Hades. What would it be like to go down to the Underworld, the lowest reaches of Erebus, with only the Sibyl for guidance? What is it like when you get there and find that it's not a dream sent from the Gates of Horn but is forever? What is it like to be one of the dead, squeaking like bats, as Homer says, with no substance, longing only to drink blood and be reborn?

"I hope I'm not interrupting. There are just one or two questions I wanted to ask."

She had hoped to be able to do her hair in the ladies', but it wasn't a ladies' at all; it was an evil smelling shed with men as well as women in the queue, and when you got inside there was only a hole in the ground and no light and no paper. Luckily there was a woman in the queue with her own roll. They had had a nice little chat. But now she has the great Michael Thorpe-Smith all to herself. He is really handsome, even better (of course a bit older) than he looked on the back of *Horace, The Man as Lover*. She did hope he wasn't involved with that Fenella; but she didn't think so, because she was sure he was married to that chat-show woman, Tabitha something or other. How wonderful to be married to a man like him. She looks at the grey hairs on his chest. She imagines her head resting on it.

"There's this question about..." He holds up his hand.

"Look at the water," he says quietly. "All the answers are there. And the questions too." He throws his cigarette into the pool. "That's for you, Charon old chap. No point in not smoking where you are."

How wonderful to be so unpredictable. She is already storing up anecdotes for her friend.

But she doesn't have him to herself for long. They have been to the lavatory, had their coffee, peered into the lake and are ready for the next. Here is Miss Aitchinson moving along quite swiftly with her stick, Colin Jones holding the wooden box by a brown handle in its top. The fat lady and the one in the red tracksuit are taking photos. Penny is putting a lavatory roll (somewhat diminished) away in her knapsack. Percival has a tape out and is taking measurements. William is allowed to hold his tape. Others who are looking forward to getting to the hotel have already returned to the coach. To tell the truth, they find the lake rather disappointing; it's only March and it is not warm, even for Italy. Time to get a move on.

Finally they are all gathered into the coach, all, that is, except Gerouin. Somebody has seen him acting suspiciously in the Sacred Grove. Red Trouser Suit fills them in, however.

"I saw him having a pee," she said. People move uneasily in their seats. Michael sits down next to Fenella.

"Did you see it, Fen?" he asks, "the lake, or were you too busy STT?" STT is short for Fenella seeing to things. Fenella is very good at her job, and Michael likes people to do things well.

"No," she says, "I wanted to come and find you, but there were problems with the loo." He takes her hand.

"It's a very frightening place," he says, "particularly being mixed up with the cult of Hippolytus. I don't like Hippolytus, all purity and sexlessness, Fen. The cult of Hippolytus is far more dangerous than the cult of Dionysus, don't you think?"

Fenella hasn't seen him over the last two years (except once) although, of course, like everyone else she has seen him on television. This is the first time they talk together, and he doesn't talk about his broken marriages or ask her what she has been doing. He talks about Hippolytus. She smiles.

"Tell me about him," she says. He seldom speaks of his wives anyway and she wishes, and yet does not wish, to hear of the other women in his life. He, too, has a great respect for her privacy. He would not dream of prying into her private life.

He strokes her hand absently and looks into the past.

"Well, there's the play by Euripides where Phaedra, Hippolytus' stepmother lusts after him unbearably. She tries to fight against it - but she cannot, Fen, just like you couldn't in that cave on Ithaca..." He smiles at her, remembering how she had tried to pull his hands away, and had come all the same. "So, she tells him how she feels and, when he repudiates her, she hangs herself, leaving a note for her husband Theseus, saying Hippolytus had raped her. Theseus appeals to Poseidon, and he sends a great white bull to scare Hippolytus' horses, and they throw him from his chariot and he dies. God, I wish I could have a fag. You've done well to give up, Fen."

"Go on telling."

"Well, okay, it's a bit of a shock to find your stepmother wanting to fuck you, but it's the way he rejects her, Fen, with a kind of hatred for her, for it. It's so violent, so unpleasant, and, of course, he's into orphism as well... You have got nice hair, Fen."

"Orphism?"

"Orphism was the first of the Greek religions. It was concerned with Chaos, Darkness, Night and Tartarus, ritual, mysticism and the ultimate punishment of the individual in the Underworld. He loves punishment, Hippolytus, punishing himself, punishing everyone else too. It's this exaggerated respect for purity, for chastity too. What's so great about it?"

Fenella starts gathering things up. They are getting near Gaeta and the hotel. She smiles at him.

"I liked being chaste before I met you," she says.

He is going to reply but Gino is asking her something about parking the coach, so she turns her mind to STT, as Michael calls it.

Chapter III

Pillow Talk

"I had forgotten, Fenella, how much I desired you."

"I had not forgotten."

"They're so swelling. So fecund, so warm. So big." He punctuates this with a bite of increasing intensity as they lie naked on Michael's bed.

"You too are big, very big," she whispers, reaching for him.

But Michael, who has made love to her for twenty years, has taught her himself, knows she is not yet ready for him. He needs to excite her further.

"Perhaps too big. You will not be able to bear me thrusting inside you."

"Oh, yes. Please. Please."

"So big and hard, moving within you."

"Yes. Yes. Yes. Ah." Fenella moans as he enters her, this man that she loves so much. Michael, too, is not silent, although he no longer expresses his thoughts in words. Fenella excites him more than any woman he has ever known.

"Happy, darling?"

"Silly question!" He lies sprawled on top of her, wetly inside her, and reflects that it is indeed a silly question. What man would not envy his present position on Fenella. Not only is she still (after twenty years) extremely beautiful, schooled in those arts of love-making that he himself taught her when he took her virginity on Ithaca twenty years previously, but also possessed of a kind of dumb, primitive passion that he has not found in any other woman, certainly not in either of his wives (satisfactory in other ways as his first wife, Jemima, was). He cannot imagine why Fenella's marriages were such failures: Mark going after other women and finally leaving her with the two children, and the marriage to that wanker Graham, or Gordon, or whatever his idiot name was, dissolved. Whenever he is with Fenella he cannot imagine ever wanting to fuck another woman. Perhaps she had found a grand passion with lovers, of which he imagined she must have had a large number, being the way she was.

"Fenella Sykes," he raises his head and strokes her hair back, "am I unappreciative? Do I leave you wondering whether or not I have come?" He withdraws and reaches over her for cigarettes.

"No," she says sadly, "it's just that every time we make love on a course, you go home and marry someone else."

"Fen, you know why."

"Yes, I know about Jemima. She had a rich daddy who would publish your books and make you famous and give you lots of leisure for research and..."

"Something like that," he says brusquely.

"But there was Tabitha too." She isn't being reproachful; she is simply puzzled. She stares at the picture of Mount Vesuvius hanging askew on the opposite wall.

"Yes, well, I wanted to be a media person, a television personality. Who better to marry than a chat-show hostess?" He sits smoking. "But," he adds, "let me tell you this: she was nemesis to my hubris. I got my come-uppance with her. Cold and mean. She'd have fixed a price tag on every fuck if she could. It lasted six months."

"You'd have been better off staying with Jemima then."

"Infinitely." But he doesn't add that he would have preferred Fenella to either of his two wives.

There is always this barrier between them, a sort of impasse. He will never tell her that he loves her, and there is Jemima too, his first wife. Once Fenella had thought she could get him away from Jemima. She had even thought he would come and claim her back as she walked up the aisle with Mark; but he hadn't. Every time she had run a course with him in the early days she thought he would leave his wife for her, but he hadn't.

And then he had gone to the States and she had married Graham because he was kind, because he was persistent, because she wanted a father for her children, and because he promised he wouldn't bother her in bed. And then he had married Tabitha. It was a cold consolation that it was not for love and had been disastrous. Now, however, he was free. She too. Graham had not kept his word. That marriage was dissolved some five years since.

She, however, must say nothing. Michael is a free spirit, not to be shackled with reproach and demands for restitution. There is nothing to do but hope and wait, and love as she has always loved, ever since he took her virginity against her will in the cave of Nymphs on the island of Ithaca, some twenty years ago.

A sort of shadow crosses his face, a kind of ripple of pain.

"What is it?" asks Fenella.

"Nothing," he replies, his face restored, "absolutely nothing. Now," he beams at her, his mood changing as it does so often, "who's the worst of the course, course members, I mean?"

"Oh, Michael, they're not bad."

"Of course they are. Who's the worst?"

Fenella laughs in spite of herself. It is not in her to dislike people.

"Well?"

"Oh well, Percival Jeavons probably. He will dislike me because I'm a woman, and you because you're successful. What was he doing with a tape measure at Lake Nemi?"

"God knows. Probably going to write a learned paper on the height of the bulrushes in the Ancient World. And that old girl with the stick, I don't think she needs it at all. I saw her with it tucked under her arm positively bowling along."

"Perhaps," says Fenella wickedly, "it comes into its own under cover of darkness."

"Ah yes," he says, "not everyone is as fortunate as you, having me to satisfy them at night."

Fenella laughs. "There's Colin Jones with his box," she says. "I wonder what he's got in it?"

"Don't you know?" His hand explores her gently. "You do feel nice, Fen.!"

"Good," says Fenella, parting her legs a little. "No, I don't know."

"We might have a bet."

"How much?"

"I wasn't thinking of lire."

Fenella laughs; it is such a happiness to her to have him back again, like your favourite book that you come across after a passage of time. And although you know the story and the episodes you reread it again avidly, recapturing your old delight, finding words you had never realised were there before. Thus she feels as she holds him.

Suddenly he smiles, gets out of bed and walks around the room.

"Very green this room, Fen, like a pistachio nut. No sea view either." He picks up a hair comb from the floor where it has fallen when they were making love and deftly twists up her long curly hair and fastens it on top.

"Shut your eyes, and don't cheat."

"What are you doing?"

"I'm... hang on a minute... I'm... can you guess what I'm doing?"

"You're fastening something round my neck."

"Correct. Don't look. Come and look in the mirror." He takes her hand and conducts her to the dressing table.

"What do you think?"

She opens her eyes and they both look in the mirror. Fenella turns to kiss him, but he turns her back again.

"Lapis lazuli," he says, "like your eyes. No, don't say anything, it's hideous wondering what to say when people give you things."

He stands behind her as they look in the mirror; he gathers up her breasts in his hands.

"'Nam modo nudatis mecumst lucata papillis. Interdum tunica duxit, opertu moram.' Do you know what it means?"

She feels his penis hardening behind her.

"Yes," she says, for although the only two words she recognises are *nudatis papillis*, she knows he is not talking about the Latin. The blue pendant swings above his hands, glinting as it catches the light, and falls into the valley of her breasts.

"You'll stop me if I hurt you?"

"If I give you pleasure," says Fenella, "the pleasure becomes mine too." She can feel him hardening and hardening against her, his hands crushing her breasts.

"Even if I give you pain?"

"I cannot distinguish between them," says Fenella. Indeed, it is true; so much have pleasure and pain been part of her love for him.

Afterwards, in bed, he is contrite.

"I think I hurt you, Fen. I am so sorry."

"It was Dionysus, not you," says Fenella, stroking back the lock of hair that falls so insistently over his eyes. She is only happy that he is happy. She is, however, conscious of duty and sits up.

"It must be frightfully late. Do you have an alarm clock?" He smiles.

"What a mistress of bathos you are! Yes, I do, under the Propertius. What time shall I set it for?"

"I ought to be back in my room by six."

As he grimaces she reaches out to turn off the light, but he stops her.

"Please not."

It shows how long it is since they have slept together. How can she have forgotten his fear of the dark, how he always has to sleep with the light on, and how it is difficult for her at first to sleep, even tired out as she is with passion? He likes to sleep sprawled on top of her, and, even though her breasts are unbearably sore, she doesn't try to stop him. Instead she says,

"Michael, I love you."

"Sweet," he says. But she does not know to what he refers; is it her love that is sweet, her, what he has just done to her, does he feel love for her or is it just a sop? She is just dropping off to sleep when he says, "How would it feel, underneath the black waters, going down..." he lifts his head up a moment from her tender breasts, "going down to Erebus like Aeneas or Theseus or Heracles or...?"

"Or Odysseus," says Fenella sleepily, who has learned a great deal about classical mythology in the last twenty years of her life.

"It would be terribly lonely, wouldn't it, Fen? Black and lonely."

"Not if I was with you," says Fenella stoutly. "Now go to sleep."

"Fen."

"Mm."

"I like being in bed with you."

If Fenella had been less forgiving, she might have asked him why, in that case, he had been there so seldom over the last twenty years. Instead, she replies, "Do you, darling? I like it too."

Chapter IV

At Gaeta

It is as well that Fenella is back in her own double-bedded room by six, as there is no peace to be had thereafter. The first to knock is Miss Aitchinson minus the stick, so great is her haste to tell Fenella that she has no plug to her basin, that she has not had time to collect it. But Fenella is firm. Has she not been running courses for twenty odd years?

"Oh, Miss Aitchinson, I'm just about to have my shower."

"I'm afraid I must ask you to provide me with a plug straight away."

"Reception is your best bet, Miss Aitchinson." Fenella is clutching her towel round her; Italian Easters can be very chilly.

"Impossible, I'm afraid. With my leg..."

"Oh yes, your poor leg. How are you managing without your stick?"

Miss Aitchinson is momentarily put off course by this cunning mention of the stick, and hesitates. Fenella pursues her advantage.

"I'm sure Reception will be only too pleased to help." Smiling brightly, she shuts the door. She is, in truth, very tired.

After her shower Fenella feels refreshed. She mentally makes a list of things to be done before eight o'clock, prime among which is to wake up Michael, who was none too happy when the alarm went at six, and flung himself across the bed into a new and heavier sleep.

There is another knock at the door. Miriam Whitbread is standing there in her dressing gown, clutching a photo.

"Oh, Mrs Sykes."

"Fenella," says Mrs Sykes, "call me Fenella, and come and tell me all about it. I'm sure we can sort it out, whatever it is."

She leads her firmly to the bed and sits her down. She hates to see anyone distressed. She remembers that Miriam has young children and how guilty she herself had felt when she, too, had left her children in the care of her mother to go on whatever course she could be on with Michael. Fenella takes her hand.

"Tell me, my dear..." she says.

It all comes pouring out: Timothy and Joe, Timothy a difficult birth, had to have a Caesarean, doctors thought he wouldn't have Joe on antibiotics, the husband's inability to give medicine at the right time. Will he defrost the chicken? You can't do it properly in the microwave. Joe's tears when she went, Timothy crying "Mummy, Mummy," insidious influence of her mother-in-law. She will look through cupboards. The strange noise made by the washing machine. She herself not knowing any Latin, teaches Classics in translation. Joe's pyjama bottoms missing. Better to go home. Wants to go now. Will insurance pay? Can she go from Naples? Will someone take her? Frightened of flying too. Is sharing a room with lady and her stick. Had fallen over it, nasty bruise, lady not very sympathetic... hasn't had children. People don't understand when they haven't had babies. Oh dear, has Fenella? Oh she has, well then she knows... No bath plug...

Fenella sees that none of this is very serious. She takes on board Miriam's elegantly polished nails and neatly lacquered hair. She plans to sit her next to some unattached man on the coach. Perhaps William Thornton would do. That, however, will come later. Now she speaks words of comfort. Miriam must try another day because she will enjoy it. No, the insurance won't pay up. What dear little boys. A new room, perhaps, sharing with that nice girl Caroline? Now, how about phoning home, here and now, from Fenella's own room where she won't be disturbed? Everything will be fine. Fenella will put the call through herself. Then Miriam is to come down to breakfast. Ah, here it is, ringing for her. Miriam to stay there just as long as she wants.

The next port of call is Michael. She pauses momentarily from the door to look at him in all his vulnerability, sprawled across the bed. She had forgotten (after all, it has been two years) how he makes the bed his own; it does not seem that he sleeps in a bed, but rather that the bed is there as an extension of his ease; it is party to the massive conspiracy on the part of people, events and even, it seems, furniture, to make his passage through life a pleasant one. He sleeps not vertically, but horizontally, as if to gain more from it this way. He lies neither in nor out, but he lies as if he has mastered the bed, has imposed his presence upon it, and indeed upon the room as a whole.

There he lies, the man she has loved for twenty years. The man who has deceived her, cheated her and occasionally, perhaps, loved her.

She notes for the first time he is beginning to look his age. The lock that falls over one eye is a little thinner, a little greyer than before, his closed eyes reveal the bags beneath. Even in size (he is six foot two) he looks a little less somehow than before.

The sight of this massive man who has been such a power in her life, lying exposed and defenceless, stirs up a deep tenderness within her. The sight of a naked arm hanging over the side of the bed gives her a rush of feeling that she last experienced when newborn Felicity was placed in her arms eighteen years ago, hers alone to provide for, a perfect specimen of humanity that was flesh of her flesh. She feels tremendously protective towards him because he is older. Some of his clouds of glory have been dimmed; and this makes him more approachable, less god-like.

She sits down on the bed and shakes him gently by the shoulder. He wakes immediately. She had forgotten how quickly he makes the transition between sleep and consciousness. Effortlessly he pulls her down on top of him.

"Michael, I can't, I've got breakfasts."

"Of course you can." He is undoing her skirt. "I love it when you look all organised and bossy. And somehow," he adds, putting his hand between her naked thighs, "I don't think you will be able to resist." Fenella has, after all, been unresisting for more than twenty years.

Going down in the lift some minutes later, she encounters three new course members, or rather two and their child, an unpleasant-looking boy of about ten. They had come over last night from a three-day course in Rome. There had been a lot of coming and going and discussion about his presence on the course. It was felt that a small boy would not go down well with the course members. Fenella, looking at Nigel now, feels that this sentiment was probably correct. He is kicking the side of the lift, fondly watched by his mother.

"Don't do that, Nigel," says his father irritably.

"You're all set, then," says Fenella to the parents, who rejoice in the name of Box, "for coming to Terracina this morning?" The mother is a nervous woman.

"Oh yes, I think so," she gasps. "I just hope it won't be too tiring for Nigel."

"It's boring, sitting in coaches," says Nigel.

"Don't be stupid, Nigel," says Mr Box. "This course has cost me a lot of money; I want you to learn all you can."

He is not, however, looking at Nigel, but at Fenella, and in particular at Fenella's breasts. He is an unpleasant looking man, thin, with too-short trousers and an apology of a beard. Through thick glasses he devours Fenella's breasts. He would like to have them in his hands.

Mrs Box smiles uncertainly; unattractive as her husband, dressed in a jumble of ill-assorted clothes, she shares her anxiety with Fenella,

"He doesn't like the food," says Mrs Box.

"It's pigswill," says Nigel. Fenella notices he has an unpleasant thin pinched nose.

"I've brought some of his favourite cereals from home," says Mrs Box. Mr Box makes an inarticulate noise of irritation.

"Here we are," says Fenella, as they get off at the ground floor. "Enjoy your breakfast, Nigel."

Caroline Jeffery has spent a long time doing her hair. Her mother always says it is her great glory. It is certainly very long and very ginger. An unkind friend had once said that if Caroline's hair had been ten times thicker it would be quite nice.

At first she thinks she will put it into a French plait, but that makes her look very severe and school-marmish. Then she thinks she will wear it loose, so she can toss it about when she speaks to him. But there again they will be outside a lot, and it does tend to look rather greasy and unflattering if it's windy or rainy. No, she will wear it caught at the nape with the pearl slide.

She has made for the first table inside the dining room so she can waylay him as soon as he comes in. She has her question ready, 'Wasn't it Terracina that Lucius Vitellius attacked? I seem to remember it in Tacitus.' She spreads her bag and camera over the table to deter others from joining her. She has been sharing a room with Penny Diver. Penny had told her to go on down; she would be a little time in the bathroom. Caroline is not pleased to see Kate Small lumbering into view. Unlike the others she makes no concession to the age of trouser. She is clad in a brightly garlanded dress of many colours. She is a flower bed, or, indeed, a whole garden all on its own.

"Is there anyone sitting here?" she asks. Caroline opens her mouth, but Mrs Small sits down anyway. It seems she occupies both chairs opposite Caroline.

"Have you finished?" she asks. Again Caroline is too late. Kate Small scoops the entire contents of the breadbasket on to her plate.

"I love Italian bread," she says.

Percival and William are sitting together at the table by the window. William is eagerly pouring out coffee for his august companion.

"Sugar, Percival? No. Right. Some milk? Oh, not too much. Quite right."

"You may be interested," Percival is saying, "to hear what Strabo has to say about Terracina and Formiae. Of course you will know the origin of the name of our present abode, Gaeta."

"No, I don't think..."

"Surely you are familiar with the passage in Virgil, book seven, with its reference to Aeneas' nurse Gaeta?"

"Now you come to mention it I..."

"Strabo tells us that Formiae comes next after Terracina; this was, in fact," Percival leans across to William as if imparting a great secret, "formerly called Hormiae because, of course, of its good hormos." He looks triumphantly at William.

"Gosh," says William, "I didn't know that." But out of the corner of his eye he sees the tearful Miriam looking for somewhere to sit. There is no time to be wasted.

"Excuse me," he says, "I wonder if you would like to join Percival and me? We're just talking about the good hormos."

"Oh," says Miriam. She is feeling better now. Fenella had been so kind and caring, and she'd spoken to Joe on the phone, and his knee was much better, and Granny wasn't coming until the next day, and now here was this nice young man asking her to join them.

Percival rises from the table. This he cannot stomach at any cost.

"Do you have the key to the room?" he asks coldly.

Jane, in her red tracksuit, is approaching. Ever since the lavatory queue she has taken against Miss Aitchinson.

"You want to be careful where you put that stick. Someone's going to go a purler over it soon. When are we leaving, Fenella? The sooner the better, I'd say."

Caroline has been watching the main door avidly while Mrs Small chomps her way through the *panini*. And at last she is rewarded. There he is at last, a lock of hair falling over his forehead, wearing his beautifully cut jeans. She is so busy beaming her welcome that she doesn't notice a private-looking door at the side, opening, and the thin man who lost his mackintosh emerging.

"Oh, I am so glad I've found the dining room," he is saying. "I got lost." And he sits down thankfully next to Caroline. Caroline glares at him.

"There's no bread left," she says as she sees Michael receding from her.

"Oh, it doesn't matter," says Gerouin. "I'm used to going without."

Michael finds himself a place next to Colin Jones and the wooden box.

"Hi," he says, "who are you?"

Colin is desperately shy and blushes and mumbles.

"What I want to know," says Michael, "is what you have got in that box of yours."

Colin leans over and vouchsafes Michael a confidential reply.

"Ah," says Michael, "I shouldn't tell Fenella if I were you. She might make you put it in the safe."

Fenella is busy with lists. She has now accounted for everyone, including those who transferred last night along with the Boxes from the

Rome course. There is a small man with a lot of beard and a north country accent called Joe, and, more confusingly, there are three women all called Brown. Two are sisters-in-law, and spell their name with an 'e'. They are both dowdy and middle-aged. It is difficult to tell them apart. The third is rather younger and attractive in a heavy sort of way. Fenella cannot work out what their relationship is to each other.

Chapter V
Tiberius' Grotto

Michael works them hard at Terracina. He takes them round the Forum Aemulium inch by inch, he explores the genealogy of Aulus Aemulius, its builder, he shows them different styles of building and makes even the loathsome Nigel able to recognise the *opus reticulatum,* the regular arrangement of stones on a wall. He builds temples for them. Arcades and arches rise out of ruins before their eyes. He shows them Lucius Vitellius, its captor (just as Caroline had known). Fenella, coming back from phoning the office (not an easy undertaking), observes him. She sees he is very happy; she thinks he is as happy at finding a stretch of *opus reticulatum* as he is at making love. He really loves the Romans, he loves their building skills and their poetry. He can see their world as clearly as his own, but it is a private world, not one into which Fenella will be able to follow. He has found a bit of the Appian Way.

"Cicero walked here," he says. He loves to think his foot is standing on the very same stone.

Finally, he releases them and they skedaddle off like beads from a broken necklace. Fenella chases after them, taking their orders for *panini*, for on this first day they will have them paid for. It is not easy however. Some cannot eat salami, others cannot abide cheese; some want two, others none. But at last it is sorted and Anna is despatched to purchase them at a nearby *panetteria*. Anna, wearing the same tight black dress and looking very sulky indeed, goes stomping off. Gino stretches out in the coach.

Percival is looking for William. He is looking forward to treating him to a lecture on the identification of the temple to Jupiter Anxur, but he is nowhere to be found. He has, in fact, gone to buy stamps with Miriam. She is very anxious to send off two cards to Joe and Timothy. William, too, it transpires, has a young son and is missing him (he does not mention missing his wife, just as Miriam does not mention missing her husband). They sympathise with each other, and their delight knows no bounds when finally they manage to purchase stamps and send their cards.

Irritated by the absence of William, Percival goes to put Michael right on a thing or two, but even there he is unsuccessful: the frightful ginger-haired girl is raining questions on him. Where exactly did he think Horace had met up with Virgil? What, in his opinion, had been the actual date of construction of the forum to the nearest five years? Had Aulus Aemulius paid for the buildings himself? If so, how much would he have paid? Each question has been accompanied by a toss of the orange hair (the slide has slithered out and been abandoned).

Michael is feeling a little worn down by all this cross-questioning and wondering where Fenella is, and if she will come and rescue him. But Fenella is inside the cathedral lighting a candle and making a prayer.

Michael is, in fact, rescued by the tracksuited Jane who says,

"For heavens sake, let the poor man have a rest. It's all in the bloody guidebook."

Michael is further rescued by Jupiter himself, for the clouds that have been looming and grey suddenly open and steady rain ensues. The course members reach for their waterproofs (except Gerouin, who no longer has one). They would actually like to get back on the coach, but nobody wants to be the first to suggest this.

Finally, Fenella rounds them all up and allows them back on the coach. Anna is handing out *panini* and paper cups of wine. This is causing much trouble as she invariably gives out the wrong *panini* and people who are given red wine want white or water. Anna looks even crosser. Then Fenella finds that mackless Gerouin is missing and also the three Boxes. She sets off into the rain. Gino and Michael are engaged in animated Italian. Caroline thinks it looks a very male conversation.

Fenella finds the Boxes at the stamp kiosk. Mrs Box is trying to buy something for Nigel.

"Oh dear," she is saying, "They don't seem to have any Mars Bars; he doesn't like anything else." Fenella, in rapid Italian, buys the nearest thing to a Mars Bar and enquires if anyone has seen Gerouin. Mr Box says he thinks he has seen him taking refuge in the church. He adds that he looked very wet, and he couldn't think why he didn't put an anorak on. He stares at Fenella. Great boobs on her!

Fenella returns to the cathedral and extracts Gerouin from a group of unruly Italian children and escorts him back to the coach. She gives him a *panino* and sits him next to Penny. Perhaps she will be able to dry him off with the lavatory paper.

The steady rain means a change of plan. They cannot now stretch their legs and picnic at Monte Circeo; they will make for Tiberius' grotto at Spelunga.

"Da otto mesi non piove. Appena arrivati gli Inglesi e piove, Pa pioggia, la portono con loro!" says Gino to Mrs Small (he has taken a liking to her, she speaks Italian and reminds him of his own vast Neapolitan mother).

It is as if Gino's words set the tone for the afternoon. A feeling of gloom seems to permeate the coach. They had come all this way, leaving their Timothys and Joes, leaving their homes and their schools, to come to the sunny shores of Italy. Although the ostensible reason was the pursuit of erudition, a desire to increase their classical knowledge, to develop a new awareness of the Ancient World, there is hardly anyone who, in truth, was not lured hither by the sunshine and glamour of Italy. And now, what happens? It is cold and wet, there is white wine instead of red, no water, salami in the *panini* when one is vegetarian and horrible Italian chocolate instead of Mars Bars. They had expected the solace of a cup of hot coffee from the wonderful machine on Gino's modern coach, but Anna, herself sunk in gloom, announces '*machina è rotta*' and goes off to sit by herself at the back. Percival finds he has been deserted by William and joined by the man with the box. Its edges obtrude and dig into him every time the coach turns a corner. Nigel feels sick and Gerouin is very wet. Penny thinks how the whole thing is a waste of time; she will never find a husband here. Caroline is worried about the unflattering effect of the rain on her hair. The three Brown(e)s, too, appear hostile. They keep themselves to themselves and converse *sotto voce*. People suspect they are saying unpleasant things about them. Fenella has a splitting headache; she rummages in her bag for paracetamol.

Only Michael is happy. The ambience is perfect for his purpose.

"Spelonga," he says sonorously, "the cavern of the Emperor Tiberius." Michael has written a book on Tiberius. He believes him to be both a homicidal maniac and schizophrenic. He lingers on Tiberius' massacres and touches on his unnatural practices. He reads to them from Tacitus. He regards their gloom with glee. Something of the spirit of Tiberius has remained.

Gino, also permeated by the gloom, stops the coach uncomfortably far from the grotto.

"Almost as if he'd done it on purpose," says Miriam to William. She doesn't like getting wet.

They beat their way, clad in anoraks and plastic macs, to the grotto. Within, all is as dark and murky as Tiberius himself. As they stumble inside, among rugged and gloomy recesses, Michael's voice declaims, "All through his son's illness, Tiberius attended the senate. Either he was unalarmed, or wanted to display his will-power. Even when Drusus had died and his body was awaiting burial, Tiberius continued to attend."

The sides of the cave bear in on them, the interior is black-green in its murkiness. Outside, the rain falls into the *piscinaria*, the fishing pools. Suddenly there is an electric flash from the recesses of the cave. It can be traced to the bearded Joe. He had apparently promised himself for years an opportunity of photographing here. He is to take a lot of photos over the week.

"Piscinaria," says Michael, with a light in his eyes. "Let's go and look at Tiberius' fish ponds," and he leads them forth into the rain. "Hortensius," he says, "fell in love with one of the lampreys in his fish pond, or so Pliny tells us, but I can't help thinking it must have been an unconsummated love." (a little gasp from Caroline). "I have a mass of fishy stories," he says, "and I'm going to tell you all of them." He draws them after him like the Pied Piper. "Do you know, Nigel," he says, "Drusus had a wife called Antonia and she used to dress up her favourite

fish in earrings and all the nobs used to come and see?" Nigel pauses in the mastication of gum. He reckons Michael's all right.

After the *piscinaria* they visit the museum. One after another they file past the nude sculpture depicting the giant Polyphemus. Miss Aitchinson looks firmly at the torso, Colin wonders whether men do have penises that size. Jane hoots with laughter,

"He's in good shape," she says.

Miriam pretends not to look, but nevertheless glances downwards at William. Mrs Small comments enigmatically "ah," but whether from desire or some more subtle emotion nobody knows. The three Brown(e)s have much to say *sotto voce* among themselves. Penny thinks it is too long since she has glimpsed such a sight, Percival looks long upon it; he reflects on the beauty of the male body. Mrs Box tries unsuccessfully to hurry Nigel past.

"What a whopper," says Nigel. His father thinks his own thoughts.

Fenella looks at Michael and smiles. There is something relaxed and abandoned in Polyphemus' attitude as he lies back with an arm thrown across his body, leaving his penis to do as it will. The legs are muscular, the one folded behind. It is the post-coital Michael. Only Gerouin does not see Polyphemus; he has returned to the coach, having lost his way to the museum; but he wishes he had sought out the museum after all, as Gino is embracing Anna in the back seat. Gerouin doesn't know where to look.

If they imagine Michael will allow them back to the comfort of the hotel after so much culture, they are mistaken. Indeed, Miss Aitchinson is reaching for her stick as Gaeta hoves into view, but Gino, who is now restored, is singing snatches of song and drives straight past the hotel. ("I want to get out," says Nigel. He speaks for the majority.)

"Now," says Michael, "I want to show you the tomb of Munatius Plancus. "I want you to look at the Doric frieze," he says, "and tell me what battle it commemorates." He almost has a revolt on his hands. Most are comfortably ensconced in the coach; they have no desire to see the frieze. Percival is telling Colin Jones that the hill itself was supposed to be the grave of Gaeta, the nurse of Aeneas. Colin takes out a notebook and writes this down. Percival feels gratified.

"Now," says Michael, "for Formiae and the tomb of Cicero. Let me read you the passage from Livy. Hang on a tick while I find it. Ah, here we go, 'As he thrust his head out of the litter and held his neck steady, he was decapitated. Nor was this enough for the brutish cruelty of the soldiers. They also cut off his hands, reproaching them for having written something against Anthony. Thus the head was brought back to Anthony and, by his order, placed between the two hands on the rostra.'" Miriam gives a little cry. William pats her shoulder. "How horrible and brutish they were, the Romans," says Michael reflectively. "What a barbarous people."

Everybody is relieved to find that they do not have to get out at Formiae, which is a horrible shanty town, the sort of Italy they do not like to think of.

Off they set once again, through the marshlands of Minturnae. "Malaria-ridden swamps," says Michael, "a veritable death area. Here it was that Marius foiled his assassins."

He forces them off the coach, not at gunpoint, but by the power of his will.

"I want you to see the theatre," he says. "Come with me." He takes some but not all. Fenella catches up with him by the remains of the theatre.

"Michael," she says, "they can't take any more." He comes back to her from many centuries away. He has been watching Plautus' *Mostellaria* in the theatre. A smile spreads across his features.

"Yes, of course," he says. "Home, James, and don't spare the horses."

Chapter VI

Fenella is Tired

That night there is no feeling of *bonhomie*, no desire to carouse in the apology of a bar, only a feeling of immense weariness. As Jane says to Kate Small,

"We've had Tiberius' dodgy grotto, the tomb of Munacius Plancus, the death of Cicero and the assassination of Marius. That's about as much as I can take in a day."

Fenella for one is totally exhausted and has retired to her room. She also has paperwork to complete.

Only Michael is not exhausted. He has a couple of stregas in a bar down the road and goes off to his room. He is on a high. He has been delighted by everything, the *opus reticulatum*, the tomb of Munacius Plancus, Minturnae and the Pontine marshes. He also has a boyish delight in imparting his knowledge. He is pleased that the horrible Nigel had stopped chewing for long enough to ask, "Who is Cicero, then?" He knows there is another reference to the *piscinaria* somewhere in the Martial. He is determined to find it. He lights a cigarette and sits down in the comfortable easy chair that superior hotel rooms offer. He has forgotten how good Martial is.

At last he shakes himself and returns to the twentieth century. It is time to go and see Fenella.

Fenella is fast asleep in bed. She has tried to stay awake, but it is now eleven o'clock and she has been on the go since six. She is not as young as she was, and she has fallen asleep.

Michael looks at her wonderingly. Just as she had felt touched by his vulnerability when she had gone to wake him in the morning, he is now forced to see Fenella as a separate person, a being without reference to himself.

When he saw her asleep during the night she was an adjunct of himself, a partner in pleasure, an addition, an embellishment to his bed. And now she lies fast asleep in a world of her own, as lost in her dreams as he has been in the Martial. She is where he cannot reach her.

He also notices how much older she looks. To be honest, he cannot remember exactly how old she is; he supposes she must be about forty-two or three, but when he thinks of her, as he does from time to time, he thinks of a sort of composite Fenella, a Fenella made up of a collage of experiences that they have shared, so a twenty-one-year-old Fenella wearing an impressive suntan and a spotted bikini is superimposed on another Fenella sitting across the table from him in a Soho restaurant, and finishing her crème caramel, saying, "You're going to marry Jemima?" or a Fenella who sits at her desk wearing her reading glasses and writing him letters saying 'Dear Dr Thorpe-Smith, Classic Tours are planning their summer season. We are wondering whether you would be available at all in July for a lecture tour? We would hope to increase the remuneration from that of the 1989 tour...'

He sits down, (Fenella also has a superior room with an armchair) and gazes at this amalgam of Fenellas.

Perhaps he should have married her when she imagined he would, when she was twenty-three and he couldn't get his books published. But Jemima's father ran a big publishing house. It had seemed the logical step to marry her instead. In a funny sort of way (and although Fenella had been very, very upset) he believed that she had understood the necessity in it too.

Fenella stirs a little in her sleep and groans a little. She doesn't look particularly pretty at the moment, but he doesn't hold this against her. After all who does look their best asleep? Anyway women need make-up and she's taken hers off for the night. If TV viewers could see his second wife, Tabitha, without her make-up on, they wouldn't recognise her. It had come as enough of a shock to him. But initially he had not been able to resist the lure of Tabitha, chat-show hostess, half his age, all the media world at his feet. It had been flattering to own a woman whom five million viewers saw twice a week and lusted after.

Of course he was drawn by the glamour, of course he wanted to see his face on television and read about himself in the gossip columns; but it wasn't as simple as that. In the first place, his marriage to Jemima was quite satisfactory, his lifestyle suited him. Furthermore, he had two daughters and disliked causing any of his family pain. The glamour he could have resisted; what he could not resist was this opportunity, perhaps the same opportunity for which he had married Jemima. For he believed that he could bring the Ancient World alive to millions of people and show them the things that mattered to him. He could show them that Classics wasn't dusty and dead, but bursting with people like themselves, ready to tell them what life was really all about.

But it had not been possible. He found instead the world of the media, people whose interest was not in ideas but in themselves. He came to dislike his wife intensely. Cold, ambitious and self-centred, she soon lost interest in the Romans and in him. They separated after six months. The new series he had started on was dropped. He had failed.

And here was Fenella lying asleep, probably with nothing on except her watch, Fenella, who had loved him through two husbands and two marriages of her own. Fenella was always there. If he was an exotic flowering morning glory, she was the wall upon which he climbed. His flowers might wither, his leaves fall to the ground, but the wall stood firm for him to climb upon another year.

He is about to undress when he is struck by a thought. He feels remorse for his behaviour of the previous night; he lifts the duvet and winces at the damage he has inflicted. He is angry at the pain he has caused Fenella, and the bruises on her breasts seem to symbolise what a destructive influence he has been on her life. He remembers Fenella's words spoken in the coach as they were approaching Gaeta, "I liked being chaste until I met you." How badly he had treated her always. Fucking had been of little significance in his life. Perhaps it had come too easily to him. Always there had been women willing and eager. He had taken them as he took on board any new experience. They gave him pleasure and he returned the favour. He would as soon, though, write an elegant translation of a poem by Catullus. But it wasn't like that for Fenella. He replaced the duvet gently over her. Fenella fucked him because she loved him. What had she said? "I get pleasure from your pleasure." He leans down and kisses her forehead. "Sorry, Fen," he says. Pain catches him underneath his heart.

He has only just returned to his room and found his cigarettes and emptied the ash tray into the bin, when there comes a knocking at the door, almost as if someone had been waiting for him to return. He is intrigued.

It is Caroline in her nylon dressing gown and fluffy pink slippers. She has obviously just washed her hair. She stands breathlessly on the threshold, her eyes darting into the inner recesses of the sanctuary.

"I wonder..." she says. She seems nervous.

"Come in," says Michael, looking for the ashtray. "What can I do for you?"

She comes into the room and folds her arms over her small breasts as if to hide them within the recesses of nylon.

"I have one or two questions to ask... about, about Munacius Plancus." She dares not look at him. She fixes her eyes on his copy of Martial. She can sense how silly she must sound, how tenuous her excuse must be to him.

"What do you want to know about Munacius Planks?" he says, smiling. She raises her eyes to look timidly at him.

"I don't think you're in the least interested in Munacius Plancus," says Michael lightly, "and quite right too, he wasn't a very interesting person. Shall I tell you what I think?" She nods and clamps her arms more tightly over the yellow folds of the dressing gown.

"I think," says Michael, "you've come to check out how I compare with Polyphemus. Is that right?"

Caroline is struck dumb. This isn't as she had planned, although, true, she had only planned the initial stages in detail, but there didn't seem to be any initial stages.

"Well, actually," continued Michael, sitting down in the chair, "I'd say quite well really, seeing as I'm not a giant like the cyclops. But, there again, it's not really for me to say, is it? Do you like fucking?" he adds mischievously.

She had not thought of Michael in connection with the sexual act, nor, indeed, putting it to use, particularly not in reference to herself. After putting an arm round her, he might perhaps have kissed her (even on the lips); he would hold her hand when they went round sites together and eventually (but this, even in her wildest imaginings, she had to admit was not very likely) he would divorce his wife and marry her.

But now there is this ugly word. She can hardly believe he has used it. Why, he has asked her if she likes doing this... this activity, much as he might have asked her if she liked shopping. What does he mean? What will he do?

Michael has been looking for another packet of cigarettes and has finally located one under the Martial. Only then does he look up and see the hideous embarrassment on her face.

"Oh dear," he says, "I've put my foot in it - well, better the foot than... Are you a virgin?"

Caroline has never thought of herself as such, indeed the word in her mind only exists in relation to Mary. She teaches at a convent school. She hears a lot about the Virgin Mary.

"Well," says Michael, adopting a paternal tone, "you stay that way until you meet your Mr Right, your Mr Munacius Plancus. And don't go throwing yourself away on old reprobates like me. You'll find the right man; you might even find him this week." He casts around for something to soften the blow. "And with hair the colour of yours, you're sure to have a nice passionate time."

He gets up to open the door for her. It will be good for her to go before she gets hysterical. He has encountered academic virgins before. They are bad news.

She hesitates, however. She must ask him this one question.

"Is it... is it very nice?"

"Sex? Oh yes, brilliant, almost as good as standing on the Appian Way. Now off you go. Not that you need your beauty sleep, but we've got a busy day tomorrow. Cumae and Baiae. Cumae's probably the most magical place in the world." He pats her shoulder avuncularly and politely holds the door for her.

"Where have you been?" asks Miriam suspiciously. She is lying in bed reading a magazine. She is still missing Joe and Timmy, of course, but somehow not nearly as much as she was yesterday. It's so lucky she has met William; he's really nice. She looks forward to tomorrow.

"Oh, just to the loo," says Caroline, unwrapping the yellow layers of dressing gown and climbing into bed.

"Shall I turn the light out?" she asks. She has a lot to think about.

Chapter VII

Letters and Postcards

To Miss Grey:

Arrived safely. Leg very painful. Lucky I have my stick. Hotel fair but I had a very disturbed night with a great deal of noise from the next room. There is too much getting on and off the coach too. I feel worn out already. Hope you are well.

Yours,

Margaret Aitchinson

PS A lot of rain.

To the Editor of the Classical Society:

Dear Sir,

I am presently engaged on a tour of Southern Italy in the company of other academic colleagues (Michael Thorpe-Smith is one.) Stopping at the Lago di Nemi, I had occasion to note that the bulrushes were unusually tall (some 75½ cm). I take this as an indication of alluvial deposit thereby placing volcanic activity many kilometres further north than hitherto believed.

I am sharing these preliminary findings with you as I believe they may be of no small importance.

On another subject, I am still waiting to hear whether I have been elected to the Steering Committee of LACA. You will appreciate I have many calls on my time and should therefore appreciate an immediate reply.

Yours sincerely,

Percival Jeavons (BA)

To Stephen Fowler:

Italy is CRAP. Food is disgusting. Saw a giant with a massive great dick.

See you,

Nigel

To Jennie Browning:

I can't believe I'm here! The hotel is really luxurious but best of all, Jennie, is the fact that he's here. You know how we were wondering if he would be like the back of *Horace, the Man as Lover*. Well, he is! Even more gorgeous if that's possible. I know this sounds like boasting, well, perhaps it is, a bit, but he said, well, implied really, that he liked my hair and said he thought I must have a passionate nature!! What do you make of that?

I've taken lots of useful slides for UVA Class. Civ. I know a lot more now about Munacius Plancus. Michael (imagine me calling him by his Christian name!) and I talked a lot about him...

Lots of love,

Caroline

To Mrs Stover:

Dear Mother,

I am sorry to tell you I lost my mackintosh at Ciampino Airport. The nice courier woman tried to find it, but couldn't. Do you think I can claim on the Insurance? I can't seem to find the forms. Do you have them? I've also lost my pen, the one with the silver knob. Perhaps I can claim for that too.

The hotel is very nice, but complicated to get the hang of. This morning I found myself in the staff kitchen. By the time I got to breakfast I found a fat lady had eaten all the bread!

I know what they mean about the Italians having a passionate nature now! Our driver, Gino, has his girlfriend with him, and he wasn't at all pleased to see me coming back early to the coach! (I hope you're not shocked by this.)

There is a lady on the party who has got a bad leg. I don't know exactly what's the matter with it, but I think it could be the same as yours. How is it, Mum?

To Tabitha Price:

... no, I'm not prepared to discuss your divorce spoils or wrangle about who gets what, in the middle of running a course in Italy...

M

To Susan Hall:

... having a great old time. Seen Terracina, Formiae, Minturnae and Grotto of Tiberius. Got loads of slides that will be useful for next year. Suspect the courier girl of having a fling with the charismatic Michael Thorpe-Smith. Don't blame her; wish I was in with a chance.

Love,

Jane

PS That red tracksuit's been a godsend – it's been pissing down here.

To Mr Jones:

Dear Dad,

I am trying very hard to overcome my shyness, but not very successfully. A nice lady tried to sit next to me in the coach, and I was trying to explain how I would move the box, when she went off again. However, I have met a man called Percival Jeavons, who seems very important; he knows an awful lot of useful facts and learns ten lines of Virgil (a Roman poet) every day.

You will be pleased to know I have the box safely with me. I haven't told anyone (except Michael Thorpe-Smith) about it. I hope to pluck up enough courage to open it perhaps soon.

Yours,

Colin

Three letters to Stuart Browne:

... jolly interesting course, especially Terracina, got several snaps of that. Your sister is being a bit of a pain as usual, but Jennie is doing a good job at keeping the peace between us... What a good person she is.

Sally

... are you wearing your thermal long-johns? It's very cold here so I'm sure you must be even colder at home. And you've always felt the cold so badly, haven't you? Do you remember when we were ten and we had that terribly wet holiday in Wales? Sally is being very trying but Jennie is keeping the peace between us. What a pity you couldn't be here too.

Alice

... I wish, I wish it could have been the two of us here like we planned. It's ironic really, isn't it, to come here with your wife and sister? They quarrel all the time and I am hard put to it to keep the peace between them. Imagine, if they knew!

To Timothy Havers:

Darling little Timmy,

Mummy misses you very, very, very much and Joey and Daddy too, but she'll be back very, very soon. There are some very nice people here. I saw a big giant yesterday with no clothes on! Wasn't that rude?

Lots and lots of love,

Mummy

To Felicity Sykes:

Darling,

Are you and John managing all right? There are loads of meals in the freezer and money on the top of the fridge. I shan't see either of you before you go back. Hope the term goes wonderfully for you both.

Your heart-throb sends his love, etc. He is looking a bit older...

Look after yourself,

Mum

Chapter VII

Cumae: The Most Romantic Place in the World

Mrs Small goes lumbering across the bedroom to open the curtains. She is clad in a vast white winceyette nightdress. She grunts softly to herself with the effort of pulling the curtains across. There is a tiny balcony outside the window on which somebody has optimistically placed a chair. They had not seen Mrs Small. The window gives out on to a street full of garbage and parked cars. Yesterday it had been a gloomy prospect indeed; the squashed tomatoes had looked like raw flesh and the black plastic bags sinister, as if containing decapitated bodies; the cars had looked battered, squalid, even threatening, parked, as they were, almost menacingly about the street. But today everything is changed.

"Jane," she cries, in her small shrill voice, "Jane, the sun's shining!"

Jane, who is snoring rhythmically, is not immediately aware of this excellent news. It takes another sibilant cry of "Sun shining!" and a shaft of light to fall, giving positive reinforcement, before Jane blinks, sits up and cries,

"This is more like it." She is out of the bed instantly. She touches her toes and sways from side to side with one arm in the air. She is clad in a pair of boxer shorts and a tee shirt.

"Cumae today, then," she says. "Have you been before?"

"Yes, many years ago," says Kate. "My husband excavated part of the Cumaean Acropolis."

"Why, so he did," says Jane, pulling the tracksuit on over the boxer shorts and the tee shirt. "Roy Small. I never made the connection."

"No, people don't," says Kate Small. For some reason people don't expect her to be married to the most famous archaeologist of the twentieth century. She doesn't mind. It is enough for her that she is. They are a devoted couple. "He is hoping to join us for the last few days of the course. He is presently finishing off a dig in Turkey."

They stand at the window and gaze out, Jane now dressed for the day in the red tracksuit, Kate with her labours all before her.

"Oh look," says Kate. "There's that man with the funny name."

"Who's that?" asks Jane. She is pulling a comb through her short brown hair.

"The one who lost his mackintosh. It's something like Gawain or Geraint."

"They see him advancing through the sunlight; he is staring at the hotel as if to identify it. He hesitates a moment and then walks on past.

"Well, he's lost the hotel now," says Jane cheerfully.

"Oh," says Kate, "what a shame! I hope he won't miss his breakfast today, like yesterday."

"Why did he do that?" asks Jane, putting her glasses on her prominent nose. "Miss his breakfast?"

"Oh," says Kate, "I'd eaten it all."

"Well, I'm not taking any chances," says Jane. "I'm off down."

As Kate heaves herself into the shower, she reflects that in spite of sharing the same room with Jane for two nights, she has not yet seen her apply soap or water.

It is a measure of Percival's growing ascendancy over Colin Jones, and of Colin's acceptance of this, that he takes Fenella aside as he is leaving the dining room.

"Excuse me," he says, "it's my box..."

"Cricketer, are you?" says a north-country voice. The bearded one is making his presence felt. Colin blushes scarlet. "I was wondering if they have a safe here, where I could lock it away." (Percival has grown tired of being biffed by its edges).

"Yes, of course," says Fenella. "Shall I take it for you?"

"No," says Colin, "if you would just come with me to reception and explain."

"Surely," says Fenella. She, too, feels cheered by a good night's sleep and the warm sunshine. "What have you got in there? Is it something precious?"

A crafty look comes over Colin's face. "I've been advised not to say," he says primly.

Michael, who is standing talking to Marco, the waiter, by the reception desk, pauses in his fluent Italian to greet Fenella with a light kiss. Some people feel this is unseemly behaviour even for Italy. The kiss, light as it is, does not escape the notice of Mr Box. Caroline, who is refastening her hair slide fortunately misses all this.

She is feeling very shy of him this morning. She doesn't quite like to think about last night. Michael winks at her.

"There's Munacius Plancus over there," he says, indicating the beard. But Caroline has only eyes for one man, it is not the bearded Joe. Penny, however, has other ideas.

Yesterday was a depressing day, full of tombs and death and useless men. It had rained all the time and she seemed to be saddled with Margaret Aitchinson and stick for good. But today a new strength had come to her along with the sunshine. It is time to take stock. That little dark girl, Miriam, had got her claws into William, that was obvious. Percival was obviously queer or gay or whatever they were called nowadays, and that Colin Jones was probably that way too. Anyway he had snubbed her yesterday with his silly box, so she could count him out. Michael was out of her class, she had to be realistic. She was forty-two, on the large side, with glasses. Anyway he was probably sleeping with Fenella. Who else was there? Well, she was hardly likely to steal Mr Box from under the eyes of his wife, and, besides, she wished to be at a distance from Nigel; she had enough trouble with boys at school. There was Gerouin, but he was a useless sort of specimen and, anyway, too young, probably late twenties. So that left bearded Joe. Now there was hope there.

Penny is not a very good teacher, nor is she a very good Classicist, but she is extremely conscientious. Indeed this had been shown in her recent appraisal: 'Mrs Diver always prepares her lessons,' it said, 'to the best of her ability.' Nor is she just conscientious in the work field, no, this quality has permeated all aspects of her life, hence the good supply of lavatory paper, hence the preparation in advance on Joe. She has noted his vulnerability, his aloneness, and coming from the other course he wouldn't have worked out yet who was who. Nor did he have bonds of friendship with the others from that course. The three ladies seemed to keep themselves to themselves, and he obviously didn't like the Box child either.

What about the opposition? Well, Jane in the red tracksuit wasn't exactly a *femme fatale* any more than Mrs Small. Miriam was busy with William. Miss Aitchinson? She could dismiss this spinsterly person. That left only Caroline. She had shared with Caroline the first night, before Fenella had made them all shuffle round. She suspected Caroline of having a crush on Michael (silly idiot, she stood as little chance there as she did herself). But, and here was the danger, once she realised that Michael was beyond her grasp, she might veer round and see what else she could lay hands on, and that object might well be bearded Joe. Also, she was probably ten years younger than Penny. She did have the red hair too, but then, it wasn't very nice hair, it was all thin and stringy, but there was no telling what men might like. She thought sadly of Patrick and the PE. teacher. She was a plain woman if ever there was one. So, it behoved her to move quickly. Speed was of the essence.

"Hello," she says, moving purposefully forwards, "I don't think we've met. My name's Diver, Penny Diver."

"Hello," he says, "it's nice to meet someone who's a bit friendly. No one's spoken to me since yesterday." Sunshine pours from above.

Fenella cannot believe she has got them all aboard the coach, but look, she has! There is Gino at the wheel looking very pleased with himself. Even Anna looks less disagreeable than usual, although she is still clad in the black dress, the cardigan and the crucifix.

Fenella herself is looking efficient and elegant. She sports a pair of white jeans and a tee shirt with the logo 'Classic Tours' The C of Classic hovers over one breast, the T of Tours over the other.

Gerouin has noticed the tee shirt. He thinks Fenella is a most attractive woman. She was very kind too, looking for his mackintosh. Michael picks up the microphone.

"*Otiosus*," he says, "at leisure, on holiday, *securus*, free from care, *luxuriosus* even, though that has a naughtier nuance, but that is how I want you to be today when we visit Baiae, the Blackpool, the Brighton of the first century. And look, even the sun shines on us. But that's a treat in store. Let's turn our minds to Cumae now. Listen!" He holds his hands up for silence. He doesn't need to; they will listen anyway, even Percival will listen; he is anxious to fault Michael. He dislikes his empathetic approach. He should concentrate more on the facts. Michael prepares to read the Latin. It is something he knows that he excels in, and he loves the sound of the rolling hexameters, but Fenella has told him they can't understand the Latin. "But Fen," he says, "they're all Classicists." Fenella smiles.

"Don't spoil it for them," she says. So he reads the translation instead.

"'But the god-fearing Aeneas made for the shrine where Apollo, Sits throned on high, and that rusty cave, the deeply received, Crypt of the awe-inspiring Sibyl, to whom the god gives, The power to see deep and prophesy what's to come.'"

("It's a pity he's using the C.D. Lewis translation," says Percival to Colin, "the Penguin is far superior." Colin nods sagely and makes a note in his pad.)

"'There's a huge cave hollowed out from the flank of Cumae's hill, a hundred wide approaches it has, a hundred mouths, from which there issued a hundred voices, the Sibyl's answers.' This," says Michael, "is what we are going to see in about an hour from now. Do you remember how Petronius tells us about the Sibyl, an old withered woman hanging up in a bottle, who cried 'I want to die!'?"

"Excuse me," says Caroline, blushing scarlet, "but doesn't Robert Graves use it in *I, Claudius*?"

"Absolutely," says Michael. "Well done, Caroline..."

She blushes to the colour of her hair.

"Let's go back," he says, "among the Chalcidiani and Aeolians and find out who got to Cumae first."

He tells them of Hieron of Syracuse (he rolls the name around his tongue) and the valiant people of Cumae defeating the Etruscan fleet.

"And I'm going to read you Pindar's Victory Ode celebrating this, even though," (he adds wickedly), "Fenella tells me I shouldn't – in the original Greek." They are both right really, he is right because it is good to do something you do well and which you enjoy doing, and she because they do not (always excepting Percival) understand it at all.

He tells of raids by the Saracens and the revenge of Naples. He tells them of Cyclopean walls and trapezoidal passages, "Six galleries," he says, "filtering the afternoon light." Fenella knows how magical he finds it. He tells of the temple of Apollo, hijacked by the Christians, the temple of Jupiter that became a five-sided Christian basilica. "Here," he says, "are the great primordial cathedrals of early man. When the sun plays on the ruins there is stillness broken by a rustle of lizards and the murmur of the sea beneath. You will never," he says, and he holds them with his magnetic glance, "you will never go to a more romantic place."

Caroline gives a little gasp, Nigel thinks he's all right really, not like these other poofaces; even Colin murmurs something to Percival, but Percival shakes his head sadly: Colin has a lot to learn.

"Tabloid stuff," he says, "juvenilia. If you look back to *Classic News,* 1968 you will see that I have written a paper on the depth of the *dromos* at Cumae."

"Jolly good performance," says Jane to Kate.

Only Fenella knows it is not a performance: it is a passion. He has seen the Etruscan kings and the Sibyl hanging in the bottle. He will take them to the edge of his imagination, he will let them paddle their toes in it but he cannot, or will not, take them inside. Fenella knows that he will not even take her, and that he has never taken either of his wives.

Once released from the coach he gives them their head; some make for the echoing trapezoidal caverns beneath, others prefer, like the lizards, to bask in the sunshine that plays on the ruins of the temples. Like eddies in a pool, they form little groups and disperse. Momentarily and quizzically he watches them, knowing they will gain something, but not very much.

Cumae is a magical place high on a cliff top. The great ruins lie, sprawled amidst olive trees. There is a warmth, a balminess in the air, a light breeze blows and there is a scent of thyme. Wild geraniums spread themselves over grey stone, small yellow flowers rear anxiously from the remains of the temples. Below, the sea murmurs softly in the bay. Fenella stands looking down at it, her still-blond hair blown gently in the breeze. From the back she could still be the Fenella of twenty years ago.

"Come on, Fenella," says Michael, putting an arm round her shoulder. "We can't come to the most romantic place in the world and not be together!" Fenella turns and smiles. Great gusts of happiness break within her.

"Come and sit down," he says. "I'm going to read you some Virgil – in the original."

"But shall I understand it?" asks Fenella. "It's twenty-five years since I was at university."

"That doesn't matter very much," says Michael. "What matters is that we are sitting together in the sunshine in the oldest Greek colony in Italy."

"Read me the bit about the souls waiting to cross into the Underworld, then."

"No, no," he says. "This isn't a dead place. This is a place of light and life. Listen."

Fenella listens and finds she hasn't forgotten her Latin after all. She looks down at the sea and sees the Trojan warriors delighted at finding this peaceful bay, tying up their ships and tumbling out onto the beach, rather with the same enthusiasm that the coach party had disgorged themselves onto the Cumaean slopes. She sees them lighting fires and drawing water. She sees them armed with bows and arrows, hunting wild animals across the hilltops. She sees Daedalus, he of the bird's wings, hovering gently in the air above.

"I have written numerous papers on the excavations at Baiae," says a grating voice. "It might be advantageous for me to lead the party this afternoon." It is Percival addressing Michael. He has not waited for him to finish. He stands with his back to Fenella. He wishes to exclude her from the conversation.

"Oh I think..." says Fenella. She resents this self-opinionated man breaking in on Michael's dreams and their quiet together.

"I said," he raises his voice to exclude Fenella and gain Michael's attention, "I will lead the party at Baiae this afternoon." But Michael is watching Daedalus hovering above them in the sky.

"Fine," he says.

"Very well," says Percival. "I shall return to the coach and look over my notes."

"Super," says Michael; he is passing into Diana's grove with its gold-roofed temple.

"But..." says Fenella. Percival darts a look of triumph at her and takes his departure to the coach, where he will lock himself away from the most romantic place in the world and look at his facts and figures on Baiae.

Michael arrives in the twentieth century with a jolt.

"My god, what did I agree to?"

"You've just given him *carte blanche* to bore the pants off everyone at Baiae this afternoon!"

"Oh, Fen, I haven't."

"Yes, you have." She is laughing fondly at his discomfiture.

"Oh well, I'll tell them all about Baiae in the coach; and then let him do what he wants! Come on, I'm hungry. Let's find a spot for lunch."

Chapter IX

Pranzo al Fresco

This time Fenella has made them buy their own *panini* before they got on the coach at Gaeta. Some have bought nothing, but helped themselves from the bread basket at breakfast and shamefacedly open up rolls wrapped in hotel napkins. Gerouin is looking enviously at Colin's cache; his own lunch has mysteriously disappeared.

"I didn't eat anything at breakfast," Colin says, stung by Gerouin's stare. He has four rolls. He does not offer Gerouin any. "Have you seen Percival?" he asks.

"He's sitting in the coach," said Gerouin. He doesn't like Percival and hopes he has suffered the same embarrassment that he experienced on the previous day.

Mrs Small comes lumbering up after Jane, carrying a huge folding canvas stool. Veteran of many of her husband's digs, she knows it to be an invaluable adjunct. She is also clutching a vast bag of victuals. Gerouin looks longingly at them.

"Have you lost your lunch?" asks Jane of Gerouin. She is used to taking school parties on excursions. Nothing surprises her. Gerouin nods miserably.

"Come and share mine," says Kate surprisingly. "I've got enough for all Aeneas' men here, but then," she smiles, "I've got a lot to fill!" Nobody includes Colin in the invitation. He has removed himself from them behind the barricades of lunch bags and Percival's erudition.

Searching for A level grassy spot where the folding canvas stool will be safe, they come across Michael and Fenella, who have also attracted

Caroline and Miss Aitchinson. Like Colin, Miss Aitchinson has brought the breakfast rolls. She eats them dry, sitting on a piece of temple with the stick propped up beside her.

"Kate, come and join us," shouts Michael. "What's Roy doing these days?" Fenella is amused; there is, she thinks, a sort of freemasonry amongst the established, which even extends to the most disparate characters. (Michael has been with Kate's husband, Roy, in Turkey when he discovered a bronze sword.) Kate slowly assembles her canvas stool next to Michael, tests it for safety, and cautiously lowers herself into it.

"Well," she says, opening her enormous food bag (Gerouin drools), "he should be here in a couple of days; he is finishing off at Hissarlik."

Caroline feels rather resentful at this intrusion. She was just going to ask Michael about the Temple of Apollo. She hasn't asked before because she still feels shy addressing Michael after the other night, and has only just plucked up courage. She also hadn't liked to sit too close to him, and now the space between them is filled up with the bulk of Mrs Small.

"Oh dear," says Fenella, "your *panini* look very dry, Miss Aitchinson."

"I find a plain diet best," replies the other. "Rich food causes my leg to become inflamed."

"What exactly is wrong with your leg?" asks Gerouin. He is the happiest he has been for three days: he holds in his hand a *panino* crammed with salami, since the disappearance of his rolls he hasn't mislaid anything, he has people round him so he can follow them to places and not get lost. He is also sitting in close proximity to Fenella, his eyes are glued on the Classic Tours as they move up and down. And here he is engaged in conversation with them all. "Only," he adds, "my mother has a bad leg too."

"I doubt it's the same," replies Miss Aitchinson. "Mine is a very rare malady."

"So's my mother's," adds Gerouin eagerly. "She says..."

"I prefer not to discuss it," replies Miss Aitchinson coldly. She is always on difficult ground when people go on this tack. She has found it wisest to change the direction of the conversation. This has the dual advantage of making people too embarrassed to ask for further details and creating the impression that she is a woman of great personal courage.

A little of Gerouin's happiness recedes. He has put his foot in it again.

"Caroline," says Miss Aitchinson, "how did you fare last night?"

Caroline blushes scarlet. How can Miss Aitchinson know? Did she see her going to Michael's room? What does she mean anyway? She couldn't have known...

"When I was sleeping in that room with Miriam, I was awakened by the most terrible groans from next door. Didn't Miriam mention it?"

"No, I..."

"Terrible groans, accompanied by a whimpering noise. I've never heard anything like it."

"How dreadful," says Gerouin, who is anxious to make amends for his previous *faux pas*.

"Whose room is it?" asks Jane. She is squatting down unattractively on a piece of outcrop.

"I really have no idea," lies Caroline, who wants to allay any suspicion of her own nocturnal visit.

"Fenella would know," continues Jane. Fenella, who has been listening to Michael and Kate discussing digs, hears her name.

"What would Fenella know?" she asks.

"Who has the room next to Miss Aitchinson?"

"I think it's the Brownes," she says. She hopes they are talking about Miss Aitchinson's new room, the one she now shares with Penny.

"No, no," says Miss Aitchinson, banging her stick up and down in irritation, "not that room, the other one, 501. Who is next door to 501?" Michael, who knows nothing about the reporting of the nocturnal noises says innocently,

"My room's 500."

Jane slaps her thighs and roars with laughter. "Thought as much," she says.

"Were you ill in the night?" asks Miss Aitchinson, turning surprisingly sharply to Michael. But Fenella has spilt her wine all over Miss Aitchinson.

"Oh, how clumsy of me! I'm so sorry. Let me dry it with this tissue."

"We could do with that Penny Diver here with her lavatory rolls," says Jane, tucking heartily into her lunch.

"Let me give you some wine," says Fenella solicitously to Miss Aitchinson. "It's white."

"Falernian," says Michael, pouring some out. "It's a bit like Riesling." He turns to Caroline. "Will you try some, Caroline? Do you like Riesling?"

Caroline goes scarlet; it reminds her so horribly and clearly of the previous night's question, when he had asked her 'do you like...?' She does not look at him in case he thinks of it too.

Gerouin looks at Fenella nervously; he has been racking his brains on how to get into conversation again with her since the mackintosh.

"I wonder why that person was groaning," he says to her at last.

But he has erred again; for some reason Fenella looks irritated. "I've no idea," she says. "Michael, do tell us about the Sibyl."

Only Michael and Mrs Small talk about the Sibyl, everyone else is busy with their own thoughts. Caroline is wondering if Michael has some dreadful illness that he hasn't told anyone about. But there hadn't been any noises last night. Perhaps she'd ask Miriam. It does seem odd... Miss Aitchinson senses she has hit on something very suspicious indeed. There is more to this than meets the eye. Fenella decides that when they move to Pompeii she will arrange for Michael and her to have rooms miles away from the rest of them. Gerouin wonders if he has upset Fenella; he gazes sadly at the Classic Tours. Jane wishes she had a chap groaning away on top of her. She had once; it was jolly good. But that had been a long time ago. She didn't suppose she would again.

"She was little more than a fortune-teller, really," says Jane, "the Sibyl, I mean."

Then Mrs Small says a surprising thing,

"I can tell fortunes."

Suddenly they are all jolted out of their private reflections.

"Can you really?" asks Fenella.

"Yes, I really can," says Kate.

"How do you do it?" Even Michael is intrigued.

"Well," she says, in her sibilant voice, "it all started when Roy and I were on a dig in Crete. There was this old peasant woman, her husband was one of our workmen, kept coming up to me and asking me something. Well..." she shifts on her stool, "my Greek wasn't very good then, and I couldn't really understand what she was saying, and I brushed her off I suppose. The next year we went back again, and I'd learned a good deal of Greek and I could understand a lot more, and this peasant woman pops up again..." Five pairs of eyes fix themselves on Kate. "Anyway, now I could understand what she was asking, she wanted me to tell her if she would have a baby, and I said, 'I don't know'. But the odd thing was, as soon as I said I didn't know, I was sure I did. I knew she would have twin boys, so I told her and, so I wouldn't be caught out, I added, 'but not for five years'. We didn't go back to Crete for eight years. That woman had three year old twins."

"You're having us on," said Jane.

"Am I?" asked Kate. And there was a twinkle in her eye.

"Why don't you.. I mean, would you tell our fortunes?" asks Caroline. She feels immensely excited.

"You can't tell fortunes in the sunlight," says Michael.

"But you could in the Sibyl's cave," says Jane. Like Caroline, she feels a frisson of excitement. Miss Aitchinson taps her stick.

"It's dangerous to play about with the supernatural," she says severely.

"Go on," says Jane.

"Well," says Mrs Small, heaving her bulk off the stool, "if you bump into me in the Sibyl's cave, I might, but, there again, I might not." And off she lumbers. Her bag of food is empty.

Miriam and William have already been to the Sybil's underground cavern. Poor little Miriam had found it very spooky and scary. Once or twice she had almost caught hold of him; he had to put his arm round her more than once. She seemed to find it quite comforting. It was a good thing that Colin Jones had taken his place with Percival. It might be a good idea if those two shared together when they moved to Sorrento.

William is thinking he would like to have a room to himself there, somewhere where Miriam could come if she needed his help.

Gerouin thinks he will follow in the wake of Caroline and Jane who, after a brief conversation, have set off purposefully (though not, it would seem, in the direction of the cavern). He comes panting up to them.

"That was an interesting conversation at lunch, wasn't it?" he asks them. He feels almost confident now. But they are not very friendly.

"Yes," says Caroline curtly.

"Down here," Jane says to Caroline. They quicken their steps.

"I say," says Gerouin breathlessly, "you do walk fast."

"That bush over there," says Caroline. Their speed increases.

"I say," says Gerouin, "the cavern's down there, you know."

Jane stops in her tracks and stares at him. "Well, why don't you bloody go there, then?" Gerouin is taken aback at this hostility.

"I thought we could all go together."

"Well you can go if you like," says Jane, "but Caroline and I are going to have a pee behind this bush."

"Oh... I... I'm terribly sorry... I... I..." But he is talking to thin air; they have both disappeared. What an awful mistake. What must they think of him? How embarrassing. He mustn't hang around or they'll think... actually a pee isn't such a bad idea. Have to make sure its not near them, though...

Fenella and Michael continue sitting amidst the cyclopean walls of the Temple of Apollo. They feel idle and there is half a bottle of Falernian left. Michael runs his finger lightly across Classic Tours.

"You know what I'd like now."

"Yes, but you're going to have to settle for a fag instead."

"Nice in the thyme with the echoing caverns beneath."

"Reverberating round Miss Aitchinson?"

"What was all that?"

"She thought someone must have been ill in the night. They were making terrible groaning noises. They seemed to come from your room."

"Oh Fen!" Michael pulls a face, puts his arm round her and draws her to him. "I don't make all that much noise, do I?"

She turns and kisses his neck.

"Well," he says, putting a hand between her thighs, "you're not exactly silent yourself. Anyway," he withdraws a hand and lights a cigarette, "that's what life's about, isn't it, fucking, and going to places like this? Did I tell you Caroline came and offered herself to me last night?"

"No, really? Did you accept?" Fenella knows she has nothing to fear from that quarter.

"Well, Fen, you may well imagine how tempted I was. I came to make love to you, and there you were, fast asleep. So, hot with passion, I return to my room to be assailed by a red-haired virgin, thrusting herself upon me."

"What did you do?"

"I asked her if she liked fucking, and she was so scared she fled."

"What would you have done if she had said yes?"

"Ah! That we shall never know! Fen, look at the sea down there. Aeneas brought his boat in there."

"Yes, Michael, you told me."

"Oh god! I'm going senile. I've got Alzheimer's. Cast me away. Lock me up. By the way, I know what's in the box, so at least I haven't forgotten that!"

"Box?"

"Colin Jones' box. We had a bet on the contents."

"I get confused with all these boxes: Mr and Mrs Box and Nigel Box and Jones' box. Anyway, I shall find out."

"I doubt it."

"Have you been cheating?"

"Now, Fen, would I?"

"Yes, you would." She inserts a hand inside his jeans and explores gently.

"Does this indicate you intend paying your debts now?"

"No."

"No, I thought not, Fen. I want to have you here, in Apollo's temple."

"What about the Boxes and the Browns?"

Fenella looks at him as he sits there with his back against a broken column, cigarette in hand. The sun glints in his hair, no longer blond and shoulder length as it was so long ago in Ithaca, but still appropriate. He has always looked the part; always he has been conversant with trends, but effortlessly. It is this strange mixture in him, his love for the Classical world which has taken him among the dull and the dry, coupled with his looks and charm, his intense longing to recreate the past and his ability to be of the moment, at the same time. He is smiling at her with glee in his eyes, the way he does when he is contemplating something outrageous, and knows that she will acquiesce.

He gets up and unzips her jeans.

"It'll be wonderful, Fen. Apollo is the Archer god, you know. He'll make sure I fire my arrows absolutely," he caresses her, "on the target." His lips are brushing her neck. He unzips his trousers, unconcerned for possible passers-by. He moves against her. "Do you like my arrow, Fen? Shall I..." his fingers play with her, "shall I...?" They both know she will be unable to resist him.

Nobody sees them except for Gerouin, who had got lost after his pee. Now he comes upon them suddenly. He retreats in haste.

He is very shocked indeed. All right, he had seen Gino and Anna up to something of a similar nature in the back seat of the coach yesterday, but he hadn't really seen that much, and, anyway, they were foreign and you expected that sort of thing from foreigners, especially these Italians (passionate nature, he'd mentioned it in his letter to his mother). But Fenella in her white jeans, and married too, and being responsible for all of them. Of course he wouldn't say anything, but any of the others might, that Percival, for instance, you could imagine him complaining. And Michael! Of course that wasn't so surprising really, a dashing chap like that, he could probably get women whenever he wanted. But he was married, married to that chat-show woman. It wasn't very good really. And then all this sex! Well, he'd seen quite a number of videos – there was a useful shop just round the corner at home, he used to watch one when his mother went off to her patchwork classes on a Wednesday. So the sex bit was nothing new to him, but it was different really when you knew the people concerned. How could he look Fenella in the face now, knowing how she'd looked? And then he feels immense envy, how lucky these people were. Other people's lives were so easy; they didn't get lost all the time, and have children laughing at them in school. Why couldn't he just meet some girl and have sex with her without things going wrong all the time? It is all so unfair.

Thinking these sad thoughts Gerouin finds himself eventually back at the coach. He casts a circumspect look over it, but can see no Gino and Anna, only Percival. He thinks he will get back on the coach himself, at least he won't get lost that way. Anyway, he didn't want to go and have his fortune told. It would be all bad news after all.

Chapter X

Fortune-Telling

Percival has spent a great deal of time going over his notes on Baiae. Not that he needs to. His own writings are far more familiar to him than those of any other author. He feels elated, too, at the thought of leading the group at Baiae (it would look well on his CV). There had been too much frivolity under Thorpe-Smith's leadership. It was time that people learned some hard facts. He takes out the rolls he had removed from the hotel breakfast bread-basket and eats them without enjoyment. They taste old and stale. A disconcerting thought flickers in his mind that they are like himself. He is angry for permitting himself to entertain such thoughts. The fact of the matter is of course, he has been too bright, too learned, too erudite for people. People wanted froth nowadays, frivolity, 'fun' (he snorts), they wanted coffee-table books and TV programmes with loud pop music. There was no room for scholars like himself. It was the same in schools nowadays. There was no discipline. And what had happened when he had tried to instil a little discipline? Pushed out without a reference. Perhaps he had hurt the boy a little.. his tongue passes swiftly over his lips... perhaps he had, pain was a good adjunct to discipline. People didn't understand that. Moreover, at fifty-five he was too old to be in the job market. It was university teaching he was most suited for with his extensive knowledge. There was another miscarriage of justice! When he should have obtained a first, he obtained only a third. He remembered now the insulting comments of his tutor. "You know a great number of facts, Mr Jeavons. What a pity you can't apply any of them!" Ah, but he had proved him wrong. He was on the committees of at least four Classical Societies, probably five when he heard back about the steering committee of LACA. He had published papers (not all at his own expense, either). He had some hundreds neatly stacked in his room waiting for ordering. What had that man Thorpe-Smith got that he hadn't got? Rich wives! That was the kind of man he was, living off women! He thought of Fenella with her Classic Tours tee shirt and shuddered. She was another; she was like a bitch on heat. He had seen her looking at Michael. There was only one thing in her mind. He would have them whipped, all of them.

He has finished his two dry rolls and thinks his miserable thoughts. He has been through his notes on Baiae. He has several pages of pleasing statistics. For a while he stares out of the window at the grass where the sunshine plays on grey stone and wild geraniums grow. He feels no desire to go out there now; he feels hunger, he wishes now he had bought food. He would also like something to drink. He looks disconsolately round the coach: they are an untidy lot, these Classics teachers, muddle and rubbish everywhere. And there, lying in the aisle is, of all things, a Tesco bag! Yes, in Southern Italy, a Tesco bag, and spilling out of it are two *panini*, one with cheese, and the other with ham. There is also a bottle of mineral water and a bunch of grapes.

In the echoing underground cavern of the Cumaean Sibyl, sinister happenings are afoot. Strange sounds echo and reverberate from trapezoidal wall to trapezoidal wall. A weird new hieroglyphic appears on the rough granite rock. But, as so often, the mystical has a mundane and rational explanation. The reverberating sounds are not from the Sibyl hanging from her bottle speaking in a hundred voices. They are Nigel Box rushing up and down the passages trying out different vocal effects to frighten all the poofaces. The hieroglyphics with the letters NB are carved with a Swiss Army knife belonging to Nigel Box.

It is one of the Brown(e) contingent, though, none of whom has hitherto been noted for community spirit, who now takes action and taps Mrs Box on the shoulder.

"You'll do us all a favour," she says, "if you take that child out of here."

Mrs Box utters a tremulous "Oh dear." She knows she ought to do something but doesn't quite know what. She looks hopelessly towards her husband.

"Bugger off," shouts Mr Box. "Nigel, bugger off out of it."

"Oh dear," repeats his wife hopelessly. He glowers at the cowering Mrs Box. "Can't you even see to the child?" he says. "Can't you ever do anything right?" On the side of the cavern, where he has his hand, there is a raised nodule. He touches it with his sweaty fingers, and moves his finger on it. It puts him in mind of a nipple; he has been imagining Fenella's inside her Classic Tours tee shirt. He takes the nodule between finger and thumb and presses it hard.

A strange apparition has appeared in a recess in the rock. It cannot be a ghost for there is nothing of the shadow about it. It has substance, it has bulk, it is female; it is not, however, the Sibyl, but Mrs Small on her folding canvas stool. She is telling fortunes.

Unlike the Sibyl, her words are not written on leaves, nor does she speak with a hundred mouths. Her proclamations are laconic, curt even. Nor does she (true to the oracular tradition) offer any explanation for her words.

William and Miriam (in spite of Miriam being almost too frightened) decide to return and put the prophetess to the test.

"You go first, William," says Miriam. William sees it behoves him to be brave.

"Wait here, Miriam, there's a little light coming through. Now, don't worry. I'll soon be back."

"Oh, William..."

"I shall be right back, don't you worry." In spite of his bravado, he experiences some trepidation at the awesome sight of Kate on her canvas stool.

"I see," says the sibyl, "a dark-haired girl..."

"Ah," says William, thinking of Miriam.

"She beckons and..."

"What do I do?" asks William. "Am I there? Do I go?"

"Alas," says the sibyl disappointingly, "the clouds are coming over. I cannot see."

William doesn't think much of this. He knows about the beckoning anyway.

"I wouldn't bother," he says on his return to the anxious Miriam. "She didn't say anything much."

But Miriam thinks she will bother. There is something she would like to know. She is to be surprised.

"I see," says Kate, "a tall dark stranger crossing your path."

"Are you sure?" asks Miriam. William is short and fair and rather bald.

"I see what I see," replies the sibyl.

Penny thinks it's all rubbish, but you never know. It makes a break from holding Joe's tripod anyway.

Kate is all smiles.

"A letter," she says, "a letter coming from overseas."

"Oh," says Penny, "I hope it's good news."

"Excellent news, excellent news," hisses Kate, but she will not or cannot divulge what it is.

Nigel Box, once more upon the scene, is taken forward by his mother.

"Smart new uniform," says the sibyl. "Crest on the blazer pocket."

"That's stupid," retorts Nigel. "We don't wear uniform at our school."

"Oh, hush, dear," says Mrs Box. She does not consult the sibyl herself. There is nothing she wants to know about the future.

Miss Aitchinson, too, is to be seen advancing towards the sibyl.

"Stay. Approach not too near," cries the prophetess. "I see a rod. I see it lie cast upon the ground. I see a woman walking straight and upright like a sapling. I can see no more." Miss Aitchinson moves thoughtfully away.

Jane leaves roaring with laughter.

"I see," the sibyl has proclaimed, "a bar of soap and a basin of hot water."

Fenella is coaxing them upwards into the light. She wants to get them on the coach as quickly as possible now.

"No sibylline prophesies, Fen?" asks Michael.

"No," says Fenella, "I can see the future, or, at least, the immediate future, very clearly. I can see Gerouin wandering lost and Percival sitting gloating over the prospect of Baiae."

"Go on," says Michael, "don't be chicken," and he moves her firmly into position, placing his hands on her shoulders, before a kind of modesty prompts him to leave her to it.

Kate looks at Fenella in a kindly way.

"I see," she says, "much sadness and much happiness."

"But which is there more of?" asks Fenella.

"I cannot see," replies the sibyl. "They are mixed together."

"Ah," says Fenella. It has been the same for twenty years.

Michael, too, to Fenella's surprise, goes to consult Kate. He is only just in time, she is packing up the folding stool.

"Well?" says Michael. He is about to quote 'her fey heart swelled in ecstasy, larger than life she seemed...' but, given Kate's size, it doesn't seem very tactful. She is certainly enormous, awe-inspiring, even with the canvas stool. She looks at Michael as if she does not recognise him; a sort of shudder passes across her body. She gathers up the stool firmly and says:

"Sorry, Michael, Apollo has left me. The gift of tongues has gone."

"Oh, that's a shame," says Michael. "Couldn't you get him back again? Couldn't your foaming mouth make another utterance?"

"No," says Kate firmly. "I'm tired."

"All right," says Michael, smiling his golden smile. "Let me carry your stool for you, then."

Gerouin climbs into the coach and goes to find his place near the back. He nods politely at Percival as he passes him. But something arrests him. He stops in his tracks. Has he too seen a supernatural apparition? Not at all. He has seen a Tesco bag. It is stretched across Percival's knees. There is also an empty bottle of mineral water, half a cheese *panino* and the remains of a bunch of grapes.

"Hi," shouts Gerouin, goaded out of his usual lack of confidence by a surge of anger, such as he has not felt since Next Door's dog took a piece out of his ankle.

"Hi, you've stolen my sandwiches!"

"Don't be ridiculous," says Percival, holding the uneaten half of a *panino*.

"*In flagrante delicto!*" exclaims Gerouin.

This remark is, perhaps, not strictly applicable to Percival's behaviour with the *panini*, but recent sightings have brought this expression to Gerouin's mind.

"Red-handed," he says. "I have caught him red-handed." For now the coach is filling up. People look towards Percival's seat; they sense drama.

And lo! Whether it is Cumae or the recent lascivious sightings, or the combined loss of the mackintosh and silver-knobbed pen, or anger itself, a new Gerouin is born: no longer a lost soul wandering in the wake of the pee-ers, a sojourner in the sculleries of hotel kitchens, but a tall straight figure, a man demanding justice.

"Eating my sandwiches," he cries. Percival puts the uneaten piece of bread down on the Tesco bag. He feels distinctively uncomfortable. This is not an auspicious start to the Baiae lecture.

"Are those Gerouin's *panini*?" asks Jane. "Have you pinched his lunch?"

Percival feels a sense of vertigo as this great red-trousered woman stands over him.

"I may have made an error, taken his in mistake for my own..."

"Balls," says Jane. "I saw Gerouin carrying that Tesco bag, because I thought, how odd to have a Tesco bag in the middle of Italy. And Kate was with me. We saw him coming back from the shop."

Another one of the Brown(e)s (they appear to be becoming more vocal) volunteers that she has also seen Gerouin with the bag.

"Do you think there will be a fight?" whispers Miriam to William. He pats her shoulder reassuringly.

Miss Aitchinson volunteers that all sorts of odd things seem to happen on this course.

Bearded Joe, too, adopts a public voice.

"Here," he says, "did you nick his sarnies?"

"Yes, he did," says Gerouin triumphantly, snatching the half-eaten *panino* and holding it aloft. "And he drank my mineral water." A murmur goes round the coach. This is a crime indeed. Gerouin is becoming a hero. Five minutes ago he was despised by all and sundry. And now? Peripeteia, a reversal of fortune. Never has he stood as the object of so many people's sympathy all at once.

Colin Jones, recently embarked on the coach, sees the fall of his hero from his dizzy height. But he is a time-server; he doesn't leap to his defence. Anyway, the man might have stolen his box.

Nigel is heard asking his mother if the police will come, and don't Italian policemen have guns? Will there be a shoot-out? He starts making suitable noises.

"Belt up, Nigel," says his father. Mrs Box trembles.

Caroline is wondering what Michael will say. She can see him from the window, walking along in earnest conversation with Kate Small.

Nobody knows quite what to do. The Brown(e)s converse frantically together, and at last the youngest Brown says:

"If he took them instead of his own *panini*, where are his, then?"

This piece of logic meets with universal acclaim. It is a neat syllogism, something of the kind could be found in Plato.

"He must be made to pay," says Mrs Box surprisingly. All the insults to Nigel and the anger of her husband combine within her to give her voice.

"Like in Homer," says Miriam, "when they demand blood money for a murdered relative."

This analogy, though not exact, voices the feelings of the assembled course members. There is angry murmuring. The feeling of the crowd is dangerous.

And at this moment (when anything could happen), Fenella, all in white (trousers and Classic Tours tee shirt) appears on the scene. She has not been in the travel business twenty years for nothing.

"Fenella!"

"His sarnies!"

"Mineral water, too."

"And grapes."

"Tesco bag."

"Not very nice."

"Would rather not sit on that side of the coach."

"Fenella!"

"I hope," says Fenella, even more brightly than usual, "you have all enjoyed Cumae. Now we are about to set off for Baiae. We're just waiting for Michael and Kate. Any little problems can be sorted out in a minute, I'm sure. Please sit down, Miss Aitchinson, and you, Gerouin, thank you. Ah! Here's Michael. We're all waiting, Michael, to hear about Baiae, the place to go when you are feeling *otiosus*."

"Absolutely," says Michael, cognisant of the appeal in Fenella's look.

Chapter XI
Baiae

"Baiae..."

While Michael speaks and the simmering dies down, Fenella goes and sits next to Gerouin and listens to his whispered anger. He is so elated by his own heroic stance that he doesn't think at all about his last sighting of Fenella. She is very nice to him, and sits next to him all the way to Baiae. He feels enormously happy.

"Well, of course, we shall reimburse you for your lunch," Fenella is whispering so as not to interrupt Michael. But, while she is whispering, she is also turning a number of problems over in her mind: will it be appropriate for Percival to lead the group at Baiae? What will happen if he does? Does Michael actually know about the stolen lunch, and, if he doesn't, how can she explain it in full view of everyone? And, anyway, it is tactful to remain seated next to Gerouin as a sort of official voice of approbation of Gerouin and disapproval of Percival. Perhaps Michael will forget anyway.

"It was from Baiae to Puteoli," Michael is saying, "that the wicked emperor Caligula built his bridge of boats. Suetonius tells us that he anchored them two deep, covered them with a layer of earth, and for two days rode across this bridge in a gold zoot-suit on a resplendent horse. Lots of reasons were given for this extraordinary exercise..."

He wonders momentarily why Fenella is sitting next to Gerouin; laughs at himself for feeling something possibly akin to jealousy - of Gerouin, of all people, thinks of the Temple of Apollo and smiles at the memory.

"Some thought it was a kind of PR exercise to scare the Greeks and Britons – if he could do that, what wouldn't he, and couldn't he, do to them? Suetonius, though, has a different explanation: Thrasyllus, the astrologer had told Tiberius that Caligula was just as likely to become Emperor as he was to ride on horseback over the Gulf of Baiae. It seemed as good a way as any of proving him wrong."

"People had this idea of Baiae as being a degenerate sort of place, where you went for a dirty weekend," (Miss Aitchinson looks disapproving) "sort of place like Brighton used to be in the fifties maybe, a kind of marine Soho.

"Cicero has stern things to say about Baiae. Let me read you – Fenella says I mustn't read in Latin – This is taken from Pro Caelio: 'The accusers are dinning into our ears the words debauchery, amours, misconduct, trips to Baiae, beach parties, feasts, revels, concerts, musical parties, pleasure boats ...' You see, going to Baiae is almost synonymous with low moral standards.

Propertius can't stand the thought that his girlfriend Cynthia's gone off there:

'As soon as you may, abandon decadent Baiae, Those beaches bring so many separations, Those beaches so hostile to virtuous girls'."

Caroline, who is listening avidly, is reminded of his words. "You're a virgin, aren't you?" Baiae, then, is another of those scary places, like smoky pubs and school discos.

"'Oh perish seaside Baiae, love's corruption.'

"Seneca has lots of stern things to say about Baiae, too, but then, he would, wouldn't he? And! Just one more thing. Pliny tells us, one Lucius Crassus, who was the first inventor of shower-baths, used to fit out houses in Baiae and then sell them off. A property developer making a quick buck! Perhaps a touch of California about Baiae!" Fenella wonders how Michael got on in his years in the States. She imagines the Americans would have loved him. He seldom talks about them however. Indeed, he seldom talks about his experiences at all. "It's all very boring, Fen," he says when she asks him. Whether he really regards them as boring or whether he doesn't want to share them with her, she can never decide. Perhaps he is only really interested in things that happened over two thousand years ago.

"Now, as it was such a fun place to be, you'll forgive Gino and me if we go off and visit the flesh-pots! I shall leave you in the capable hands of my colleague Percival Jeavons..." Fenella groans; there is a disturbed rustling in the coach. Fenella stands up quickly.

"Of course," she says, "if you prefer to go out on your own that's absolutely fine. I think Michael has some maps and plans up at the front there!" It is the best she can do. She also has no idea what Gino and Michael are up to. She is about to ask Anna when she remembers she hasn't turned up today. "*Non le piacciono le vecche pietre*," says Gino. Fenella doesn't say anything about the defunct drinks machine and Anna's duties with it being part of the bargain.

At Baiae they pour rapidly off the coach and disperse in little murmuring groups. It has been a very exciting day one way and another – there were the echoing caverns at Cumae and then the fortune-telling, and all the drama of the stolen sandwiches. There is a feeling of disappointment among some that more didn't come of it. Then there is a sense of the wickedness of the place they have come to. It may well be little more than an unattractive small town centred round a railway station now, but wicked it once was.

There is a manifest desire among the righteous to show their disapproval of the sandwich stealer by absenting themselves from his guided tour. This too fits in quite neatly with their own abhorrence of listening to a man whom they consider arrogant, patronising and boring.

"Come on," says bearded Joe to Penny, "let's go and have a drink. I don't want to listen to that prat."

Gerouin is standing outside the coach, once again on his own. He senses his moment of glory has passed. But no! Jane approaches in her red tracksuit.

"Come on, Gerouin," she says. "I'm going to buy you a *gelato*."

"*Gelato*? Oh you mean an ice cream. Oh, are you? Oh, thank you." He is amazed.

"I'm sorry I was sharp at Cumae," she goes on, taking him along in her wake, "but I was dying for a pee. And you know how you can't think of anything else when your bladder's bursting."

No woman has ever spoken to Gerouin like this before. He tries to take it all in.

Colin Jones feels in a quandary. He has sat apart from Percival on the coach so that no one can imagine him to be in any way implicated in the crime, but, on the other hand, he has not spoken to anyone really on the course except Percival. He is much too shy to approach anyone else and, anyway, since Penny Diver tried to sit next to him on the first day nobody has shown any interest in him at all. It could well be that he is now totally ostracised from the group, and a stark choice faces him: reunion with Percival, or complete isolation.

Percival has spoken to nobody since the accusation fell so heavily upon him. Indeed, he seldom speaks to others unless it is to lecture at them. He does not like conversation as such. He has no use for other people's views. The incident was certainly an uncomfortable one, but it had passed. He does not doubt that many people will wish for the benefit of his erudition. To this end he is gathering up his briefcase full of notes.

"Got any sandwiches in there?" shouts Nigel. Mrs Box, who was surprised by her own outspoken words against Percival, feels a new inner strength and says firmly,

"Come here, Nigel. Don't speak to that person." Kate Small, exhausted by her fortune-telling, elects to stay in the coach.

William and Miriam are walking off together.

"It's very difficult," William is saying, "sharing with him. I shan't know what to say."

"Say nothing," says Miriam, "he's a horrible man. He taught at a prep school near us, and I'm sure there was some scandal. I can't think what it was now. I keep trying to think." She purses her lips and furrows her brow. It is the sort of little problem she likes.

"I shall insist on a different room when we move to Sorrento," says William. "I shall see if I can have a room to myself."

"Good idea," says Miriam. It is strange, but she hardly thinks about Joe and Timothy at all, nowadays.

Caroline is watching Michael, who is engaged in animated Italian with Gino. There is also much physical joking with Gino, and Michael is making strange gesticulations which end in loud laughter on the part of both. Fenella is standing by, not entirely of them, nor yet separate. She looks moderately amused. Caroline thinks she will go and join them. She remembers Michael said he and Gino were going off to the flesh-pots of Baiae. But surely he doesn't mean that seriously? Modern Baiae looks a very un-flesh-potty sort of place and, anyway, surely men don't go off to flesh-pots in the afternoon? And, after all, Fenella is with them. It would be nice to go off in a foursome. Fenella could walk with Gino while she went with Michael. She feels quite bold about him again.

But alas! It is too late. Just as she is about to go over and join them, Gino and Michael take off together. They push at each other in a very silly way. You would think Gino would be more respectful to Michael really. Fenella herself goes back on to the coach. There are things she wants to sort out. STT as Michael calls it.

There remains Margaret Aitchinson who has paid for her culture and is going to get her fair share of it, even if it means listening to Percival Jeavons instead of Michael Thorpe-Smith. Actually she has a sneaking sympathy with Percival over the eating of the *panini*. After all, Gerouin had left them lying about. Percival probably thought he didn't want them. It was the sort of action she might well have done herself. Anyway, Gerouin had kept them all waiting at the airport when he lost his mackintosh. He obviously wasn't worth bothering about. She sets off with the maps Fenella has provided. The site is behind the station.

Percival has assumed that they will all come and follow after him. He is unable to put himself in other people's shoes. He knows that he would be only too pleased to be in the happy position of hearing his own lecture. He assumes others will feel the same. He has dismissed the sandwich episode from his mind.

He feels no need to guide others towards the ruins. That is their responsibility. He will talk at them when they get there.

Caroline is now at a loss, her plans foiled. Kate Small occupies two seats near the back of the coach. Fenella sits at the front with her reading glasses on. Neither wants Caroline. She decides to follow Miss

Aitchinson. Colin has decided he, too, has no choice. If he follows after Caroline (at a safe distance), nobody will think he has colluded with Percival.

Percival stands at the Scavi di Baiae and waits. First to arrive is Miss Aitchinson, but he has no desire to speak to her, nor she to him. They stand some yards apart and look in opposite directions; neither evinces any interest in the ruins. Next to arrive is Caroline. She smiles in a sociable way and makes noises suggestive of anticipated enjoyment. Percival turns his back. Miss Aitchinson pokes at a bit of imperial *palatium* with her stick. Colin Jones arrives. Neither Miss Aitchinson nor Caroline know his name; they feel they should by now, but, as they do not, they think it wiser to say nothing. Colin cannot bring himself to speak to any of them. Percival does not wish to speak to him because he wants to punish him for his desertion after the sandwiches. The four of them spend many minutes in silence. At last Miss Aitchinson says,

"Are you going to start?"

"I am waiting for the others," comes the reply.

"There aren't any others," says Caroline.

He discounts her words, firstly because she is a woman, and secondly, because he does not wish to accept them. In his heart of hearts he knows nobody else will come. Then he starts to rationalise this. Why won't they come? Answer: because they are too stupid. They know they will not be able to stand the force of his erudition. It is a compliment to him, in fact. Out of the whole party there are only three that are capable of understanding, or rather trying to understand what he will say. It is all right now.

"Octagonal without and circular within, it preserves four niches and part of its domed roof. Systematic excavations began in 1941."
He does not even look at them, these swine before whom he casts his pearls. So it is that shortly afterwards, Miss Aitchinson takes herself and her stick off back to the coach. Caroline and Colin hesitate momentarily and then follow after.

"These buildings appear to have made up a thermal complex, principal among them is a great circular hall some twenty-two metres in diameter."
He looks up for the first time. There is nobody there.

****

"Have another *gelato*," says Jane. "You need to put a bit of flesh on." She grins at him encouragingly. He grins back. It has been an exhilarating day. First he was the hero of the hour, and now he is being – what is the expression? – 'chatted up' by this lady. He looks at Jane across the Formica top, the dirty glasses and the overflowing ashtray. It isn't perhaps the nicest of cafés, or the most romantic, but then, what is happening, is! He has to be honest: Jane is not the most glamorous woman in the world. She has very short brown hair, and her teeth, ears and nose have a distinct prominence, each vies with the other for the onlooker's attention, but, there again, he is no oil painting himself, and she may well have a good figure under that tracksuit. Again, she may be a little older than he. But what is wrong with an older woman? And she has obviously taken a shine to him. She has bought him an ice cream, is offering him a second one, has even enquired about the loss of his mackintosh, and best of all, is loud in condemnation of Percival's heinous crime.

"He's a pain in the arse, if you ask me," says Jane. Gerouin likes this expression very much. He stores it away for future use.

"Mind you," she adds, "there's quite a number on this course that fit that category." Extraordinary! She is saying exactly what he has been thinking himself.

"Yes," he agrees eagerly, knocking over the overflowing ashtray, "that Colin Jones is one. I share a room with him and he never speaks at all. And he's got some funny box with him."

"Yes," says Jane, "I wonder what he's got in it. Have you asked him?"

"Well, I did sort of say something, but he kind of muttered and I didn't like to ask again."

"I hope he's not going to blow us all up," says Jane.

"You don't think...?"

"No. Not enough guts." A thought strikes her. "We've got another half an hour. Let's have a drink. What do you want?"

"I suppose they don't have tea?" Even he is conscious that this is not a very audacious reply.

"You don't come to Italy to drink tea," says Jane. "Let's have an amaretto."

Gerouin is not sure what this is, but it is a day for living dangerously. "Yes, let's," he says.

Jane's Italian is very good, or so it seems to Gerouin. Anyway the amaretti are brought along with some macaroon biscuits.

"Let me..." He sees the waiter (a surly character) standing, threateningly it seems. He gets his purse out. "Put that away," says Jane, "before you lose it. I'll do this. Hey, don't drink it all at once!"

He feels abashed and takes a small sip. He's not really quite sure about it and searches about for something to cover up his ignorance. An extraordinary sentence forms itself on his lips.

"I saw Fenella and Michael having sexual intercourse at Cumae."

He has succeeded beyond his wildest hopes in interesting Jane. She bangs the glass of amaretto down on the dirty table.

"No! Where? In the coach?"

"No, in the temple bit."

"What, Apollo's temple?"

"Well, I think so."

"How did you know?" asks Jane, leaning forward pruriently. But before he can answer this difficult question, she sees Miriam and William hovering hesitantly in the café doorway.

"Here," she shouts, "come and have a drink and hear Gerouin's amazing bit of gossip."

Whether William and Miriam would have preferred to be alone, is a matter of conjecture. But now they are all four sitting round the Formica table. Sometimes William's leg brushes a little against Miriam's. She doesn't appear to notice.

"What are you drinking?" she asks.

"Amaretto," says Gerouin knowledgeably. "It's very nice." He takes an impressive gulp to prove his point.

"I think I'll have one of those," says Miriam.

"So shall I," says William. He's glad to see Miriam likes a drink.

"*Per favore, per favore,*" says William to the waiter. The evening classes have not been in vain.

"Tell them," says Jane to Gerouin, "what you told me." He suddenly feels rather shy.

"I... I saw Fenella and Michael... they–"

"Were having it off," says Jane, "in the Temple of Apollo."

"Gosh!" says William, "in the Temple of Apollo?"

"Did they have their clothes on?" asks Miriam. This is exactly the sort of conversation she likes. It is even better than talking about Joe and Timothy. They all look to Gerouin for enlightenment.

"Well, no, I mean, they had their top halves on."

"How did you come to see them?" asks William. There is a momentary pause while the waiter waits to be paid for the amaretti. He adds a few thousand lire on this time.

"Well I was lost, actually," says Gerouin, "and I..."

"Now wait a minute," says Miriam, taking a substantial sip of amaretto, "now I understand!" She takes another little sip. They all wait to hear what she has to say. She gives a little pat to her short layered dark hair and says, "I don't know whether I should, really." She gives a little giggle.

"Spit it out," says Jane.

"Well..." says Miriam. It is so nice to be the centre of attention again, just like she is at home. "You know the first night I was sharing with that horrid old woman with the stick?"

"I don't think she is that old really," says William.

"Never mind that," says Jane.

"Well, she took forever getting to bed and fussing around, I've never seen such a palaver, and she put her stick for me to fall over, and I'm sure it was on purpose."

"Yes, yes," says everyone.

"Well, eventually she got into bed and I said could we turn the light out, and she said yes – only she fussed around making me wait, and I'd just turned the light off when all these noises started coming from next door. There was this couple making love and they were really going at it

– like some people do," adds Miriam. "Well, I'm quite broad minded, I mean you are when you've had babies, but..."

"It was Fenella and Michael!" says William.

"Well, yes, it must have been, only I didn't know his room was next door; I thought it was, well, Italians, I suppose..."

"Were they making a lot of noise, groaning and so on?" asks Jane. There is a touch of envy in her voice. "Miss Aitchinson was going on about it while we were eating lunch; I thought then it was Fenella and Michael."

"That was very perspicacious of you," says William. "How did you work that one out?" But Miriam doesn't like other women being complimented by William, even if they do look like Jane.

"I haven't told you about Miss Aitchinson," she says. "She kept saying, 'Miriam, what's that noise?' It never crossed her mind what it really was, I was so embarrassed, I just burst into tears, and then she said, 'Do you think someone's ill?' And I pretended to be asleep, and it went on and on; and the next morning she went on about it again. Apparently it had happened again in the morning, only I'd been asleep. But she had no idea."

"Oh gosh!" says Gerouin.

"What?" asks Jane.

"Well, they were talking about it at lunch, and just to make conversation I asked Fenella who she thought it was, because I thought it was someone being ill."

"And what did Fenella say?"

"Well, she was quite sharp really. I can see why now."

"I think she's known him for years," says Jane. "They must have run other courses together."

"I expect so," says Jane.

"But they're both married," says Gerouin.

"That doesn't always stop people," says William.

"No," says Miriam. "Sometimes it makes people all the keener."

"Yes," says William.

"Ah," says Jane.

"Oh," says Gerouin.

The waiter comes up all smiles now with the bottle. Unasked he pours out more amaretti. The lire are entering six figures.

The four of them feel quite well-disposed towards each other; they feel bound together by their discovery. The air is full of sexual nuance and ambiguity. They are enjoying the course immensely.

****

Fenella is anxious to get them all on the coach and back to Gaeta. It is a long way, and they will become fractious like tired children.

First to return are Caroline, Miss Aitchinson and Colin Jones. They are, and are not, together. They appear to come from the same direction and yet they do not seem to speak to each other.

"Did you enjoy the site?" asks Fenella brightly.

"Well, it was very..." starts Caroline.

"No," says Miss Aitchinson. Colin Jones says nothing. They all go and sit down, but not together. Caroline gets up. There is something she has to ask.

"Er, excuse me, Fenella, where has Michael gone?"

Fenella looks up and smiles. "Pinball machines," she says. "Gino and Michael are pinball wizards."

"Oh," says Caroline. She adds, "thank you."

It doesn't seem right really, a famous Classicist playing pinball machines, especially with the coach driver.

"Michael's good," says Fenella, "but I expect Gino's better. Ah! Some more on their way."

The Brownes and Boxes are returning together, perhaps united by older ties. The Boxes stop by the front seat. Apparently Nigel feels sick; Mrs Box asks Fenella if she has a spare plastic bag. While Fenella (who is always equipped with such things) rummages about, Mr Box looks at the downward curve of her breasts, he clenches his fists.

Penny and Joe return together. Joe is carrying a tripod; he has taken a lot of photos. Penny looks rather weary.

The party from the café return, they are rather loud. They have a racy air about them. People suspect them of having been drinking.

Michael and Gino return. Michael looks sheepish.

"Was it good?" asks Fenella.

"Era magnifico," says Gino.

Percival is mounting the steps, bag in hand. Michael, who still knows nothing of the sandwich saga, asks him,

"How did the tour go? Did you get lot of punters?"

"A sizeable party," says Percival. "I believe I may have drawn their attention to one or two items of interest... I have also been following a line of my own. I have taken the measurements of the *tempi dell'ecco*. I believe there may be an error of some centimetres in the diameter."

Chapter XII

La Donna è Mobile

Miriam is lying in bed reading a magazine she has brought with her. She has put all sorts of twiddly little bits of wire in her hair. She offers to lend some of them to Caroline,

"You'd have no problem with your hair if you curled it a bit," she says.

"I don't have a problem with my hair," says Caroline. She thinks of her mother's words 'your great beauty'.

"It's very easy," says Miriam. "I'll show you if you like."

"It's all right," says Caroline. "I like my hair straight."

"Oh," says Miriam. She manages to include a great element of surprise in that 'oh'.

Caroline is fed up with Miriam; she wishes she was still sharing with Penny. What particularly irritates her about Miriam is the fact that she will go on and on about her husband and boys and how much she misses them, and at the same time she is busy flirting with William. Also Caroline finds out that Miriam's course fees were paid for by her school whereas Caroline has had to save up and pay for hers, herself. And Miriam isn't a bit interested in any of the sites. Fancy bringing some awful woman's magazine to read when you could be reading the Latin texts, or at least reading one of Michael's books.

She wonders what Michael is doing now. Probably some research, because he's had his bit of fun in the afternoon with the pinball machines; now he will be writing or reading – not that other horrid 'ing' word anyway. He was only teasing her. He liked her hair. He wouldn't want her to put curlers in it. Perhaps tomorrow when they go to Capua she can talk to him about Mithraism. He has such lovely blue eyes, and the way that lock of hair falls over his forehead...

"You'll never guess what I learned today," says Miriam. She has been filing her nails and is now regarding them critically.

"Which site are you talking about?" asks Caroline, jolted out of her dreams and climbing into bed.

"Cumae," says Miriam, "the Temple of Apollo actually."

"Oh, how interesting," says Caroline. Perhaps she has misjudged Miriam after all. "The Augustan part or the fifth century Christian church? I always think..."

"Oh," says Miriam, "it wasn't any boring old archaeological thing. This was far more interesting." She imbues the last sentence with great emphasis. Caroline flinches at the heresy, but says nothing.

"Don't you want to know what it was?" asks Miriam. "It concerns your favourite."

"My favourite? What can you mean, Miriam?"

"I don't think I shall tell you," says Miriam irritatingly. "Shall I use the 'rose blush' on the 'crimson hint'?" She surveys her bottles of nail varnish. "My husband loves to see me with my nails just done! One day Joe and Timmy took my nail varnish and they painted the wash basin with it. They thought they had made it look pretty. I couldn't be cross with them."

"What were you saying about the Temple of Apollo?" asks Caroline. She wishes Miriam wouldn't keep wittering on. She would like to turn the light off now and think 'things'.

"It wasn't the Temple itself – I think I'll use the rose blush – it was what was going on in it. Gerouin told us."

"What do you mean?" asks Caroline. She has a feeling of foreboding and unease.

"Fenella and Michael," says Miriam triumphantly. She shoots a look at Caroline. Silly bitch, serves her right. But she still doesn't understand.

"Fenella and Michael? What were they doing?"

"Three guesses," says Miriam. Silly cow with her stringy red hair and Latin texts.

Caroline feels a stab of pain somewhere just below her heart. "Were they... fucking?" she asks. The word that has been so much on her mind since last night, and been suppressed and hidden away comes bursting out.

"Well I shouldn't like to use that word myself," says Miriam, "but, yes, that's what they were doing."

"Perhaps, perhaps... I mean, I expect Gerouin got it wrong – he seems a muddled sort of person, I mean, his mac and the sandwiches. I don't think..."

"They've been doing it for years," says Miriam smugly, "and, anyway, I heard them the first night. They were both in his room next door. They couldn't get enough of it, and she was as bad as he was. If you don't believe me, ask Miss Aitchinson."

"But she said..."

"Well, I don't think she knows a lot about sex," says Miriam, "and, of course, when you're not married there is a lot you don't know. Shall I turn the light out?"

Caroline turns her face to the wall. The blow is so tremendous she cannot register it. Michael. She sees the face that she has looked at so long on the back of *Horace, The Man As Lover*. That is the essence of Michael, that is, Michael the Holy Ghost, and she had come on the course to see Michael made flesh and come to dwell among us. And, indeed, initially it had seemed that her prayers and dreams would be fulfilled. For there he was, talking down the coach at her, showing her the kingdom of heaven. But thereafter things had started to go wrong, fall apart. It all stemmed from her visit to his room, when he had used that word. And now these terrible tidings about him and Fenella doing this terrible unknown activity in the full view of twenty Classicists, not caring if they were seen – and in the Temple of Apollo. How could this brilliant, this scholarly, this erudite man behave in such a way? It was as if Christ had said to Mary Magdalene, "Do you like... that dreadful word?" She felt that he had deceived her personally. He had taken an interest in her, singled her out, commenting on her hair, and now to snub her. Awful reverberations of Miriam's words echo through her mind 'they couldn't get enough of it'. How could he wish to embrace Fenella? She probably hadn't even got A level Latin. How can she look at him now, knowing what she knows?

And she had asked him what it was like and he had said brilliant, and he was thinking of Fenella; better than standing on the Appian Way, he had said. Oh, the unendurable misery.

****

Fenella too is in bed, dozing lightly. It has been a tiring day one way and another. She would like to go to sleep, but doesn't want to miss Michael like last night. She thinks longingly and sleepily of him; she thinks of Baiae and the Temple of Apollo and how making love to him there had been right, just as he had promised. Now he is older and virtually divorced, will he turn to her at last, after twenty years of waiting and loving? But he is elusive, like a beam of sunlight playing for a short space of time on the landscape of her life. He is like a fish that a child tries to catch in a rock pool, one moment within his grasp, the next gone. And where is he now? Gino has taken him for a return game on the Gaetan pinball machines. "Please, Fen," he had said, the lock of hair falling over his forehead, "I won't be late; and it'll be the last time. Please."

"Remember Polenza," she had said. They had been running a very erudite course on the Battle of Numisium. Polenza was a horrible post-war urban sprawl, as horrible a place as only the Italians know how to make. There was nothing to do in the evenings. It was then he had discovered pinball machines. He had eschewed all the learned and erudite members of the course in favour of a crowd of idle, ignorant, loafing Italian youths. He played for hours and lost a lot of money before he became better than they were. He had not yet published his first big coffee-table book; he was still relatively unknown. Various important people on the course had taken it upon themselves to criticise his behaviour. He had lost his temper, partly because he was young and arrogant, but mainly it was this other thing.

It was part of his creed that research into the past had only one real purpose, and that was to understand how best to live life, not to count the number of ivory dice discovered in Italy, but to understand how certain urges and fascinations are timeless. When he next read a reference to

Roman soldiers playing dice, he would be able to feel a sympathy, a oneness with them. They were doing the same as he, they with their dice, he with the pinball machines, and in each there was a glorious delight to be found in the glamour of the unexpected. There was a continuity in the spirit of man. And that these austere men used their scholarship for only limited, blinkered ends; that was what he could not stand.

She stretches out in her double bed. It is a lovely soft comfortable bed, the coverlet is shiny and pink. At home she would have thought it flashy and vulgar; but here, in the heart of Italy, she likes it. The pink walls glow. Pictures of putti hang from them. Her eyes close, a pleasant drowsiness creeps over her.

It is Verdi. Verdi fortissimo. It starts beneath her window with *La Donna è mobile*, and then goes on to *Aida*, although it strikes her that Aida sounds more like Fenella, celeste Fenella. She opens her eyes and listens. There are two male voices and the singing is not of the highest order. There is also a great deal of laughter and noise; and something seems to hit her window. She gets out of bed, puts on jeans and a sweater and pads downstairs barefooted. She does not wait for the lift but runs downstairs to meet them. She notes that neither is steady on his feet, but of the two, Gino probably has the better chance of remaining upright. They seem to find Fenella's appearance a matter of great wonder. They express their amazement to each other in Italian, but they seem to find gesticulation an easier mode of communication. Fenella is stern with them.

"Siete molto tardi – tutti i due. Dov'è Anna?"

"E sparita," replies Gino. Suddenly he becomes grief-stricken. He weeps.

Fenella deposits Gino with Marco who fortunately appears on the scene. She will find out about Anna tomorrow.

Going up in the lift Michael wants to sing.

"Be quiet, Michael," says Fenella. "You'll wake everyone up."

"That's very true," says Michael, lurching against her. "You're a very wise woman. You are a wonderful woman, a beautiful woman."

"Shut up, Michael," says Fenella. "I'm going to put you to bed."

"Your bed, Fen."

"Yes, my bed."

When they get to her room, he leans against the wardrobe and surveys her.

"You are a beautiful woman, Fenella, you..."

"Take your clothes off, Michael, and get into bed."

"She orders me, she commands me to her bed... lots of buttons, Fen. Why do they make shirts with lots of buttons? Buttons."

Fenella undoes his shirt buttons and takes off his shirt. She undoes his belt and flies.

He lurches against her.

"You are a beautiful..."

"Yes," says Fenella. "Take your trousers off."

He has to concentrate very hard to do this. Eventually hc sits on the edge of the bed. His boxer shorts defeat him. Suddenly he says,

"I'm going to be sick, Fen."

Ever resourceful, Fenella reaches for the waste bin.

Fenella is not at all revolted by the vomiting. She has brought up two children, she has cleared up a lot of sick in her time. She gets her flannel and wipes his face. She also empties the waste bin.

"Now, into bed," she says.

He lies down. "Fen hold me. Hold me tight."

"Yes, darling."

"Fen, I don't want to die."

"You're not going to die."

"Put your arms round me, Fen."

He is sick several more times, mostly in the waste bin, and every time Fenella empties it out. Every time she sponges his face with her damp flannel. At last he turns towards her and buries his head between her breasts.

"I want to sleep here," he says, "for eternity." She strokes his hair until he falls into a soundless sleep. There is no greater happiness for her in the world than to hold him in her arms.

Chapter XIII

Gaeta

It seems there has been a change of plan. Instead of leaving for Capua at nine they will now leave after lunch.

There is much muttering at this juncture (Fenella makes the announcement at breakfast). They could have got up later, now there will not be time to go to Lake Avernus, the museum and Pozzuoli. They have paid hard-earned cash for this course. It is also true that, however much people do not want to visit a place on holiday, once they are told that the opportunity has passed from them, there is an enormous feeling of resentment. Miss Aitchinson is thinking of composing a letter of complaint to Classic Tours, listing her different grievances: disturbed nights, no proper tour at Baiae and now done out of Lake Avernus, the museum and Pozzuoli.

When, however, Fenella explains that Michael is unwell: 'a touch of his old trouble', the mood changes. Michael is universally (with the exception of Percival) liked and approved of. They have spent three days with him, he is like part of themselves. He is, after all, leader of this little English colony in the middle of alien Italy. They feel concerned for him, and shortly afterwards, as is the way with human nature, they feel concerned for themselves. Is it infectious? Is it a tummy thing, a bug that could spread?

Mrs Box, in particular, is concerned: Nigel didn't feel well on the coach yesterday. Could it be the start of something serious? She has heard Mr Thorpe-Smith say that in Roman times there was a lot of malaria in the swamplands of Minturnae. Fenella is able to reassure her. Michael is merely overtired. He will be restored to health in a few hours.

"Sounds like a hangover to me," says Jane to Gerouin. They are having breakfast together.

Fenella says that this extra morning in Gaeta will give people an opportunity of doing a little shopping, or even revisiting the Tomb of Munacius Plancus (she can arrange a taxi there should anyone wish to do this). It is also an opportunity for people to come and talk to her privately (she will be in the bar from ten o'clock) and tell her what arrangements they would like to make for the rest of their stay when they move to Sorrento. There are, she understands, a few single rooms to be had at a small extra cost. That is the most interesting thing Fenella has said so far.

Before ten o'clock Fenella must fly here, there and everywhere. She waylays Marco the waiter and pumps him on the health of Gino, the fate of Anna and anything else that she can think of. Marco is only too ready to inform her.

"*Signor Michael aveva bevuto molto, perchè Gino è stato desolato dalla partenza di Anna. Lei era tornata a Napoli, meno male! Anna era... Lui non pronunciarebbe la parola davanti a Fenella. Si, Gino va bene stamattina. È pronto ad uscire, ma, Signor Michael non va bene? Era forse perche era si 'simpatico' con Gino. Aveva bevuto con lui. Era stato molto commosso da Gino. Lui farebbe ogni sforzo per il Signor Michael. Lo amava da fratello...*"

"If Gino could send up black coffee," says Fenella, not waiting to hear any more protestations of undying devotion. She goes back upstairs to see how Michael is. He had been sleeping when she had gone down to breakfast.

He is better. This is apparent from the fact that he is standing up with a cigarette.

"Fen," he says, "I was revolting, horrible. You won't ever want to speak to me again. Fen, *mihi ignosce.*"

"Of course I forgive you," says Fen. "Anyway, it is not the first time you've thrown up all over me. Remember the magic mushrooms."

"They were truffles. But seriously, Fen. Can you forgive me?" He stubs out the cigarette and walks over to her and takes her face in his hands. "I'm nothing but bad news to you, Fen. I always have been."

"Balls," says Fenella. She rests her forehead on his chest. "I just love you, that's all." He turns away, dislodging her head.

"Don't say that."

"No." She smiles. "Go and have a shower; you smell all sicky."

"I'll make it up to you, Fen."

What will he make up to her? Last night? Her life? The last twenty years?

"Of course you will. And now," she continues briskly, "I'm going to sort them all out downstairs."

"Do you feel all right? After all, you can't have got much sleep last night." She is touched by his concern; and, oddly, she is all right. She has slept peacefully with the man she loves between her breasts.

"Marco's sending up coffee. Do you want something to eat?"

"No, I don't think I shall ever eat again."

"Or drink?"

"I only drank to share in Gino's sorrow."

"So Marco said."

"Kiss me, Fen, even though I am all sicky."

They kiss until Fenella breaks away and says,

"I have to go."

"Yes," says Michael, "otherwise Miss Aitchinson will be after you with her stick."

"Oh, did you hear the sandwich saga?" asks Fenella.

"No."

"Well, I shan't tell you. Not unless you tell me the contents of the box." With that she leaves. She will have a gruelling hour ahead.

When she has gone, Michael picks up the telephone. It is fortunate his Italian is so good.

It is amazing how many people have problems about sharing rooms with other people. It is not, however, amazing to Fenella. She has been running courses for twenty years.

"You see, Fenella, the man has barely spoken to me in the last two days. He is appallingly rude. And ever since that business with the theft of the *panini*... I–"

Fenella listens patiently. It is best to say nothing. Sooner or later they will grind to a halt.

But William is nowhere near finished yet. There is another problem. Apparently, as a married man, used to a double bed, he finds it impossible to sleep in a single. Would there be a spare room with a double bed? He doesn't mind paying over the odds. He is sure Fenella, as a married lady herself, will understand.

Fenella will see what she can do.

Jane, on the other hand, doesn't beat about the bush... Gerouin and she, she says, have taken a shine to each other. She doesn't see much point in a lot of humbug and creeping about in the night. She'd like a room for the two of them.

Fenella will see what she can do.

Kate Small needs a room with a double bed as her husband is joining her at Sorrento. Fenella, looking at her, wonders if one will be enough, but Kate reads her mind.

"Good thing Italians have big beds," she says merrily.

Mrs Box seems in a great state of anxiety: she and Mr Box must have a room separate from Nigel (they have all three hitherto shared). After all, she whispers to Fenella, Mr Box is a 'married man'.

Fenella will see what she can do.

Gerouin arrives next. He would rather not continue sharing with Colin. He is obviously not party to Jane's plans for them both. Momentarily Fenella is thrown. She will, however, see what she can do.

Neither of the two Brownes with an 'e' wish to continue sharing with each other. Each wishes to share with the Brown without the 'e'. She, it appears, wishes to share with neither.

Nobody wants to share with either Miss Aitchinson or Percival. Fenella thinks it is a pity she can't put them in together, perhaps with Nigel Box thrown in.

Caroline does not want to go on sharing with Miriam, but nor does she want to speak to Fenella. Miriam's wishes are unknown; she has taken advantage of the free morning to go to the hairdresser's.

Joe doesn't mind who he shares with – as long as it's not that poofter Percy.

****

Joe wants to visit the tomb of Munacius Plancus again, Penny sighs as she trudges along behind. He does sites very thoroughly.

She is on the horns of a dilemma really. She has allied herself to Joe, rather in the way that Colin had allied himself to Percival. Consequently she is now cut off from the rest of the party. There is no solace, either, to be found in her room-mate Margaret Aitchinson. She has also used a whole roll of Penny's lavatory paper.

"Look at this inscription, Penny," he says. "I must have a shot of that. It will be dead useful for when we do inscriptions at the end of Unit 3A in the Cambridge Latin Course."

"Yes," says Penny.

"How much time do you spend on inscriptions?" he asks, setting up his tripod.

"What?" says Penny. She ought to have asked Fenella if she could share with someone different.

"Inscriptions. Just hold this steady, will you? There's so much material in that course. I'm hard put to get through it. We start Latin in Year 7. When do you start?"

"Oh, um..."

"We only have three thirty-five minute periods a week. Just pass me the light meter, would you? Ta. Yes, only three thirty-five minute lessons in Year 7. But last year... Bugger, I moved that. Have to take another one. We had a fifty percent pass rate with twenty-three percent grade A or B. What do you think of that?"

"Are you going to be much longer?" asks Penny, "only I should like to find a loo."

"Go behind the mound," says Joe. "I shall be a good half hour before I've finished."

As Penny relieves herself behind the orange tree next to the *opus reticulatum*, she thinks of the high hopes she had started off with, coming on this course. She thinks of how Colin Jones had snubbed her with his box and how she was stuck now with this boring man with his beard, his camera, his light meter and his classroom talk.

But, on the other hand, he was quite presentable. He seemed to have accepted the fact that they would spend the course together (albeit, it would appear, platonically). It was good to have a man at hand, even if he was immensely boring. Poor old Caroline never seemed to have anyone to go with.

"I'll just take a shot from up here, Penny. I tend to take slides, but I like the photos for reference, don't you?"

"Yes."

"I use a lot of slides in my lessons. I get through an average of thirty-five a lesson, that's one a minute you see. 'Course, you spend longer on some than others. You can tell it paid dividends by the results I get for GCSE. I've got six going on for A level this year, and I've built up a Class. Civ. class from nothing. I tell you, Penny, when I went to that school three, no four, years ago now, there was no Class. Civ. You'll not believe me when I tell you I built up a Class. Civ. class from nothing to twenty in two years. And next year, if I'm not mistaken, we'll have two streams in Year 8. How many streams do you have?"

"Shall we go back now?" asks Penny. She wonders whether he is married or not.

Chapter XIV
Capua

Fenella has quite a job hustling them aboard the coach. There is a sort of *fin de siècle* feeling.

To start with, twelve o'clock is a bad time to leave. What about lunch? Do you eat it first at eleven o'clock (I ask you), or do you take it with you and eat it on the coach at risk of indigestion, or do you wait until you get to Francolini or Capua or wherever they are taking you? (As Miss Aitchinson says, with so many odd things going on, you don't know where you are) There again, if you don't eat at eleven, or on the coach, when will you eat? You might not get a square meal at all, or even a *panino*, until eight o'clock at night. It is all very difficult.

And, besides, they've had enough of getting on and off coaches. This unexpected free morning has brought it home to them. They are tired of Gaeta. They want to get to Sorrento now and get settled in there and finished with all this coach travel.

"It simply does not suit Nigel," says Mrs Box to Mrs Browne. Does she have children herself? No, it appears she doesn't. She also looks at Nigel in a nasty way and says she has no regrets on that score.

Miriam solves the problem by not going at all. She is standing in the hotel foyer nonchalantly touching her hair, which, since this morning's visit, has gained a reddish tint. She advises Caroline to go to the hairdresser's while they are here. "Italian hairdressers are wonderful at giving body to hair." Unfortunately, though, sitting under the dryer has given her a nasty headache. She thinks it wiser to stay in the hotel this afternoon, doesn't Fenella agree? William is quite concerned; he thinks it better if he stays too. After all, he has been to Italian classes and will be able to send for a doctor if need be.

Nobody has seen Percival. He is, in fact, busy in his room writing to a Classical Association: '... being asked by Michael Thorpe-Smith if I would lead a group of academics round the ruins at Baiae in view of my specialist knowledge of the area...'

Michael has appeared. He looks perhaps a little subdued, but wonderful nevertheless. He has an open-necked cream linen shirt, a cashmere sweater (or a sweater that looks expensive, who can be sure exactly what cashmere is?), and a pair of elegantly cut trousers which obey all the rules of the latest in men's fashion. Fenella wears a long rust-coloured dress and has her hair up. She looks very proper indeed.

The fact that Miriam, William and Percival are to absent themselves, raises questions in the minds of others who have not regarded non-attendance hitherto as a possibility. The Boxes have seen a cinema in Gaeta. Mrs Box thinks she will take Nigel.

"Would you like that, dear?" asks Mrs Box.

"It will just be some crap Italian film," says Nigel, "but it's better than boring old sites." They decide to go to the cinema, although Mr Box (who is unexpectedly called Robin) will come on the coach.

Even though they have the solace of their virtue in not truanting from culture, the feeling of the party is not altogether a happy one. It is often a mistake to feel that doing one's duty brings its own rewards; the coach is not that comfortable and the coffee machine is still broken, and, anyway, there is no longer Anna to tend it. There is many a one who envies William, Miriam, Mrs Box and Master Box, and even Percival.

"*Villae*," says Michael, picking up the microphone, "country estates. Let me read you a little something to set the scene." He looks around at their dull, cross faces and feels wickedly inclined to read a great deal of the Lex de Agraria, which is about the most uninteresting text he knows. Fenella, however, gives him an admonitory look. She knows very well (none better) that a firm eye must be kept on him. He puts the Lex de Agraria down regretfully.

"I'll kick off with some Martial," he says. "'Here, when November is past, and winter is now at hand, the unkempt pruner brings home late grapes. Fiercely in the deep valley roar bulls, and the steer with brow unhorned itches for the fray. All the crowd of the untidy poultry yard wanders here and there, the skull-cackling goose and the spangled peacocks.' Quite nice," he adds meditatively, "'Spangled peacocks'. 'Greedily the pigs follow the apron of the bailiff's wife and the tender lamb waits for its dam's full udder...' Martial has a lot to say about the delights of country living – it's so fantastic, he tells us, that even the wanton, long-haired eunuch delights in work. Was it really that idyllic, or was it big business? Think of the *latifundi*, with the gangs of slaves chained together, spending their nights in underground barracks. I have put together a selection of extracts, mainly from the First Century. I would like you to read them before we reach Francolini, so we can look together and decide."

Francolini contains the recently excavated remains of a Roman farm. Frankly, there is not a lot to see and, although Michael tries hard to bring it before their eyes, conjuring dovecotes and fruit from out of broken bits of stone, they do not have the eyes that see the slaves bound together digging the soil, the bee-master with his honeycombs, and the *dominus* lounging inside with his Greek statues. Michael loves Roman machinery; he has found a winepress; he examines its workings. They are dreadfully bored. They want to get to Capua and have some lunch.

Sadly, he watches them move off eagerly in the direction of the coach.

"They didn't like my winepress, Fen."

"Well, perhaps they're not machine people."

"But it's wonderful, it's a prototype. Nothing better's ever been invented. It's..."

"Darling, they want their lunch. So do I, or a drink at least."

"I never thought of you as a philistine."

"No. Just a laywoman."

He comes back to the twentieth century. "A laid woman would be better. Let's see about that when we get back, shall we?"

"All the more reason for getting on to Capua."

"Bags I sit next to you on the coach then."

However, he doesn't get the opportunity. Robin Box slides in next to her. He sits very close. His breath smells unpleasant. He has wet patches underneath his armpits. Fenella smiles brightly.

"I though I must take this opportunity of complimenting you on your efficiency." He moves a little nearer to her and breathes in her face. "Mrs Box and I have been so impressed with the organisation."

"Thank you," says Fenella.

"We are, of course, anxious to have a room to ourselves in Sorrento. I am sure as a married lady," he breathes in Fenella's face, "you will appreciate..."

"Quite," says Fenella, getting up, "You must excuse me, there are one or two handouts I need to sort out."

"And I thought," he often makes an unpleasant clicking noise at the end of a sentence, "I should have the pleasure of sitting next to the prettiest little lady in the coach." He leers at her; he would rather be sharing a double bed with her than with his wife. He'd bet she'd have her legs open soon enough.

Michael takes her place. "I'm going to bore you with my wine-press," he says. Mr Box smiles unhappily.

Caroline stares out at the rolling Campanian countryside. It is the week before Easter and the fields are full of flowers. There are orchards full or orange and lemon trees. There are bullocks grazing in the pastureland. Sometimes they pass an old, black-clad, ambling Italian woman with a single cow before her. It is all the Italy she has dreamed of, and there he is, sitting next to Mr Box, this man whom Miriam says... But perhaps, suppose Miriam is lying. Caroline has heard nothing from next door, and she has spent the last two nights there. There has been absolutely no noise. You would hardly know anyone was there. And when she had gone to see him that night, Fenella wasn't there then. Perhaps Miss Aitchinson was right. Perhaps he had been ill. After all he was ill last night apparently. Then there was that talk about Cumae and the Temple of Apollo – but that was just Gerouin's silly talk; he could easily get the wrong end of the stick. It could have been someone else. It could have been... now, wait a minute, suppose it was Miriam herself! And William. Trying to cover her tracks having been caught by Gerouin.

You could see what Miriam was like, pretending to be all pathetic, and missing her children, and all the time carrying on with William. Gerouin had seen her and William carrying on and she wanted to allay suspicion by getting in first, and everybody would believe her, not Gerouin, because he was such a twit...

The more Caroline tests the theory, the more she likes it. She looks to the front and sees Fenella in her long dress with her hair up, sorting through handouts and looking the picture of respectability. Was it likely that this proper and efficient lady would have been cavorting naked in Apollo's Temple? It isn't Fenella who is forever painting her nails and having her hair done. And look at Michael there, earnestly talking to Mr Box on some classical subject. Does he look like a naked cavorter? All right, he said that word, but he was only teasing, probably embarrassed. And Fenella had written very kind and helpful letters before the course when Caroline had difficulty finding the last instalment. She had maligned them both, Michael and Fenella. Should she warn them about Miriam and these slanderous rumours? The thought of Miriam makes the blood boil. The hypocrisy! The bare-faced lying. Little did she think when she came on this course that she would meet with... with whores and liars.

"I've got us a room together," says Jane to Gerouin as they approach Capua. Gerouin is looking for his purse (he feels sure it was in his anorak pocket) and doesn't hear what she says. At least, he hears, but it doesn't register.

"I've got us a room at Sorrento," says Jane, "together."

"Oh," says Gerouin. A thousand thoughts rush into his mind at once. What can she mean? She can't mean... No. Suppose she does? But how can he tell? What should he say? Sharing a room? What would he... how would he?

"Together?" he echoes.

"Yes," says Jane. Jane, who lives on her own, is accustomed to making her own decisions without consulting anyone else. Now she wonders if she ought to have asked him first.

"Is that all right then?" she asks.

"Oh yes, I... I didn't want to go on sharing with Colin... I..."

"That's not quite the point, though," says Jane snappishly.

"No, I suppose it isn't," says Gerouin. Suddenly everything is becoming difficult again. He can't find his purse and he has to share a room with this lady in the red tracksuit. What will she expect him to do? Will he have to... ? A snippet of one of his Wednesday evening videos appears before his eyes. He really can't see himself... But inside that tracksuit is a woman's body (probably; it seems open to question). It's not as if it were Fenella or even Miriam.

"Well, do you want to, or not?" asks Jane.

"Yes please," says Gerouin. He is actually being propositioned by an older woman (there was something of the kind in *Sexy Pussy Cats*). Here is something he can't put in his daily letter home.

Fenella tells Gino she's sorry about Anna. Gino makes a sort of spitting noise and alarmingly takes both hands off the wheel to make an obscene gesture. Fenella thinks the subject is best not pursued, Gino does not seem at his best; any further gestures may well endanger all their lives.

"I'm going to take you," says Michael, abandoning Mr Box and picking up the microphone, "into a Mithraeum – the sacred temple of Mithras. Mithras, the soldiers' god, Mithras who comes from the degenerate East, Mithras the god of light and truth who triumphs over the forces of evil, Mithras who kills the mighty bull whose blood has the power to give life and death." He pauses momentarily. "There were seven grades of initiation into Mithraism, each with its own secret ceremony. Perhaps you would lie in a pit with your life ebbing away under the weight of mighty stones crushing the breath from your body; perhaps you would be branded with an iron brand. Then you might become the Raven, the Maiden or the Lion. But whatever you did, you needed courage, loyalty and secrecy. Let us go deep beneath the earth and see Mithras himself."

Gino has some difficulty parking the coach, and eventually leaves it across a narrow street, thereby totally stopping any ingress or egress. Fenella and Michael exchange glances. He is best not crossed at this juncture.

"We shan't spend too long at the Mithraeum," announces Fenella through the microphone, thinking of the *carabinieri* and massive bribes having to be paid by Classic Tours.

They go down and down (led by Miss Aitchinson, feeling the way with her stick); all is murk, all is gloom. Michael has a torch which he shines suddenly straight ahead. Fenella thinks of another occasion more than twenty years ago when Michael had carried a torch. She remembers the light had shone on his shoulder-length hair and how he had said with perfect decorum, "May I kiss you, Fenella?".

Mithras stares at them with his sightless eyes, with his hands he throttles a massive white bull. There is evil here in the barrel-vaulted ceiling, there is evil amidst the benched walls. There is evil emanating from the painted figures on the walls. It is not a place to linger (even if you weren't dying for a *cappuccino* and feared the *carabinieri*).

Michael is quite pale when they emerge again into the light.

"It's horrible," he says to Fenella, "all dark and deathly. Ugh." He shudders. "Don't you feel it, all the death round you?"

"No," says Fenella, "but I don't have your imagination."

"It's not imagination. It's real, it's palpable, tangible." He stares at the steps leading down.

"Come on," says Fenella, "time for a drink."

But even the word 'drink', which so often galvanises him into action, seems to have lost its power. He stands, quite white, staring into the gloom.

"It's all round me, Fen," he says, "the underworld; it subsumes me."

"Well," says Fenella, becoming very sensible, "let's get Gino to move the coach, otherwise we shall be subsumed by the *carabinieri*." She takes his hand and he follows obediently. He smiles.

"You must be a marvellous mother," he says, "so firm and stern."

"I try," says Fenella.

"How old...?" he asks. He really ought to know by now.

"Nineteen and twenty," says Fenella, "the same age as your two."

"Ah," he says absently.

Only Penny and Joe remain in the Mithraeum. Joe has many photos to take and needs Penny to steady the tripod.

"This is perfect, perfect, Penny, for use with Stage 32 in the Cambridge Latin Course; there's a whole section on ancient religions. I devote a whole week to it, a whole week, and all that entails; you're with me – to ancient religion. I have been only devoting a small time to Mithraism but now I shall have to rethink... just move to the left a bit... rethink the whole week. I have an excellent set of handouts – I could send you one."

"Thank you," says Penny. "Shall we go and get something to eat now?"

"Something to eat? What, when there's the Musea Campano to see with the series of Deae Matures from the temple of Mater Matura..."

"Well," says Penny, rebelliously, "I'm going to get something to eat. I'm hungry."

He mutters a bit, but eventually follows in her wake. She has learned this afternoon that it is better to be assertive.

Chapter XV

Flower Power

Fenella's bedroom is full of white roses. There are roses on the dressing-table, roses on the armchair, roses on the bed. There are, (Fenella counts them) forty-three. There had actually been fifty, but the hotel manager has been having trouble with his wife ever since the last baby. He has taken a modest seven in the hopes of gaining a little of what has been so long denied him. Fenella anyway would have been the last person to begrudge him that.

White roses in March! Forty-three white roses that will have to be transported to Sorrento tomorrow. Even now they look a little tired. Italians have more use for the plastic variety. Nobody has thought of putting them in water.

There is a note on the pillow: '*Me paenitet*' it says, 'I'm sorry'. Was this then what he had meant when he has said he would make it up to her? Had she hoped that he had meant it in a more general sense, with reference to the future?

Forty-three white roses, that had probably cost more than a month's salary, roses that would be dead tomorrow. *Me paenitet.*

How mundane she had become, how mealy-mouthed, how ungracious, how petty. What he had done was a lovely thing, a gesture that cut through the small-change of life. He knew the roses would die, that the Italians would not bother to put them in water, even that Fenella could have done with the money. But all that he had ignored because none of it mattered. All that mattered was that he acknowledged how he had always buggered up her life, whether by marrying other women or by being sick in her bed. He wanted to say sorry in a way that she would remember until the day she died.

She gathers up the roses and puts them in the basin, filling it first with water. She picks up the phone and rings his room. He answers almost immediately. She wonders if he has been waiting for her to ring.

"Michael," she says, "there are forty-three white roses in my bedroom."

"Gosh," he says, "do you have a lover?"

"Yes," she says, "he's taking me out to dinner tonight."

"Really?" he says. "Where is he taking you?"

"He hasn't told me yet."

"Well," he says, "shall I ask him?"

"Mm."

"He says," says Michael, "he is taking you to the most expensive restaurant in Gaeta... wait, he's saying something else... he's saying the most expensive restaurant, on one condition."

"Which is?"

"Well, he says it's very important to him that you wear some flowers in your hair. Apparently you and he used to listen to a song about going to San Francisco."

"Darling, I... I..."

"Why are there only forty-three roses, Fen? You were always useless at maths. Your friend says nine o'clock."

She lies on the bed a long time. Her body aches. Eventually she is roused by a knocking on her door. Caroline with her long, stringy, red hair, stands outside.

"Fenella," she says breathlessly, "I've come to warn you."

"Warn me?" Bomb scares dart through Fenella's mind.

"It's Miriam. She's saying horrid things about you. About you and Michael. She says..."

"Yes?"

"Well... Well... Just things."

Fenella smiles soothingly. This situation is not unfamiliar to her.

"Thank you for telling me, Caroline." She waits politely.

"Aren't you going to ask?"

"No," says Fenella. Caroline really can't make head or tail of all this, but she sees she is supposed to go, and is about to do so when something arrests her attention.

"Roses. You've got hundreds of roses."

"Not hundreds," says Fenella, "just forty-three." She turns round and they both look at them.

"I can smell them," says Caroline. "Where did they come from? I mean, roses at Easter; they must have cost a fortune."

"An old flame," says Fenella.

"And he found you," asks Caroline, "in the middle of Italy?" It is the most romantic thing she has ever heard of. "He must be very fond of you," she adds boldly.

"Oh no, I don't think so," says Fenella. "It was more by way of saying sorry, really."

"Gosh. It must have been something big to say sorry for." She longs to know.

"Oh no," says Fenella, "something quite unimportant really." She pauses, seeing Michael's face of twenty years before. She smiles pleasantly at Caroline. "Would you like some? There are plenty here?"

"Oh no," says Caroline, "they aren't my roses, you see."

****

"You choose," says Fenella. "I can't cope with all of this."

"Balls," says Michael, "you probably know far more about it than I do. You just want me to be masterful."

They are indeed sitting in the most expensive restaurant in Gaeta. It has mosaics on the walls and marble-topped tables and aggressive-looking pot plants in antique urns. Waiters hover round, eager to remove and replace Michael's ashtrays. Fenella looks most attractive in an extremely low, rose-coloured dress. Her copious blonde hair is caught back by a single white rose.

"It's worse than Classic Tours," says Michael.

"What is?"

"What are! Your tits straining out of that dress at me. How can I sit opposite them for two hours without touching?"

"You could tie your hands back and be fed by slaves."

"Who shall I have? Nigel Box and Caroline?"

"Oh, by the way, Caroline came to warn me people are gossiping about us." Fenella takes a sip of Campari.

"Caroline seems given to visiting our bedrooms by night. How curious that she never finds us together."

He orders in rapid Italian. The waiters are impressed. They double their attentions with the ashtrays. "It doesn't bother you, does it, the gossip, I mean?"

"No. People have gossiped about us for twenty years."

"They don't have much in their lives, do they, most of the people on the course?" She is surprised; he would never have said that, or even noticed in previous years.

The antipasto arrives. It is a hundred different delicious bits. It will not be cheap.

"What's Gordon up to these days?" asks Michael unexpectedly, forking an artichoke heart.

"Well, that's an interesting piece of lateral thinking," replies Fenella, "only, if you are referring to my second ex-husband, his name is Graham, not Gordon. You've always got that wrong."

"Yes, I should have remembered. Not a gin man."

"Well, he's married again. She seems very pleasant. I hope they're happy."

He looks at her quizzically. "It beats me, Fenella, why both your husbands went after other women when they had you."

She would be quite justified in retorting that that was exactly what he had done; but it is not Fenella's way to make sharp retorts and, anyway, the reason is so simple that she is amazed he does not know it after all this time, but she will not tell him. It is her secret. So she smiles and says, "These squiddy bits are nice."

"There's squid on the mosaic there. I've seen it before somewhere." It would be anathema to him to pry into the intimate details of Fenella's two failed marriages.

"Herculaneum, I think," she says. "Women's baths."

"Brilliant. You should be doing the lecturing instead of me. Shall we swap roles and I'll do the Boxes and the Browns?... No, *non porte via il portacenere. Per piacere lo lasci...* And what about Mark? What's happened to him?"

"Oh, I think he's on his third wife. There's always a better one coming with Mark."

"Why ever did you marry him, Fen? I only saw him once and thought him a real wanker." The hovering waiter refills their glasses.

"I expect I wanted to show you I could marry other people too."

"But you could have married anyone, Fen. They were all after you. They used to be wildly jealous of me. It was a lovely feeling. What do you think of the wine? I hope you like it. It costs about ten million lire."

"You had just married Jemima. So I thought I'd get married too."

"Yes, you sent me an invitation, just for me, not Jemima."

"Yes, that wasn't very subtle, was it? Anyway, you didn't come."

"I did, actually."

"You did?"

"Yes, I stood at the back next to some awful woman with blue hair. I didn't stay though. I didn't like it much."

"Why not?"

"I thought you were marrying the wrong man."

They smile across the table at each other and he takes both her hands in his. He puts them back and lights a cigarette.

"I saw Mr Box after you."

"Were you wildly jealous again?"

"Insanely. There may well be a murder tonight. A *crime passionel.* Curtains for Box. Box in the box."

"Who would be the chief suspect, do you think? Miss Aitchinson? She's the only one with a weapon."

"No. No. You forget the other box."

"Nigel?"

"No. The secret box. The one whose contents you do not know, yet are known to me, and to me alone."

"Ah, well then, suspicion will fall on you, you and your partner in crime, Colin Jones."

"But I may well set up Percival, because everybody would lie through their teeth to get him locked away, so they wouldn't have to hear him lecturing again."

"And, of course," says Fenella, "he's got a proven history of crime behind him. You still haven't heard the sandwich saga. Oh, and I know what else! I must tell you. Jane has asked for a double room for her and Gerouin."

"Does he know?"

"No, I don't think he does."

"Well he probably won't find his way there anyway – I suppose we shouldn't laugh."

"You've become very concerned about people. You never used to be."

"An unkind cut. Yes, you are right, Fen, I was quite ill last summer; had tests and things. Everything fine of course. But I got to thinking – I've always been lucky; I haven't been kind to you. You deserved better. You spent your time hanging around for me." The waiter pours out more wine.

"No I haven't," says Fenella. "I've been married twice. I've had two super children."

"You've certainly made a good job of them. I hear John is set to get a first and Felicity's doing great things at RADA. My two don't do anything: leisure studies and beauty therapy. I ask you! Anyway, they don't speak to me since Tabitha. That was a bad mistake, Fen."

"How is the divorce?" She tries to sound casual.

"Almost through. She wants all my money. She's a real bitch, Fen. If only people knew what she is really like when they see her on that show. Hard as nails. Cold as ice. Have some more wine. You're not eating. Don't you like it?"

"You know I can never eat when I'm with you."

"Yes, I'd forgotten how I always buy expensive meals for you not to eat. Shall we skip the main course and take the bottle back with us?"

"You'll have to pay for the meal."

"No, I shan't. Look ill."

Much rapid Italian ensues. Many waiters come and go. Michael smiles a lot. They all end up on excellent terms. Michael takes the bottle. They walk back along the harbour front to the hotel. He puts his arm round her shoulder. It is almost Easter.

"Warm enough, Fen? You can have my jacket if you like." She shakes her head.

"Look at the lights on the water, Michael."

"Yes. It's one of those things you think of as timeless. But it's not; it's very twentieth century. The Romans would have had virtually no lights on the water. Think how dark with no moon."

"You never liked the dark."

"No. I like the light, don't you?" He turns to look at her. In the strange orange glow from the harbour he looks ten years older. Suddenly he scoops her up and carries her to the water's edge. "I'm going to drop you in, Fen," he says.

"I'll do anything," she pleads in mock horror.

"Anything?"

"Well, almost anything."

Only Kate Small sees them going into the hotel. She is still waiting to get through on the phone to her husband. She looks long after them. Then she returns to the telephone booth. She is so large she has to leave the door open.

****

"Shall I put my sexy nightie on?" asks Fenella. There is a huge vase of white roses on either side of the bed.

"No," he says. "*Non iuvat in caeco Venerem corrumpere motu.* Art cannot improve upon nature. You're still lovely, Fen."

"I'm not so sure about the 'still'," says Fenella. She sits on the bed and hugs her knees. She is watching him undress. Perhaps this, more than anything else, brings back the past. He can undress so quickly, walking away from his clothes. He bends over her and bites a nipple.

"You're so desirable, Fen," he says.

"And you to me," she says, pulling him down on top of her.

"I'm sorry, Fen," he says, entering her. "I can't wait."

"You will not," says Fenella, "be too quick for me." It is true, were he to think of it. It is the power of his orgasm that arouses her. His desire has always become hers.

Afterwards her face is wet with tears. He dries them with his fingers.

"Why do you cry, Fen?"

"Because I love you."

"Is that something to cry for?"

"No. It's because the happiness and the sadness get all mixed up." She strokes his hair.

"Like the pleasure and the pain? You said..." he takes his head from her breasts, "you said you couldn't tell them apart."

"What rubbish I talk," says Fenella, embarrassed. "As long as you're still you."

"I'm still me, or rather I'm still I." He rolls off her and gropes about for cigarettes. "Are you still you?"

"Definitely."

"Well, you've given up smoking."

"Mmm." She plants kisses in the hairs of his chest.

"Do you mind that I still do? I haven't your will-power, you see."

"I have never minded anything."

"Yes you have, but you generally don't say."

"Would I be more interesting to you if I had?" She looks up from her kissing.

"You are always interesting to me, Fen."

"All those years between courses, when you never contacted me."

"That's not to say I didn't think about you. I did have a wife, quite a good one, in fact – but I always wanted to see you. I looked forward to courses as much as you did. I nearly always did them when you wrote and asked me."

"And that was enough for you, wasn't it?" she says sadly. "To fuck me every two years."

"Fenella, stop it!" He gets out of bed. "Don't reproach me. Don't."

He stubs out a cigarette and lights another one. "Please." He turns an anguished face towards her.

A kind of giddiness seizes him and he sits down abruptly. The pain on his left side burns a little. He grimaces, but it passes as quickly as it had come.

"What is it, darling?" asked Fenella, alarmed.

"Nothing. Nothing, sweetie." He doesn't tend to use pet names or terms of endearment. Fenella knows he uses it now as a kind of barrier to distance himself from her question. Whatever it is, he doesn't want to pursue it.

"I'm sorry," says Fenella, "I should have smelt the roses and not looked back at the past." She gets out of bed and puts her arms round him.

He stands, running his fingers through her hair, his expression unfathomable. Suddenly he opens his eyes very wide at her and says,

"Go and put your sexy nightie on. Revitalise my satiated appetites."

"What about my appetites?"

"Oh, you're too easy, Fen. Look at you, just now. Instant arrival."

"Shall I put it on then?"

"Most certainly. Does it scoop your breasts up, and fight a losing battle in retaining them?"

"Something like that. Shut your eyes, then. Don't cheat."

"Of course not," he replies. He lies back, smoking and watching her. The nightdress is as he has described. She runs her hand down it and plays with the hem. It is a very, very short nightdress. They look across at each other. Neither speaks. At last she says,

"Come and get me."

He stubs out his cigarette, folds his hands behind his head and replies, "On the contrary, you come and get me." She holds out a little longer and then gives in. She has never been able to resist him in anything for more than a few seconds. He folds her into his arms.

"You are the best of them, Fen," he says, enigmatically. It is perhaps the nearest to a declaration of love she has ever received from him.

Chapter XVI
In the Bar at Sorrento

Everybody likes Sorrento. How could they not? The sun sparkles on the water. And the hotel is luxurious beyond the dreams of those whose sights are bounded by the concrete walls of school buildings. Indeed, those who have stolen *panini* from the breakfast bread baskets at Gaeta are now afraid to do so, so terrible is the aspect of the hovering waiters. They themselves have seldom inspired such terror into the breasts of their recalcitrant pupils.

Spring is in the air. Double rooms and beds are upon the mind, Latin texts are in the pocket. All is set for phase two of Classic Tours' Southern Italy Course.

Some (the loved), have mail awaiting them. Suddenly they are returned to their former personae. For a short time Miriam forgets William's attentions, and when she pulls out of an envelope a crayoned picture with LOVE JOE in uneven letters, she sees him as a creature of no importance; she is back in her true role of mother, even dutiful wife. A flash of William's former life, his pre-Italy life, appears in the form of a letter from his wife who bids him 'not to be a silly Willy'. She is not unlike Miriam. The days of the course are diminishing fast. Soon he will be back in the land of nappies, broken nights and small but expensive jars of baby's first apple purees.

Neither Miss Aitchinson nor Percival receives any letters. Miss Aitchinson does not really expect any. There is nobody but the woman next door, and they do not always see eye to eye. In the very depth of Percival's heart is a knowledge that nobody will want to write him a letter, but he is adept at pushing things into the depth of his subconscious. He tells himself he is astonished that he has received no reply to his letters to various Classical Societies and committees. He even insists they check again at Reception. He sees scorn written on the face of the handsome male receptionist.

Fenella receives many, many communications from the office, many forms to be filled in and a number of faxes. She will be kept very busy. She also receives a letter from her daughter. 'Give him all my love,' says Felicity, 'and tell him I'm waiting in the wings for when you move off centre stage.' Felicity's metaphors have all been to do with theatre since she has gone to RADA.

Gerouin hears from his mother:

'Dear Gerouin,' she says, 'I hope you are having a nice holiday. I hope you are meeting some nice people too.

'I have found that trainer shoe you lost behind the waste bin in the kitchen. Do not ask me how it got there. There is also a funny card come asking for the return of a video called *Sexy Pussycats*. I expect it is meant for next door's Adam. He looks a funny one. I am looking forward to seeing you safely back again. Do not get lost. Remember to leave enough money for the whisky.

With love, Mum.

PS My leg is still bad.'

Gerouin does not think it will be easy telling his mother about the course, or indeed about anything else.

Mrs Small receives a fax from Turkey. '... have found a shard with Linear B script. May be held up.'

"You'll have to look to your clairvoyant skills," says Jane to Kate, "to find out when he's arriving." She herself has received a dirty postcard from a girlfriend on holiday in Blackpool. Gerouin hardly knows where to look.

Michael receives a letter from Tabitha telling him she has put the house on the market. She reminds him that it is in her name. He screws it up. He also receives another letter. He checks the postmark and puts it away in his pocket unopened. He will not yet think of its contents. Like Percival, he has become adept at putting things to the back of his mind.

The three Brown(e)s receive three letters in identical writing. They collect them separately.

Penny is astonished by the writing on the envelope of her letter. She takes it to her room and remains there for some hours. Later she goes downstairs to use the telephone. She does not want Miss Aitchinson listening to her very private conversation. Bearded Joe looks in vain for her. His wife has forwarded him a publisher's list of new editions of the Cambridge Latin Course.

Nigel Box receives a letter with a ten pound note in it from his Granny (Mrs Box's mother).

"Granny's a pooface," he says. "I can't spend this. It's all stupid liras here."

"Don't speak of your grandmother like that, Nigel," says Mr Box. But Mrs Box promises that Daddy will speak to Fenella and get her to change it into lire.

"Go on, Dad, find Fenella now," says Nigel. "I want my lires." Mrs Box looks anxiously at her husband, but he says they mustn't bother Fenella when she's busy. He will find a time to catch her when she's on her own. Mrs Box smiles nervously.

Colin receives a letter that causes him to be mindful of the box again. It is a heavy responsibility.

Caroline receives a card from a girlfriend. 'I'm keeping my fingers crossed for you.' it says. There follows some heavy deletions as if the writer has thought better of her words. Caroline can only decipher the word 'legs'.

****

The bar is very frightening. Well, the whole hotel is really, with its great staircases and lifts and balconies. But the bar! It stretches out in a massive half-moon shape. The walls are of black and white marble and there are great sofas to sit upon (which in itself is scary, for you do not know who will choose to place themselves in such close proximity to you).

By and large they are not venturers into bars in England, Italy or anywhere else. Only bearded Joe and Jane are comfortable in a pub.

Miriam, it is true, is more familiar with this ambience. Sometimes, when they can get a baby-sitter, her husband takes her out for a nice little meal.

Miss Aitchinson has not been to a pub or a bar for the last twenty years. Percival has visited bars, but they are generally rather specialist ones.

But it does exercise a fascination. It is so large, so splendid. It would be interesting to have just one drink there after the meal. In Gaeta there was only a poky sort of corner to Reception, and anyway one hardly knew people to speak to. But this is Sorrento. It is a time to be bold.

Gerouin is embarrassed because he would like to buy Jane a drink, but he hasn't been able to find his purse. He knows he hasn't lost it, but he just can't find it.

"Don't worry," says Jane, "it'll turn up. Anyway we shan't be here for long."

"Oh," says Gerouin, "why not?" He quite likes it here with all these people. Also it puts off the evil hour of going to the shared room.

"Early night," says Jane with a wink. She has marked this *rite of passage* with a different tracksuit, same design, but navy this time. Gerouin has stood in the lavatory while she changed.

"Look what little Timmy has done for me," says Miriam. She shows Miss Aitchinson the precious crayoned drawing. Miss Aitchinson looks unimpressed.

"And look, he has written 'love Timmy' in big letters on it."

"He shouldn't be writing in capitals," says Miss Aitchinson. "He should learn small letters first."

****

There are cosmopolitan-looking Italians staying. They smoke cigarettes and laugh a lot. Two of them are glamorous-looking girls. Mr Box looks covertly at them. The two glamorous-looking girls do not notice Mr Box, but they do notice Michael, who is talking to bearded Joe.

They smile at him. "Ciao," he says, with a smile, before turning attentively to Joe.

"You'll not have done much school teaching," Joe is saying to him.

"Hardly any at all, I'm afraid," says Michael politely. He does not, however, look as if he regrets having missed this experience.

"You see, what worries me," says Joe, leaning forward at Michael to give emphasis to his words, and then leaning back again as he gets caught up in the smoke from Michael's cigarette, "is the calibre of my pupils in this day and age." He pauses to take stock of the impact of his words on Michael.

"Quite," says Michael. He wonders where Fenella is.

"Let me give you just two examples," says Joe.

"Please do. I should be most interested," says Michael. He wears his sympathetic face.

Caroline is sitting on an adjacent sofa. She has worked out that Michael will eventually be released from Joe. Then perhaps he will join her. She looks with scorn at Miriam with her son's crayoned picture in her hand. What a hypocrite!

"You don't mind me joining you, do you?" It is Mr Box, sitting down next to her (Mrs Box is trying to coax Nigel to bed; they are all sharing a room again). Robin Box has looked in vain for Fenella. Caroline, of course, is not in the same league, but she has a great bum on her. It is pleasant to feel the warmth from it. He does not think he will buy Caroline a drink. After all there is equality of the sexes nowadays; perhaps she will buy him one. This course is costing more than he has anticipated.

"Oh, actually, I'm just going," says Caroline, getting off the sofa. She could weep with vexation.

"And I thought I was going to be sitting next to the prettiest little lady in the room," says Mr Box.

William has got rather tired of seeing Timmy's crayoned picture. It seems to be usurping the place recently occupied by himself. He plies Miriam with amaretto.

Penny sits down on the arm of Kate Small's sofa. There is no room on the sofa itself.

"It's good news, isn't it?" says Kate in her sibilant tones. "I told you it would be, at Cumae, but you wouldn't believe me then!" Indeed, Penny is transfigured. She even looks different physically: she has put a little powder on her nose, a little colour in her cheeks, she wears a spotted dress. The effect is not displeasing.

"I'm thinking of flying back home tomorrow," says Penny. "Bother the expense. I just want to tell him it's all right. I've already spoken to him on the phone. He'd got my address from school, you know," her face positively glows. "I won't say anything about it, I mean I won't go on. She was such a horrible woman, always wore a tracksuit... not..." she adds hastily, catching sight of Jane, "that there's anything wrong in that."

"I shouldn't go back early," says Kate. "I should enjoy the rest of the course if I were you." She looks in the direction of bearded Joe. Michael is easing himself from his grasp. "After all, he's kept you waiting long enough, hasn't he?"

Penny smiles. Perhaps Kate has a point.

Miriam is becoming rather silly under the effect of all the amaretto. She laughs at everyone: Miss Aitchinson, alone in a corner with only her stick and the Blue Guide to Southern Italy for company, Caroline fleeing Mr Box (fancy wearing a red dress with hair that colour!), and Kate Small on her sofa. "I wonder it doesn't go through the floor."

Jane gives her a look.

"I'm off upstairs," she says. "Coming, Gerouin?"

"Yes, in a minute, Jane." Cold fear grips him.

"Don't be long, then." She goes striding off past the glamorous Italian girls. They find her very funny. Only then does Gerouin remember that Jane has the key and he cannot recall the room number. There is also no Fenella to consult.

"Oopsy daisy," says William, helping Miriam up. "I think I'd better give you a hand upstairs."

Even though he is on his way to find Fenella, Michael stops to have a word with Margaret Aitchinson.

"How are you enjoying the course?" he asks. "I can see you have the Blue Guide there." What can it be like to be an elderly virgin whom nobody wants even to talk to?

"Some of your lectures have been excellent, Dr Thorpe-Smith. I am afraid the same cannot be said about Mr Jeavons' guided tour of Baiae."

Michael gives the smile that he has so often given in the course of his career, when people have implied that others are less able than himself: it combines a gracious acceptance of their estimation of his worth with a hint of goodwill towards the one less favoured. He neither believes nor disbelieves what he implies. He has simply become used to doing it. It serves its purpose.

"And what is your specialism, Miss Aitchinson?" This is another rule of the game. You must not linger on the compliment, you must return it. He smiles encouragingly.

Margaret Aitchinson is taken aback. People are seldom pleasant to her; indeed, seldom even notice her, least of all the glamorous and successful. She looks covertly at the man; she observes his beautiful linen trousers, his open-necked shirt, his soft sweater, his large blue eyes and the unruly lock of hair that falls so insistently over them. Some dim recollection of another life comes upon her, a pre-virgal life when she had no need to depend on props, when happiness had seemed more of a possibility. She has not always been a middle-aged stick wielder. Once she had been young, once she used to laugh, but that had been a long time ago, when she thought she might marry Stuart.

"I am particularly interested," she says, "in First Century building techniques. I was most interested in your words on *opus reticulatum.*"

"Well then," he says, "you and I must walk round Pompeii together. I shall want to show you *opus testaceum, opus incertum, opus quadratum* and *opus quasi-reticulatum.*" He smiles his warm and friendly smile. Nor is it pure altruism. He relishes the idea of sharing his enthusiasm with another.

After fifteen years a man has asked her to go for a walk with him. Margaret Aitchinson smiles. "I shall look forward to that," she says, "very much indeed."

Colin has hung around for a while on the periphery of the group, blushing furiously. He thinks he may offer to buy Caroline a drink. He almost spoke to her at Baiae when they were coming back from Percival's awful tour. She has nice red hair and looks about his age; he edges towards her and some Italian girl, who doesn't notice him, bumps into him.

"*Scusi*," she says.

He blushes furiously. He rehearses words in his mind. 'Would you like a drink? My name is Colin Jones,' or 'isn't it crowded?' It's all so complicated. And then there will be the actual purchase; that will be another nightmare. Perhaps he should have opened the box before, just as his father had advised.

"It'll get you talking, Colin," he had said. A wise and kind man, he is concerned for his son's ineptitude.

He is, however, saved all this worry by the arrival of Mr Box on the very bit of sofa he had earmarked for himself, but it seems Caroline isn't staying. She is walking right out of the bar. Oh well. Perhaps it's a good thing really. He'll go back to his room and read up on Greek Naples, ready for tomorrow. It appears that he isn't sharing with Gerouin any more. Who can he be sharing with? It must be Joe. He seems a nice enough chap. Perhaps he can strike up a friendship with him.

Gerouin thinks it best to go to Reception and ask about the room. Reception is difficult to find, but, when at last he does find it, walking past, and into, unfriendly Italians, his courage fails him. Behind Reception sits an extraordinarily handsome and arrogant Italian. It is at such moments Gerouin becomes conscious of his own thinness and his clothes, the ones that seem all right in the shop, but somehow don't look quite right when set against the context of other people's. He notices that people don't seem to wear very narrow trousers nowadays, and his sports-jacket with the leather patches on the elbows looks distinctly odd compared to, say, Michael's linen jacket.

"*Si, signore*?" says the handsome Italian from his elevation behind Reception. He gazes with arrogant impassivity at Gerouin. Gerouin smiles nervously.

"A room," he says.

"*Si*, you are wanting a room in this hotel? You wait. I see." He looks as if he doubts Gerouin will be able to afford it. He picks up the telephone. The glamorous Italian girls walk past. They turn and stare after Gerouin.

"No. I have a room. I..."

"You say you want room."

"It doesn't matter," says Gerouin, miserably. It is all too complicated to explain anyway. He will go back to the bar and ask William or someone what to do. The handsome receptionist shrugs. What can he do?

It is difficult to find the bar again. When he does, there are no familiar faces to be seen. It is full of sophisticated-looking Italians. He sets off again, he knows not where. But the gods are with him; what he takes to be another glamorous Italian is in fact Michael, who is on his way to Fenella's room.

"Oh, Michael," he cries, "I don't know what to do." Michael stops and looks at him quizzically.

"How can I help?" he asks pleasantly. Gerouin pours out a tale of woe and Michael sees how it is.

"Let's go and ask Fenella," he says. "Fenella knows everything."

"But I don't know where..."

"Come with me." Then Gerouin remembers Baiae and is encouraged. Michael will know where Fenella is.

"I expect Jane will be awfully cross," says Gerouin.

"Jane?"

"Yes, the lady I'm sharing with. She generally wears a red tracksuit."

Michael, remembering Fenella's words, stops in his tracks. They are walking down a long marble corridor. He takes in the thin narrow trousers and the sports jacket, sees a mental picture of Jane and is filled with compassion.

"Do you have condoms?" he asks at last. Gerouin shakes his head miserably. Michael draws a packet out of one of the many pockets of his linen jacket.

"Surplus to requirements," he says, "but in case you need more – I hope you do – you know the Italian?"

Gerouin does not know the Italian. "*Prophylattici*," says Michael. "Can you remember that?" Gerouin nods. It has a pleasing Classical ring.

Fenella has been doing the invoices, checking the bookings, writing to the office (the fax machine is not working) and generally oiling the wheels of Classic Tours. But eventually all is accomplished, she bathes and changes into her very short nightdress. She is brushing her hair, which is long and curly and perhaps less naturally blond than it once was. The figures of Michael and Gerouin appear in the mirror.

"Heavens!" says Fenella. She is horrified by the apparition of Gerouin.

"Gosh, I'm sorry. I didn't mean..." He seems doomed to see Fenella in a state of undress. That nightdress, gosh, and Fenella was leaning over. It's so tight you can see her breasts, almost the nipple in fact, and the bottom of the nightdress. It's *Sexy Pussy Cats* all over again. He mustn't stare. It's rude.

"Gerouin's lost his room," says Michael. He sits on the bed in a proprietorial sort of way and lights a cigarette. Gerouin tries to absorb all this. But his eyes return to Fenella. The nightdress is black and shiny; it hardly covers ...well. She's got lovely... fancy holding those in your hands. Her hair touches them too; blond hair. Would it be blond everywhere?

"Let me just check the number for you," says Fenella. She regrets not having a dressing gown and is anxious for Gerouin to be gone. The black nightie catches between her legs as she walks. Gerouin feels a sensation that he sometimes feels on a Wednesday night when his mother is at the patchwork class. As she bends over the list he can see the shell-pink nipple trying to escape.

"Three-five-eight," says Fenella. "Is that a key you have in your hand?"

"No, it's a... *prophylattici*."

"Good for you," says Fenella, smiling in spite of herself. Suddenly Gerouin wishes that he was not wearing such tight trousers. It's very embarrassing.

"Will you be able to find your way?" asks Michael. He is smiling too. Has he noticed the trousers?

"Oh yes. thank you." He can hardly reach the door quickly enough.

"May Jane never know how much she has to thank you for," says Michael as Gerouin makes a hasty departure.

"I didn't notice my nightdress having the same effect on you," says Fenella, who is putting papers back on her dressing table.

"That's because I don't have the crotch-hugging trousers," says Michael. "Anyway, I've got a new girlfriend now."

"Has Caroline come back in your life?" asks Fenella.

"No, Miss Aitchinson. She and I share a passion for *opus quasi reticulatum*. We are going to look at it together in Pompeii."

"Well, I have two admirers," says Fenella. "Not only Gerouin but Mr Armpits Box, Robin to me. He called me the prettiest little lady on the coach. So there." She picks up her hairbrush.

"Stop arsing around over there and come over here," he says. Suddenly he feels tired. "Just come here, Fen. Please." He extracts her breasts from the nightdress, and kisses each gently.

"Did you ever hate me, Fen?"

"No." She starts undoing his shirt buttons.

"Not when I married Jemima?"

"No. Nor when you married Tabitha."

"What did you feel?"

"Acute misery; bottomless despair. No," says Fenella thoughtfully, "the first time I thought I'd get you back anyway, and the second time I had the children. They have always been very important to me. Why do you ask?"

"I just needed to know."

He gets up and takes the rest of his clothes off in silence. She takes his shirt and turns it the right way out; then, laying it down, she says, "I've always loved you, Michael, I could never stop just because you treated me badly. It isn't a virtuous thing or even a stupid thing, it's something I just have no control over – like I can't help having blue eyes and big tits. It's just the way it is."

"Get into bed, Fen. I want to lie next to you very straight and solemn like those Elizabethans on tombs in cathedrals; you know, the man in his ruff and a severe-looking wife next to him and lots of little children in ruffs all round the outside."

She snuggles down next to him. "I thought you wanted to lie very straight and still, so 1 don't know why you are doing that."

"Don't you, Fen? Don't you?"

"Well, yes, darling, yes."

"Will you always love me, Fen?"

"Yes."

"Whatever?"

"Yes."

"Will you keep your arms around me when I'm asleep – not take them away?"

"Yes."

Suddenly he smiles; the worry has passed. He devotes himself to satisfying the woman who loves him so unreservedly. In his jacket pocket is an unopened letter.

Chapter XVII

Naples

Fenella has said they must take nothing of value with them to Naples. There are gangs of youths on mopeds with knives. They will slash the straps of shoulder bags; pickpockets will be found at the station. Even children will attack them. Nor will anything stolen be recovered by the police. She urges them to make use of the hotel safe (Colin Jones has already lodged his box there) and leave even wristwatches behind. By and large they obey her. Percival takes no notice. He scorns Fenella and her advice. Michael also does not avail himself of the hotel safe; but then Fenella's advice is not directed at him.

And now she has them all on the platform at Sorrento Station (Gino and his coach have been released for a few days). Gino has disappeared soundlessly into that unknown Italy that is so alien to them, the Italy of peeling apartment blocks, narrow streets smelling of garbage and passages where dirty children play and women wear very tight black skirts. Even his coach has gone.

"Perhaps he will get the coffee machine mended now," says Miss Aitchinson to Colin Jones.

He blushes but makes no reply.

Fenella is very proud of herself: she has counted them and has them all assembled with their tickets on the platform. She does not even have to fear the losing of Gerouin. Jane has him by the hand. They are standing slightly apart from the others. Jane has a little colour in her cheeks and you hardly notice her prominent features. Gerouin too has a more assertive stance. You feel he will not lose many mackintoshes today.

Ah! Here is the train coming. This is the worrying moment for Fenella since the platform is jam-packed full of Italians bound for Naples. She must be careful not to allow any of her little band to be engulfed or swept away.

Miss Aitchinson has been watching keenly. She can see that seats will be at a premium. She is prepared to use her stick if necessary.

Mrs Box is very worried about Nigel. Something can so easily happen to him. Percival gets on further down the train.

Caroline again is fated not to stand next to Michael in the crowded train (only Miss Aitchinson seems to have a seat). Caroline turns her back on Colin Jones who is strap-hanging next to her, and gazes fondly towards Michael.

The crush is tremendous. Human beings of all shapes and sizes are squeezed against each other. There will be no respite until Naples.

Blushing furiously, Colin finds himself pressed firmly against Caroline's large hips. There is absolutely no escape.

However, as the train rushes on its uneven course, as is the way with Italian trains, Colin begins to experience a sensation which is not unfamiliar to him, but which he has seldom, if ever, realised in any place other than in the seclusion of his bedroom. A large evil-smelling woman behind him propels him into Caroline's spreading hips. The large woman holds him there as if in a clamp. The jolting of the train causes friction to occur between Caroline and Colin. Caroline herself is held in place by the hips of two large Italian girls; she is also gazing towards Michael, lost in her own thoughts. She is unaware that the rhythmic thrusting of something hard against her hips is anything other than the general crush behind her.

Colin breathes into Caroline's red hair (worn loose today); the sensation of pleasure is exquisite.

At Naples, Fenella experiences anxiety as she stands in the middle of the platform with her clipboard held up in the air ("Like an Aquilifer," says Michael – "A what?" says Fenella distractedly – "The standard-bearer in the Roman army," says Michael). She can see Mrs Box with Nigel, but not Mr Box – oh, there he is, standing behind her. There's Miss Aitchinson too, clearing a path towards her with the stick, there's

Jane and Gerouin; Kate Small is impossible to miss. Three Browns in a huddle – Joe with an enormous camera and Penny looking surprisingly glamorous; Percival, further down the platform, William standing near, but not with, Miriam.

Now, who's missing? Caroline? No. There she is. You can tell by the red hair. Colin Jones? What is he doing? He seems to be facing a wall and zipping up his coat. What does he want a coat on for today? How odd. Fenella gathers them to her, issuing stern warnings about pickpockets. They are bound for the Museo Nazionale.

Many people wish to attach themselves to Michael at the museum: Miss Aitchinson now regards herself as specially favoured; Miriam, too, standing at a distance from William, eyes Michael. She doubts she will be able to wrest him from Fenella – they have obviously been lovers for many years, but he might like a little variety. Who knows? Caroline obviously makes a beeline for him, followed by Colin Jones who still wears his coat zipped up over his trousers. Joe thinks he might have a few words with Michael about the Cambridge Latin Course as they go round. Fenella however is at hand to fight off the predatory if need be.

In the event he surprises them all. Casting round for an ashtray in which to stub out the inevitable cigarette, his eye lights on Nigel Box, who is engaged in kicking his mother's shins. His father is unaware of this as he makes a close scrutiny of Fenella's breasts from his vantage point at her side. His hands clench and unclench.

"Come on, Nigel," says Michael, "you and I are going to look at a few things together." He flashes his golden look at Mrs Box. "Can you spare him for a few minutes?" Mrs Box nods, dumbfounded (so few people appreciate Nigel), as she sees Michael propelling him onwards to the Grande Atria dei Magistrati and disappearing from sight.

Michael places a hand on Nigel's shoulder and stands him firmly in front of a sarcophagus.

"Now," he says, "you take a look – no, a proper look, and tell me what you see." He waits politely for Nigel's words.

"Some sort of bloke making something," says Nigel. He's not sure about all this.

"Take another look," says Michael, "and tell me what he's making."

"A sort of a bit... like a person," says Nigel.

"Well done," says Michael. "Let's walk about and look at things and I'll tell you about the man doing the modelling. Have you ever made anything out of clay?"

"Yeah," says Nigel, "I made a dog once at school."

"And was it difficult to make?" asks Michael.

"Not for me," says the objectionable Nigel.

"Well, it was very difficult for this chap (his name is Prometheus by the way) because he was making the first human being out of clay and bits of animals, and when he had finished making him, he gave him something very important. Can you guess what?"

Nigel can't.

"Fire," says Michael. "Think of it! Before then man had no heat..."

"Or light," says Nigel, wanting to show Michael a thing or two, "and he couldn't do his cooking."

"Absolutely," says Michael, "only Zeus... do you know who he was?"

"He was like the boss god, wasn't he?" says Nigel, staring all round him at the statues.

"Zeus was angry with Prometheus," says Michael.

"Why was Zeus angry?" asks Nigel.

"Because..." – they stop in front of a statue of a naked woman – "... because, oh, that's Aphrodite, by the way; she looks a bit like Fenella, doesn't she? Because Zeus wanted to keep man under his control. So he devised a horrible punishment for him. Those statues there are Harmodius and Aristogeiton, murderers actually..."

"What was the punishment?" asks Nigel. "What did Zeus do to him?"

"Do you really want to know?" asks Michael, standing still and turning to him politely.

"Yes," shouts Nigel, "go on, tell me."

"Well," says Michael, so quietly that Nigel has to listen very carefully, "Zeus chained him to a rock and sent an eagle to eat his liver. Just imagine how much that would hurt! And every night it grew back again."

"He would have died," says Nigel.

"Ah, but he couldn't," says Michael. "He was immortal. Every day his liver was eaten, and every night it grew back again – for hundreds of years."

"What happened then?" asks Nigel. He likes this.

"I'll tell you later," says Michael. "Now I want you to look at these two. He's called Orpheus and he's such a good musician that even animals follow after him to listen. And that's his wife Eurydice. He's going to fetch her back from the Underworld because she's died and he loves her."

"He's got a nice face," says Nigel. "Does he get her back then?"

"Well, yes and no," says Michael. "I'll tell you later. There's Hercules. Do you know about his labours?"

"No. Go on telling. Tell me!"

Michael turns to Nigel politely. "Tell me?" he echoes.

"Please," says Nigel reluctantly. It is such an unfamiliar word. Michael smiles his golden smile.

"It will be a pleasure," he says. "Oh, there's Achilles! Let's go and have a look at him, shall we?"

Fenella has been regarding the couple with amusement. Why does he do it? Has he to got to make everyone his slave? But these are all too easy for him: Caroline, Miss Aitchinson, Miriam – oh, she has seen Miriam looking at him – Gerouin, bearded Joe, Nigel Box. They will all die for him a little. How lightly he has accepted her own devotion, not without gratitude, she must not be unfair, he has thanked her for her favours and complimented her on her person. He has made his sexual enjoyment of her body abundantly clear. He has sent her forty-three white roses and demanded her wholehearted and eternal devotion. He has latterly indicated his need of her. He has placed himself in her hands and asked her to look after him. But never once in the last twenty years has he told her he loved her. Sometimes she has believed that he does and other times she has known that he does not. And now she is forty-three and none the wiser.

Michael's groupies will not yield him to the Box child for long. As they arrive together at the entresol from the grand staircase, Miss Aitchinson is waiting, the stick tapping nervously on the ground.

"Mr Thorpe-Smith, come here," she shouts (Nigel wonders if Michael will make her say 'please' too), "I have found some superb *opus secule*. I must show it to you."

Caroline, too, emboldened by Miss Aitchinson's unashamed accosting of him, asks for clarification on the mosaic with the musical instruments. She wishes that Colin Jones wouldn't keep breathing down her neck. Joe is showing him the very mosaic that is reproduced in Unit 3A of the Cambridge Latin Course. Miriam mentions that she feels a little faint.

He has a smile and a word for everyone, nor does he abandon Nigel Box.

"Look at the crocodiles on this mosaic, Nigel. Look at the teeth on them."

Indefatigably he takes them on upstairs. He leads them amidst satyrs and dancers and the double Hermae. He takes them to the Pompeian artefacts room, and shows them the inhabitants of Pompeii all unaware of the catastrophe that is to overwhelm them: here are the youths playing knuckle-bones – "That's because they had no pinball machines," he says, with a sheepish look at Fenella, "and here are the theatre tickets, ivory for the rich; here is a man sitting writing and here is a doctor with his forceps and catheter. Here is a statue of a satyr and here an iron strongbox." (Everyone looks at Colin; he blushes furiously and retreats a few paces from Caroline) He wants them to see the Pompeians as he can see them himself, with the humdrum drudgery and the touches of splendour of their lives, the lives that will be lost all at once under the ash of Vesuvius.

Best of all he likes the Campanian wall paintings.

"Look at Paquius Proculus," he says, "and look at his wife; look how they fix their eyes on us." He turns to whoever happens to be standing next to him. "Do you think they will join our party? I have never, have you..." he fixes his blue eyes on Caroline – something she will remember for always – "seen such a look unless it is on the face of the lady in the Arnolfini wedding!

"And here is the brawl in the Amphitheatre at Pompeii. Do you remember Tacitus tells us how the Pompeians were forbidden by Nero to hold any more shows for two years?

"And the port at Puteoli, the flat boats, the square walls, pure Caneletto. And the girl from Stabiae gathering flowers; look how delicate she is, look how gracefully she moves."

Fenella knows that faraway look in his eyes; he is being momentarily unfaithful to her with the graceful girl from Stabiae.

"Meleager and Atlanta. And Iphigenia. Do you know the story, Nigel?" He sweeps them all round with him. People from other parties, or individuals, be they Italian or German, attach themselves to the group. Joe sees Miss Aitchinson glowering (her fingers tapping on the stick), and warms to her.

"We can do without the Krauts," he whispers loudly. Miss Aitchinson nods fiercely.

"And here is Perseus and Andromeda. It is supposed to be a copy by Nicias. Not one of my favourites. Andromeda looks so ungrateful for being freed from her rock. If I were Perseus, I'd be inclined to go away and leave her there." One of the Brown(e)s frowns; this is heretical talk indeed. Another Browne smiles. What a very sensible remark of Michael Thorpe-Smith's. "And look at the three girls playing knuckle-bones. Is there something reminiscent of a Leonardo cartoon there? And here are Venus and Mars caught in bed together; do you remember the wonderful story told to Odysseus by the Phaecian bard Demodocus? How Hephaestus made a splendid invisible steel net and trapped them in bed together...?" Jane whispers something to Gerouin who looks embarrassed, "And all the gods came and laughed except Poseidon who was extraordinarily po-faced about the whole thing.

"And here is Hercules about to shoot the centaur Nessus who has just tried to rape his wife. Moral of the story, 'Never leave your wife alone with a centaur'. And here's Theseus about to make off with Andromache. For a mighty hero he's singularly poorly endowed. But there," adds Michael cheerfully, if a little complacently, "Greek artists seemed shy of a large penis." Colin blushes furiously and Caroline casts down her eyes. She can't understand why Michael has to keep using these unpleasant words.

"And just to finish off," says Michael, "here's a jolly old Bacchic orgy with a very pretty boy in the midst. A scholar of note, whose name I shall not mention, speaks of his 'charming vivacity'. I am sure," he opens his eyes wide and grins wickedly, "you will appreciate his meaning if you look closely."

Fenella thinks it is time to move them on. Michael shouldn't say things like that. Poor Miss Aitchinson's stick is tapping up and down in embarrassment. When, however, she comes to count them, she finds Percival missing. Perhaps he has stayed behind for a private viewing of the boy with the charming vivacity.

Fenella has taken them all off by this time, a feat over which she has experienced no little trepidation, but which, in the event, has worked out well - only Colin has found it a less rewarding experience than his earlier journey. She has taken them to Virgil's tomb. This is less than successful: there is in fact very little to see, and Michael says cheerfully that he's sure it's not Virgil's tomb anyway. Only Miss Aitchinson is rewarded by the sight of a pillar made of *opus reticulatum*. Furthermore, they are hungry; it is past their lunch time. They are tired from the museum. There are many tempting shops and cafes. Nor do they evince much enthusiasm for rediscovering Greek Naples. Basically they want to be left to their own devices. They have their train tickets; they can get back to Sorrento under their own steam.

Chapter XVIII
Rebellion

Fenella has not been running Classic Tours for twenty years without being able to sense possible insurrection. She gives way graciously: she is sure Michael will be glad of the extra free time and will, of course, be available to talk to anyone on this fascinating subject. Perhaps (she turns to him with polite interrogation) this evening? Michael will be delighted to share what little knowledge he has on Greek Naples. Possibly the early evening would be best. Fenella warns them again of the dangers of pickpockets and muggers. She urges them not to go anywhere alone. Then she casts them adrift like so many paper boats. She wonders how they will fare, battling against the currents and tides of Naples. She hopes they will find themselves safely wafted back to the shores of Sorrento.

As is so often the case, the desire is subsumed in the act. A dictator is murdered, Julius Caesar for example, but what are the conspirators to do next? The course members have won a mighty victory against Fenella and her tyrannous ways. She has been vanquished and accepted defeat, and now she is retreating with her ally Michael, apparently towards the Museo Nazionale.

Like post-Communist States, they feel the lack of control and order. Also, with Fenella there, there was safety. She held up her clipboard, and lo, all might shelter beneath it. Now they realise what they have lost: Fenella was wise and kind, Fenella knew where lavatories were and how much *panini* should cost. Now they wish for Fenella back, even at the price of having to walk round Greek Naples. All around them lurk murderers and thieves; one must be sure to have lunch with another, even if that other is not one's boon companion.

There are two members of the party, however, who do not share these sentiments. One is Miss Aitchinson; she has her stick to protect her. The other is Percival Jeavons. He is glad to see Fenella's tyranny smashed. He trusts he knows Naples as well as Fenella. Neither he nor Miss Aitchinson require the spending of money on lunch. Each sets off in the direction of the harbour, but not, of course, together.

It is difficult for Miriam without William. They no longer seem to be on speaking terms. She is so terrified of being left on her own that she attaches herself to the Boxes. Mr Box finds a distinctly insalubrious restaurant, 'dirty', Miriam would have called it, if she could have spoken her thoughts instead of having to smile at the loathsome Nigel and go whither she was bid. Mr Box says that there is no point in spending a lot of money and Mrs Box agrees. Nigel won't eat anything anyway. Mr Box orders them each a plate of greasy *gnocchi*. The very smell of them makes Miriam feel sick. She only eats a few although she is very hungry. Mr Box says if she's not going to eat them, he might as well finish them up.

"No point in letting good food go to waste," he says, scooping it on to his plate.

He has been eyeing Miriam up in the absence of Fenella. Those little dark ones liked a bit between their legs; better than that plain red-haired girl too. When Mrs Box takes Nigel to the lavatory, Mr Box moves his chair towards Miriam. She begins to wish she had been a little more accommodating to William.

William is similarly lost without Miriam and is now regretting some over-zealous behaviour of the previous night. He thinks he will attach himself to Gerouin and Jane, but they seem to have disappeared. They are in fact hot-footing it back to Sorrento and the shared room. Gerouin has not done anything so successful since gaining his lower second in Classical Studies.

Penny and Joe have gone off to take photos. Joe has all sorts of equipment with him. The Brown(e)s too have departed, bent on some mysterious business of their own. There remains only Caroline and Kate Small, with Colin Jones following after.

"Can I carry something, Mrs Small?" asks William. He will have to become willing again.

Fenella and Michael have had a lovely time in the Museo Nazionale. Fenella did her degree in Art History and is still quite knowledgeable. Unlike many people who themselves teach or lecture, Michael is happy to listen.

Coming out into the sunlight they head for a cafe; unlike Mr Box's, it is not cheap. They sit on the gaily painted chairs on the pavement outside and share a bottle of wine and eat *cartoccio*.

"You used to take me to the National Gallery - in London, I mean, Fen - and try to educate me. I still go and look at Monet's Waterlilies and think of you."

"I bet you don't," says Fenella, "because that was simply ages ago." She is saddened because she remembers their last visit to the Waterlilies very well, because it was just before the lunch in Soho when he told her he was going to marry Jemima. But Michael, who is unaware of Fenella's lateral thinking, pursues the subject.

"You were awfully keen on art then. I don't know why you didn't get a job in a gallery or something, instead of slaving away for Classic Tours."

"Well, it was because I was meant to be looking at the art that I went to Ithaca and got involved in travel."

"There isn't any art on Ithaca."

"No, but there might have been. Doug Easterwood wanted me to..."

"I think we can imagine what Doug Easterwood wanted you to do. Do you remember he tried to beat me up when he found out I'd had my wicked way with you?" He pours them both more wine.

"Oh yes, so he did. Poor Doug. Well he'd asked me along to look into the art; the organising of the accommodation for the dig was only really inventing a job. I would never have thought of going into organising tours and things if it hadn't been for him!"

"I remember him saying in his pompous way, 'This beautiful young girl, this innocent virgin...'"

"Well, I was."

"Yes, it always beats me, Fen, how you could have spent three years at university..."

"Four, actually. I did a Masters."

"Four years without going to bed with anyone; especially looking the way you did."

"How did I look?"

"Amazing," He opens his blue eyes wide at her. "Why didn't you go to bed with anyone?"

"I told you. I was waiting for the right one."

"How could you be sure, that night in Ithaca?"

"Well, you didn't give me much choice, really."

"Oh, Fen, what a pig I've always been to you."

"No," says Fenella, "you've just been you." She smiles at him.

"Why are you smiling, Fen?"

"I was just remembering when you first arrived."

"I nearly didn't, you know," He smiles at the waiter, "*Un'altra bottiglia di vino, per favore...* I was in Turkey and I nearly stayed on. As it was, I arrived two days late."

"Yes," says Fenella.

She remembers it all so incredibly clearly; the dreary set up in Ithaca, a painstakingly tedious dig where everybody knew really there was nothing to find; several elderly men and the requisite number of novice archaeologists and two stout unpleasant women; and Fen 'to advise on art' because pompous Doug Easterwood had fancied her and invented a job for her on university money. She was to organise accommodation, drive the jeep and see there was lavatory paper available. She envisaged three ineffably dreary weeks ahead. People spoke of Michael Thorpe-Smith doing great things in Turkey, a brilliant scholar, the up-and-coming man. She imagined he would be like the rest. Nobody told her he would have shoulder-length hair bleached gold by the sun, azure blue eyes and a suntan from weeks of working in Turkey; that he would have a necklace of shells, washed-out jeans, and a smile that had the power to undress her. She had given herself to him that first Ithacan night under the stars near the Cave of the Nymphs; and she had been giving herself to him ever since, although the bleached hair had been long ago cropped and turned from gold to grey.

"You were like Apollo," she says. "Is there any more wine?" The waiter appears as if by magic and pours it out.

"And you were," says Michael, "like Aphrodite. They all fancied you rotten. Did I tell you I once caught Doug Easterwood watching you in your bikini and jerking himself off?"

"Poor old Doug. What happened to him?"

"Oh he did very nicely for himself, got himself a chair somewhere, wrote a couple of mildly tedious books. I meet him on committees and things sometimes. He's so incredibly pompous that I often feel tempted to remind him of Ithaca. It would be such fun when he's holding forth about A level grades and assessment committees to say 'Are you still wanking?' It was a brilliant summer, wasn't it, Fen?"

Fenella smiles; for him it had been a 'brilliant summer', for her it had been the most stunning thing that had ever happened, evoking feelings in her that she didn't know she possessed. She had been caught in the spell ever since. Their eyes meet over the *cartoccio*.

"You taught me to make love," she says. Even now she has to cast her eyes down. He reaches for her hand across the cluttered table and strokes it gently.

"You were an apt pupil. The only trouble was you wanted only to give pleasure, not to receive it. I remember you fighting and fighting against an orgasm and sobbing with shame when you came."

Fenella cannot look up; she plays with the *cartoccio*.

"I was very silly."

"No, you were very sweet. You have great douceur as well as great passion." He takes her hand to his lips. He smiles gently at her; then he says, "Do you remember that cove with the cliffs that came down sheer, that you could only get to by boat?"

"Andri. We made love on the edge of the shore that night after the storm, in all the surf and seaweed."

He grips her hand. "God, Fen."

"And in the November you married Jemima." She doesn't mean to reproach him; it is just that the scar is deep.

"Yes." He lights a cigarette.

"I never thought it would last," she continues. "I thought I'd get you back. I even married Mark to get you back. It didn't work though, did it? You never even thought of leaving Jemima for me, did you? Not even after the Rome course, when you had been married a year and we did it all the time." He tucks a stray piece of Fenella's hair behind one of her ears.

"She was pregnant, Fen. I couldn't leave her. Anyway, you were pregnant yourself soon after. I often wondered whether John was my son."

"No, I don't think so," Fenella smiles. "He looks exactly like Mark now."

"I'd have liked a son," says Michael, "but I don't think I'm very good father material. I was useless with Chloe and Octavia."

"Why?" asks Fenella; she pours him out more wine. All this is unexplored territory to her. She knows it as forbidden ground.

"Why? Because I was never there; and, when I was, I spoiled them, undoing all Jemima's good work. After we bought the place in Berkshire, I stayed in the flat in town all week and often at the weekends as well. And then I had the sabbatical in the States. I was away two years."

"Why didn't Jemima go with you?"

"Well, she didn't want to uproot the girls; they had just started some new school or other; and then there were the horses. Jemima lived for her horses. I know you think she was dull and stupid."

"Not at all. I thought her very pleasant when we met; she obviously understood you very well and she had lots of..."

"Money? Is that the word you are looking for?" he asks angrily. He pours himself some more wine; he doesn't pour any for Fenella.

"I'm not a materialist, Fen. I don't want riches *per se*... no, listen. What I wanted was the freedom to get inside my subject. I do love the Ancient World, Fen, and I wanted to study it in my way; not through limited little tunnels built by university grants, but how I knew I could do it best. I wanted to get into the mind of Horace; I wanted to know how Propertius felt. I knew I was good; but I needed time, and time cost money. I'm delving, Fen, deeper and deeper into the minds of people living two thousand years ago. It matters to me. Can you understand that?"

"Yes, darling." She reaches over the table to him. "I can understand."

"And you, Fen. No, I didn't think of leaving Jemima for you. No, don't look like that. I'll tell you. You were me, Fen. You were, are, an extension of me. We think alike, we don't disagree on anything fundamental. You are an extension of my sexuality. You are part of me. It doesn't matter that you're not always there. You can't use all of yourself all of the time; when you're writing an article you're not making love; when you're giving a lecture you're not thinking about your children – but all these facets are there, waiting in the wings, and you're one of them, one of the parts of me. I don't think of you as extraneous to myself." He lights a cigarette and sighs, "I don't explain myself well."

"But, Michael, I am not part of you. I'm me and I've spent my life waiting to be more than a facet of you that you might want that day. I love you." Perhaps it is the wine she has drunk that allows her to ask the unpermitted question. "Do you love me?" He pours out the dregs of the bottle into her glass.

"I don't know what you mean." He speaks almost angrily. "Are you talking Eros? Do I feel very strongly, very passionately about you when I am inside you? The answer is yes, I do. Are you talking Biblical love – when Christ talks of selling all you have and following after him. No, I wouldn't do that for you. Do you mean liking? Yes, I like you enormously, probably more than any woman I've ever known – "

"You'll never give me a straight answer."

"I don't know the answer. I don't think it matters very much."

"It doesn't matter?" she asks angrily. "You say that, but you demand my love."

"That's different, Fen. You're a woman." He leans over the table and kisses her. "My woman. And you taste of *cartoccio*. Come on, let's go back." He is ridiculously generous with his tip.

Chapter XIX
When You don't Listen to Fenella...

Leaving the tomb of Virgil, Percival steps out smartly. He is not actually quite sure where he is heading for, but he has a shrewd suspicion Miss Aitchinson is coming along behind, and he wishes to show that he is full of purpose. Eventually he comes to the tunnel leading to Fuorigrotta. As he walks through it, holding his briefcase in one hand (the Baiae notes are inside) he has an uneasy recollection of Fenella's warnings. It is pleasing to find them quite ungrounded, another indication of female hysteria and Fenella's ineptitude.

Halfway up the steps to the Parco Virgiliano, he encounters seven children aged between eight and ten. They look none too clean and not at all friendly. A boy, larger than the others, holds out his hand.

"*Soldi*," he says. Percival tries to push past, but they close round him. A small girl twists his briefcase from his hand, she opens it and tips out the Baiae notes. Two or three children scrabble through the contents, and, finding no money, kick the papers about.

A second boy joins the first in blocking Percival's advance.

"*Lire*," he says.

Although Percival has always made mention of 'a useful working knowledge of Italian', actually he has no more than a handful of words with which to instil discipline into these ragged children. They do not seem to be like the boys at the last prep school he taught at. He tries to push past. A small foot shoots out and trips Percival up, he sprawls on the ground and his purse falls from his pocket. The children light upon it with glee. They seem to want to divide the spoils there and then. As he tries to get up, a big girl kicks him. He feels fear; he wishes they would take the purse and leave him. The children with their threatening ways terrify him.

"Prego," he says, bringing out one of his few words of Italian, *"per favore."* They mock him, *"prego,"* they shout, *"per favore."*

But surely... can it be? No? Yes, there is a familiar sound, steps accompanied by a tapping. In his dazed state Percival thinks of Long John Silver. But no! It is Miss Margaret Aitchinson on her way to the Parco Virgilio.

Miss Aitchinson, well practised in looking out for potentially dangerous situations for herself, now observes another in a situation not just potentially dangerous, but actually so. Equipped with the twofold advantage of language and stick, Miss Aitchinson advances: *"Andate via, ragazzi,"* she cries and lays about her with her stick. The children, attacked physically and recognising the voice of adult authority, drop the purse and flee.

"Are you all right?" asks Margaret Aitchinson. It hasn't yet struck her what a heroic act she has just committed.

"I don't know," says Percival, easing himself up. It is perhaps the most honest thing he has said all week.

Percival stands and examines his person, his trousers have a great stain across them, his jacket is dirty and he aches all over. Miss Aitchinson, grunting with the exertion, is picking up all his Baiae papers and putting them back in his case.

"Did they take much?" she asks.

"A few thousand lires, I think," he replies. He feels weighed down with misfortune.

"We'll get a taxi," says Margaret Aitchinson, "and go back to the station. That's the best thing to do."

It seems very good to him that somebody knows what is best for him. All his life he has tried to work out what is best for himself and always he has seemed to fail. He has consulted nobody, and listened to nobody and nobody has listened to him either, nor has anyone shown any interest in him or his welfare. He has built a strong carapace round his *amour propre*, a carapace composed of Classical learning; but the carapace is cracking: for all his learning he has no job. Nobody from the world of

Classics answers his letters on erudite subjects. Not one person had stayed to hear him at Baiae, and there are other, darker concerns as well. And now a band of children knock him over and scatter his notes. He sobs aloud.

"Now, none of that," says Miss Aitchinson sternly. "Lean on that stick, and we'll get down the steps and into a taxi and take you home."

It amazes her too how freely, authoritatively, and suitably she is speaking; and, not only that, she is being listened to as well. Head held high, she leads the way; her step does not falter nor does she even need to use the handrail.

Percival Jeavons hobbles after her. He experiences the same sense of release that he felt as a child when he waited in the playground and children kicked him and teased him because he was clever and hard-working; and then, at three thirty, his beautiful mother would arrive and take him home by the hand. He even manages a weak smile in the direction of Margaret Aitchinson.

****

William, Kate Small, Caroline, and Colin Jones are on their way back to Sorrento by train. Much to Colin's disappointment the train is not crowded and there are seats for all, although William has to search further down the train. Eventually he finds one next to a vast moustached man who smokes some vile-smelling cigarettes. William thinks his own thoughts, going back in his mind over the events of last night.

He had managed to get Miriam into his double-bedded room comparatively painlessly; indeed he had even got her onto the bed – such was the power of the amaretto. Unfortunately for William, there is little time with him between the anticipation of the act and the act itself (his wife can vouch for this), and under these circumstances a new William appears, not the helpful altruistic William we know so well, but a William with one thought in his mind and a determination to equal the thought. Miriam has enjoyed the kissing and is lying back in anticipation of some more, when she sees William advancing upon her, intention obvious upon his person. From the haze of amaretto ancient bells sound. She sits up but William pushes her down, firmly pulling at her knickers.

"Come on, Miriam," he says, "you know you want it as much as me." This comment was a mistake. Miriam would perhaps have agreed to William's demands if she had been made to feel she was awarding a mighty prize. If he was a knight errant and she his lady. But to be told she actually wanted it; that she could not accept.

"Get off me," she cried, as William tried to get on top of her. "I'll scream. I'll tell everyone you raped me."

William knew when he was beaten. He got off her. "Bitch," he said, "fucking dick-teasing bitch."

This is the scene that goes through William's mind as he stares out of the window at the tenement blocks and Martini advertisements in the world outside. It is difficult to know what to do really. He could still be in with a chance; some women like masterful men and he has paid a lot of extra money for the room with the double bed. It seems a pity to let it go to waste. He considers Caroline, whom he can see further up the train talking to Kate Small. She's not much cop really, probably wouldn't be much good either, although you never knew. After all his own wife was a case in point. But Caroline is really very plain with her stringy red hair and that Colin Jones, with his coat done up, keeps staring at her. Good big hips, though. Then Miriam could turn nasty. He has an inkling that she's really rather an unpleasant person. Best keep a low profile. See how the land lies.

"And when is your husband arriving, Kate?" asks Caroline, not because she wants to know, but to avoid having to talk to Colin Jones, who seems to be constantly present.

"I think," says Kate, "but I don't know, it's just a feeling that I have, that he'll be at the hotel when we get back."

"Gosh, how exciting," says Caroline. "How long since you've seen each other?"

"Four weeks," says Kate, smiling at Caroline from her two seats. "He's been in Turkey."

"What's he been doing?"

"He found some Linear B tablets. He's always lucky in Turkey; he found a bronze sword there once, that was twenty years ago. Michael was with him."

"Michael?" Caroline's ears prick up.

"Michael?" echoes Colin. He is getting better at conversation.

"Yes," says Kate, "they found it together, but Michael let him claim all the kudos from it because he was just leaving for Ithaca."

"Ithaca?" says Colin.

"Yes," says Kate carefully. "That's where he met Fenella." She watches Caroline out of the corner of her small eyes. They are almost lost in the folds of fat in her face.

"They have known each other for twenty years then," says Caroline tremulously.

"Yes," says Kate deliberately, "they are very old friends."

"Old friends," says Colin. Caroline turns to him furiously.

"Oh, shut up," she says. Tears start to her eyes. Kate pats her hand consolingly.

"That's the way it is, my dear," she says. Colin blushes furiously. He won't venture any more remarks and he'll change his trousers when he gets back too.

Chapter XX

Bedrooms

"What have you done with my pills, Pamela?" whispers Robin Box. He and his wife are preparing for bed. Nigel is asleep in the bed opposite.

"Oh dear," comes the whispered reply.

"What do you mean, 'oh dear'," says Mr Box, forgetting to whisper in his anger.

"I... I threw them away," says Mrs Box. By the light of the bedside lamp he can see her smiling the familiar smile of one who has acted foolishly yet again.

"You did what?" he shouts. Nigel stirs in his bed.

"Oh hush," says Mrs Box, nervously clasping her hands. "You'll wake Nigel... I was afraid, I was afraid Nigel would eat them. They look so pretty." She looks pleadingly at him.

"You stupid fool," says Mr Box, getting into bed. "Why didn't you just give them to me?"

"Oh dear," replies Mrs Box, getting into her side of the bed, "I didn't think." She is struck by a bright idea. "Perhaps we can get some more, Robin."

Her ineffectiveness and her stupidity infuriate him.

"That's very likely, isn't it," he says. "Please, Signor Chemist, have you got some pills to stop my husband wanting to fuck everything in skirts under ninety?"

"Oh dear," says Mrs Box, "what shall we do?" For a minute Mr Box lies silent, then he says nastily, "Well, you'll have to work overtime, won't you?"

Mrs Box looks anxiously at the bed opposite. "But Nigel..." she says.

"Sod Nigel," says the father, "get working." He turns out the light.

Lying in the dark with his glasses on and his wife at work upon him, he substitutes Fenella for her. He remembers how she refused him a separate room for Nigel, saying he would have to pay extra, speaking patronisingly at him with her nipples taunting him, how he has heard whispers of her baring her body to her lover at Cumae. He feels the familiar urge to get on top of his wife.

"I'm going to fuck you, Fenella," he says. "I'm going to fuck you hard."

He is just at the very point of accomplishing his purposes when Nigel, alerted perhaps by the combined sound of the whispering and the bed springs, wakes up.

"What are you doing, Dad?" he asks, sitting up.

"Oh dear, oh dear," says Mrs Box. "You'll have to stop, Robin."

"Stop what?" says Nigel, amazingly wakeful from his bed.

So near and yet so far. Mr Box cannot bear to stop. He's under the duvet after all.

"Go to sleep, Nigel," he commands in a voice of thunder. He continues to move up and down on the top of Mrs Box.

"I know what you're doing," responds his son. "You're like that dirty old satyr Michael showed me on a Greek vase. He was sticking his dick into a wood nymph." But Mrs Box is no wood nymph and she bursts into tears.

"This is the last time I take you two on holiday," says Mr Box, climbing off Mrs Box. "the last fucking time."

****

Michael is asleep across Fenella with his head buried in a pillow. Fenella has woken up, probably because she is not used to sleeping on her back and the weight of Michael (which is not great, he is still slim) is pleasantly unfamiliar. She waits for sleep to return to her and strokes his hair. She has promised not to take her arm away from him while he sleeps, so she won't.

It is then that he starts to mutter. She cannot catch what he is saying, but he is obviously distressed. She continues to stroke his hair.

"It's all right, darling," she says. Then he begins to thrash about and move his head from side to side, muttering increasingly. She wonders whether to wake him. Then he lifts his head up and, still lying on top of her, stares at her with open eyes. He speaks clearly and distinctly,

"*Lapsa cadunt folia aut ad terram, gurgite ab alto, quam multae glomerantur aves, ubi frigidus annus, Trans pontum fugat et terris immitit apricis.*"

She does not know if he is awake or asleep. It would be like him to dream in Latin. His head goes down into the pillow again, but he twitches convulsively. Fenella strokes his back.

"Hush, darling," she says, "it's all right, I'm here."

"It's dark, dark," he says.

"No," says Fen, "the night light is on; it's not dark. I'm here, Fen." He starts to tremble again and Fenella feels her hands getting wet where she is touching his back. She decides that, whatever textbooks may say to the contrary, she is going to wake him.

"Michael," she says, taking his shoulder in her hands, "wake up, darling. Come on."

Suddenly he wakes, and, as always, he gains consciousness immediately.

"Hello, Fen," he says, "have I been dreaming?"

"Yes," says Fen, "let me stretch a minute... that's better. Only you would dream in Latin."

"Latin?" He looks puzzled. "Latin?"

"Yes, I think it was the bit in Virgil about all the souls waiting to get across to the underworld."

He rolls off her and sits up, running his fingers through his damp hair.

"Oh, Christ," he says, "it's always the same, always going down to bloody Hades. Sometimes I'm Orpheus going down to get Eurydice. I've been Alcestis dying instead of Admetus; but unlike them, I know I'm not going to get back; and I'm back to Orpheus and Hippolytus, I'm to be punished. I'm to lie in the dark in the mire with my soul imprisoned in my body like Plato says. And I go down and down to Tartarus that's twice as deep as Mount Olympus is high... and I want a cigarette." She passes the packet over.

"I don't think your sins are very great," she says. "I don't think you'll merit great punishment."

"Hubris, overweening pride, a belief I could do anything; the reason I married Jemima and Tabitha so I could explore the past, become part of it and bring it back to the world. I suppose like..." he lights a cigarette, "like Hercules bringing back Cerberus from the Underworld; but, of course, I couldn't. You can't get back into the past alive and bring it back, and all I got was two failed marriages."

Fenella says nothing. She cannot rejoice in his failure, but in the failure there may be hope for her own future. She kisses the greying hairs on his chest. She wonders silently if his dreams ever include her. As if he read her thoughts, he says

"It wouldn't be so bad if you were there."

"I'm always there," says Fenella.

As so often, his mood changes. Suddenly he rolls over and smiles at her.

"Do you know what I want to do now?"

"Yes."

"Do you want to too?"

"Why don't you find out?" says Fenella.

****

In the room that contains Gerouin and Jane there are a large number of *prophylattici*, but whether they have been used in an orgy of passion, or whether they have been the result of unsuccessful application, cannot be known. Suffice it to say that Jane snores comfortably in one of the two single beds and Gerouin lies next to her. Because he is so thin there is plenty of room for both of them.

Chapter XXI

Capri (The Villa Iovis)

There is something awfully exciting to the British about 'going on the water'. Perhaps coming from an island we feel an affinity with the sea, or perhaps it is for the opposite reason, the island has provided shelter; to venture off it requires skill and daring. There is danger involved.

Be that as it may, there is certainly a feeling of excitement amongst the party as they make their early-morning way along past the souvenir-shop-ridden streets of Sorrento down to the harbour. It is quite a long walk (Fenella intends working them hard today; they have had their treat at Naples, and now they must be prepared to rise to the challenge).

Miriam and Caroline walk along together, not through a desire for each other's company, but through extraneous circumstances. Miriam is determined not to be stuck with the Boxes again and the only unattached male seems to be Colin Jones, and where Caroline is, there is he too. He's quite a nice-looking lad really and his clothes are quite stylish (Miriam notices such things). It's a pity he's so shy. He was better in the beginning when he had his box. Miriam is pleased to see Caroline looks even more unattractive than usual. In fact she looks downright miserable. This in turn cheers Miriam up.

"It seems to be a very long way to the harbour," she remarks. "I find long walks very tiring. My husband always makes me take the car at home. He worries about me a lot."

Caroline makes no reply and hastens her footsteps to get away from Colin.

"Is anything the matter, Caroline?" she asks.

"I think I owe you an apology," says Caroline, slowing down (Colin has got stuck behind the Boxes). "I thought you told me something that wasn't true, but it was, and I'm sorry."

"Oh, you mean Fenella and Michael," says Miriam, who is very quick on the uptake where such matters are concerned. "Oh yes, everybody knows. I think it's disgusting really." A scene in a double bedroom passes before her eyes. She thinks she won't pursue this train of thought.

"I suppose she's very pretty," says Caroline sadly.

"Fenella?" Miriam can't bear to hear of another woman being praised. "I don't think so. Mutton dressed as lamb if you ask me, and you can tell her hair's dyed."

"Can you?" says Caroline miserably. They both look ahead towards Fenella, who is walking with one of the Brownes. Perhaps there is some truth in Miriam's words. She is certainly dressed more provocatively than usual. She has a very tight blue skirt on and a stunning blue frilly top, rather low in the front. She is, in fact, obeying orders. A little smile plays around her lips as she recalls the scene in her bedroom that morning.

"Wear something tarty, Fen," he had said, "so all Capri lusts after you."

"Will this do?" Fen had asked, turning to him in her blue.

"Absolutely. Tiberius would have paid millions of sesterces to have you in his Villa Iovis."

"I thought he was only interested in boys."

"No, no, Fen; he was very broad-minded indeed. He was terribly happily married to Vipsania Agrippina; it was only when Augustus made him divorce her and marry that scrubber Julia that his problems started. When he saw Agrippina in the street afterwards and knew he could never have her again, he used to weep."

"I know how he felt," she had said.

"Anyway," says Michael, who had chosen to ignore this, "the point of my not particularly erudite excursus was to say that I like your blue skirt very much, and even better the blue droopy top – ' a careless disorder in the dress' – as Herrick says. Can I sit next to you in the hydrofoil and grope you?"

"Only if you tell me I'm the prettiest little lady in the boat."

"Ah, my rival, Mr Box. Do you know, Fen, the boy would be all right if he was taken away from that awful pair. He's got a bit of spark, quick on the uptake. If he went away to school somewhere..."

"Oh, Michael, you're not going to perform one of your appalling acts of altruism, are you?"

"Absolutely not. Charity begins at home, in this room in fact. I'm going to give you..."

They are approaching the harbour steps; there are a lot of these. How will Miss Aitchinson get down? There appears to be no problem. Even if she does not exactly glide, there is a lightness in her step. Sometimes she slows down for the limping figure at her side to catch her up. She has become quite a celebrity, a heroine in fact. She has told the story many times now, and, as is the way in the development of myth and legend, a whole new version has emerged. Even Percival himself has emerged with a new clean character, his old crimes expunged by this fresh instance of Nemesis.

"What a wicked attack on poor Mr Jeavons," says Miss Alice Browne. "How much was taken, Mrs Sykes? I heard it was two million lire."

"Oh no," says Fenella, smiling out of her blue, "I don't think it was much really. I had warned people not to take much money."

"Of course it wasn't two million lire," says Sally, the wife, "that would be something like eight hundred pounds. He would be hardly likely to take that, would he?"

"I don't think you'll find two million lire is eight hundred pounds, Sally," says Alice. "It's quite simple to convert lire really."

"So he didn't lose much," says Jennifer, the friend.

"A gang of gypsies, wasn't it?" says Sally. She is not unlike a gypsy herself with her untidy grey hair and dark staring eyes.

"No, dear," says Alice, "it was two men with knives."

"I think it was children actually," says Fenella.

"Children!" They all stare at her. For the first time that week they are all three in agreement. It certainly wasn't children.

There is a tang of salt in the air. For those who are not seafarers (most, in fact) hardly comprehensible words, partially understood concepts form themselves into actualities. This is a waterfront, these are wharves, here are berths and mooring points. Here are boats of all descriptions and there indeed is the very hydrofoil which they will journey in. They may not yet embark. Nautical things are being done aboard: decks are being scrubbed, ropes are being heaved up and down, engines are being examined. They must stand on the quayside and wait. The tension mounts. Nigel Box, who sports a nautical cap (worn back to front), nearly falls in. Mrs Box gives a little scream, but Mr Box doesn't even notice; he is watching Fenella in her blue filmy blouse that falls in folds over her breasts.

And now there are Italian sailors who look just like sailors in story books (Miriam thinks of Timmy's book *Sinbad the Bad Sailor*), and these sailors are bidding them embark. It is a moment for anxiety; to leave terra firma and to commit oneself to a frail bark. To show Jane he is unafraid, Gerouin sings 'what shall we do with the drunken sailor' - and, indeed, there are one or two who look decidedly that way; let it be hoped they are not in positions of responsibility.

"Put him in the scuppers with the hosepipe on him," responds Jane robustly, so robustly that Alice Browne, who is of a nervous disposition, jumps.

It is, however, no time for hanging back. Italians are not given to standing aside and letting others through. Miss Aitchinson and Percival give no quarter. They make a formidable pair; even without the stick Margaret Aitchinson is adept at beating a passage forward. What she cannot achieve is completed by Percival who does have the stick, and has no compunction about using it.

Surely the boat is sinking a little lower in the water? But no, it is only the association of ideas as Mrs Small embarks, for not only has she her own bulk to install but that of her husband as well. For, indeed, she had been right: on her return yesterday from Naples, there was Roy Small, standing in the bar with his beard and his smile.

To say that Mr Small is built on the same scale as his wife would be an exaggeration. Nobody is as large as Kate. He is, perhaps, half her size. He is a large man. He is a happy man. What he likes best in life is to be sifting through fine soil for a shard; next to doing this he enjoys the company of his wife to whom he has been married for thirty years, and who has borne him six successful children.

Anchors swing and engines purr. Farewell to the land.

Some people are born sailors, others not. Most of the party belong to the latter category. It amazes William that he can feel so ill and still be alive. Colin wishes he had died on that train, next to Caroline. Caroline's complexion, which is naturally pale, takes on a greenish tinge, and Miriam, who is used to the supportive arm of her husband under such circumstances, clutches at the nearest man. It happens to be William.

Even Jane, the strong, is leaning over the side, and Gerouin is beyond words.

Others are made of sterner stuff, Joe is taking photos of Procida. "You see that island, Penny. Michael told me that's the one that looks like Sirens coming out of the water. Probably that that gave rise to the Odysseus legend. This will be very useful for my GCSE Class. Civ. class. I do the Odyssey option on Paper IV, combined with the Sophocles. What do you do?" But Penny cannot speak. She is, anyway, longing for the course to finish and to go home. Her husband will meet her off the plane.

Michael, standing at the prow, is showing Fenella the sirens. He had wanted to show the rest of the party, but Fenella says they will be unreceptive.

"Imagine, Fen, you are Odysseus, you're tied to the mast while your men, with their ears plugged up with wax, row you past. You think you hear them singing, promising you everything you've always wanted, and yet you can't get to them because you've instructed your men to bind you tighter every time you plead. It's all within your grasp almost and yet you can't have it."

"Yes," says Fenella.

"But all the time," says Michael, "you're wrong about them because they're not going to give you your dream, they are going to smash you to pieces on the rocks."

"Perhaps," says Fenella, "before they smash you to pieces they give you a glimmer, a glance or taste of something so wonderful that there's no point living on. You accept the dying."

"I don't imagine many people accept the dying," says Michael.

Oh, to feel ground beneath your feet that doesn't move. Not to smell oil in your nostrils and not to be standing next to someone who is groaning and retching. Suddenly life is good. You are alive after all. You have reached Capri.

Fenella leads them to a quayside café. She tells them they must drink a little brandy if they still feel poorly. She has to admit that she herself does not feel entirely one hundred per cent. People smile; it is good to find Fenella as frail as themselves. William has been weighing up odds in his mind. Eventually he decides to take a gamble.

"Can I get you a brandy, Miriam?" he asks.

Miriam, too, has been thinking things over. Yesterday with the Boxes had been frightful. Today, standing next to Caroline while she retched over her carroty hair, had been pretty bad too. There are simply no available males; she takes her hat off to Penny having cornered Joe (she doesn't know how boring he is). She briefly reconsiders Colin Jones, who is quite nice looking, but seems almost incapable of speech, and, anyway, he seems (for some extraordinary reason) to be mooning after Caroline. There is really no alternative to William. Furthermore there are only a few days of the course left. It would be fun to have a fling; she's on the Pill, so no problem there. She wasn't actually at all bothered by William's behaviour *per se*, only annoyed that he was trying to take it on his terms rather than hers. Of course he had called her a nasty name, but that was a compliment to her really; the strength of passion she had inspired in him. And she had punished him by not speaking to him yesterday. It will be pleasant to have his attention again, all the while making it clear that she hasn't entirely forgiven him.

"Thank you, William," she says, "I think I could manage a very small one."

Fenella explains carefully that they will be taking the funicular railway from Marino Grande, where they are at present, to the town of Capri. Yes, she has their tickets. From there they will walk up to Tiberius' villa. Now, this is a long walk and there are people who, after their adventure yesterday (she smiles in the direction of Miss Aitchinson and Percival, who graciously acknowledge this reference to their suffering with nods of the head), might prefer to rest at the restaurant which is halfway up, and either make an early lunch (Kate Small smiles) or come on later. When they reach Tiberius' villa (properly called Villa Iovis), if they would be good enough to gather round, Michael will tell them all they've always wanted to know about Tiberius and have never dared ask.

"She's a good lass, Fenella," says Roy Small to his wife.

"Perhaps too good," says Kate.

"What do you mean?" asks Roy. He has long appreciated his wife's views on human nature are generally right.

"She could have had Michael years ago if she'd been less good," she says.

"Well perhaps she'll get him now," says Roy, who is an optimist – he has been confident that he will crack Linear A for twenty years. "Michael's marriage to that awful chat-show woman has broken up, hasn't it?" Kate makes no comment. She is looking forward to an early lunch.

The ascent to the Palace of Tiberius is steep and not all course members have attained the top. Even the faithful Caroline is missing. Struggling up on her own (she is unsurprised to see William giving his arm to Miriam), she senses Colin behind her. She feels sad and dispirited. While she could believe Michael to be Fenella-less, he could always be obtainable; everywhere she went it was always possible that he would turn to her and say, no, not those disconcerting words spoken in his room at Gaeta, but... well, something to show her she was chosen, special; but now she can see how it is: Fenella wears her flimsy blue blouse and at night he will take it off her and they will engage in that activity he has described as brilliant, better than standing on the Appian Way.

Caroline is interested in Classics; indeed she was in love with Classics before she was in love with Michael. And this course, with its combination of both, has proved a heady brew. But now Michael has, as it were, removed himself from the arena of the possible, the sites themselves have lost interest for her. The spotlight has been turned off. She does not care whether she sees Tiberius' palace or not.

As she senses Colin behind, she thinks she will turn round and say something nasty like 'do you mind not following me?' when it is his voice that speaks instead.

"I like your hair," he blurts out, blushing scarlet. "I've been walking behind you, I don't expect you noticed, and I've been looking at it." He has been rehearsing this for some time now.

"Oh," says Caroline, turning round. She looks at Colin for the first time and it strikes her that, if his face was less scarlet with the blushing, it would be quite a good-looking face. It is also tremendously soothing to have her hair admired. True, Michael commented on it, but Miriam has always spoken of split ends and lack of body. Now her great glory (she remembers her mother's words) has been restored. Suddenly she can see the sea glinting between the cypress trees. The sun is warm and balmy. Life holds possibilities again.

"Do you want to see this villa place?" asks Colin boldly.

"Not really," says Caroline.

"Shall we, I mean..."

"Have lunch now?" says Caroline. "Yes, let's."

****

"They don't want to hear me on Tiberius, Fen," says Michael, "not even the dirty bits."

He is actually quite aggrieved. Fenella knows he goes to a great deal of trouble to research what he will say. Also, it seems unforgivable to him for anyone to choose to miss out on a great chunk of Roman social history. He lights a cigarette and goes and leans on the rail overlooking the sea and the sirens.

"I want to hear you, darling," says Fenella. She cannot bear him to be hurt. "Anyway, you've got more than Percival had at Baiae." Michael smiles absently at her and flicks ash down on the rocks hundreds of feet below.

"Look, Fen," he says, taking her by the shoulder, "you see that sheer bit just there, no, there. Tiberius used to stand here just where you and I are, and watch victims being thrown into the sea, after what Suetonius calls '*protracta exquisitumaque tormenta*'. He had sailors down there with poles to whack at them in case they weren't dead enough already, poor sods. Why did he do it, Fen? Why was he so unhappy?"

"Perhaps it was being married to Julia instead of Vipsania. Being married to the wrong woman can have an awful effect on a man."

"Touché; but, no, that's not it. Women always attribute everything to relationships; he probably didn't have time to brood on it; he had the whole Roman Empire to run, for god's sake. Like being Clinton and Gorbachev all rolled into one."

"I thought he had Sejeanus to help him."

"Shut up, Fen. You're not meant to know anything. I do the talking." He brushes his lips briefly against her cheek. Nobody notices – except Robin Box.

It has been a long steep walk up to the Villa Iovis, but now there is a sense of achievement. Far below the sea beats against the rocks, sending up a milky spray. The sun has come out and the water glints. They stand amid the grey ruins where Tiberius brooded nearly two thousand years ago.

"A few days after he came to Capreae (that's Capri, Nigel), a fisherman suddenly intruded on his solitude by presenting him with an enormous mullet which he had lugged up the trackless cliffs at the rear of the island – in other words more or less exactly down there. Tiberius was so scared that he ordered his guards to rub the fisherman's face with the mullet. The scales skinned it raw, and the poor fellow shouted in his agony, 'Thank heavens I did not bring Caesar that huge crab I also caught'." Michael pauses. "Tiberius sent for the crab and had it used in the same way."

"Yuk," says Nigel.

"This was the man," says Michael, "who built the palace or Villa Iovis. I want to take you up the steps and show you the guardrooms."

As he takes them up the steps, Fenella knows he sees the Praetorian Guard standing there, the picked men of the army, the élite. He will make the course members see them too, a little. And, along with Tiberius sunk in debauchery in the baths, he shows them the Imperial rooms, even the kitchen ("I want you to imagine roast peacock being prepared here."). Even the broken mosaic pavement, too, he rebuilds for them. They see it glowing in reds and greens before them.

"How did he die?" shouts Nigel, who has been regaled with some of Tiberius' less heinous crimes.

"Slow poison," says Michael, his eyes dreamily fixed on the scene; suddenly, however, as is his way, he gives a little shake and returns to the twentieth century.

"And on that note, ladies and gentlemen," he says, "let's go and have lunch."

Chapter XXII

Joe Takes a Photograph

The lunch-party is a jolly one. The restaurant (rather expensive) is built on a promontory in the hillside; a big table has been laid out for them, covered in a blue and white check cloth. Kate and her husband, Roy, are well ensconced, they have eaten huge plates of *sgombro en cartoccio*, but are not at all averse to embarking on further dishes.

The general festivity of the party is increased by the sensation that they have all deserved this: they have weathered a long voyage, have climbed up a very steep hill, have absorbed information and now they can reasonably expect to be rewarded.

"Would you like some more wine?" asks Colin of Caroline. They have been sitting with the Smalls. All four have eaten and drunk well. Colin has ventured one or two sentences.

"Yes, I would," says Caroline. There is a warm breeze; it catches becomingly at her 'great beauty'.

Miriam looks reproachfully at William. If Colin Jones can offer Caroline, of all people, wine, the very least William can do is to follow suit.

Percival, too, has purchased wine; as he pours it out for Margaret Aitchinson and the Brownes, he feels he is being drawn into society again. It is a pleasant feeling.

Michael is happily catching up on Turkey with Roy Small, who is embarking on a plate of *maile al latte*. Kate, who has finished hers, looks wistfully at it.

"Where's Jane and Gerouin?" asks Penny. She is slightly tanned now; she is wearing her contact lenses instead of glasses and the effect is a pleasant one.

"They've gone by taxi to the Blue Grotto," says Fenella, smiling. "It's got a reputation for being a most romantic spot." They exchange glances. They can both afford to be indulgent.

"I don't recall anything about Capri in the Cambridge Latin Course," says Joe.

"Thank god for that," says Penny.

"Well... I..." Joe is temporarily stunned, then he grins.

"I suppose I do go on about it a bit," he says ruefully. "Shall I take a photo then, Penny?"

"Yes," she says, "take a photo of us all sitting here."

There is much business with the tripod (yes, he has carried his tripod across the sea and up to the palace).

"Say cheese," he says. And there they are; he surveys them through the aperture: Percival, who certainly is not going to say 'cheese', but who is getting out some measurements he has taken (even with his injuries) to show Margaret Aitchinson. She is frowning slightly as if in anticipation of finding something to criticise. Kate Small is thoughtfully holding a forkful of her husband's *maile* mid-air; she occupies the whole of one end of the table. Michael is lighting a cigarette and Miriam is drawing back from it towards the attentive William, who is pouring wine for her. Caroline will come out badly because she is in the midst of tossing back her hair. Of the two related Brown(e)s one smiles, the other frowns; the remaining Brown has a placatory look on her face. Fenella looks decidedly sexy in her blues and Mr Box is staring fixedly at her. He has drunk a lot of wine – Mrs Box smiles nervously. Nigel is pulling a horrible face. There they are; caught for eternity.

Fenella says they must all be at the quayside at five, ready for the return voyage. They may like to ascend Monte Solaro in a chairlift; they may prefer to go back to the town of Capri and do some shopping. At all events they must return to Capri by funicular railway, for which she has the tickets. The lavatory? Ah, that is some way down the path to the left there. It may not be very salubrious.

Gradually they disperse, some to the lavatory, others down the winding path that leads to the funicular railway. Kate Small says she will not be taking the chairlift. She is quite happy about her size; so is her husband; they set off arm in arm.

"Do you want to do the chairlift, Fen?" asks Michael.

"Why not?" says Fenella, "I have to go to the loo, but I'll catch you up if you like." She hands him the clipboards and the apparatus of her trade and makes her way to the evil-smelling hut down the winding path to the left. It is as unpleasant as she has imagined it would be; but not as unpleasant as what awaits her in the narrow passageway outside.

"I am very angry with you, Fenella," says Robin Box, "very angry indeed." He stands at the end of the passageway, blocking out the sunlight. Fenella feels fear but exercises her habitual self-control. She looks at him coldly.

"I'm sorry to hear that, Mr Box," she says. "Perhaps we can discuss it as we walk down to the railway." She wants to dislodge him from the end of the passageway, but does not want to approach him.

In his mind he has rehearsed the angry speech he will make to Fenella. He will tell her how she has prevented him from having sexual intercourse with his wife by refusing to give Nigel another room. He will tell her, too, how all the world knows of her shame at Cumae. He will speak of the sin of adultery and upbraid her for wearing wanton clothes. In his mind all his attack has been verbal. Now, however, Fenella looks at him haughtily, as if she regards him of no account. She speaks to him coldly, she calls him 'Mr Box'. And all the time her breasts stick out at him provocatively; he can see the fullness under the flimsy blue stuff, he can almost feel the nipples touching his lips. He has drunk a great deal of wine; his thoughts and vision become blurred; he sees this wanton woman, who has denied him, with her fullness and her curves. He feels quite mazed by it all and there is an unbearable tightness in his trousers. He undoes his flies. He lurches forward to grab the breasts, to bruise them and hurt them, and to revenge himself on Fenella in a way that seems overpoweringly right and necessary.

****

"How does this shard tie in with the stirrup cup from Orchomenos?" asks Michael, who is carrying all Fenella's paraphernalia and talking to Roy Small on the way down to the railway. "Is the syllabery like the Blegen tablets?" Once he and Roy had tried to crack the code of Linear A together. Michael had subsequently moved towards the Roman and Etruscan but he is still interested. He thinks how good it would be to be young and strong again and be sifting through the soil of Hissarlik for bits of the Trojan War. He thinks how second rate it is lecturing about things, when you should be on your hands and knees discovering them first-hand for yourself.

"Well," says Roy; he slows down a bit, partly because he wants to illustrate his point and partly because he is short of breath, "you know the ideogram for a wheeled chariot, well, on this shard (they're calling it the 'Small Shard'), there's what looks like an upside-down chariot with the wheel on top like this,"... he withdraws his arm from his wife and circumscribes an unlikely sketch in the air.

"Like a helicopter, you mean?" says Michael. "Early evidence of visitors from outer space." They both laugh comfortably.

"I want you to see it, Michael," says Roy. "Why don't you come to Turkey with me in the summer?"

As Michael thinks about this, Kate suddenly grabs his arm.

"Fenella!" she exclaims, "where's Fenella?"

It occurs to Michael, too, that he has not seen Fenella for quite some time. Panic is infectious, there was something about Kate's grabbing of his arm that alarms him.

"I'm going back," he says.

"Run," says Kate. " Something's happened."

As he approaches the restaurant, he sees Robin Box making his way downwards towards him.

"Hey," says Michael, "have you seen Fenella?" But the man merely glares and quickens his step. Various thoughts form themselves horribly in Michael's mind.

Chapter XXIII
A Very Italian Scene

There is the usual coterie of loafing Italian men at the table recently vacated by the course members. There are bottles of strange looking liquids on the table. As it is outside, there is also a mangy-looking dog and three small Italian girls with long plaits. They stare with interest as Michael approaches with Fenella. Michael's arm is round her shoulders. Fenella is wearing Michael's sweater; her skirt is wet at the hem.

"Vai a cercare tua madre," Michael shouts at one of the girls. "*Mia moglie è stata ferita. Fai presto.*"

The men break into conversation all at once. "*Che cosa è successa? Dovè le fa male? Perchè ha la gonna bagnate? È caduta*?"

"No," says Michael, "*è stata violata. Non era un Italiano era un Inglese.*" Much shocked murmuring. A large black-clad matron appears and takes Fenella within. Michael makes to follow her; she gestures him away. It is the first gesture Fenella has made. Her eyes look expressionless.

A perfect torrent of conversation ensues, Michael is made to drink the colourless drink; he is bombarded with questions. There hasn't been so much excitement in the Casa Tiberia for years. It is also particularly pleasing that the rapist is English. It confirms all their views of that nation. And then again *la donna è bellissima.* "*Ecco il marito ingiuriato.*" Inside is the woman. Michael will want the *carabinieri*; the man will be imprisoned for two hundred years, he will be fed on bread and water, flogged, locked in solitary, executed by the *cosi nostri*.

Michael has been turning over the question of the police in his mind very rapidly. He knows Italian police; he thinks them quite capable of arresting the whole party – and they will be Caprian police. He thinks of Baiae and the temple of Apollo. It will not look good for Fenella. It will come to light that Fenella spends her nights with him. And then again, he has called her his wife why did he do that? He doesn't know. And, anyway, he doesn't really know what has happened. Fen won't say. And what will be come of the liaison between the Italian police and the English police? He imagines Fenella appearing in the tabloids; her children shamed, her job gone.

"No," he says. "I will deal with the matter myself."

This meets with universal approval. The original six Italians have now been joined by at least a dozen more, as if summoned by some invisible bush telegraph. There are also two aged crones and four bold young women with babies. They cannot get enough of gazing at Michael. He is good to look at, he also appears rich and has a commanding air; he is an English milord. Byron's name is mentioned. The woman's beauty is rehearsed again. *Ha i cappelli biondi; la figura...* There is a little salacious whispering which is violently castigated by the man who has emerged as the leader. It is his wife who attends Fenella. Her credentials are vouched for by five or six others. She delivers babies, lays out corpses, makes herbal brews, wears the evil-eye averter. *Il signor* could not have placed his wife in better hands. As if on cue Maria herself appears from within, an anticipatory hush falls; a small boy who laughs is soundly clouted and cries instead.

"*Sua moglie dorme. Ha bisogna di pace. Si, le ha dato un sonnifero?*" *Il signor* must not enter. This is a woman's world; the men must not approach; it is as sacred as the mysteries of the Dea Bona.

All look now at Michael. They wish to know what he will do. They are not short of suggestions. Some are for killing the rapist; a short man with a moustache volunteers himself for the job. Suppose he escapes, will he hide out in Capri? No, Michael says he will return to the hotel at Sorrento. The hotel has his passport. Much nodding and adulation of the wisdom of this hotel, and hotels in general. The leader quells them with his withering scorn, "Is this a time to be talking of hotels?" Others are for hiring thugs to take care of the man.

"You know what Tiberius did here on this very hill?" says Marco the leader. All respect Marco and listen.

"Yes," says Michael, who does. The curiosity of the crowd, however, knows no bounds.

"Gli ha forzato la vittima a bere l'acqua in quantità e poi ha legato i genitali."

Much shaking of the head, some maintaining this would be too good for *questo rapitore inglese*, others rebutting this horror.

There are yet more for whom it is a fear lest he escape justice altogether. They would like to form a party and hunt him down themselves.

It is actually a worry to Michael as to what Robin Box will do, but he reckons he will have to rejoin his wife and son; his first concern must be with Fenella.

The two aged crones enlist the Virgin Mary on their side. The young women, privy, by virtue of their sex, to the secret within, converse among themselves in low voices. It is a treat for them to be in possession of such privileged information. They intimate that such secrets as are theirs are not for men's ears.

One man indicates to Michael that it is not difficult to arrange a death: Michael can see how close they are to Sicily.

Some are disappointed by Michael's non-activity. It confirms their opinion of the English. Others commend his patience in staying near his beloved wife and hint darkly that, in the present company, he may well be advised to do so.

Gradually a malaise creeps over them; the colourless liquid has long gone, the afternoon is less warm, and it is apparent there will be no further drama. There begins to be a drifting away. And then Roy Small is sighted puffing up the hill. At once the flagging interest is revitalised; those who have set off down strange passageways, retrace their steps. There are those who maintain that Roy is the rapist returning to the scene of his crime, others, who point to his size, either as proof of overwhelming strength, or, conversely, of impossible torpor.

The crowd watch as *i due Inglese incontrano*. They stand aside, not because they do not wish to intrude – they do, but they wish to show their deep respect.

There is speculation about *il grasso*, some maintaining he is Michael's *fratello*, others see him more in the light of the godfather. Those with a smattering of English nod their heads knowingly as they catch the odd word.

Roy thinks, like Michael, that the police are best left out of this; he will make sure the course members get back to Sorrento. Michael must stay with Fenella as long as she wishes. With regard to Box, they will take no immediate action. There is, of course, Mrs Box and Nigel to consider. Michael winces.

"And you, Michael," says Roy, "you'll not do anything silly."

Chapter XXIV

Fenella Tells her Secret

'Rumour, the swiftest traveller of all the ills on earth,
Thriving on movement, gathering strength as it goes at the start
A small and cowardly thing, it soon puffs itself up,
And walking upon the ground, buries its head in the cloud base.'

So says Virgil, and never was it more true than in the case of the party assembled on the quayside at Marino Grande. How can they possibly have an inkling of what has happened? But they do, or, at any rate, think they do. From what thin strands have they spun this skein of conjecture? Such strands as: Miriam (always interested in such matters) has seen Mr Box looking at Fenella in a very funny way. And where is he, Robin Box? He has been seen talking to Mrs Box, but has now disappeared. Mrs Box looks tearful and frightened; even Nigel is subdued. Mr Small himself has perhaps been unwise in his words,

"Fenella has suffered an accident. Her life is not in danger, but she may have to remain on Capri for a while. Michael is with her. Mr Box will not continue to be a member of the party." He advises them not to discuss the matter.

"Fool," says Kate.

Little groups form; Caroline says to Colin that Mr Box has sat down very close to her, unpleasantly close. Colin blushes scarlet and says nothing, but he thinks of the train journey to Naples. Miss Aitchinson says it has been an extraordinary week. She mentions the noises in the night and several people look uncomfortable; they feel this complicates the issue. William thinks of the incident of two nights ago in the double-bedded room. He vows never to do so much as converse with Miriam again. Percival says nothing; he knows what he thinks. Penny, who is feeling rather irritable, says to Joe that she doesn't suppose anything in the Cambridge Latin Course has prepared him for this. Of the Brown(e)s, Alice says she fears they will never see Fenella again, Sally replies that she expects to see her at any minute. Jennifer says she believes she will return tomorrow. Nobody speaks to Mrs Box and Nigel.

Into the middle of all this appears a totally extraneous element. It is as if fate has chosen this moment to play a wild card. A taxi draws up and out tumble Jane and Gerouin, wreathed in smiles.

"Look," shouts Jane, "look at this, folks!"

People turn their heads slowly; they wish to give the impression that weighty problems rest very much on their shoulders at this present time, and that they do not consider it altogether seemly to be distracted from them. They feel that Jane's gleeful shouting strikes a discordant note. They are enjoying the dramatic and tragic turn of events, there is a feeling of bathos about Jane's shouting jollity; a spuriousness. It is as if, at the end of *Hamlet*, Fortinbras were to remark there were five pounds off whisky at Tesco.

And what is all this gleeful shouting about? Only that Jane wears a ring with a garnet on the third finger of her left hand.

"We're going to be married," says Gerouin, amazed to be again the centre of attention. The thought of the ceremony is already a terror to him.

"I wonder if she'll wear that tracksuit to the church," asks Miriam of William. But William frowns slightly. He feels it is not the time for levity. He moves away.

It is Miss Aitchinson, however, who expresses the feelings of the party.

"I am sure we are all very pleased for you," she says, "but at present we all have more important matters on our minds."

Gerouin is conscious of having said the wrong thing again.

"What's going on, then?" asks Jane. She is a little disappointed that her news did not meet with a more encouraging response, but she is used to making do and accepting second best (viz. Gerouin).

"Fenella has been raped," says Alice.

"Rubbish," says Sally.

"Hurt," says Jennifer.

"Some very odd things have happened on this course," says Miss Aitchinson. "On the very first night I heard..."

"Don't forget my sandwiches," says Gerouin, "how they were stolen."

"It's a good thing I've taken plenty of photos," says Joe. But nobody understands the relevance of this. Percival comments that there are others who have been physically attacked this week too. Colin, who did philosophy as part of his degree, considers whether he himself is morally guilty of raping Caroline. He could have prevented those glorious minutes.

Miriam adds that she can't imagine what her husband will say. Caroline thinks it would almost be worth being raped if you had Michael to comfort you afterwards.

But Kate Small tells them it is time to board the hydrofoil back to Sorrento.

Mr Box is seen slipping on at the last minute, and going to join his wife and son. They all three stand together. They seem to have nothing to say to one another.

****

The room is whitewashed and there is a crucifix hanging on the wall, the shutters are closed, and the room is so dark that Michael can hardly make Fenella out as she lies with her hair all brushed and spread out on the pillow.

"Fen," he says, "may I put the lamp on?" She nods, and he floods the room with light.

Fenella has been given what is obviously the marital bed; the coverlet is made of white lace, the sheets are white and Fenella herself has been given a nightdress of some creamy material. There is no sign of Fenella's blue outfit anywhere. Fenella herself looks expressionless; she might be lying in her coffin.

He goes and sits on the bed, but when he tries to take her hand she moves away.

"I'm sorry," she says, "it's just that I can't..."

"I know," he says. He looks at her through the silence and has difficulty in relating this still figure to Fenella, Fenella who is always busy, Fenella who has never moved away, who has always reached out her arms to him, who has lain holding him when he has bad dreams. At last he says,

"You have to tell me, Fenella." She turns to look at him.

"What do you want to know?" she asks dully.

He is ashamed of what he wants to know. Why is it that incessantly his thoughts form themselves into a single question? What difference can it make? Is it possible that his attitude to Fenella can change if she has been penetrated by this man? As always she reads his mind.

"No," she says after a pause, "I was lucky. He came before he got inside me." She pauses. "That's what you want to know, isn't it?" Again she speaks flatly, dully, in a matter of fact way. She has become aware that this is what matters to men; she has seen it. There is no reason why Michael should be different.

Michael feels an almost physical sense of assault, that Fenella, lying there in her cream nightgown with hair brushed out, can utter these expressions. He realises she does not feel words matter. The violation has occurred. She may regard Michael's question as prurient; but she is not surprised by it; men are what they are.

"Yes," says Fenella, "he undid his flies and grabbed at my breasts. He kept kneading at them and trying to get my knickers off and get his penis inside me; but he couldn't wait, there was this great stream of stuff, my skirt was covered in it. Then he went. Is there anything else you would like to know? Have I omitted any salacious detail? Oh yes, he used a lot of four-letter words. Shall I enumerate them for you?" Suddenly her eyes fill with tears and she turns her head away.

"I'll kill him, Fen," he says. She continues to face away from him.

"Oh yes," she says, "that will make it all right again, won't it? A fucking to be answered by a killing. That is male logic."

Michael continues to sit on the bed in silence, trying to understand this Fenella who will not reach out to him, who will not be comforted or even placated by him. Always Fenella has listened to him and accommodated herself to his words. Now she distances herself from him.

"I will do nothing, Fenella, that you do not wish me to do."

"Why are you so different from him?" asks Fenella. "You fondle my breasts and put your penis inside me."

"Because you want me to, Fenella. You cry aloud in delight."

"Ah, how horrible," shudders Fenella.

"Why horrible?"

"You have never understood, have you, how I've felt? Why should you? You're a man and I never told you. Why do you think I never had anyone at university, why my marriages failed? Because I hated it, hated the violence," she moves her head from side to side, "the sex, the degradation, the filth."

"But you let me love you, Fen, the first night."

"I let you fuck me; I did the loving." She moves her head on the pillow and draws her hair back.

"You see, I loved you and I found that I wanted this dark thing, this dirty thing; I wanted it because I wanted you. It was the only way I knew of reaching you, and when we made love, this thing that was so disgusting, was so lovely that I couldn't..."

"It was lovely for me too."

"Lovely, but not love. For you it was a fuck, for me it was love. I could only ever think of sex with you. That was really why Mark went after other women. You didn't know that did you? Because I was so useless in bed; I found it so repugnant."

"And Graham?"

"Oh he knew what I was like before we married; he was like it himself, an old woman. He wanted a companion, a helpmeet. He was rich. I took a leaf out of your book. Married for money. Anyway he found he couldn't live like that in the end, so he went, the marriage was dissolved." She moves restlessly. "Please may I have some water?"

"Did you never take lovers?"

"Why should I?... Let me sit up myself... Why should I take lovers? You haven't understood, have you? I only ever wanted it with you, for you. It was all bound up with my feelings for you. At those times I have felt such love, and sometimes I thought..." she takes a gulp of water, "I thought that you loved me too. And all the things you taught me, those shameful things, seemed not shameful but part of love and you. But now I've seen how it is, a spasm and an ejaculation of white stuff."

"Fen..." She moves impatiently.

"It's like, like Lake Nemi, when the waters all look sparkling and magic, but really there's only slime and mud and filth and stench there."

"But that doesn't mean the magic doesn't exist." He feels so strongly that he gets up and walks about. "Don't you remember having babies, Fen? How much blood and gunge there was at the birth, but when they put the child in your arms you didn't think of that. That's how it is. Because we are human beings, dirty scrubby creatures, we have to use our dirty scrubby bodies, but out of them comes this glory, like finding a ruby buried in the ground, a mushroom on a dung heap." For the first time a glimmer of a smile appears on her face.

"What a talker you are," she says. "Michael, I'm so tired."

"Now," says Michael, "listen to me. First I am going to plait your hair for you because it is worrying you. No, I shan't touch you anywhere. I won't kiss you... turn round and I'll plait your hair." Fenella obeys slowly, as she always obeys. She feels his hands on her hair. They are very gentle.

"What will you do?" she continues sleepily, "I mean, what time is it?"

"It's late," he says. "I shall stay here. No. Don't worry. I shall be in that chair with rugs, cigarettes and a copy of the Aeneid. Sit still. I've nearly finished."

"Where did you learn to plait hair?"

"I do have two daughters. I am a father as well as a lover."

Fenella's eyes fill with tears as she thinks of Michael's daughters that are not her daughters, of how he must have been present at their births, and how they were the fruit of his union with his wife; and how, after all the loving she had done with Michael, her most vivid memory is of Robin Box's penis squirting white stuff over her skirt.

"What will happen to him?"

"I don't know yet, Fen. We thought the police were best kept out."

"Oh yes, not the police."

"But justice will have to be done, Fen." He thinks of Robin Box grappling with Fenella in his desire to get inside her, and he feels a desire to inflict pain. He has not only violated her, but has taken her from him and revealed her unhappiness.

"Michael, why did you tell them I was your wife?"

"Because you're *univira*."

"What's that?" But she sounds half asleep. Michael suspects she has been given something strong. He tucks her in, and feels about in his pocket for cigarettes. "The Romans," he says, "had a special respect for a woman who gave herself to only one man, the man who had her first. As far as you were concerned, Fen, you married me that first night in Ithaca. I suppose that's why I called you my wife. I must have known all the time how it was for you."

But Fenella is asleep.

Chapter XXV

Michael Reflects

Michael lights a cigarette, picks up the rug and settles himself into the chair. It is not a very comfortable chair, but he is glad of the discomfort; it is something that Fenella lies asleep in the ease of the vast marital bed, while he, the instrument of her sufferings, indeed the sufferings of many, sits in the cold night air in the hard chair. He thinks of Robin Box trying to get inside Fenella and his mind veers away; it is unthinkable. He thinks too of other problems of his own, in particular of the unopened letter in his pocket. This too he puts to the back of his mind. Then he considers instead the twenty years of Fenella's life when he unthinkingly created misery for her.

When he had received the invitation to Fenella's wedding, his feelings had been mixed; he had been relieved that she had, as it were, closed the episode, had spared him the scenes and reproach he might have justly expected, had made things easy for him. She could, after all, have contacted Jemima and told her enough to upset their engagement; but she hadn't. She had found someone else. But the male in him had been angry that she had (as he then thought) replaced him so easily, that another man would hold her breasts in his hands and enjoy her, she who had become so proficient in the art of love as a result of his teaching. But it was not like that. Only now did he understand. She had not conferred upon her husband her skill and her passion because she was only able to give them to her first lover.

Now he could feel sorry for this man whom he had disliked on sight, he felt for him marrying the beautiful voluptuous Fenella imagining the heaven in store for him, only to find a cold unresponsive partner, no, worse, one who, it was apparent, found him unpleasing, repugnant even. That Fenella had fought against this, he did not doubt. She was good and kind, she did not like to inflict pain. She would have tried to hide her antipathy, tried to oblige; but this in itself, would be worse than the other. Michael attempts to imagine making love to a woman who was trying to do her duty. At least Tabitha had not even tried, she just looked on sex as a bargaining ground.

He is interrupted in his thoughts by the entry of Maria with coffee, strega and rugs. She is pleased to see that Michael does not usurp his wife's bed. That is as it ought to be... She touches his shoulder and nods her approval. She indicates the lamp, and asks,

"*Spegnerò la lampada*?" but Michael shakes his head, now more than ever he wants light. She smiles at the eccentricity of the English and takes her departure.

Michael gasps at the bitterness of the coffee and a pain grabs at him beneath his heart. He breathes heavily for a few seconds and it passes.

And perhaps all would have come right in Fenella's marriage had she not started to work for Classic Tours and subsequently written and asked him to lecture. Whose idea had that been, Fenella's or her boss's? He had never asked. They had gone to Rome; it had been a year after his marriage, his own wife, Jemima, was pregnant and he had fucked Fenella for a fortnight. Fenella's first child, a boy called John, was born a year later. Under what circumstances was he conceived? Had Fenella, in some strange way of her own, looked on John as his child? And what an odd twist of fate it was that Fenella's two children, born of the uninteresting and disappointed Mark, should be so gifted and successful, while his own should be so dull and mediocre.

Fenella moves in her sleep and mutters, her eyes are open and she says, "No"; but she is not awake and she subsides again into quietude.

A year later they had taken a course to Crete; that had only been a week. Fenella had not liked leaving the baby; but they had fucked and fucked. It seemed that Fenella could not get enough of him. He winced to think how he had teased her. He remembered saying to her, a bottle of retsina by the bed,

"Marriage has certainly given you a taste for it, Fen. Your husband must be quite a stud." She had made no reply. He understood now that she feared she would not see him again. Her passion was born of fear and a desperate attempt to hold him through her sexual skills. Again he had not understood. How deeply stupid and insensitive he must have seemed; and yet she never said; it was not her way. His wife was pregnant for the second time.

After the birth of Fenella's second child, Felicity, her marriage began to break up, not because of Michael, Mark would not have suspected – why should he be suspicious; he knew Fenella for a cold woman; but because he wanted a woman who found him attractive. Michael lights a cigarette; he can understand that Mark needed to prove that he wasn't repugnant to women, that it was only Fenella that found him so because of her prudery. And yet, apparently Mark's second marriage had not been successful either. Poor Mark. It presumably was not enough that another woman found him desirable. Perhaps Mark needed to go on and on proving that he was not repugnant to women. He needed to convince himself that Fenella was wrong. For this too, he, Michael, was responsible.

Once Fenella was divorced, it did not occur to him that he might marry her. His own wife was accommodating. He spent most of his time in London. It was a fruitful period for him. He was writing his most successful book *Horace: The Man As Lover*. He was writing for the serious Sundays and had been offered the Chair at his university. He had a flat in town and a pleasant house in the country, two charming daughters and the world was his oyster. And, besides, Fenella was always there. As he had told her in Naples, he felt that she was part of himself. He imagined she felt much the same about him. In her thirties, too, Fenella had matured into a beautiful woman; he had imagined as a divorcée she would be greatly in demand.

They ran courses every year or two, and they sometimes met in between. He rang her from time to time to talk, mainly when bothered by things. She had made it a rule not to ring him. She always listened and advised sensibly. Nor was it all one-sided. Once, when he found she was worried about school fees, he motored down to John's school, interviewed the bursar and paid the fees for the next two years.

Then he had gone to the States for two years, and when he returned he found her married to Graham.

He gets up and goes down the passage to relieve himself. It is the first time he has left her. He is worried that she will wake and find him gone. It is all right however; she lies on her stomach, her plait hanging over her shoulder. He is reminded of watching over his daughter, Octavia, on one of his infrequent stays at home.

There is a jug full of water and a basin for him to wash in and a bar of plain soap. Its primitive nature and its simplicity delights him. He washes himself quietly and continues to think of Fenella, how she has lived uncomplainingly all these years, bringing up her children lovingly, doing her job dutifully, allowing him to maintain his illusion that she takes sex when it comes her way; but all the time living only for him, *univira*. He sees how terribly he has wronged her. Why couldn't she have told him? But would it have made any difference? Would he have left Jemima, eschewed Tabitha if she had said, "I can't make love to anyone else because I have given myself to you?" Perhaps, at first, she herself hadn't realised; after all she had married Mark. She must have believed she could make it work. Perhaps the truth had come as a shock to her too.

And what about Graham? But he knew what she was like. She had told him what he could expect. Why had she married him? Because she was lonely when he disappeared off to the States? Because she wanted a father for her children? Because she wanted to show him that she could manage without him? At any rate she had told Graham how it was with her. Perhaps he did not believe her, perhaps he believed he could live with only her companionship. But he was wrong; the marriage was dissolved. Another life he has ruined.

He goes and opens the shutters quietly; they are old and creaky, but Michael is deft and quiet. Gradually they open and reveal the bay. As he has said to Fenella at Gaeta, there is a spurious timelessness about lights twinkling over the dark sea. Really there is nothing but the blackness. What Fenella has been is the light in his darkness, the light that he has assumed will always be there. He gazes out; the night air is chilly and he wraps the rug around him. And what has he been to her? Both darkness and light. There was darkness in the horror she felt for the sexual act, yet light in the love that she felt for him that blotted out the darkness and shone most gloriously. And now what has this man done? Has he taken the light from Fenella, showing her only the darkness, making her think of the light as an illusion?

And what the hell is he to do now? He feels the darkness closing in on him and he pulls the shutters to. They make a little moaning noise and Fenella moans a little too in her sleep. The pain that sometimes catches him beneath his heart makes him take refuge in his chair.

As his eyes close and fitful sleep approaches, many images form and reform themselves in his mind; Fenella lying before him in the bed she now sleeps in expressionlessly, saying, "He kept trying to get my knickers off, then there was this stream of stuff"... Twenty-one year old Fenella with downcast eyes, saying, "I don't know much about sex"... she is cataloguing shards ... Fenella in the Soho restaurant with her *crème caramel*, saying, "You're going to marry Jemima, but you were married to me." The images become mixed up and Fenella stirs the shards into the *crème caramel* and, smiling shyly at him, says "but I am married to Robin Box." The pain drives him into sleep.

****

Fenella awakes. She stretches out in the vast bed and is conscious of warmth and ease. Here is no man with a penis to penetrate her or arms to take hold of her, or hands or teeth to bruise her breasts. The bed is hers. There is safety within the white folds. She thinks of Robin Box, but it seems very distant, unreal, that episode, as if it had happened to someone other than herself. She feels she cannot bother with it. He has gone and has taken the darkness with him. Perhaps, later, she will feel differently, perhaps the horror will return, but now she feels conscious only of warmth and comfort. She sees Michael, awkward in the hard chair and she thinks how ironic that now it is she who is at her ease and he who is in discomfort. She has told him the thing that she had vowed she would never tell him; how she could make love to no one else but him; and because of this they had ,between them, ruined many lives. Between them. The blame was not his any more than it was hers. What effect will her words have had upon him? Will he blame himself, will he wish to make restitution, marry her even, this thing that she has wanted so long. But now she cannot bear to think of him doing this to her that Robin Box had wanted to do. She does not want to have that darkness engulfing her again.

But he stirs and groans. Instinctively she gets up and goes to him. At first she is part of his dream; he is Aeneas reaching out to the ghost of his dead wife, Creusa; and, like Aeneas, he cannot grasp her, for she moves away. She cannot yet stand to be touched.

"Fenella," he says.

Last night he had felt shame for his actions and the misery he had brought on other lives, he had suffered in his waking and in his dreaming; but now Fenella stands before him in her creamy night-gown with her hair tangled and her cheeks flushed with sleep. Full as he is of yesterday's horror, cramped from the night's discomforts, he is conscious of one overriding thought: she is immensely desirable to him, perhaps because of yesterday, because she has been a temptation to another man, because she has confessed to him that, of all men, only he can satisfy her. He would like to satisfy her now, hear her moan and call out his name the way she does when she is about to come. He would like her to satisfy him too, in the way she does, better than other women because she loves him more. And immediately he is ashamed.

"How are you?" he asks gently, easing his cramped body from the chair.

"I am well," she says, "and you, in that horrible chair?"

"I am well too," he replies. And they smile at each other. They both realise there are things that have happened that they do not at this moment want to speak of.

"Darling," says Fenella, "what am I going to wear?"

"Well," he says, stretching his legs, "you have my sweater and a skirt of Maria's." He hesitates a moment. "I told them to burn yours."

"I bet she doesn't," says Fenella, smiling.

She is, of course, quite right. Maria's granddaughter Marcia has seen the blue skirt and top and has earmarked them for her own. She will wear them at the procession on Easter Sunday and "*le sui cugine, quelle grasse vacche si rodessano dalla gelosia.*"

Chapter XXVI

Mrs Box

It is rumoured that Fenella and Michael are back; nay, it is certain because Fenella has been seen by the Browne contingent.

"Wearing a very strange sort of long peasant skirt," says Alice.

"No, dear," says Sally, "those are very fashionable these days."

"Anyway she was wearing Michael's sweater," says Jennifer. "I remember because we were discussing whether it was cashmere or not."

This piece of interesting information is relayed round the party with amazing rapidity. It is a particularly welcome diversion as the trip to Pompeii that Mr Small was going to lead has been cancelled; (but for no more sinister reason than the fact that it is pouring with rain), and time hangs heavy on their hands. There is nothing to do but speculate.

Nobody is sure whether Mr Box is still with them or not. Penny thinks she has seen him coming out of a lavatory, but she only saw the back so she can't be sure. Mrs Box and Nigel are certainly here; Mrs Box has been seen crying. Nobody is sure what to do about this; they do not wish to be associated in any way with the criminals. After all, whatever Mr Box has done, Mrs Box must be in some sense an accessory.

Mr Small seems to have generally taken command. He has been seen talking to Mrs Box and has also been sighted at Reception a great deal. Miss Aitchinson says to Percival Jeavons that she thinks he takes too much on himself. Percival nods; he couldn't agree more. Once he had written a letter to Mr Small, listing two hundred and forty ideograms. Mr Small had not even bothered to reply. In fact both Miss Aitchinson and Percival Jeavons feel rather aggrieved at recent events. After all, up to yesterday they had been the protagonists in the week's drama. People had asked them many times to relate the story of the attack at Naples. They had both enjoyed the novel experience of people actually wanting to hear what they had to say. It is sad that new events have now overshadowed this. They are therefore inclined to take a censorious attitude towards those involved. Miss Aitchinson speaks of unsuitable dress and Percival says he is none too sure whether Thorpe-Smith's views on the Villa Iovis are sound. He has himself taken some measurements which were at variance with Michael's remarks.

Jane, too, is just a bit resentful of having the limelight stolen from the engagement. There is also the fact that the whole business seems a poor omen for the future of her matrimonial happiness. She wonders what all the fuss is about, "just because Box had a bit of a grope at Fenella." She doesn't think there is too much to worry about. After all, it seems that Michael has done enough of that already. Her fiancée, who remembers Cumae, is inclined to agree with her.

Miriam, who would love to hint that she too had been the victim of male lust, but dare not, feels she must express strong sisterly sympathy just in case an opportunity should arise for her to cite her own experiences.

William feels a sneaking sympathy for Box. He wonders whether he got further with Fenella than he had with Miriam.

Penny and Joe come rather well out of it, taking Nigel Box into Sorrento; Joe even lets him use his camera. They take it as a measure of Mrs Box's despondent state that she lets him go without his mac.

****

"Fen, I have to go and do things," says Michael who is sitting on the side of Fenella's bed. "Shall I get Kate to come and sit with you?"

"No," says Fenella, "stay with me a bit."

He is very exercised as to what to do about Box. He has spoken briefly to Roy who says he has sent a message via Mrs Box that he is to keep to his room. He looks across at Fenella sitting up in bed wearing a big tee shirt of his, and imagines this man violating her. The male in him feels a desire to torment Robin Box; he cannot get Fenella's words out of his mind:... kneading at her breasts... there was a great stream of stuff. He imagines stamping on his genitals, electric treatment. He is, in fact, shocked at the violence of his own feelings. He also finds it difficult to weigh up to what extent he himself has a right to administer justice, how pure are his own motives? He goes to take her hand, and then changes his mind.

"I don't know what to do, Fen," he says. Fenella is just about to reply when there is a knock at the door. They look at each other. Roy has given orders that Fenella is not to be disturbed.

Michael goes and opens the door. A sorry figure confronts him. It is Mrs Box. She appears to have been out in the rain; her grey hair is plastered to her head. She wears a brown gathered skirt which features her rather prominent stomach, a grubby blouse and a cardigan with flowers on it. Her glasses drip with the rain. She is an extremely plain woman.

"Please," she is saying, "please, I must speak to Fenella. Well, and to you too, please. You see, it's all my fault."

Several thoughts pass simultaneously through Michael's mind: that she is a very poor pathetic creature and he should be kind to her for this reason; how could Box, who wanted Fenella so much, have married this? What would Fenella want him to do?

"Come in," he says. "Fenella, Mrs Box has come to see you."

"Pamela," says Mrs Box, "my name is Pamela." She looks at the big spacious room and Fenella sitting up in bed, and sighs.

"You see, he didn't have the pills," she says. She looks round the room fearfully.

"Here," says Michael, drawing up the armchair, "sit down."

"Oh no," says Pamela, "I won't sit." She begins to talk very fast. "You see he has these pills and if he takes them he's all right but I was afraid Nigel would eat them thinking they were sweets - they are a nice orange colour. So I flushed them down the toilet." She looks at them helplessly. She knows how useless she is, her only hope lies in their acceptance of this.

"Go on," says Michael.

"I flushed them down the toilet," she says. Michael thinks irrationally how she would have to say 'toilet', lacking the confidence to say lavatory or loo.

"I flushed them down the toilet," she repeats almost triumphantly, as if she has taken a perverse pleasure in showing them the extent of her stupidity. Then she continues, gabbling in her anxiety to make them understand. "I didn't realise he needed them really, because he never said. You see, he's got what people call..." (she lowers her eyes and voice) "... a high sex drive. It's all right most of the time... but then you see I knew he, well I mean, I saw him looking at Fenella, and he blamed Fenella for not giving Nigel another room."

"But I told him he could have one," says Fenella weakly, "but he would have to pay. I couldn't do it for nothing."

"No, no," says Pamela. She has found a handkerchief in a pocket and is wiping the rain from her face. "But you see, if there's a lady he likes, he pretends it's them when he, you know... me, and he thought he was you know... Fenella, and then Nigel woke up and he couldn't sort of satisfy himself," She looks at them vaguely; her glasses are still all wet. She can hardly see.

"Good god," says Michael. The male in him sees a horrible sort of humour in Mr Box calling Mrs Box 'Fenella'. Fenella herself says nothing.

"And then," continues Pamela, wiping her glasses, "you were got up so pretty yesterday, Fenella, all in blue with that very low blouse..."

Michael remembers his words 'wear something tarty, Fenella, so the whole of Capri lusts after you'. Was he, then, responsible for all this too?

"And," says Pamela, turning the knife in the wound, "Nigel kept saying how good Michael was at talking about gods and that. Well, Robin has always told him about that sort of thing..." (Mrs Box is at a loss talking about the Ancient World. She knows nothing of Classics), "and he always said, Nigel I mean, it was boring. It hurt his pride as a teacher." Fenella sighs. The female in her can see how Mrs Box has been hurt by this more than by anything else. Mrs Box knows that she is plain and unattractive to the opposite sex; she has long known that. She knows that her husband is in the habit of lusting after other women, she is inured to it; but, through all this, she has buoyed herself up with the belief that, for all his faults, her husband is a clever man, skilled at his job, deserving of respect for this. Indeed, this makes up for his other faults. It is an illusion dear to her, and Michael has smashed it effortlessly, thoughtlessly. Michael shakes his head, but Mrs Box hasn't finished yet. She looks from one to the other, nervously.

"Then Miriam said that at Cumae… oh dear, I don't know how to say it, you and Fenella…"

"I think we follow your drift," says Michael grimly.

"Well, he kept thinking about it, you see, and he thought if Michael could… you know, all out in the open with Fenella, why shouldn't he? Of course I know it was wrong…"

She seems to have come to an end. She looks helplessly at both of them, Fenella sitting up in bed, Michael smoking on the window seat.

"So, what are you asking exactly?" asks Michael brutally. He hates woolly thinking and he feels a mixture of irritation and pity at the sight of this poor creature standing there in her ill-assorted clothes, pleading for her husband, twisting her wet handkerchief in her hands.

"Please… it's not, is it, I mean…?"

"What?" says Michael thunderously.

"You won't get the police, will you?" She has finally brought it out, her fear, the thing that will bring her life, miserable as it is, crashing about her ears. She clutches the handkerchief.

"No," says Fenella decidedly from the bed. Michael looks across at her; he would not have committed himself so readily.

"But justice must be done," he says, "and there is the question of the deterrent. If he can do this to Fenella, what is to stop him doing it to other women or girls? What sort of school does he teach at?"

"Oh, it's a boys' grammar school," says Pamela eagerly, "and there are hardly any female members of staff, only Miss Dibb and she's worse than me – I mean to look at." She says it without rancour, simply as a fact of her existence. Fenella, who has been admired all her life, wonders what it must be like to have to accept that you are one of God's unsuccessful creations.

"What about the rest of the time?" asks Michael, "when you're not there?"

"Oh, but I always am," says Pamela brightly. "Robin doesn't like women working – that's why he was cross with Fenella – he thinks women should be in the home. He likes to come home for lunch, and it's best like that; if he feels it coming on, you know... he can just do it quickly in the kitchen and then he's all right again." Both Fenella and Michael are amazed at Mrs Box's comparative lack of embarrassment on this subject. They suppose it must be due to its familiarity in her life.

A grotesque picture forms itself in Michael's mind. Mrs Box with her brown gathered skirt held up, standing against a fridge, while Mr Box penetrates her, sandwich in hand. He reflects on the extraordinary nature of other people's marriages.

"And then, there's the pills. They're very good. It would have been all right this week if I hadn't thrown them away; oh dear." She looks as if she will start crying again.

"What about the hurt to Fenella?" asks Michael, stubbing out a cigarette. He feels irritation at Mrs Box's one-sided view of things. But Pamela has spent twenty years satisfying Mr Box's urges; it has taken the edge off her sensibilities. She has obliged so many thousands of times herself, she perhaps feels that one occasion isn't of much moment.

"Well, I know it must have been upsetting, but, I mean, he didn't ...you know, did he?"

"So that makes it all right?" says Fenella grimly from the bed.

"Well, no, no, of course not," says Mrs Box; but they both have the feeling that Mrs Box thinks it does.

"How does Nigel fit into all this?" asks Michael suddenly.

"Oh well, that's very difficult too," says Mrs Box. "He's very strong-willed, you know and Robin says I spoil him; but he doesn't really get on with his father and I try to make it up to him; but he's so naughty sometimes. That's why I threw the pills away. There was nowhere to lock them away in the room." She takes her glasses off again and has another wipe at them.

As Fenella looks at her, she sees how Mrs Box has spun a web of muddle and disaster around herself, and yet still continues to go blithely through life. She even smiles a little now as she senses that things will be all right.

"Have you ever thought of sending him away to school?" asks Michael.

"Oh yes, Robin often mentions it, but we couldn't afford it, not on Robin's salary."

"There are scholarships," says Michael, "assisted places and so on. You have to think of Nigel."

"Oh yes," says Pamela hopelessly.

"Now, Pamela," says Michael, swinging his long legs off the window-seat, "listen carefully. Fenella has very generously said that she does not wish to involve your husband with the police. However, it would be intolerable for Fenella to have to meet him again. He must go home as soon as possible; but not only that, Roy and I will wish to interview him and extract a number of undertakings from him. We would be very much to blame should another such incident occur."

"Oh yes," says Mrs Box brightly, "so can I tell him it's all right, then?"

"No!" exclaims Michael, so loudly that both women jump. "You bloody well can't."

"I think, Pamela," says Fenella, "that Michael has explained what is to happen. Perhaps you would tell your husband. I should like to rest now."

Chapter XXVII

Mr Box and the Eumenides

Downstairs people are making their dispositions for the rest of the day. The rain is easing off and most feel a great desire to be outside. There is a feeling of claustrophobia and uncleanliness within the hotel. They have discussed and gossiped enough. Now they would like to be up and doing.

Penny and Joe, who have just come back from the town with Nigel, prepare to sally forth again.

"Do you want to go to Mount Vesuvius, Nigel?" asks Penny.

"Don't mind," says Nigel, who actually wants to go very much. Michael has told him how a giant lies chained inside the mountain and sometimes wakes up. He might be lucky and see him.

Jane and Gerouin are having a slap-up lunch in Sorrento, and Jane is talking weddings.

Caroline, with Colin in attendance, has undertaken to join Penny and Joe on their way to Mount Vesuvius and agrees to share a taxi with them.

Miriam has gone to get her hair done again. She rather likes the male hairdresser.

Percival is writing letters in his room. He will soon be off to post them.

William has been co-opted by the Brown(e)s to play bridge. Apparently the three of them are in the habit of playing with the missing male member of their party. They argue incessantly.

"I can't imagine," says Alice, "why you took me out of three no trumps, Sally. It was stone cold."

"Four spades was the contract," says Sally.

"Why didn't you make it, then?" asks Alice.

"A very difficult distribution," says Jennifer. She and William are doing extremely well together.

"I hope you won't forget we have agreed to play Stayman," says Alice to Sally, "like you did last time."

"I didn't forget," says Sally. "I could see it was an inappropriate response, and you shouldn't have opened a no trump on that hand anyway."

But William is asking them if they would like him to get them a drink.

Margaret Aitchinson is waiting for Percival. Perhaps they will go and measure something together.

****

"Actually, Roy, I want to hurt him quite a lot," says Michael. He and Kate and Roy are awaiting the advent of Robin Box. Kate is comfortably ensconced on a sofa, knitting. The hotel has put a special room at their disposal.

"Yes, I expect you do," says Roy evenly. He is sitting in a large green armchair. He seems to fill it.

"You see," says Michael, lighting a cigarette, "Fenella has a very strict view about sex. To Fenella the whole act is extremely repugnant."

Roy raises his eyebrows and looks towards his wife.

"Did she find it repugnant with you?" asks Kate. She has put down her knitting. Michael looks at the ash on the end of his cigarette.

"No," he says quietly; then he looks up and adds, "if she did, she found something else so good, that it outweighed all the rest. And that is what this man has taken. She can see only sordidity."

"She doesn't want you to touch her, does she?" says Kate.

"No," says Michael sadly. "She flinches away if I so much as take her hand."

"That'll pass," says Roy the optimist, "it's only natural for her to feel like that at the moment."

"I don't know," says Michael. "Things go very deep with Fenella." He stubs out his cigarette. "And that's why I want to hurt this man. To be honest, I would like to slice off his cock."

"Because you can't make love to Fenella?" asks Kate coldly.

"No." He turns round sharply to face her. "Because she can't make love to me. I can fuck anyone anywhere, Kate. Fenella can't. She can only fuck me."

"Then you've treated her very badly over the years."

"But I didn't know. She had husbands; I assumed she had lovers. She never said."

"And you never asked," says Kate.

It was true. Women had always fallen for him and he took what was on offer without question. He liked the company of women, but better, he liked his work. Of all things it was the work that mattered to him most. Fenella was dear to him. He had fucked her for twenty years, but not regularly; they lived some three hundred miles apart, he in London, she in Newcastle. Mainly they had made love on courses and occasionally when she came down to London. He was always delighted to see her, but there was so much else in his life, the books, the research, the television programmes, the lecture tours, the university; his wife and daughters too took up a certain amount of time.

"You would like to meet violence with violence?" says Roy. "I think you need to think back over your Aeschylus."

"The Eumenides," says Michael.

"Tell me," says Kate. "I've forgotten all about Greek tragedy."

"Well," says Roy as Michael lights another cigarette, "when Agamemnon returned from Troy, he was murdered by his wife and her lover, Aegisthus. She in turn was murdered by her son in revenge for his father's death. Dying, she invoked the Furies, the Eumenides, against her son; and thereafter they hounded him, demanding justice and his death; eventually they allowed him to be tried in the Athenian court of law, the Areopagus. The votes were equal and Athene placed the casting vote, that the bloodshed should come to an end. What does she say, wait, I'll have it in a minute..." he ruffles the hair on his enormous head, "it's something like this: 'Nothing that strikes a note of brutal conquest. Only peace blessings, rising up from the earth and the heaving sea...' There's a lot more about sunlight and..."

There is a knock at the door and Robin Box enters. As if he were indeed in a court of law he has put on a clean shirt and a pair of cord trousers. He looks remarkably small and insignificant. His glasses seem to dwarf his face; and his tiny beard seems to all but have disappeared from his face as if he has tried to shave and has lost heart. It is hard to imagine him assaulting anyone. Roy bids him be seated and explains that he has arranged a night flight for him, his wife and child, for which he will be expected to pay, even if it is in instalments. He himself feels a letter of apology to Fenella would be something. He does not know what further action Michael will wish to take.

Robin Box lifts his head to stare at Michael who is sitting astride a chair watching him.

"You," says Robin, his whole body seems to twitch and throb with rage; it is as if the whole of his person is dwarfed by his anger, "what have you got to do with it? She's not even your wife. She's your bit of stuff. Oh yes; it was fun for you to flaunt her at us all, wasn't it? It was all right for you to fuck her, you the famous Michael Thorpe-Smith..."

"I think..." says Roy.

"No," says Michael, "let him have his say..." he pauses, "like Orestes at the Areopagus."

"You fucked her out in the open for everyone to see, you made so much bloody noise fucking at night that everybody was talking about it. And she wasn't even your wife. You've got a wife, another one who flaunts herself on television. Lovely for you with millions of men lusting after her. You saying, 'she's mine. You can't have her.'" He pauses for breath. "What's it like for me? There's nothing glamorous in my life. Every day I go and teach a lot of kids who don't want to know, and then go home to my wife. You've seen her. That's my life. Envy me, do you? No little ladies with big tits waiting for me." Roy makes a gesture to indicate that enough has been said. Robin, however, hasn't finished.

"I've never tried to rape any woman before, and I'll never do it again, but she was like a symbol to me of the unfairness of life, my life. Why should she open her legs for you and not for me? What's so different about you? Why should you have sexy women and nice clothes, and your picture on the back of books? You've got no better degree than me. I got a first, did you know that? You make me sick, appointing yourself as an agent of justice. What's so bloody marvellous about your behaviour? And I bet there's times you've fucked her when she hasn't wanted it. I bet you've done dirty things to her. You're no better than I am. You're just luckier."

All the time Kate and Roy look from Robin to Michael, but mostly at Michael. Roy moves to the edge of his chair, ready to intercept Michael if he makes any move in the direction of Robin. But Michael sits with head bowed. Then he says equably,

"Much of what you say is true, not all of it, but some of it. I am not without sin, I cannot cast the first stone. But you miss the point," He looks at the man for the first time, and the old confident Michael returns. "My feelings don't matter, it's not about me. It's about Fenella. Fenella has a sort of purity that you and I cannot begin to comprehend. That's what you have violated." He has had enough; he will leave the rest to Roy. He feels old and ill and dreadfully tired. He wants to go and lie down and sleep.

Chapter XXVIII

Ithaca

Initially it had struck him as grossly unfair when Box had accused him of fucking Fenella against her will. There had been times over the last twenty years when Fenella had demurred. Perhaps she had a period, or was feeling unwell, or in a hurry and he had always respected her feelings unequivocally. But what about Ithaca, the first time? How blameless had he been there? Or had he acted exactly as Box had acted, with less provocation and with equally critical results?

He had not expected to find a Fenella on Ithaca. He nearly hadn't come because of the find in Turkey, but he generally carried out what he had undertaken to do, and he arrived on Ithaca without great expectation either of the dig or of the archaeologists. So Fenella was a very pleasant surprise. He was aware that he cut something of a glamorous figure and he imagined that Fenella would undoubtedly fall for him, but even he did not think it would be on the first night.

They were staying in rooms in the village of Stavros close to the dig. They had all eaten together at the taverna, drinking a fair amount of ouzo, when Michael asked Fenella if she would like to go and see the cave of the nymph by moonlight. She smiled in agreement. One or two people exchanged glances. Michael's reputation as a womaniser was well known.

He was good at creating atmosphere and excitement even then when he was comparatively young. He had taken a torch with him (he always needed light) and let it play over the stalactite formations of the cave.

"That's the staircase where the nymphs come and go," he said, "and sometimes the gods come down too; but mortals must never go that way, there is a separate passageway for us. Shall we go and see, Fenella?"

He had no plan for seducing her; he never made such plans; he never had any need to, but when he brushed against her in the darkness of the cave, it occurred to him it would be very nice to make love to her.

"Look," he said, "that's where Odysseus put all his presents from the Phaecians, lots of cauldrons and ingots and bronze swords; did I tell you I found a bronze sword in Turkey?" Fenella shook her head and smiled. She had a very sweet smile. He put the torch down; it created an eerie effect in the cold echoing cave. He smiled at her. He was not unaware that he was immensely good-looking.

"May I kiss you, Fenella?" he asked politely.

"Yes," said Fenella softly. And when he felt her breasts heavy against him he knew he would have to have her.

"I would like to make love with you, Fenella," he said. "Would you like to make love with me?"

Fenella made no reply, but her eyes were enormous in the torchlight. He undid the zip of her dress and eased her out of it. He undid her bra and took it off. Her breasts filled him with unendurable desire.

"You are very beautiful, Fenella," he said. "Come outside under the stars." He took her by the hand, in the other he held the torch. He remembered how soft and grassy it was outside.

He undressed rapidly, walking out of his clothes in the way that Fenella was to know so well.

"Look at the effect you have on me," he said. He was fitting on a condom. She turned her head away.

"No," said Fenella, "Michael, no," but she didn't move.

"Show me your body, Fenella." The torch lay on the ground, glimmering over Fenella's beautiful body. Her nipples stood out hard against him; he bit each gently and felt a shudder go through her body. He attributed it to desire.

"Lie down, Fenella," he said, but when he got on top of her she began to struggle.

"No," she said, "no, not that."

"Yes," he said, "Fenella, yes."

She cried out when he entered her. It was a strange cry, not like that of any woman he had had before. The feel of her huge breasts, like those of some earth goddess, and the eerie torchlight and the fascination of the cave excited him unendurably, and although he had meant to hold back and give her pleasure too, he came almost immediately.

"Sorry," he said afterwards, "but you shouldn't be so beautiful." He withdrew and kissed her lightly on the forehead. But she said nothing; he could feel her trembling.

"Are you cold?" he asked. "Put my sweater on; here."

"No," she said quietly, "I'm not cold." Something in the tone of her voice attracted his attention. He shone the torch on her and saw her face.

"Oh god," he said, putting his arm about her, "it wasn't the first time, was it? You weren't a virgin?" She nodded.

"Oh, Fenella," he said, "I'm terribly sorry. You should have said. Was it awful? And I was so bloody selfish." He was vexed with himself. He began tying his sweater round her. "Can you forgive me?"

"Come," she said, "let's get dressed and go back now." They held hands going back, and neither referred to what had happened.

The next day he wanted to see her and apologise. He felt he had behaved badly, but it was difficult to catch her on her own. They all depended on Fenella for everything from feta to false teeth, but at last he found her in the hut classifying some shards. He came and put his arms around her.

"Am I forgiven?" he asked. He looked wonderful with his bleached hair and blue eyes smiling at her.

She smiled up at him and he was surprised at how pretty she was; he had been carried away the previous night by the whole experience; it was her breasts he remembered chiefly. He had been going to say that he wouldn't touch her again, but now he altered his decision.

"Yes," she said, "of course." She went on looking down, "I was very silly. It was just that I didn't..."

"I know," he said, smiling his irresistible smile. Then she said a surprising thing.

"I don't know what to do, you see," she said, fiddling with the shards. She looked up and gazed at him directly. "I mean I don't know much about sex, but I would like to give you pleasure."

Michael, with all his experience of women, had never encountered such an offer from such a beautiful, yet innocent, woman. For a moment he was speechless and then he said,

"I should wish to please you, Fenella, in equal measure; there is little pleasure unless it is mutual." Fenella shook her head in disbelief.

He sat down beside her and took both her hands in his.

"You must have had boyfriends, Fenella."

"Oh yes," she said, "but no sex."

He could not believe what he was hearing; she was so pretty, so sexy, voluptuous even.

"But you've fondled and petted and so on?"

"No."

"But they must have tried..." Fenella smiled.

"Yes," she said, "but they didn't get very far. They knew if they wanted sex, they must go somewhere else."

He shook his head in amazement.

"Why?" he asked.

Fenella smiled.

"Because it had to be the right person," she said.

"Am I that person?"

"Yes," said Fenella simply and unhesitatingly.

But even then he didn't understand how it was for Fenella.

"I was very stupid and ignorant." She looked down at the shards to avoid looking at him. "Please, will you teach me what to do?"

He felt enormously touched, that this beautiful girl, whom he had taken against her wishes, not only forgave him, but apologised to him for her inexperience.

"Put down those stupid shards," he said. "It's lesson time."

The third time, she had an orgasm; he was much more pleased than he was at his own. Only the intensity of her passion alarmed him slightly. He also put the thought of Jemima to the back of his mind. He had then, as now, the ability to disregard unpleasant things. How would Fenella react to the news that he was virtually engaged? It would be too difficult to get out of the engagement now. And, anyway, he needed Jemima's father to publish *Horace: The Man As Lover* which he had been sending round agents for the last two years. A deal had not exactly been struck, but all three of them understood that Michael's book would be published with due attention to publicity about the time he married Jemima. He hadn't particularly wanted to get married, indeed he had spent the last eight years avoiding marriage, but he had seen how it was. No marriage, no book. And it wasn't just the one book, there were others he had written; and then again, Jemima was an only child and her father immensely rich. He would be able to devote a great deal of time to research. He liked Jemima. She was a nice girl, moderately pretty, perhaps a little on the plump side and not so very bright, but agreeable enough. There was also a flat in London.

He couldn't help becoming aware as the weeks passed that Fenella was very much in love with him. He liked her a great deal; she was calm and efficient, bright, interested in Classics, extremely pretty with the most wonderful tits in the world. Whoever married her would be extremely lucky.

After Ithaca he had to return to Turkey for a while and then he returned to London for the start of the university term. Fenella had all these dates in her mind. It was a question of meeting as soon as possible.

They met at the National Gallery and she took him to see Monet's waterlilies. Afterwards he took her out to lunch in Soho.

"I have something to tell you, Fenella," he said.

He was afraid she would make a scene she turned so white, but she merely echoed in a mazed way, "You are going to marry Jemima? But you were married to me."

He thought it an odd thing to say; he attributed it to her distress. She left at once. She married a month after he did.

How could he possibly pass judgement on Robin Box?

Chapter XXIX

Resurrection

The Boxes are going; their departure is witnessed. Some turn their backs when they see Robin Box waiting in the foyer for the taxi that is to take him and his family to Naples for the night flight. It is pleasant to assert one's own moral superiority by such gestures. It also seems appropriate that Mr Box, doer of terrible unexplained deeds, should go by night. One or two people say goodbye to Nigel who is standing kicking at the cases; he doesn't answer but says to his mother,

"I want to say goodbye to Michael. I like Michael; he's my friend."

"Oh hush, dear," says Mrs Box, "I'll buy you some sweets at the airport."

"I don't see why we have to go anyway," says Nigel. "Nobody else is going."

"Shut up," says his father.

Mrs Box smiles nervously at people waiting in the foyer. She thinks she ought to say goodbye, but doesn't quite have the courage. Nobody speaks to her.

"Do you know," says Miriam, enjoying the feeling of virtue conferred upon her by her sentiments, "I felt like spitting on them, both of them. I'm really upset over the whole business."

William inclines his head in sympathy, but refrains from patting her shoulder.

At last the taxi arrives, driven, in fact, by Gino's second cousin. He must know all about it too, because he stands pointedly not helping them with their cases. Roy Small stands, and sees them off the premises, as it were. Only Jane, the joy of her engaged state overriding such moral distinction, shouts after them,

"Good luck, see you at the wedding."

But the doors have been slammed to, and they are swallowed up by the night.

The departure of the Boxes seems to usher in a new feeling, almost one of hilarity. It is as if the Boxes, like the rain, have contributed to the general malaise and depression. The course members have been through the long dark night of the soul, and have come out in the morning. A great weight has been taken from them. On a more mundane level it will be good not to encounter Nigel holding his nose when you come out of the lavatory. Mrs Box certainly hadn't contributed anything of moment, although Gerouin says he thought she had spoken up at the sandwich-stealing. Jane nudges him. Apparently they mustn't mention that any more.

Even before all this raping, or whatever it was, Mr Box had been a figure to inspire fear. Caroline tells Colin how he pressed up against her on the sofa.

"Anything could have happened," she says darkly.

"Yes," says Colin.

It is felt generally that a move towards the bar is a good idea. And lo! What more to complete their happiness than the sight of Fenella in her rust-coloured dress and her hair in a plait sitting in the bar with a glass in her hand. She is restored to them. She looks perhaps a little pale, a little washed out, but otherwise obviously sound in mind and limb. They are delighted to see her because she fulfils a dual role; there are two sides to her persona: firstly she is the centre of drama, a tragedy queen, an Iphigenia sacrificed on the altar of Box's lust, and, as in the legend, Artemis has snatched her from the jaws of death, or the hand (or worse), of Box, and restored her to them. There will be a lot of mileage to be gained, and not a few salacious details, from the asking of tactful questions. And there is her other quite opposite role: that of restorer of calm, resolver of crises (viz. the sandwiches), holder of tickets and adviser on diarrhoea tablets. Her presence inspires a wonderful feeling of calm and security. How right Fenella always is; did she not advise against thieves and scoundrels in Naples and was she not proved correct? True, Fenella may have indulged in some form of licentious behaviour with Michael, but allowances may be made for this; he is a figure of glamour and they are old friends.

They also feel a new closeness towards her. It is as if Fenella the lioness has kept wolves at bay far from the course members, her cubs. But suddenly a rogue lion appeared and snatched their lioness away, leaving them all unprotected. But the males of the pride have sought out the rogue male and destroyed him; they have brought back the lioness, bloodied but alive. Now is the time for the cubs to bring food to the mother, she who has fed them for so long. One by one they bring their humble offerings.

"I don't know whether you would like the use of my stick, Fenella," says Miss Aitchinson. "My leg is so much better I hardly need it at all." Fenella is most grateful for the offer, but can manage very well. She is glad Miss Aitchinson's leg is so much better.

Joe, rather like the poor shepherd boy in the Christmas carol, has little to offer of value, but what he has, he offers: his publishers' list of the latest editions of the Cambridge Latin Course. Fenella is most welcome to browse through it.

Jane shows her the guest list for the wedding: Fenella's name is in red at the top. Fenella asks when the wedding will be. Apparently that is not yet decided as Gerouin is uncertain about dates.

Alice Browne offers a restorative tonic without which she never travels, Sally smiles pityingly and offers powders. Jennifer brings half a bottle of Campari which she has bought out of her bridge winnings.

Miriam offers a lace handkerchief, one of three given her by Timmy for her last birthday. Fenella however cannot possibly take such a valued possession (she can appreciate the sacrifice, having had children of her own). She returns it to her. Miriam is in the happy state of basking in her own sense of generosity, without having incurred the discomfort of loss.

Even Percival. Yes, Percival has a gift to bring. His own notes on Baiae as Fenella was not fortunate enough to be able to join his little tour.

All these gifts Queen Fenella receives from her royal throne in the bar. Each subject is rewarded with a word and a smile of approbation. It is a happy time.

But the surprise of surprises is yet to come. It is time for the opening of Colin's box. As Jane says, "One box closes, another opens." Scarlet in the face, he makes a little speech. Caroline is at hand, perhaps to prompt if need be.

The box is brought with great aplomb and placed in the centre of the bar by the Handsome and Arrogant Young Man from Reception. Like all Italians, he enjoys a drama, and stays to watch. Gerouin is surprised to see him smiling and drinking. He has supposed him not capable of such human activities. Colin stands up in their midst. He has gained a new presence. Miriam wonders why she hadn't made an effort to get him away from Caroline, standing there with her stringy orange hair, all puffed up with her own importance, and she feels intense irritation.

"My father," Colin is saying, "is a worker in metals..."

"Like the god Vulcan," whispers Michael to Fenella.

"So when I knew I was coming on this course, I thought, I mean, I wanted to give..."

"He asked Fenella for a list of everyone's names," prompts Caroline who is already privy to the secret.

"Yes," says Colin, a little tetchily. Nervous as he is, the moment is his, and he doesn't want anyone else taking the limelight.

"Fenella sent me a list with everyone's names on, so I got my father to make everyone a pewter mug with their name etched on it and the words 'Southern Italy Course Easter 1994' and 'Classic Tours' in brackets." He gulps. It is a long speech. Gerouin wonders where he last saw Classic Tours written and remembers with a feeling of pleasure how it had been displayed between Fenella's ample breasts. Immediately he feels guilty. He is virtually a married man now.

"How very kind," says Fenella graciously. "I'm afraid it must have involved you in a lot of expense."

"Oh no," says Colin, blushing furiously.

It is very dreadful to Miriam to feel that Caroline may have caught a man rich as well as good-looking. And there is Caroline by reason of her privileged position as friend and companion of Colin already receiving her mug.

"One for Fenella," Colin is saying, "one for Miss Aitchinson..." How tall he stands, giving out his cups.

They gather round, each a little exercised in case there should be an omission in the case of their own. But no! All are there. There are three untouched.

"I wonder what he'll do about the Boxes' cups," says Jennifer.

"I think they should be sent them," says Alice. "After all, they have paid for the course."

"Oh no," says Sally, "they couldn't possibly be allowed to have them. It would be condoning Mr Box's behaviour."

"Perhaps just Nigel," says Jennifer.

The Handsome and Arrogant Young Man from Reception is seen examining the remaining three Box cups.

"Perhaps he'll get them," says Jane.

Everyone is very pleased to be a recipient of such unexpected bounty. There is much thanking of Colin and much blushing on Colin's part and much (Miriam feels) patronage exercised by Caroline.

There is, however, a limit to the amount you can say about a pewter mug with your name engraved on it, even if it does have the additional words 'Southern Italy Course Easter 1994 (Classic Tours)', especially when (circumstances being as they are) you mustn't think too much about where you have last seen these parenthetical words written. People are anxious to be seen to be grateful: they pick the mug up and examine their names (some commenting on the evenness of the letters), then they put it down again. Some even mime a drinking action. Others wrap them in tissue paper again as if they fear too much light may be harmful. But the situation is a tricky one; when you have exhausted all these actions, it seems cavalier to go on sitting there and ignoring your gift. It is perhaps best to pick up one's prize and make an early night of it. There is nearly a nasty incident when Percival Jeavons erroneously picks up Gerouin's in place of his own.

"That's mine," says Gerouin, "you're not having that as well as the sandwiches."

People are amazed at how masterful and audacious Gerouin has become since his engagement.

"I beg your pardon," says Percival. People see a change in him too, a change for the better. It has been noticed how he offered Fenella his Baiae notes. They attribute this to the benign influence of Miss Aitchinson.

****

Fenella is sitting at the dressing table and Michael is plaiting her hair ready for the night. It is typical of him, she is thinking, to have hit upon the one action that is acceptable to her. It is a kind of timeless ritual which brings order and dignity in its wake. Nymphs with braided hair dance in ordered lines round Greek vases. There are statues of Roman matrons too, formidable and stately with braided hair. He understands that loosened dishevelled hair will remind her of the Bacchic, of sensual frenzy. It is right that it is he who tames the locks.

"There is a recalcitrant tendril here," he says, "that refuses to be brought into line." He holds it in his fingers. Fenella gazes at them both in the mirror.

"You look like Pasquius Proculus' wife in the painting at Naples," he says.

"But you don't look a bit like a baker," she replies.

"No," he says, "actually I'm thinking of making a career move in the direction of hairdressing. Do you think I should be a good stylist?"

"Yes," she says, "the salon would undoubtedly be packed out."

"Mm," he says, putting a band on the end of the plait, "Miriam would be there every day."

"More probably Caroline," says Fenella.

"Oh no," he says, "I've lost out to Ganymede."

"Ganymede?"

"The cup-bearer. What shall you do with yours, the goblet I mean?" Fenella sighs. "Oh, I don't know," she says, getting up. "Michael..."

"Okay, I'm going."

"No!"

"No?"

"I want you to stay. I want you to sleep next to me. I even want your arms around me. I just don't want..."

He lights a cigarette, and smiles, "You want to have your cake and eat it, or, rather, you want to have your cake, and not eat it."

"Yes." She is standing there, looking at him, in a dreadful long-sleeved nightdress he has bought for her that afternoon. He had handed it to her wordlessly. They both knew exactly what he meant.

"Fenella, although that is probably the most hideous garment known to man, it will still be bloody difficult. You are asking a lot."

"It's you I'm thinking of," she smiles, "you might have bad dreams."

"I shall have to cope with them without you next week."

It is the first reference he has made to the time that is coming; the time after the end of the course. Always the last few days of a course are torture to her with the knowledge that this man whose she is so totally, will remove himself from her, will become largely unattainable until the next course, maybe one, two, or even three years away. She knows she must not ring him at home or write. He may appear in Newcastle; he may even summon her to London for the odd night or two; but he doesn't like anything that smacks of the sordid, anything consciously connived at. The only unwritten agreement between them is that sooner or later he will lecture on one of her courses. Nor does she know the ramifications of his life; his connections in the States, in Turkey, in France; the relationships with his first wife and his daughters, his ongoing divorce with his second. He never volunteers such information, nor does she ask for fear of what she will hear.

He must have known, for example, that he would divorce Jemima and marry Tabitha when they were in Athens together, and yet he had been as loving and attentive to her as ever. It had been a shock as terrible as the news of Jemima, to receive the letter some months after the course: 'My lovely Fen, I could not ask you to forgive me if I did not know you to be sweeter and better than other people...'

It seems he had got his just deserts with Tabitha. The marriage had lasted only six months. She was everything he loathed.

This time she has thought him different: older, wiser, kinder, perhaps as a result of the recent unhappy events in his own life. She has almost dared to hope that he will make some overtures to her, with talk of the future.

And now she cannot even bear to entice him with her sexual arts, those skills which he himself taught her on the island of Ithaca, when he took her virginity some twenty years ago.

The prospect of life post-course without him is so appalling that she cannot bear to think about it, particularly since yesterday when he has been so good. It is worsened by the thought that he is almost free: for the first time since she has known him, he is not married or engaged to be married. Or is he? Fenella fears Jemima. She has obviously underrated her. It would seem that he had been reasonably happy with her and would not have divorced her without the lure of Tabitha. He had accepted Jemima for what she was, a country girl. He had approved that she bred horses; there seemed to be something timeless and worthwhile about this. She had kept a pleasant house for him, she had bred him daughters, and when he was tired of her he used to go to the London flat and stay there. Jemima was tolerant, she was kind and sensible, and not without intuitive power.

Once Fenella had come across them by accident in a restaurant in Chelsea. She had taken her daughter to London to celebrate her exam results and to buy her clothes. She saw him immediately; she would have left; she could see he was not alone, but Felicity was already through the door. He came straight over with his wife.

"Jimmie," he said, "this is Fenella who looks after me on the courses; and you're Felicity," he said, flicking his golden smile at Fenella's daughter, "because I've seen pictures of you." Fenella flinched at the pet name. She did not want to be brought face to face with this other Michael, Michael the husband of another woman. And then there was the wife: she wasn't really pretty and she could have been slimmer, but she was pleasant to look at and was expensively dressed. Fenella saw the woman appraising her. She said,

"He always said how efficient you were, but he never said how pretty."

"Thank you," said Fenella, "but I don't expect he noticed really."

Michael's wife laughed and Fenella couldn't help respecting her because the laugh said it all: she knew perfectly well that there was absolutely no chance that he hadn't slept with her, and that she bore no grudge against either of them.

"Let's all sit together," she said, "and make a party of it." She liked gregariousness, she hunted with crowds of people, she ran charity things with loads of women, she gave riding lessons for scores of children; the house was full of people doing horsey things. She had little conversation beyond the horses.

"Do you ride, Michael?" asked Felicity who felt somewhat protective about her mother. Since her step-father had left, sixteen-year-old Felicity had been on the lookout for a new man in her mother's life.

"I find considerable difficulty telling one end of a horse from the other," said Michael, smiling at her.

"He's hopeless," said Jemima, entirely without rancour.

After the meal Felicity had said, "He fancies you rotten, doesn't he?"

"Perhaps," said Fenella.

"Come off it, Mum," said Felicity, "you know what a dark horse you are. Anyway," she added, "if you don't want him, I do. I think he's absolutely gorgeous." Fenella had laughed, obscurely gratified.

"Do you darling?" she said.

She lies in bed thinking these thoughts. Michael turns his back and lies facing the wall.

"I'm not being unfriendly, Fen. It's just that..."

"I know, darling."

"If anything happens in the night, it won't be that I've willed it or accepted it mentally, it's that I find you enormously sexually attractive, more so now than at any other time. You mustn't touch me with your breasts, Fen."

Perhaps, in some small way, he could make amends to Fenella for the two rapes, for so they were – his as much as Robin Box's. He must lie next to her and, whatever primitive desires she stirred in him, he must not yield.

Chapter XXX

Pompeii (The First Day)

The rains have gone and the sky is scoured, the sun flirts with the clouds, Gino is again outside with the coach, and they are off to Pompeii.

Fenella is standing outside the front of the hotel with bottles of mineral water and intense-looking handouts. It's obviously going to be a busy day. She is looking remarkably well in a long green skirt and a creamy blouse. Gerouin averts his eyes from the blouse; it seems blasphemous really to look. He tries not to remember the nightdress with the shell-pink nipple, or the events at Cumae. He has Jane now. Fenella's hair is worn again in a plait; she seems to have taken to wearing it this way since her... misadventure. Alice Browne says she thinks it makes her look rather severe, Sally disagrees. She thinks it gives her a school-girl air. Jennifer expects it is more manageable that way.

Michael, by contrast, people think, looks rather worn. Miss Aitchinson expects the events of the last few days have taken their toll. Percival, who knows that Michael is something of an expert on Pompeii and who will undoubtedly be considered interesting, says tartly that he can't see why.

Roy asks him how he is and he says he hasn't slept well. Kate nods. The fact of the matter is that Fenella moves in her sleep and although it is his back her breasts brush against he fears for his self-control and gets up and sits smoking and thinking in the armchair. Eventually he turns her firmly towards the opposite wall and climbs back in; but sleep evades him and he wonders what the hell to do about it all. There is also an unopened letter in his jacket pocket.

Everyone is delighted to see Gino again; and it's not only Gino but Anna! Anna whom they thought had been swallowed up in the evil-smelling garbage-ridden backstreets of Naples. And what is more it is a new Anna. Gone is the tight black dress, the cardigan and the crucifix; it is an Anna in jeans, and a smiling Anna to boot.

"I 501 sono moderni, si," says Anna to Fenella, patting her large posterior. Then she passionately embraces Fenella and makes a long speech. It is apparent that Anna too has heard of the violation of Fenella. Gino's sorrow is more restrained and confined to the shaking of Fenella's hand and the kissing of Michael.

Gino and Anna have emerged to be greeted with the emotion normally given to the figures of childhood. It is so long since they have been seen (all of five days in fact, six in the case of Anna). So much has happened since, although, of course, the seeds of crime were rooted in the old days with the theft of the sandwiches. But since, there have been rapes and banishments. They look back with nostalgia for the old days, a kind of golden age of innocence when simple pleasures like the wine press at Francoline or the Forum at Terracina satisfied them, before the dark shadows fell.

Anna is trying to say something, but nobody, not even those who have been to Italian evening classes, can work out what she is saying. She seems to have a peculiarly guttural Southern accent. Fenella when appealed to, says she thinks the coffee machine is mended and Anna will be bringing round coffee. She points out that they will be at Pompeii within a quarter of an hour. She suspects that Anna will be charging quite a hefty whack. The 501s have to be paid for somehow.

The party seems very much smaller without the Boxes, and Fenella has to count them all twice to make sure they are there. It is easier, she reflects, now they have all resolved themselves into pairs, except of course the Brown(e)s who remain an uneasy threesome.

She feels a vague concern and affection for them, perhaps born out of her own troubles. How many of these new-forged relationships will endure? Will Miss Aitchinson keep in touch with Percival? Would Caroline ever embrace Colin? Would Jane and Gerouin actually get married? Perhaps Kate knew; Fenella could only guess.

Michael picks up the microphone; Fenella knows he will become happier as they near their destination. He adores Pompeii.

He looks round the coach and smiles; the shadows of the night are dissipating.

"'If some loving Antiquary, On Resumption Morn, Will not cry with joy Pompeii, To the hills return'," he says conversationally.

There is a feeling of embarrassment in the coach. Nobody can make any sense of it. Anyway, why should they? It's not Classics.

"What this neurotic, Victorian, American..." he was going to say 'virgin', but, catching sight of Margaret Aitchinson's fierce expression, substitutes 'spinster', "was trying to say, I think is that if you are not turned on by Pompeii, God help you."

There is a feeling amongst some that they would prefer a little more subtlety, a little more of the ancient; that is safer, they feel.

"What I don't want you to do," he says, "is to see old stones and measure post-holes..."

Percival frowns horribly. Oddly enough he has his measure, and post-holes were on his list.

"You have been to the museum at Naples. You have seen things that people wore and used and cherished and ate and smashed and played with and wrote with. Now you have to recreate their world from the ruins before you. I don't want you to think of them as ruins but as a sketch, a shadow, a suggestion, an etching. *You* must provide the colour."

Fenella tells them they will be entering through the Porta Maritima, which they can see on their maps. She advises them to stay with Michael this morning at least, and at any rate, to avoid the custodians who should not be offered money. Miss Aitchinson feels rather indignant. Michael had said he and she would look at the *opus reticulatum* together; she had not envisaged being accompanied by others. Perhaps the afternoon will afford a *promenade à deux*.

He takes them first to the Basilica and deciphers inscriptions for them: "'Suaris wishes to drink jars full of wine, please, he really does!' I know how he feels, don't you?" Michael winks at Colin whom he has seen previously standing by himself in the bar, downing a pint. "'*Mea vita, meae deliciae ludamus parumper; hunc lectum*'" He runs his eye quickly over the Latin and translates: "'my life, my delight – let us play this game for a while; this bed be a field and I your steed'." He avoids looking at Fenella who is anyway pointing out the judges' tribunal to Joe. Miriam clears her throat; she thinks how nearly William had been her steed. Michael marches them briskly round the forum.

"And here are the forty-eight Ionic columns of the Temple of Apollo." Gerouin wonders how he can mention the words Temple of Apollo without blushing. "And here is the treasury, and here you buy your fruit and veg, and here you go for a pee. The vats of urine will be regularly collected and carted off to the fullers where they'll be used for bleaching your toga."

He leads them over the uneven stone road, trying to open for them bits of the past. Here is the temple of Vespasian and here the building of Eumachia, the fuller, perhaps the very fuller which the vats of urine were taken to – and here they must stop. They are in the Teatro Grande and, look, there are the five-thousand spectators all in newly bleached togas, there went the awning to keep off the sun. If they look to the right here, they can see the holes the poles fitted into. They hear the words 'Cambridge Latin Course' mentioned and see Joe busy with his tripod and camera. Penny does not seem to be expected to help nowadays. Percival is extracting a tape from his brief-case.

"Imagine," says Michael, "five thousand smelly bodies in the heat of the summer, and there sat the president, resplendent in his purple-striped toga."

His blue eyes grow very still as he looks closer and closer into the past. Fenella wishes she could go with him.

Miriam looks at her watch; of course it's all very interesting and she must buy some useful slides for school, but her heels keep catching in the uneven stones and William never seems to be properly at hand to help her. It won't be so long to lunch, and if she takes a long while eating it, there won't be time for too much trudging around in the afternoon. She yawns. But they are on the move again. It is early in the season and not very crowded. Nevertheless there are parties of earnest Germans who take endless photos, being herded around by a custodian; there is a group of extraordinarily badly behaved Italian school children who put them in mind of Nigel Box. There is also a courting couple whom they seem to meet round every column. Percival curls his lip, but Miriam glances surreptitiously after them.

"Here's the gladiators' barracks," says Michael. He finds himself wishing that Nigel were there; he would have seen the gladiators.

"Look," he says, moving past the walls, "female and phallic hermae; come and look at this glass case."

They gather round. William is careful not to stand too close to Miriam. Gerouin and Jane hold hands. The Smalls stand at the back; they do not want to obstruct anyone's view.

"Here are plaster casts," says Michael, "of fugitives, made from impressions in the ash. During the eruption of Vesuvius they took refuge, I think, under the portico here, because the air was full of showers of pumice stones – do you remember how Pliny tells us they tied cushions on their heads? Well, they come to take refuge here, but the fumes get worse, they are huddling together – there, do you see how their bodies contort? But it's no good; they die by suffocation." He goes quite white; it is intolerable, to him, that people should suffer so. Fenella touches his arm.

"Let's go and see the House of Menander," she says. But this is worse: the family here had been crushed by the falling roof. Jennifer Brown has made a sketch. It's rather good.

"Will you show them at school?" asks Fenella kindly. Jennifer Brown gives a mysterious smile. Fenella reflects that she's not unattractive.

"No," she says, "I shall give it to a friend."

"I expect she means Mr Royce, the Art teacher," says Alice. "He's always had a soft spot for her."

"Don't you mean Mr Sant?" says Sally. "Mr Royce does CDT."

Jennifer shoots a peculiarly triumphant look at them.

"You are both wrong," she says, "you would neither guess who I shall be giving it to."

"Gerouin! Jane!" It is Kate Small, puffing towards them; she finds the going hard, even in her rope-soled sandals. "I want to show you an inscription," she says; they follow in her wake as she rolls ahead, clad in a dress of many colours.

"Look!" she says at last. "There it is: *amantes ut apes vitam mellitam, exigunt.*"

"Ah!" says Jane, "that's one for us, Gerouin, 'lovers like bees live a honeyed life'." Gerouin smiles wearily; he wonders how honeyed life will be when he tells his mother about the engagement.

"Bit of Soho here," says Michael, "a thermopolium serving hot drinks and hot ladies; look, here are their names, Arellina, Smyrna, Maria and Aegle." Miss Aitchinson thinks there's too much Soho and not enough *opus reticulatum*.

"Now here's the house of our respectable baker friend, Publius Paquius Proculus. When did we meet him last?" Caroline knows, because she always listens to Michael.

"In the museum at Naples," she says, "a beautiful mosaic." Fenella knows too because Michael said she looked like the wife, when he was plaiting her hair with gentle hands.

"Imagine dining here," says Michael, leading them into the ruins of the house. "Look at the walls of the *triclinium*. Here is the big, big giant Polyphemus with Odysseus' little tiny boat, and here is his girlfriend Galataea - do you know the poem by Theocritus when he tries to woo her with cheeses in baskets? Idiot! No woman was ever won with cheese! And here is Perseus and another cross Andromeda, and you see this - this carbonised object; this isn't just a stump; it's a beautiful tree - an olive, do you think, or a palm, perhaps a cherry tree?"

They gather round to see the summer dining room that exists only in the words of Michael. Caroline thinks she can see it and Penny catches a glimpse because she's happy, Percival sees only a tree stump which he longs to encircle with his measure, Miriam is wondering how long before they have lunch. Joe is setting up his tripod. Roy has gone round the back to look at the shop of Felix the Fruiterer; he's damned if he'll fall under the spell of Michael's blarney. Jennifer Brown is doing another sketch; she will have quite a little dossier with which to present her mysterious friend.

"I'm hungry," says Kate. "I've got a lot of space to fill."

Miriam perks up.

"About time too," she says to William. "It's very late."

"Only just gone twelve," says William. He has been anxious to distance himself from Miriam since the Box episode. He is also beginning to find her extremely irritating.

"Well, I'm not used to all this standing about," she says. "I'm really not very strong."

"Balls," says Jane who's standing nearby. "Look at all those amarettos you knocked back the other night."

Caroline nudges Colin.

"She's quite right," she says to him, *sotto voce*, "she's never tired at night either. She keeps the light on for hours doing her nails and things, when I'm dying to go to sleep."

"Oh," says Colin. He thinks of Caroline lying in bed, but as an image it doesn't have the same force as her standing in the train with her hips pressed against him.

Fenella thinks it best if they all meet back at the Great Palaestra at two o'clock. If anyone misses them or wants to walk round on their own, Gino and the coach will be back at three.

Miss Aitchinson thinks now might be the time to catch Michael for their tour of the *opus reticulatum*, but, when she looks round, sees him way ahead. He has Fenella by the hand.

"Come on, Mrs Proculus," he says, "I'm going to buy you lunch."

Miss Aitchinson, having lost Michael, looks for Percival but he is still busy measuring the tree stump and making copious notes, so she attaches herself to the Brown(e) contingent. Apparently Alice has something to ask her; was she at Norchester University in 1960 and was she known as Maggie? Miss Aitchinson, who has almost forgotten she was ever known as Maggie, grudgingly agrees. It is much more difficult to be grudging without the stick.

"I think you knew my brother," says Alice. There is a touch of pride in the words 'my brother'.

"What, Sally's husband?" asks Miss Aitchinson.

"Yes," says Alice, "his name is Stuart."

Stuart Browne! Stuart whom she had once thought she might marry, but who, in the end, had never quite managed to ask her.

"No, I don't think so," says Miss Aitchinson after a pause, "I'm sure I never knew anyone of that name." She wishes she still had her stick.

****

They buy *panini* and a bottle of Chianti and sit in the summer *triclinium* in the House of the Moralist to consume it. A uniformed custodian comes up to castigate them, but so great is the power of Michael's colloquial Italian, the number of his contacts in the world of archaeology, the beauty of his girlfriend and the value of the proffered lire note, that the custodian leaves them undisturbed. Michael is making crumbs and throwing them out for the birds.

"Not that there are any," he adds, "the Italians shoot them all and eat them."

"That sounds like one of your tall stories," says Fenella, smiling. She finds it impossible to eat when she's with him.

"You're looking very pretty, Fen," he says. "No woman has the right to look as pretty as you at your age."

"You make me sound about a hundred."

"No, no," he says, "Fen, when were we in Pompeii last?"

"'74," she says. "You'd just had Chloe."

"Well, Jemima had; and we talked nappies all the first night."

"And afterwards we hardly talked at all," says Fen. It was true. It had been a difficult course, a woman had been taken ill, there was a man in a wheelchair and Fenella hated hearing about Michael's babies. They fucked a lot.

"You know what you said the other night, about your marriage to Mark?" He chucks the rest of the *panini* into the box hedge and lights a cigarette. "Is it true, that it broke up because you couldn't make love to him?"

"Well, I suppose that's putting it a bit strongly," says Fenella. She drinks Chianti out of a plastic cup taken from Anna's coffee machine.

"I mean, I didn't refuse him or anything – I had two babies, after all, but I couldn't bear it. He said to me once, 'Why do you have to make it so bloody clear that you don't fancy me?' He was very good about it really, and after a while he went and found someone who did fancy him."

"That didn't last long, did it?"

"No, I suppose he's always been trying to find a wife who fancies him a bit more than the last one; he can never be sure, you see."

"I suppose that's my doing too," he lights another cigarette.

"No, I don't think so; the buck has to stop somewhere."

"You mean you can't blame Agamemnon's murder on Pelops for eating his children?"

People walk by and look curiously at them as they sit at the stone table of the summer *triclinium*. Michael lights another cigarette and says, "Odd coincidence. Roy was citing the Eumenides for letting Box go. I wanted to do bad things to him, Fen."

"Why didn't you?"

Michael gets up and shakes the crumbs off his sweater.

"Because I believed myself as guilty as Box. I couldn't speak about justice, doing what I had done."

"What had you done?" Fenella speaks softly and looks across the table.

"I raped you, Fenella, and I set in train events disastrous for many people over two decades: the misery of your husband and his wives, the disgrace of Box, but above all..." and he sweeps his hand across the hills, "the ruining of you, Fen, and I never knew, never thought." Fenella stands up and puts her hands on his shoulders.

"But, darling, you weren't to blame. You weren't to know I was as I was. I didn't know myself. I thought I would marry and have sex and forget all about you. It was just... it was just that I found that I couldn't. It was only possible for me with you. I know it's not like that for other people..." He sits next to her on the stone bench and puts his arms round her.

"Tell me."

"I know it's different for other people. You, I'm sure, can look at the dark side and..." She screws up little pieces of bread into balls. She keeps her eyes fixed on these, "... ignore it, or even accept it – like it, even; but to me it was always there, like a mixture with arsenic. But given the right proportions, mixed with other things, it could be strong and beneficial, like when it was you and how I felt for you, it was magic; but Box took that; he only left the grains of arsenic." She looks up at him shyly, almost as she did when he knew her first. "I should have been more normal."

"No, no, no. It's that you're better, purer than other people. And I was so stupid I never saw it. I thought you fucked about like I did. You always looked so amazingly sexy..."

"Perhaps I was always thinking about you."

"Fen..." But Miss Aitchinson appears through the colonnade.

"Ah, Mr Thorpe-Smith, I thought I should find you here. I've found one or two pieces of *opus reticulatum* that will interest you." Fenella sees anguish on Michael's face. She smiles her sweet smile.

"I'm sure Michael will be delighted to go with you, Miss Aitchinson. We'll wait for you at the amphitheatre; I expect everyone's coming back from lunch now. It's a lovely warm afternoon, isn't it?"

On her way to the amphitheatre, Fenella walks on her own through the ruins of the House of the Marine Venus. With her creamy blouse falling in folds over her ample breasts and her long green skirt swishing from her hips she excites interested glances from passing Italians, two of whom try to pick her up. She quells them with a glance. With Mediterranean sensibility they understand she is another man's woman.

Fenella stops before a fresco of Venus floating in her shell, and then she looks at the picture of the god Mars beyond the peristyle, and thinks how they were lovers too.

Joe is just folding up the tripod; he is jubilant, he has some wonderful pictures of the amphitheatre to supplement his teaching of Stage 5, Unit 1. Here it was that the fatal brawl took place in AD 59.

"I don't know whether you've noticed, how that business with the Nucerians is broached in four different ways; there are two unseens – one may be a comprehension, I forget; there is the famous wall painting and the extract from Tacitus."

"Yes," says Penny; she is sitting in one of the spectators' seats on the edge of the amphitheatre, "I've taught it for fifteen years." She turns her face to the sun. It is a lovely warm afternoon and her husband will ring her again tonight. Kate was probably right to dissuade her against going home as soon as she received his letter. She should not be seen to be too forgiving too soon; but it will be wonderful to have him meet her at the airport and to have a proper life again. Joe is saying something. What is it? Is he going to go through all the stages of the Cambridge Latin Course? No, he is putting the camera away in its plastic bag and saying something quite surprising.

"He's a lucky bloke, that husband of yours, Penny, having a nice woman like you to come back to." While Penny is trying to think of a suitable reply to this remark, he continues, "I did think that you and I might have had a bit of a fling, sort of, when I met you first, but..."

"Well," laughs Penny, "I thought the same really, but you only ever talked about the Cambridge Latin Course."

"Well, I know," He is fiddling about, adjusting the strap of the camera case, "the fact of the matter is, Penny, my life's not very interesting really; the wife teaches Latin too; we don't seem to have a lot else to talk about."

"You don't have children, do you?"

"No. Cheryl didn't want them and I wasn't fussy. I wish we had now, though."

"Well, it's not too late, is it?"

"No, I suppose not." He closes up the case with a snap as if that dismisses the subject. He says, "Imagine the gladiators in there, Penny. That would have been something else."

"You wouldn't really have wanted to see that, would you, all that bloodshed?"

"Not really." He sits down beside her. "Sometimes though, Penny, I long for a bit of excitement, a bit of living like that man Thorpe-Smith, married to that Tabitha Twyce and being on the television and coming out here and having it off with Fenella."

"Well I shouldn't think so now, after that assault business."

"Don't you believe it, Penny. Can't keep their hands off each other."

"Well," says Penny, "and I thought you only thought about the Cambridge Latin Course." He grins.

"Let me take a photograph of you, Penny; you look nice sitting there."

"You've just put your camera away, Joe."

"Well I can fucking well get it out again, can't I?" Penny laughs happily. How funny life is, one minute you are in despair because you have no man in your life and then Fate turns around, and you can have the choice of two. And look, here is another one coming!"

"Look," she says, "it's Percival. Let's get him to take one of both of us."

But Percival is in a great hurry; he needs a private word with Penny.

"With me?" asks Penny, surprised. She could have understood if it had been Joe.

"Yes, yes," he says tetchily, "with you." Joe stands at a tactful distance, unfurling the camera.

"I'm in rather a hurry," says Percival, "I wonder if... I understand ... I'm led to believe you, ah, have... the lavatory here doesn't have, er..."

"Ah!" says Penny, seeing the light, "it's lavatory paper you're after. Yes, I've got one whole roll left." He hovers impatiently, moving from foot to foot; snatches it off her and, without even secreting it about his person, is off in the direction of the *uomini*.

"Silly old bugger," says Joe, "got the squitters, I shouldn't wonder. Serves him right. Perhaps someone's left some poisoned sarnies about."

"Percival's had some poisoned sandwiches," says Alice, who has just arrived on the scene with her companions and overheard the remark.

"I'm quite sure he hasn't," says Sally. "I saw him tucking into *gnocchi* at the Restaurant Julia Felix."

"He's certainly in a hurry," says Jennifer. The course members are converging on the amphitheatre. They look with relish at the speed with which Percival is moving. They see Fenella approach with the air of one who has kindly advice to proffer. They see her, however, thrust out of his way. She is only one more barrier in his race against time.

"What a rude man he is," says Caroline. "I think it's horrible for a man to push at a woman, don't you, Colin?"

Colin agrees monosyllabically. He wishes this subject wouldn't keep coming up.

Here is Jane, but where is Gerouin? Nowadays where there is the one, there, it is assumed, is the other. Ah! There he is in the corner of the amphitheatre, seated right at the top. What can he be doing? Actually he has been taking advantage of Jane's absence in the lavatory to write the disturbing news to his mother. He doesn't want Jane to read the letter because there are some things a man cannot share, even with his fiancée. It is difficult to find time when Jane is not there. He has got as far as:

'Dear Mum,

I've got some surprising news for you. (How is your leg, by the way?) I hope this won't come as too much of a shock. I have become engaged (!!!) to a very nice lady called Jane. She is a Latin teacher too. She has short brown hair...'

It is difficult to know how else to describe Jane without alluding to her most distinctive features of nose, teeth and ears; he thinks of it being rather like describing an elephant without mentioning the trunk; he immediately feels guilty: he is very lucky to have Jane, it is very nice to be able to have sex every night. It's only, only that he wishes she looked a little more like Fenella. Perhaps if she were to wear a dress (he has seen one hanging in the wardrobe), she would look prettier. The tracksuits are certainly not very flattering.

But at this point, he is suddenly aware of them all assembling in the amphitheatre below, and Jane shouting up at him,

"Come on down, Gerouin. What are you doing up there?"

At school he always teaches about the good acoustics in Roman amphitheatres, but he has never known how good before, as the full attention of the course members focuses upon him. He folds the letter very small and inserts it down a crevice between the seats. He cannot risk Jane seeing it. Nothing is safe from her all-seeing eye.

"Coming, Jane," he replies obediently.

Roy Small comes ambling up with the news that Kate is digesting her lunch. She will join them later. Oh, and Miriam is resting in the coach.

At last Margaret Aitchinson appears with Michael. She looks quite girlish.

"Have you seen a lot of *opus reticulatum*?" asks Fenella wickedly.

"On 25th February," says Michael, addressing the company at large, "there will be a show by Tiberius Claudius Vetius including combat against wild beasts, wrestling matches and sprinkling with scented water, offered for the health of Nero Claudius Augustus Germanicus. You are one of the twelve thousand spectators. It's free; it's all day, and there's a fresh contingent of giraffes just imported from Africa..." He shows them beast fights and the dead giraffes dragged out from the arena with hooks, dying gladiators and lunchtime crucifixions, and the sea battles in the flooded arena.

"Thousands of bodies, dead and dying, piled up in the midday sun." He lights a cigarette; he cannot bear to think of it. Suddenly he smiles. "Never mind," he says, "they had the scented water... and Virgil and Propertius." Caroline has something to ask him. Colin stands behind her and waits.

"Let's go and see the Palaestra," says Michael, "where the playboys hang out." His smile falls on Caroline. "Come and see some graffiti," he says.

Even though they nearly all know Latin, Roman graffiti is hard to decipher; the letters do not seem the same as their representations in text books, and when you do get the gist, the meaning is often so obscene, you can hardly credit what you are translating. Michael, out of deference to Margaret, Caroline and perhaps Fenella, chooses some milder ones.

"*Crescens*, man of maidens, *retiarius*, doctor of the ladies of the night, of the day, of the others... On 9th November Quintus Postumius invited Aulus Attius to have... Perhaps not," he adds. He has whetted their appetites; the Brown(e)s cluster round a column, and Jane, who is a good Latinist, can be seen pointing something out to Gerouin.

"Outside the Nucerian Gate," says Michael, "is a necropolis, a city for the dead, but I expect you'd prefer to go straight to the Stabian baths; they're on the way back." Fenella knows he want to go and wander among the tombs on his own. She shepherds them in the direction of the baths.

"I won't be long, Fen," he says, "I have to go and see Eumachia's tomb; it's rather splendid."

"It'll only upset you," she says.

"I know, Fen, but I have to go all the same."

Kate dozes peacefully in the large comfortable back seat of the coach. The only other occupant is Miriam; she really can't face trundling round all afternoon. They aren't even going to see the nice houses today, it's all boring forums and amphitheatres. She is looking forward to going home now. It hasn't been much fun really – her first holiday away from Joe and Timmy too. Perhaps she should have let William... He's not really very nice to her now. It seems very unfair that she hasn't got a nice man when she's so much prettier than the others. There's Penny – mind you she was very sharp off the mark collaring that Joe; and then there's Colin following Caroline around with a silly look on his face – enough to make you sick; and Jane and Gerouin, well, I ask you! And even Miss Aitchinson goes round with Percival. Then of course there's Fenella and Michael. Really, she deserved all she got from that Mr Box. It was very nice for her too to have everyone fussing round her afterwards, especially after what she'd done at Cumae. Still, some people always fall on their feet! There's Percival getting on. He doesn't look very well, and what's that he's carrying? It looks like one of Penny's... oh, he's going off again. How fast he's walking! Where can he be going? Why don't they all hurry up and they could go back to the hotel, and then perhaps go shopping. There's a nice toy boat she's seen for Timmy and Joe. Only, her money isn't as plentiful as it was a few days ago: she's had to buy a lot of her own drinks now William's not around. You would think one of the other men might... Perhaps she will not buy the boat after all. It is just as she is making this decision that she looks down and sees a fifty-thousand lire note folded into the crevice between her seat and the one next to it. A fifty-thousand lire note! She casts her eyes to the back seat where Kate is gently snoring. She tries to remember who was sitting there before. She thinks it might have been Penny and Joe. She looks for clues; above the seat on the rack hangs a Tesco bag. Miriam's hand closes over the note. She thinks she will buy that nice boat after all.

****

He climbs into bed, but finding Fenella curled round to face him, climbs out and rolls her over to face the wall.

"Stay there, Mrs Sykes," he says, "move at your peril." He climbs into bed again.

"Michael," says Fenella but he is almost asleep. He is exhausted. It is not Pompeii that has tired him, unless it was his visit to the necropolis, nor even his evening lecture on Pompeian houses ready for tomorrow's visit, although it is hard to take people back two thousand years when, like Miriam, they are firmly rooted in the twentieth century. No, all that is the stuff of life to him. It was the procession, thinks Fenella, that has exhausted him.

They had all just got off the coach and there was much business with bags, cameras, guidebooks, films, tripods and souvenirs. (It is amazing how acquisitive a course member can be. In the last few days their possessions have increased four-fold) It was then that they saw the procession. The course members had not heard the figures advancing for they moved in silence, but they heard the cries of the onlookers.

A column of black hooded figures. Totally black. They wore robes of black and hoods which enveloped the whole face, holes for the staring eyes. In their hands they carried white sticks, a stark contrast to the deathly gowns. Borne aloft in their midst was Christ in agony on the cross. The image was crude, but no less powerful for that. They passed by in silence, perhaps fifty or sixty of them, and as they passed by the chanting began, monotonous, discordant, uncivilised, unpleasant, disturbing. It was Good Friday. She saw him clench his fists and force himself to watch. He made no comment.

Miriam took a photo with her dinky little camera.

"I shall tell Joey and Timmy if they're naughty boys I'll send one of the bogey men after them," she said to nobody in particular, William being so very stand-offish these days. Michael stared at her appalled.

"This is not for children," he had said. "This is the harrowing of hell."

"Oh," said Miriam; she hadn't liked to be made to look ignorant. "I'm sorry, I thought they were just some funny old Italians dressed up for Good Friday." She flounced into the hotel – but not before Percival, who had gone on ahead, almost at a run.

"Give me the heebie-jeebies, they do," remarked Joe to Penny. "Can't stand that sort of thing."

****

She is afraid he won't sleep for thinking of the harrowing of hell, but sleep overtakes him immediately. He sleeps resolutely facing the wall, away from Fenella.

It is around two when she is wakened by his cries. She can feel him trembling, and when she puts her hand on his forehead, it is wet; he starts to mutter.

"Like bats, they squeak like bats... Hermes, Lord of the Dead... Achilles says... of the dead... he descended into hell. Hades..."

"Michael," She reaches to shake his shoulder as she had before, but he withdraws from her, resolutely facing the wall and even trying to ward her off.

"Ibant obscuri sola sub nocte per umbram, perque domos Ditis vacuas et inania regna."

"Michael, it's all right. I'm here, Fen; you're not in the Underworld. Michael!"

He turns over onto his back, staring in front of him; she does not know if he is asleep or awake.

"Achilles said it's better to be a serf of a poor man, not just a serf, not just a serf... Odysseus had said he was lucky... better to be a serf, not king of the dead, not in a Necropolis. No!" She can feel his forehead hot and wet, the lock of hair that normally falls so glossily over it is sticky.

"Ibant obscuri sola... sola," He strikes the bed with his fist.

There is only one way she knows to soothe him; the way that has been made repugnant to her. She hesitates for only a few seconds. She cannot bear his distress. She reaches down and takes it in her hand, limp as a fallen flower. For a moment he resists her.

"Sub nocte per umbram." He shudders and then he quietens, his murmurings cease as the terror abates and he moans gently. Fenella takes his sleeping hand and places it on her breast.

The effect is electric; he comes instantly and drenchingly in great spasms, and moving in that moment from sleep to consciousness. As always, he is instantly awake. He stares at her in horror.

"Oh God, Fenella, what have I done?" He pulls the duvet off and gets out of bed. He searches for his dressing gown distractedly.

"I couldn't even do that, could I? I couldn't even do that for you, to lie by you. No. Did I touch you? God. What did I do?"

"No, darling, no," She was alarmed. "You didn't do anything. It was me."

"I'm going, Fen. I'm going back to my room.. You won't have to fight me off. You won't have to." He is putting on his dressing gown. He makes towards the door.

"Michael," she shouts at him, "listen. Listen! It was me. I did it – to stop your dreams. I wanted to bring you back. It was the only way... but it wasn't you. You fought me off..."

He sits down, bewildered, running his hand through his hair. "You did it?"

"Yes, darling." Suddenly she laughs. "I have done it before, you know." He takes her hand and kisses it.

"What was I dreaming about?"

"About the Underworld, like you always do."

"Yes, I remember a bit. Odysseus was there; you know in book eleven of the Odyssey when he says to Achilles' ghost how lucky he is to be king of the dead and Achilles says no, any sort of life is better than death. I can't remember the Greek..."

"Come on," says Fenella, "take that silly dressing gown off and come and lie down. I'm sleepy."

"Shall I, Fen? Don't you want me to go away?"

"No."

"Can I lie between your breasts?"

"Mm. No, come here; it's all wet there."

"Fen..."

"Mm."

"I don't deserve you."

"No, probably not."

"Fen..."

"Mm."

"I won't dream again, will I?"

"No."

"Promise?"

"Promise."

"Fen..."

"Mm."

"You've got the most gorgeous tits in the world."

"Go to sleep, Michael."

As he settles his face between her breasts and she encloses him within the circle of her arms, she feels an enormous rush of happiness, like an injection of some exhilarating drug. She cannot tell whether it is a mental or physical sensation. She only knows that it engulfs her whole body and she wants the night never to end.

Chapter XXXI

Pompeii (The Second Day)

Fenella is going to see Percival, for there are various rumours circulating about his state of health, nor has he has not been down to breakfast and she is worried about him. She is really rather apprehensive about going to visit him in his own den, as it were. She cannot ask Michael to accompany her as he is still asleep, the events of the night having taken their toll of him.

Fenella, her hair in a ponytail and wearing her white jeans and Classic Tours tee shirt, knocks briskly on his door. She knocks again, having also taken the precaution of taking the master key with her. At last a dispirited voice says,

"Come in."

Fenella detects several nuances in it: weakness, irritability, loneliness and defensiveness.

"May I come in?" asks Fenella, entering anyway, "I've come to find out how you are."

From the bed, he eyes Fenella; he hates it that she's there invading his privacy. Soon she will want to ask him about his bowels. People say that she disported herself naked at Cumae, no wonder that man tried to rape her. He regrets now giving her his notes on Baiae (even though he has another ninety-nine stapled copies with him).

"Thank you, the malady has abated."

Fenella looks around the room. She sees the ninety-nine copies of the notes on Baiae neatly piled up awaiting distribution. She reflects how sad it must have been for him to have so few who wanted to benefit from them. Many books and papers are neatly stacked, clothes folded and nothing present that speaks of warmth or of kindliness, or of human contact: perhaps the nearest indication of such is the sight of Margaret Aitchinson's stick; the only reminder of friendship. On the window sill (again neatly piled) are five of Michael's books. How he will hate Fenella to have seen that he has them; how he will fear lest she tell Michael.

"Can I get you anything?" asks Fenella. "Would you like a little breakfast sent up, a plain roll perhaps, and some weak coffee?" She knows he will not want her to look at him as he lies there, so she fixes her attention on the bedside table.

As it happens, that is exactly what he has been thinking he would like: a breakfast of rolls and coffee brought up to his bedroom. He clears his throat.

"That would be most acceptable." He feels better disposed to Fenella now and ceases to regret the giving of the Baiae notes.

"Well, I'll go and see to that now," says Fenella. "I expect you don't feel like Pompeii today."

"I fear not." His memories of Pompeii are painful; they are overshadowed by memories of the lavatory in the Antiquarium. As if she reads his thoughts, Fenella adds tactfully,

"Is there anything else you need? Some laundry perhaps?" He stiffens. He doesn't need this cross-examination; he has already dealt with his underclothes. He pictures her again at Cumae.

"Certainly not," he replies.

"Just coffee and rolls then," says Fenella brightly. "I'll go and tell them right away." And so indeed she does; but this is Southern Italy, and the waiter who is deputed to the task forgets about it and when he remembers it is too late; but it doesn't matter. "*In ogni modo gli Inglesi saranno andati a Pompeii.*" Percival waits in vain. It confirms his opinion of Fenella as feckless. He even suspects she will not read the Baiae notes. At midday he gets up and goes off to buy himself some *panini*.

It is Holy Saturday, a day to be happy in. The sun is shining warmly and Anna is still smiling; she seems to meet with approval from Gino too. He has his arms around her and slaps her bottom lustily. It is she who tells Fenella the glad tidings: there is to be a dance tonight in the hotel – a live band apparently – her eyes sparkle.

"Fenella, *hai un vestito che può prestare*?" says Anna. Fenella, pointing to her own well-developed breasts, laments the fact that she is not as slender as Anna. This is not in fact true, but Anna is nonetheless delighted.

A dance! A mixed reception greets this news. To Miriam, it is undoubtedly the most interesting event of the course. To Caroline it is of very little interest. Once she might have imagined being swept away in the arms of Michael, but now she knows this will not be. She does not think she will bother to go. Colin, on the other hand, is greatly excited by the whole prospect. Fate is offering him a second chance to be pressed close to Caroline. He thinks of it all day. Gerouin wonders whether Jane will wear her tracksuit.

Michael takes them to the house of the Vetii. He stands and smiles at them, the Easter sunlight plays in his hair, which is neither gold nor grey, but something in between. In his jeans and tee shirt, Fenella thinks him very much like the Ithacan Michael. From her position in the midst of the cluster of Classicists, she smiles back at him.

"To the right of the entrance," says Michael, "is a very interesting object. Indeed it is so interesting that it has to be kept under lock and key; it is, of course, a particularly obscene image of Priapus. Should you wish to view it, the custodian will be found lurking somewhere within the house, waiting for you to press a lire note of large denomination into his hand. No? Well then, let's go into the *triclinium* and look at the frieze of the busy cupids. It is, of course, a painting in the Fourth Style. You may remember me, rather laboriously, trying to explain the distinctions between the different styles last night." He smiles again. He does not much care now whether or not they have understood. He adds, "Such busy cupids, they put me in mind of the seven dwarves."

He takes them to see the wall paintings: "Ariadne," he says, "deserted by Theseus. 'Twas ever thus." He avoids looking at Fenella. "She was all right though," he adds, as if feeling Fenella's glance on him. "Dionysus looked after her." But Ariadne, he reflects, had been coarser-grained than Fenella. She had been all too happy to accept Dionysus' embrace when Theseus had gone off. But, perhaps, in the end they had been equally misused, for Dionysus had gone after other women too, just like Fenella's Mark. And Ariadne had ended up as a constellation in the sky, and was Fenella not his light? He pauses to look at the luminous Fenella, but she is occupied in answering some query of Caroline's. He continues,

"The lovers Hero and Leander. Now in there..." he gives a meaningful glance at a bolted door, "are what guidebooks like to describe as 'equivocal pictures', a wonderfully expressive word 'equivocal', don't you think?" Margaret draws herself up. Enough of this. Where is the serious student of *opus reticulatum*?

He takes them past the *peristylum*; he makes them stop and look out on the square of garden open to the sky.

"Look," he says, "how lovely! Look at the statuettes against the columns. Imagine jets of water spouting from them into cool marble basins. Imagine returning from the amphitheatre where you have seen a thousand men butchered to death, and walking among the columns and statues in the cool of the evening." He turns and looks at them fiercely. "How could you do both?" he asks them angrily, "relish the slaughter and love the grace? That is the enigma of the Roman. That is what I have been trying to understand for the last twenty-five years." He gazes into the *peristylum*; Fenella wonders what he sees there.

But they want to move on, to see some more. As Joe says, they have come to look at Pompeii, they're not interested in Michael's problems. Some of them have to teach, they can't afford the luxury of questioning, like Michael.

"The infant Hercules," he continues, pointing at the fresco in the colonnade at the side, "strangling the snakes. What a very unattractive child he is! One almost wishes the snakes had got him. And there is Pentheus being torn limb from limb by the Bacchantes, women possessed by the madness of Dionysus. Ah! How dangerous, how fatal to ignore the power of Dionysus." He falls silent, thinking of Robin Box, thinking of himself.

Caroline remembers he has written a book entitled *Dionysus, The Power of the Unmentionable*. He had included lots of pictures of dishevelled women, so why had she been so shocked by his question? But anyway that was ages and ages ago.

"Oh, and look, here is Daedalus showing Pasiphae the wooden bull he has made for her. Do you think he was awfully embarrassed? 'Excuse me, your majesty, I've made the bull you asked for. Would you, er, care to try it for size?'"

Alice Browne thinks him much too flippant today. Sally thinks it important not to take these things too earnestly. Jennifer finds it an extraordinarily vivid picture.

He takes them to the house of the Faun; he makes them watch the movements of the bronze statue. "Look how he dances," he says, "look how he twizzles his tail and waves his arms." He sees them looking dully towards it. He shrugs. "Perhaps you are right; he is only a small statuette made of bronze – and a copy at that." Fenella sees him looking beyond the Porta Ercolano at the Via delle Tombe.

"No," she says firmly, "it's time for lunch."

They will prefer, says Fenella, to wander at will in the afternoon. Michael will be found in the Villa of the Mysteries in the afternoon.

"You shouldn't have told them, Fen," he says. "I want to be there just with you."

****

Gerouin and Jane choose a cheapish restaurant and eat spaghetti carbonara. They always split the bill exactly in half, but Jane looks after his purse for him so he doesn't lose it. Gerouin has decided that when he has eaten exactly five forkfuls (not an easy task as its particularly sticky consistency encourages it to slide from the fork rather than adhere to it) he will tell her.

Jane is engrossed in a book she has purchased off the stand outside the Porta Marina. To open it she has had to undo a cellophane cover; it is entitled *Pompeii: The Forbidden City*. She is holding it up to get a better view.

"Hey, look at this one, Gerouin," she says, "here's a position we never thought of." The book contains pictures of wall paintings and statues that are kept under lock and key.

"It's about that really, Jane..." says Gerouin. He puts his fork down: he cannot combat the spaghetti and Jane at the same time.

"About what?" asks Jane, turning over the page. "Here's a good one."

"I don't think... I... it's my..." he starts nervously, looking at Jane. He feels acute misery.

Jane has a good degree, and if her brain was matched by her face, she would be another Fenella. But alas, it is not. She shuts the book with a snap.

"You want to call it off, don't you?" Gerouin is encouraged by the fact there is no anger in her voice.

"It's just that... I... don't think..."

"You don't want to see my face over the breakfast table every morning. Can't say I blame you." She digs into the spaghetti. She will not show him the hurt.

"It's not that, Jane..."

"Yes it is. If I looked like Fenella, you wouldn't be saying this, but then, Gerouin, you're hardly a Michael either, are you?"

They look across the table at each other. Gerouin sees Jane's great teeth, her large red nose and jug-like ears and big black glasses. The tracksuit (the navy one) bears traces of previous spaghetti carbonaras. He looks for a redeeming feature. He thinks perhaps her hair would be nice if she wore it longer and had it permed or something. What he doesn't see is enormous good nature and great sadness.

Jane looks across at Gerouin. What strikes her most is his thinness: his hands, face, body, even his hair is meagre. She has been shocked to see (in their more intimate moments) how his ribs stick out. There is so little of him, Jane reflects, he may lose himself altogether one of these days, especially now that she won't be there to look after him. She leans over the table and pats his thin hand consolingly.

"Don't worry," she lies, "I knew it wouldn't work out really."

But she had hoped it would. Chances of men, not to mention marriage, had rarely come Jane's way. There had been a chap at university, but he had gone off quite soon, probably for much the same reason as Gerouin. There was a man she sang with in the Bach Choir, but that had never really got off the ground at all. There was not really a great deal to look forward to now: there was her flat, comfortable enough, but in rather an unsavoury neighbourhood. There was her job; that was the saving grace really. It was a rough school, but she was a good teacher. She was generally respected. She supposed she was more fortunate than many people.

She had had no illusions about Gerouin; she could see exactly what he was like, a muddler, a loser; but she wasn't: she was clear-headed and efficient. She could have managed him. He afforded an opportunity, an entry into that other life that people like that feeble Miriam enjoyed, a life where you had a husband and children; somewhere you could call a home rather than 'my flat'. When people talked about their husbands or, what was that word people used nowadays? – 'partners', she could have joined in, instead of remaining silent or pretending she had work to do. She was thirty-eight. Gerouin was probably the last chance she would get. And now that was not to be. And what about him? He was a fool not to take her. He had reached the age of thirty in a state of celibacy: after her, he would be likely to return to it. He had his mother and his videos (in an embarrassed moment he had told her of them), but he didn't even have the consolation of the job. Even in the Middle School where he taught, where the oldest child was thirteen, he could keep no sort of order; he had the respect of neither staff nor pupils. She could have solaced him for that. His life would have been infinitely better under her aegis. And yet he had refused her because of the size of her ears and nose.

"It's my mother, too," he says. Jane chomps her way through her carbonara, as if she considers the matter closed. But suddenly she puts her fork down.

"No, it's not," she says, "and I don't want to discuss it any more; but I do ask one thing. Don't tell anyone – this lot, I mean, that it's off. I don't want to give people like Miriam the chance of saying she knew I couldn't get anyone – not even you. There's only a couple of days left anyway. I'll give you the ring back when we get off the plane at Gatwick."

"Oh no, I mean yes. I shouldn't want the ring back. You must keep it, Jane."

She reflects that she might as well. He will only lose it anyway.

"I shan't say to anyone, Jane."

"Well, that's all right then. Look at this one!" (She has gone back to the book) "I don't wonder this is under lock and key."

****

"Where did Dionysus come from?" asks Fenella. They are standing in the Villa dei Misteri looking at the wall paintings of the Dionysiac mysteries. The paintings are startling because of their blood-red background and mysterious figures.

"He came from Thrace," says Michael slowly, "and then on to Attica and Boetia, sweeping like wildfire across Greece. Before you could say *omophagy*, every Lysistrata and Antigone was off up the mountain, whirling about and swinging *thyrsi* and torches, snatching up animals and devouring them alive."

"Why all the flesh-eating?" she asks.

"Well," says Michael, lighting a cigarette, "I think it was a lot like the eucharist. You eat the god and he enters into you. Or rather his power does, which, in Dionysus' case, is fertility, virility, sex, call it what you will; the power of life maybe, symbolised by the phallus and the sileni and Satyrs who are all lustful creatures. He is also, Fenella, a god who doesn't like to be ignored; remember the terrible revenge he took on Pentheus."

"Allowing his mother Agape to tear him to pieces."

"All because he ignored the power of Dionysus." He smiles at her uncertainly. He realises he is on difficult ground. He senses that Fenella does not want to talk about the Robin Box episode. Perhaps by day she can be free of it as he is free of the Underworld. As if she senses his thoughts, she says,

"I have never ignored the power of Dionysus. You could say I have been in his power for the last twenty years."

"But you're no maenad, Fen. Your hair is in a dainty ponytail, not wild and dishevelled, and you don't tear things apart. You are normally settling things down. Come and have a look at this one, the satyr playing his lyre; he looks exactly like Roy Small, doesn't he, even to the beer paunch?" They stand gazing at the wall painting and Michael returns to the subject of Dionysus. "He's Lord of the Souls. There's often bits of Dionysus myth on sarcophagi, you know."

"Well then," says Fenella, taking his hand, "there's no need to be so frightened of the Underworld, is there, with Dionysus down there?"

"Be sensible, Fen," says Michael, "he's not going to do a lot for me when I'm dead, is he?"

"Oh I don't know," says Fenella, "you're pretty irrepressible."

He takes Fen's face in his hands and kisses her, then he unties her ponytail and ties her hair back in a bunch.

"I like that better," he says.

They go and look at the rest of the paintings.

"Unveiling of the phallus," says Michael, "the flagellation of the initiate, and over there the initiate tarting herself up, god knows what for. I don't wonder the senate tried to stop the rites, do you, with their *consulatum de Bacchanalibus*?" He stops suddenly.

"That's what is was all about, wasn't it," he says, forcing her to look, "the unveiling of the phallus?" They stand quite still, looking at the blood-red paintings.

"Do you remember the cove," he says, "the day after the cave?"

"Yes," she says.

"We got that boat from dodgy Iannis and..."

"No we didn't, that was another day. We climbed down that awful steep cliff."

"And I made love to you on that beach. I remember how determined I was to make it good for you and how I came too early and..."

"But you stroked me and..."

"You tried to fight it off," says Michael. "You were trying to take my hand away so you wouldn't come. But you couldn't stop yourself. I remember you throbbing under my hands and crying out."

"I was so ashamed."

"You hid your face in the sand and sobbed and sobbed; I rolled you over and your face was all covered in sand and tears. I even thought it was funny, your crying from it being so good."

"I was ashamed," said Fenella, "of the violence of my desire for you."

Afterwards they had gone swimming and played about like children in the sea, until he had finally caught her and carried her back onto the beach. And as she felt his arms around her and his penis hard against her, and his body wet with the sea, then it was that she opened her legs unasked and drew him inside her, clumsily even, she was such a novice, but she no longer fought against her shame, but welcomed it as it engulfed her. But it was also the beginning of her enslavement to Michael. He kisses her gently.

"Time to flee," he says, "like the frightened initiates. I can see Miss Aitchinson coming."

****

Miriam has taken the bold and original step of getting a train back to Sorrento. She has had enough. The course has, as it were, come full circle, bringing her back to Miss Aitchinson. She has had to spend the morning trundling round Pompeii (again, I ask you, they'd already done it once) with Miss Aitchinson. There was simply no choice. Everyone else seems to be in pairs, William having teamed up with the Brown(e) contingent. She should never have let him go really. It had been silly of her to make a fuss about that incident in his bedroom. She had wanted a fling, after all, and she had stupidly turned it down; and then she had been stand-offish and finally there had been the bridge-playing and William had got so pally with the Brown(e)s. In fact now she looks at them so much more closely she sees that Jennifer Brown is not unattractive, quite sexy-looking in a heavy sort of way. She shouldn't wonder if William was planning something there. Well, he'd better not make the mistake he'd made with her. Anyway it was all very miserable; in fact the whole course had been horrible, really boring, too. And now, having to be paired up with Aitchinson was the last straw. The stern voice had admonished,

"Look, Miriam, there's a fine example of *opus reticulatum*. I showed Dr Thorpe-Smith that one yesterday."

Silly old bitch; she probably fancied him too.

"You don't seem very interested, Miriam," says Margaret Aitchinson sharply.

"I'm tired," said Miriam.

"Tired?" had exclaimed Miss Aitchinson, "Tired? We've hardly started."

It was then that Miriam decided to take the train back to Sorrento and do some shopping. There was the boat to be bought for Joe and Timmy. She was looking forward to that.

****

Fenella stands in the garden of the House of the Small Fountain; she is looking at the *nymphaeum*, a small, recessed shrine made of mosaic and tiny shells; there are fishes and birds and miniature sea creatures. The sun glistens on it and the light that is refracted from it is so bright that Fenella has to screw up her eyes as the colours dance in the sunbeams. Michael's arm rests lightly on her shoulder.

"What are you thinking about, Fen?" he asks.

"I was trying to remember your Emily Dickinson," she says.

"If some loving Antiquary, On Resumption Morn, Will not cry with joy 'Pompeii!', To the Hills return.' Happy Fen?"

"Yes, darling, I'm very happy." She doesn't say how there are only two days left and she cannot see into the future. Nor does he.

Chapter XXXII

The Dance

Sometimes it is better to travel than to arrive; the anticipation is superior to the event itself. Be that as it may, the course members, or at any rate, some of them, are excitedly getting ready for the dance. Miriam has been getting ready most of the day: the return from Pompeii at lunchtime was ideal really. First, she had gone to look at the toy boats; she found that they were not as expensive as she had thought, and thanks to the find in the coach, she now had enough money for two. A red one for Timmy and a blue for Joe. Then she had gone to that nice hairdresser and he really had made a good job of her hair; he has been clever, creating little tendrils - really very flattering. It is obviously successful, for the Haughty and Arrogant Man at Reception smiles at her as she passes, and makes some comment in Italian, touching his own hair, which is obviously a compliment. Miriam smiles back. It is nice to be appreciated. Not that she would want to be appreciated by any of the course members. What a lot of idiots. Once back in her bedroom she has the pleasurable business of deciding what to wear. She has a wide choice. She thinks she may be daring and wear the crimson. Then she has a look through Caroline's wardrobe to see what she's likely to wear. She looks with scorn at the dull sexless clothes within. It is extraordinary to her that anyone can have so little taste. There is little to interest her there, so she thinks she will go through Caroline's drawers and have a look and see what else she's got. She's seen her surreptitiously writing a diary; always hiding it away when she sees Miriam. It would be fun to read it. She is well-rewarded.

It makes such good reading she takes it to her bed so she can lie down and be comfortable while she reads. She has a bag of toffees to eat at the same time. This is better than trundling round Pompeii!

It details her nocturnal visit to *his* room; the dreadful disillusionment inspired by her own words (Fancy! She had no idea she's created such an effect); her subsequent feelings that Miriam had lied to her (huh!). Her feelings about Miriam (Well, really, what a sly little bitch. Jealous obviously). followed by her acceptance of Fenella as Michael's chosen one; Kate Small's words being written in capital letters 'they are very old friends'. The fact was also noted that Colin seemed to be interested in her, but, 'how can I think of anyone else when he is here?' It ends, however, on a note of optimism, 'There is going to be a dance tonight. I didn't think I'd go, but I've decided I will (will wear my red dress); who knows, he might ask me to dance.' Miriam laughs. "Fat chance," she says to herself and has another toffee. Then there are her nails to do. She puts the diary back exactly where she found it. She is good at that sort of thing.

Alice Browne thinks she will wear the grey.

"Is that wise?" asks Sally. "It's not really an evening colour." But Alice thinks it better 'at our age' not to wear anything bright.

"You have to be so careful not to look like mutton dressed as lamb," she says, eyeing Sally's purple outfit.

But Jennifer (next door) takes out her black. She has a shrewd idea she will look quite well in it.

Joe is changing his shirt; it's getting near the end of the course, and it is difficult to find anything that's halfway clean, but this one looks all right.

"You know," says Joe to Colin, "you ought to do something about your redhead."

Colin, who has put on a whole new ensemble (Joe is amazed at how many clothes he has), stops in mid shoe-lacing.

"What do you mean?" he asks. He is pleased that he is bending down over his shoes; he can avoid looking at Joe.

"Well, it's no good mooning around after her like you do. You've go to do something, be a bit physical."

Colin blushes furiously as he bends to his shoes. Little does Joe know.

"And you ought to talk to her a bit more," says Joe. "Here, do you think I should wear a tie?"

"Yes," says Colin.

"You know, ask her a bit about herself and that. And talk about yourself."

"I never know what to say," says Colin. He is on safer ground now.

"Do you, like, use the Cambridge Latin Course?" asks Joe.

"Yes. Do you want to borrow one of my ties?"

"What have you got, then? That one's all right. Can I have that, then?"

"Yes. Why were you asking about the Cambridge Latin Course?"

"Well, it's a good source of conversation. I talk to Penny about it a lot. Well, I suppose she's a bit fed up hearing about it now, but it served its turn."

"Oh, I'll remember that," says Colin. He looks at himself in the mirror. In fact, with his fresh complexion and curly brown hair, he looks very pleasant. He is smartly turned out too, money not being a major problem in his life. It is people who threaten him. It is so difficult to know what to say to them, to find something to put in the enormous gulf that exists between them and him. That is why he had brought the cups. They were something to put in that empty space. But they hadn't done much really. People were pleased enough at the time, but afterwards they didn't seem to want to talk to him any more than before. Even Caroline only seemed to half-listen to what he was saying when finally he had plucked up courage to say something. She didn't seem very happy, really. Perhaps she had something on her mind, or perhaps she was just shy like him.

"Shall we go down then?" says Joe. "We could get in a few beers before the meal."

Mr Small regards his wife uxoriously. She is dressed for the evening in a dress of pansies: they burgeon over her enormous hips, they grow to enormous length over her mighty bosom; they form a positive flower bed over her stomachs. The effect is very in keeping with Easter.

Mr Small likes colour both on himself and on his wife. Perhaps in memory of the bronze sword he found so long ago with Michael in Turkey, he likes a sheen to his clothes. His shirt is of shot silk.

"Fenella's a nice girl, isn't she?" he comments conversationally to his wife who is transferring her belongings from her handbag to a bag of matching material to the dress.

Kate grunts.

"I can't think why Michael doesn't snap her up; he's been carrying on with her for years."

"Yes," says Kate.

"Mind you, I don't think he looks well; he's aged a lot. I think this rape business worried him."

"It would do," says Kate.

"I tell you what he wants to do," says Roy. "He's concerned about that Box child. Wants to send him away to school."

"Pay for him, you mean?" asks Kate. She is applying some pink lipstick. She breathes heavily as she leans towards the mirror.

"Yes, he does things like that you know. There's a couple of Greek kids he met on Samos one year. He put them through Athens University, and then there's an old woman on Naxos; he built a house for her."

"Well," says Kate, "I think he'll run out of money soon. He must have paid Jemima a lot when he divorced her, and that Tabitha will take every penny he's got when that divorce goes through, from all I hear."

"No, I don't think so," says Roy, "he's not stupid, you know. He's got himself an American lawyer because he reckons they're years ahead of us in the States over that sort of thing. No, he wants to educate the Box child, but he's not happy about his own motives; he's worried that it's some sort of revenge on Box, taking the son away from him; but he had actually thought of it before all that other business."

"So?" says Kate. She is applying a thick layer of powder.

"Well, I said I'd go and see them – the Boxes, when I got back. I could make out it was my idea."

"There's the Jebb Trust Fund," says Kate. "If he could get a scholarship somewhere, the trust would probably make up the difference."

"I'll look into it," says Roy. "And now it's time to eat. Come on, old girl!" It would be hard to say which of the two enjoys their food more.

****

"You can borrow my heated rollers, if you like," says Miriam.

"It's all right, thank you," says Caroline.

"I had my hair done at Marcello's," says Miriam, giving it a little pat.

"It looks very nice," says Caroline politely; she hadn't noticed. "But how could you bear to miss Pompeii? Michael was doing the Villa dei Misteri..."

"Oh, the House of Mysteries, you mean," says Miriam. She thinks it affected of Caroline to call it by its Italian name. "I get tired of hearing Michael. I think he just shows off."

"Oh, Miriam, how can you say that? I think he's wonderful."

"Yes, that's pretty obvious," says Miriam, "but I shouldn't think you'd get him away from Fenella. She's got her claws firmly into him."

"I don't think that's fair."

"Well you shouldn't be so silly about him."

"I'm not," says Caroline, stung. "I just admire him, that's all." She is struck by a thought

"You haven't been reading my diary, have you?"

"Didn't know you'd got one," says Miriam, blusher in hand.

"I'm going down," says Caroline irritably. "Are you coming?"

"No," says Miriam, "I've got my eyes to do yet."

****

Michael is lying on the bed smoking, waiting for Fenella to finish getting ready. He is reading Propertius.

"'Quid iuvat ornata procedere, Vita, capillo, et tenuis Coa veste movere sinus, aut quid Orontea crines perfundere murra, teque peregrinis vendere muneribus, naturaeque decus mercato perdere cultu, nec sinere in propriis membra nitere bonis, crede mihi, non ulla tuaest medicina figurae'"

"The only trouble is," says Fenella, putting on an earring, "I don't understand it."

"Come on, Fen," he says, "you've got A level Latin. *Quid iuvat ornata procedere, vita, capillo*. What's the point, my love, going out with a trendy hairdo, and swish about silk – *coa veste*, and what's the point of all the hairspray *Orontea crines perfundere murra*, and spoil your *decus naturae* – beauty with bought stuff and, well, basically not letting me see your tits; believe me *crede mihi*... well you look fantastic, but I like you better with your clothes off. Grand bloke, Propertius. Had a lot of trouble with his woman, though."

"Cynthia?"

"Yup. Tart of the first order. Claims she couldn't cope without a man *non una nocte*."

"Not like me, then," says Fenella. She speaks without rancour. He gets up and kisses her.

"No," he says, "but there's not many like you, are there?"

****

To the course members, schooled for decades by 7.30 starts to an evening, it seems incomprehensible that here it is eleven o'clock, and things are only just beginning to get under way. Even the band, when they do finally arrive, show no apparent desire to begin playing; there is a lot of greeting of old friends, laughing, joking and imbibing of various alcoholic-looking substances. In their wake come various leather-jacketed insalubrious-looking camp followers. But eventually things begin to take shape, the dining room is cleared of tables and the band earmarks a corner for themselves and their instruments. People begin to arrive too, people other than course members; there are the elegant Italian girls with their equally elegant male counterparts, not seen since the first night. There is a large party of Germans who have sometimes been sighted at breakfast and generally disapproved of, probably more by reason of nationality than anything else. As Joe says, you do not go to Italy to mingle with Germans. There are various other spurious people whom one feels do not have anything particularly to recommend them. But, be that as it may, they all are the heterogeneous members of society, the music has started, and there is all to play for.

The music favours the slow and sentimental, particularly old pop songs many years dead, now converted to the band's languorous rhythms. Occasionally however, they do allow a more lively rhythm to predominate and to such a one, Fenella and Michael are seen disporting themselves. By and large the course members are proud of the public personae presented by Fenella and Michael. They dance extremely well and in elegance and sophistication they match up to, and even surpass the elegant Italians. It has to be admitted (even by such disparate voices as those of Margaret Aitchinson and Miriam) that Fenella looks extremely beautiful. Her hair is swept upwards and outwards, a kind of winged effect which emphasises the largeness of her eyes. The dress is black, low cut, long and clinging; it falls in folds about her hips. It shows a slender waist.

Caroline gazes at them both. Her emotion is not entirely one of envy. She sees what a difference there is between her and Fenella; but she is also glad Fenella is so beautiful. It is only right that Michael's chosen consort should have beauty. It completes her image of him.

Michael has obviously had enough of the energetic dancing; he takes Fenella by the hand and leads her from the floor. They seem to be sitting with Gino and Anna. Anna, in a dress of puce, is scowling at Gino. Gino has obviously drunk a lot and seems amused by Anna's scowling. They are joined by the Smalls, and here is Roy, always with an eye for a bit of colour, asking Anna to take a turn round the floor with him.

Miss Aitchinson stays for only a few minutes. She finds it extremely distasteful. It occurs to her that she might go and see how Percival is. Unlike Fenella she has no qualms about knocking at his door.

****

She finds Percival is up and seated at the dressing table he has converted to a desk. He has a number of texts open and appears to be writing copiously; but when she approaches he hastily puts books on top of the A4 he is writing on, and frowns.

"I am very occupied," he says. For a long time he has lain in his bed listening to the sounds of festivity below. He has anyway spent most of the day in his room, only going out to buy *panini* which he brought back to eat in solitude in his room. The diarrhoea has left him weak and depressed. Fenella had come to see him on her return from Pompeii. He had taken pleasure in telling her how his breakfast had not been sent up. Of course she had seemed very sorry about it and had personally brought him up a light supper; but that was the very least she could do. And since the supper he has lain in bed. First he had to listen to everyone in the bar cavorting – even Germans by the sound of them; and later on there was the sound of the dance band. As the dining room is at some distance from his room he cannot discern any tune, only the insistent thump, thump of the beat like some African dance. Because he has been in bed all day he does not feel remotely tired. Because he has demanded supper in his room, he cannot go down and join them, even if he wanted to; he can only lie there and listen to other people enjoying themselves – as he has done all his life.

Eventually he thinks he will get up and write some notes on Pompeii: the measurements of the tree stump had yielded something interesting, but he can't remember what, now. He sits down and looks through his papers, but because he is using the dressing table as a desk he cannot avoid continually catching sight of himself. Eventually he gives up avoiding himself and stares at his reflection. He sees a man in his mid-fifties, balding, thin-nosed, small-eyed, uninteresting, the sort you would not notice in a crowd, or even in a small group. A disappointed man, unloved and unloving. He reaches behind his pile of Thorpe-Smiths and takes out a large bottle of strega. He pours himself a generous measure.

Nor was it that he was unwilling to give or receive love, it was just that he had found love only possible in unusual places, in unusual ways. And yet he loved Classics, the Ancient World, the ordered traditional ways of learning, but that too was changing: universities and schools were full of courses bent on bringing the Ancient World alive; he didn't want it alive, he wanted it dead. He liked it that way. He liked books of grammar and lists of words and diagrams of temples with their measurements. That was sufficient in itself, what matter the people who prayed at the temple or who spoke in irregular verbs? He liked its very distance from reality. He despised Michael, seeing him as a man with a butterfly net, trying to catch bits of the Ancient World and, instead of killing them with formaldehyde and mounting them in a case, stopping only to look and let them flutter by, interested only in the touch of their wings. Dilettante! He pours out some more strega. He can feel it warm in his stomach.

And what prospect was there for him to return to in England? He had no job and his redundancy money was running out. He hated signing on and drawing the dole with the idle and illiterate, he who should be a university lecturer. But not even that solace is open to him. "You know a great number of facts, Mr Jeavons. What a pity you can't apply any of them." He picks up his pen but, although he has many, many notes on the measurements of the tree stump, somehow there doesn't seem to be any point to them. He is wondering whether to go back to bed again when Miss Aitchinson arrives. He doesn't have a great deal of time for her, but considers her the best of a bad bunch.

"Are you better?" she asks, sitting down on the bed uninvited. He frowns at this liberty.

"I thank you, yes."

"Well you haven't missed much. I'd seen all the important stuff – the *opus reticulatum*, yesterday. Dr Thorpe-Smith was airy-fairy today. Very peculiar on the Dionysiac mysteries."

"That's his trouble," (it's lovely to be able to give vein to an old grievance) "too many ideas, not enough facts."

"Quite," says Miss Aitchinson, "and then tonight there's all that silly business downstairs. I think we can do without that."

"Quite frankly I have found it very disturbing in my weakened state." Miss Aitchinson's sharp eye discerns the strega. She thinks she will infuse some note of sympathy into her words.

"I'm not surprised," she says. "It's quite unnecessary. I shall write and complain to Classic Tours."

Percival warms to her. It is good to encounter another like himself whose only means of hitting out at the world outside is by writing vituperative letters.

"Would you care for a strega?" he asks. She notices he has a number of paper cups, obviously originating from Anna's coffee machine supply. There are also two more large bottles of something decidedly alcoholic-looking behind the pile of Baiae handouts.

"That would be most acceptable," says Miss Aitchinson.

Each has a brief glance into the sad and lonely world of the other. At the back of Percival's world, Miss Aitchinson glimpses strange, flitting shapes which form themselves into grotesque and lewd figures before they dissolve into a grainy nothingness.

Percival sees Margaret's life as a long line of dreary, meaningless, repetitive tasks, unenlivened even by the grotesque shapes in his own. But he is not entirely right. After the third strega she says,

"I have met someone this holiday I had never thought to meet, not in the last thirty years anyway."

"Oh," says Percival; he is not very interested in this.

"You see," continues Margaret, more for her benefit than his; she does not mind if he listens or not, "when I was at university, I fell in love."

Percival stiffens; he does not want to hear of this.

"And I thought he was in love with me too."

Percival makes no comment; he helps himself to more strega. He does not offer any to Miss Aitchinson.

"Of course, it was all very proper, you understand, nothing unseemly, but I thought that one day we would marry. And indeed, towards the end of a term, he would all but ask me. And then he would go back home – I was never asked there, I may say; and when he came back, he would be cold and distant. It took me a while, but after a bit, I worked it out. Someone at home was very possessive. At first I thought it must be the mother, but it seemed not. It was the sister. Her name was Alice."

"Ah," says Percival, "Alice Browne."

"And she won," says Miss Aitchinson, "because he never did ask me to marry him, and we left university and went our different ways; I'll take a drop more of that, if I may." Percival pours her a small amount; he pours himself a much larger measure.

"She didn't win in the end though," continues Miss Aitchinson, taking a sip of strega, "because he did marry - apparently; he married Sally."

"They seem a pair of very unpleasant women to me," says Percival. This comment serves a dual purpose; it offers a sop to Miss Aitchinson, and gives him the sort of ease he always gets from saying something derogatory about someone.

"Yes," says Miss Aitchinson triumphantly, "fancy giving me up and settling for that."

"Ah," says Percival. It is a difficult comment to make a reasoned response to. He drains his glass.

"But what I can't understand is how the friend Jennifer fits into it all," continues Miss Aitchinson. She has spent many a night while Penny writes postcards to her husband, puzzling on the intricacies of it all.

Percival makes no reply; he is back amongst his own thoughts. His hand moves to the bottle.

"I have been wondering," continues Miss Aitchinson, pursuing her train of thought remorselessly, "whether she is having an affair with *him*. And, in that case, why she is on this course with *them*."

"Does it matter?" asks Percival coldly. He feels rather odd.

"It matters to me," replies Margaret, firing up, "I've led a lonely life since I left university. I've never met anyone else I wanted to marry. I've often thought about her, this woman who put a stop to my marriage, and wondered about her. And now I've seen her - and she is nothing. Nothing," she reiterates triumphantly. "And even though he married, he never got away from *her*."

"Perhaps he will now," says Percival, reluctantly drawn into the conversation, "with this Jennifer."

"No," says Miss Aitchinson triumphantly, "Never. He has walled himself in with the sister and the wife. He is immured."

"One leads a more satisfactory life on one's own," says Percival.

"No," says Margaret, "not really. I should like to have someone, shouldn't you?" For the first time she looks directly at him.

He gives a great sigh as if his heart would burst. Suddenly he is busy putting on a jacket, checking his wallet.

"I'm going out," he says.

"But you can't!" She is shocked. "It's late, and you haven't been well. I should feel responsible." She has also been watching the amount of strega he has drunk. She has observed that it has not been meted out in equal measure.

For a moment he is almost touched that another human being is concerned about him, but then he reflects it is merely a fear of responsibility.

"I shan't be long," he says. "I'll knock on your door when I'm back, so you needn't worry." She is unconvinced.

"Remember Naples," she says, "how you were attacked."

"You must excuse me," he says. The strega is warm in his stomach. There is a place in the harbour. He has heard Gino and Michael laughing about it. And although he has no Italian, some languages are universal.

****

It is very difficult indeed for Miriam. Never did she think she would wish for the company of Miss Aitchinson, but Margaret has withdrawn upstairs and now Miriam is on her own. She looks round, desperately seeking someone to latch on to. Ah, what would she not now give for the attentions of William - any William; but he and the Brown(e)s have also disappeared. The word 'bridge' was murmured. Can you imagine anything as silly as playing bridge at eleven o'clock at night? Jane and Gerouin seem to have been joined by Joe and Penny. Miriam can hear a lot of laughter coming from their table. She wouldn't want to join them anyway. Look at Jane. She's actually wearing a dress - if you can call it that. She looks worse than she does in her tracksuits.

She doesn't dare join the Fenella and Michael contingent. She remembers how Fenella comforted her on the first morning. She feels embarrassed about that and, besides, she doesn't want to play second fiddle to her. She doesn't like Kate Small. She had made an unkind comment about Miriam sitting in the coach instead of going round Pompeii. And all the time she was sitting there herself! And though she is quite sure Kate was asleep on the coach yesterday, she makes her feel really uncomfortable. After all, if she hadn't found the money, someone else would have done. She wouldn't want to associate with that low-class Anna in her vulgar dress. So that leaves Colin and Caroline. Perhaps she can entice Colin away from Caroline. That would serve her right for accusing her of looking at her diary.

She is just making her way through the throng of Germans to join Caroline and Colin when she is accosted. Yes, actually accosted!

"You would like to dance with me?" It is the Haughty and Arrogant Young Man from Reception. He has marked her down as easy meat. It amuses him how little resistance they put up, these earnest young English women.

"You have very beautiful eyes," he says. Miriam smiles. William never told her that, nor had her husband either, come to that. It's amazing how perceptive these Italians are.

"Thank you," she smiles at him, "I should love to dance." As she is taken round the floor – he holds her so beautifully – she can look with contempt at the Carolines and Janes of life.

The band are past masters at schmaltz. They revel in it; they smoke, they drink, they play, they sing. They fill the dining room with sentimentality and bogus emotionalism. Everyone adores it.

"Roy," says Michael, "I'm going to make you terribly jealous and ask your wife for a dance." Roy nods accommodatingly; he knows Kate doesn't dance. But he underrates the power of Michael's smile. Not even Kate can resist him. Because of her size Michael puts a hand on each of her hips and guides her smoothly round the floor. She is amazingly light on her feet.

"Well," says Kate, as they move to Frank Sinatra's *My Way*, "you have always done it your way, Michael. Are you going to continue to do so?"

"You're the soothsayer, Kate," says Michael, smiling at her, "you tell me." But Kate refuses to be drawn.

Afterwards he sits very close to Fenella with his arm along the back of her chair. They have all six of them drunk several bottles of Chianti and are on to the strega.

"I find you overwhelmingly attractive, Fenella Sykes," says Michael. "I would like to make love to you."

"With," says Fenella. He is momentarily thrown.

"With?"

"You always used to say 'with'," says Fenella, "make love with rather than 'to'. I found that quite irresistible."

Anna is pulling the reluctant Gino on to the floor. She wants to be dancing. The puce dress is bursting at the seams.

"You would ask me," says Fenella, "if I wanted to make love with you."

"Too many prepositions." He bends down and kisses her neck. "Mmm?" he asks interrogatively.

"Mm," she replies, "but we can't go yet."

"Why not?"

"Because I must see everyone is happy."

"I'm not happy..."

"Yes, but you will be."

"Promise?"

She looks at him as she has always looked at him at such moments, with her eyes enormous and her pupils dilated.

"Michael..."

"Fen."

Roy Small leans across.

"Young Caroline looks fed up," he says.

They look across at her. Michael doesn't much care, but Fenella feels the tug of duty.

"You'll have to go and dance with her, Michael."

"Oh, no!"

"Yes. She must have something to take back with her. Some memory; something to tell her friends about."

Caroline doesn't like such occasions as these. Most of the time people's sexuality can be hidden beneath the surface. She can usually pretend it's not there at all. It's like putting all her books in her school bag. Generally they fit neatly inside, but sometimes they fall out, as if they refuse to be contained any longer. She dreaded it at school if the girls had a disco; even with all girls, there is this terrible simmering thing in the air. It is days before they all quieten down. She herself feels untouched by it, but frightened of it. Michael's question had been very terrifying to her. And now this dance is threatening as well. She is so glad to be there with Colin who is not like that at all – but oh dear, he is dreadfully hard work.

Emboldened by beers with Joe earlier on, wine with the meal and strega after, Colin feels a new rush of confidence with regard to Caroline.

"I like your hair," he says boldly.

"Oh, thank you," says Caroline. He has said that before, though, in Capri. This does not seem a very promising lead, and Colin is racking his brains when he remembers Joe's words.

"Do you use the Cambridge Lain Course at school?" he asks. It is quite a long question for him.

"No," says Caroline, "we use 'Marcus et Tullia'."

"Oh," says Colin. Nothing has prepared him for this reply.

"Is that good then?" he asks at last.

"Not really," says Caroline.

Then he thinks of a question so bold he is almost stunned by the audacity of it.

"We, that is, the school, has a dinner dance at the end of the Summer Term. Would you like to come? I mean, it wouldn't cost anything and..."

"You must forgive me," says Michael, "but I have to borrow your beautiful red-haired friend for a few minutes." He smiles rather drunkenly at Caroline.

"Could you bear to dance with me, Caroline?"

All Caroline's wishes and desires rush together at one fell swoop: all the emotion she has felt every time she has looked at his photo on the back of *Horace, The Man As Lover*, all the feelings of hope and disappointment she has cherished this week, all the feelings she experienced when she heard him talking in the Villa dei Misteri, all the fear she felt from his question, and a realisation that here is the consummation of all that she has written in her diary.

Her bag falls to the ground with a great clatter, her comb and lipstick roll out. What does she care?

"Oh yes, oh yes, please," she says. Colin goes and gets another drink.

"Have you enjoyed this course, Caroline?" asks Michael. He holds her close, but not very close.

"Oh yes," she says, "it's been wonderful."

"Super," he says. Over Caroline's shoulder he can see Fenella being chatted up by Gino; he has drunk enough to feel slightly possessive about her. He will take her upstairs when he's done his duty with Caroline. It will be the first time since the Box incident.

"And what has been your very best thing?" He looks down at her and smiles his golden smile. "Honestly," he says. He wishes he had a cigarette.

"Oh, well, I think it was when you took us round Pompeii," She hardly dare look up at him; she can barely believe now that she is in his arms. "You made it all so real somehow."

He is about to say 'super' again, when it strikes him that she deserves something better. This, after all, is what matters to him - to recreate the past, and it seems that it matters to this plain red-haired girl too.

"Yes," he says, "it's all there, we have to work at it to make it come alive. Sometimes it's difficult to see a house from a broken column, difficult to see a street from a house, and to see a whole town - well, that takes a superman - or a superwoman."

She gazes at him with eyes almost as dilated as Fenella's. She wants this to go on forever.

"And did you find your Munacius Plancus?" he asks benevolently. He remembers vaguely that she had come to his room and he had pointed her in the direction of someone.

"Oh yes," she says, "oh yes, I did." She grips his arm tightly.

"And here he is," says Michael, stopping abruptly by Colin. "Look, you've dropped your bag. Let me."

He picks up the comb and lipstick and puts them carefully inside, and hands her the bag.

"Thank you for a lovely dance, Caroline."

She sees him leave with Fenella shortly afterwards. His arm is round her, and his fingers move across her hips in a way that they had not done when he had been dancing with her.

"I think I'm going up now," she says to Colin. "I'll say goodnight."

"Oh, right," he says. She had completely forgotten his question.

****

"Oh god, Fenella," says Michael.

"Oh Michael," says Fenella.

They are standing just inside her room and he is pushing down her dress from her shoulders.

Fenella too is consumed with desire; she has forgotten that anything had been distasteful to her, she sees only the man she has loved on Ithaca, in Rome, in Athens, on Crete, in a score of places, whom she has desired unremittingly for twenty years, each loving and each separation intensifying the feelings she has for him. She cannot think of the future. She only knows she wants the present.

Michael, too, feels the overwhelming sense of Fenella's attraction to him intermingled with his feelings of guilt for the suffering he has inflicted on her over the years. As her head goes back, he bites her neck. He can feel her heart fluttering beneath her breasts. She reaches for him.

"Please," she says, "please..."

There is a knocking at the door. Fenella stiffens.

"Leave it," he says, his hand on her breast.

"I can't," says Fenella. "I have to... I'll get rid of them."

He shrugs and lets her go. He feels around for cigarettes.

Fenella, rearranging her dress, goes to the door. It is Miss Aitchinson.

"Yes?" says Fenella. She feels resentment, not for herself and her thwarted desire, but for him. Miss Aitchinson has prevented something wonderful. And there she stands, sexless in her candlewick dressing gown. Michael, who as if to assert his presence and deny her recognition, says,

"Where did I put my cigarettes, Fenella?"

"Jacket pocket," she replies. "Yes, Miss Aitchinson?"

"I'm sorry to disturb you," she says, looking past Fenella at Michael, who is now lighting a cigarette, "I'm rather worried – it's Percival."

"Percival? Has he been taken ill again?" asks Fenella. The weight of her desire lightens and her public persona forms itself around her.

"No," says Miss Aitchinson carefully, "at least I don't think so. He's disappeared."

"Disappeared?" says Fenella.

"He's not in his room," says Miss Aitchinson.

"Oh, I shouldn't worry," says Fenella. "There could be a thousand reasons for that." Michael has picked up a book and is turning pages rapidly, as if to look something up.

"Well, it's not as simple as that," says Margaret firmly. There is something in her tone that makes Fenella say,

"You'd better come in." Michael nods briefly from the window seat.

"We were talking," says Miss Aitchinson, "about rather personal matters. We had imbibed some alcoholic substance – and we were speaking of loneliness, and suddenly he said he was going out – it was about eleven o'clock, and I said I thought it unwise, and he said he wouldn't be long and he would knock my door to show he was back. I waited until one, and then I went and knocked, and it wasn't locked, so I went in and he wasn't there."

"Well," says Fenella. Michael gets up.

"When did you say he went?"

"About half past eleven," says Miss Aitchinson firmly.

"All right," says Michael, "I'll sort it out. You go back to your room."

"I would... Will you go...?"

"Yes," says Michael, "immediately."

Fenella looks worried.

"Do you know where he's gone?" she asks.

"I have a shrewd idea," says Michael. "Now, don't worry, Margaret. The best thing you can do is go and get some sleep." He is putting on his jacket.

"I'll come," says Fenella, but Michael shakes his head. "No, Fenella. I'll see if I can get Gino. If not, I'll go on my own. I shouldn't want you to go there."

Miss Aitchinson stands staring at them, uncertain as to what is going on.

Fenella says, "Michael."

"I'll be as quick as I can," he says, checking his pockets for cigarettes. "Sorrento isn't a very big place." He kisses her lightly and is gone. The two women look at each other.

"Will it be somewhere... peculiar?" asks Margaret.

"I think it might," says Fenella. "Shall I walk to your room with you?"

But Miss Aitchinson, heroine of Naples, doesn't need that sort of attention.

Fenella tries to stay awake, but she has drunk a lot of Chianti and eventually she drifts off to sleep, and when she wakes in the morning, Michael is heavily asleep at her side. There is a note on the dressing table: 'It's all right. He's back. Please let me sleep as long as poss. M'.

Although she is relieved, Fenella wishes he had written 'love, M'.

Chapter XXXIII

Amalfi

At breakfast there is no Percival, and people look decidedly the worse for wear. Fenella tells them they will leave at ten for Amalfi. She hopes everyone will make a big effort to be on time as there is a busy day ahead: Amalfi in the morning and Paestum in the afternoon. It should make a memorable last day. The words 'last day' have a hollow ring in her ears. As if to endorse the feeling of melancholy, the weather has taken a turn for the worse. The air is nippy and there is a light drizzle falling.

Fenella takes a cup of coffee up to Michael. He must sleep no longer.

As always in the mornings he passes rapidly from sleep to consciousness; he stares at her as if he does not see Fenella in her soft coral-coloured sweater and long cream skirt, but as if he sees something foul.

"You found him?" says Fen.

"I found him."

She hands him his coffee. Sadly she sees he does not wish to touch her.

"Was it... ?" He puts his coffee down so violently it slops into the saucer and on the bedside table, forming a murky brown pool.

"Horrible," he says. He reaches across Fenella for cigarettes. Fenella says nothing, sitting in her coral-coloured sweater on the edge of the bed with her hands in her lap.

"I don't mind," he says, lighting up, and looking through Fenella, "what people do, what their sexual mores are, but I don't want to bloody have to witness it. What I've seen, what I've seen, don't ever ask me, Fen."

And for the first time that morning Fenella knows that he recognises her because he remembered to call her by name; he is coming back to her the way he comes back to her from his dreams, from first century Pompeii and from the Underworld.

"What you said after Box, the darkness, the repugnance you felt for it all. I can understand that now."

"Drink your coffee, darling."

Gradually she comes into focus, Fenella in her soft coral-coloured sweater with her hands folded.

"You have such serenity, Fenella. You are so composed. Poor Fen."

"Why poor?" asks Fenella. She is frightened of what he may mean.

"Nothing. I didn't mean anything. I know I have to get up. We are going to Amalfi. May I plait your hair first? It would help."

She brings him brush and comb and sits down for him.

"Lot of darkness, Fen," he says as he plaits.

"How did you get him out, back, whatever?" asks Fenella.

"When I found him... when I worked out... when I... I told him the police were coming. I put my arm through his... the arm of the man who had been... I dragged him out. I pushed him into a taxi, I heaved him out at the other end. I gave him to the night porter. I couldn't take any more – then I came up here – I had to shower before I could come near you, and you were in bed, sweetly asleep, and even after I'd showered I felt I couldn't come near you; but I did anyway because I knew that was what you would have wished. And now I must get up and go to Amalfi. You look nice in coral. I like it." He shakes his hair back; he is trying to get back to normal.

"What shall we do about him, today I mean?" asks Fen. It is better to lead Michael away from yesterday.

"Oh, leave him to skulk about in his room. He'll probably write to some Classical Society or other, about the measurements of Pompeii – I don't think he'll be writing about last night. He may even have forgotten – he was very pissed. That's the bloody irony – he may forget, but it's with me for always."

Fenella nods. She knows only too well.

"Well," says Michael, "yes... it's the same for you, isn't it. But worse."

"Time to get up, darling," says Fenella, "we must go at ten."

"We must go at ten," he repeats, "it sounds like something out of T S Eliot, doesn't it?" She smiles and kisses him lightly. He runs a finger down her coral sweater.

"Last day, Fen." It is the first time he has broached the subject.

"Not quite," she says.

"No," he says and gets up. He looks very tired.

There is not much talking in the coach. There is a strange feeling of being placed between two worlds. They are travelling along the high coastal road and the cliffs drop sheer to the sea, the day is cold, wet and misty, and the combination of the sea and the cliffs and the winding road (along which Gino drives with a grim expression on his face) gives a general sense of unreality. There is a feeling that only within the coach is reality: its racks bulge with now familiar possessions (they can even identify whose rucksack is whose, whose camera has that jutting-out bit, whose mac has the belt which, hanging from the rack, takes a swipe at you as you pass). Even this reality has a kind of unreality; for, although it is home to them now, tomorrow it and they, will part, never to be reunited. Tomorrow the coach and its passengers and the bags will become part of the past; will become as if they have never been. For a while the coach will have a lingering presence in their minds, but soon too that will pass, Italy will pass, and the only reality will be the familiar grey routine that has been theirs for so long. For most, it will be a return to school life and colleagues who will preserve about their persons an awful and inevitable sameness, whose indifference to the Southern Italy Course will begin to blot it out as if it had never been.

Miriam, who usually has a magazine about her into which she buries her head and ignores Italy, is unencumbered today. She stares out at the wooded slopes and the sea below, but whether that is what she sees is another matter. Sometimes a little smile plays on her lips. Perhaps she is thinking of her two small sons and their English father, or perhaps she is not. She may perhaps be reflecting on the nature of Italy and its people.

Unlikely as it might seem, Miriam may have experienced more of the essential Italy than any of them.

From where Caroline is sitting, she can see Michael's head has moved on to Fenella's shoulder. She supposes wearily that he is tired out with making love to her (she eschews that other word). But she too has had her moment of glory; she has been in his arms, albeit briefly. It will be something to tell her friend (with perhaps a few embellishments) when she returns to school. She wonders where Miriam got to last night; she certainly wasn't with William. She had seen him playing bridge with the Brownes. Perhaps she was with Miss Aitchinson; they seemed to have gone round Pompeii together, and Miss Aitchinson left quite early last night.

Jane reflects that the hours are running out when she may be reckoned as one half of a pair. It has been sweet to have had this precious experience that comes to others so lightly. But when she looks at Gerouin, rummaging through his rucksack for something which isn't there, she thinks that perhaps things have turned out for the best.

Miss Aitchinson turns over the events of the previous night in her mind. Because of the strega she cannot remember too clearly her conversation with Percival, but she dimly comprehends that they had both touched upon something that was raw and sore within them. And then he had gone. Where had he gone, and why? She thinks of those vague and sinister shapes that had presented themselves to her when he was speaking of his life. It was not simply that he was lonely as she was. There was something discordant there. Something untoward. Why had he not come back? Where had Michael gone? Fenella had come in the morning and told her Percival was back, but not to be disturbed. Fenella had said he was unwell. There had been something forbidding in Fenella's expression.

How worried she had been! And Penny was not in bed either. She didn't get in till very late, but she was kind when she did. She had told Margaret not to worry. Everything would be all right. She seemed quite a different woman from the nervous unhappy person of last week with her rolls of lavatory paper. She had seemed quite ebullient last night, even putting her arm around her. It must be the thought of going back to that errant husband of hers. It would be nice to have a husband to go back to. (She hopes Gino knows what he's doing; the coach gave a nasty lurch there) If it hadn't been for Alice Browne she might have had one too. She would get to the bottom of the Brown(e) mystery today.

Colin thinks about the notice he had found on his door when he had reached his room (not long after Caroline). It was a piece of paper folded in half with 'Colin' written on the outside. Inside it had said, 'Could you lose yourself until about 3.00? i.e. NOLI INTRARE. Cheers, Joe.' Colin had gone out, sat downstairs for another hour and drunk another few stregas. He wished he'd never bothered bringing the cups. It had been a miserable sort of course.

Gerouin watches Fenella's coral breasts move up and down. He wishes it was his head on her shoulder.

The Smalls are both sound asleep. They occupy the whole of the back seat.

"I think you have to talk about Amalfi, darling," says Fenella, nudging Michael into consciousness, "we're about there."

He wakes immediately and smiles. His sleep has refreshed him. His cheeks are flushed and he opens his eyes wide.

"But, Fen, I don't know anything about Amalfi. It's Byzantine; I'm only a Classicist; I'm six centuries too early."

"But Michael," says Fenella, opening her eyes as wide, "you know about everything."

"So I do," he says, reaching for the microphone.

"Ladies and gentlemen," he says, "and Kate and Roy on the back seat, wake up! We are almost at Amalfi. If you're like me you won't know anything about King Roger of Naples, but he came and took a share of the pickings at Amalfi in the mid-twelfth century – sounds quite modern, doesn't it, after all we've seen." He smiles goldenly. Fenella knows he is racking his brains for something to say. But it will be all right. "At that time the doges," he continues more cheerfully, "ruled Amalfi, powerful ecclesiastical men, rogues and twisters with their fingers on the helm of state – a massively wealthy state, sending ships all over the world, trading with the orient. Imagine the spices and silks coming into the harbour here, seventy thousand people it supported. But where there's money there's strife and Amalfi fell to the Pisans and its glory was spent. And in..." he narrows his eyes and considers. Fenella thinks he is probably making this up... "1343 the ancient town itself fell into the sea. Peripeteia. But merchants from Amalfi built a hospital in Jerusalem which became the HQ of those sinister Crusader Knights. But what makes Amalfi special for me..." this will be true, thinks Fenella, "is the fact that it is the home of the luckless Joannah of Aragon, wife of the Duke of Amalfi whom we meet in Webster's horrific and magnificent play *The Duchess of Malfi*. What other play do you know whose cast includes eight mad men and contains the line 'one met the Duke 'bout midnight in a lane behind St Marks' church with the leg of a man upon his shoulder and he howled fearfully. Said he was a wolf'?"

He gazes at them triumphantly. In spite of what he has said to Fenella he knows a good deal about post-Classical history and literature. He hates narrowness of outlook, a blinkered vision, the measuring of post-holes. He loves to link things together and find continuity between one age and another.

"When you walk round Amalfi remember these incestuous dukes and doges, the poisonings, the secret midnight despatching of unwelcome courtiers; the struggle for power, the darkness of the human heart." He pauses and looks round at them and thinks of the one whose darkness he has so recently discovered.

"But what you will want to see," he continues, "will be the cathedral. You will want to go down to the crypt – you have to knock at the gate for entrance – and underneath the altar in the crypt you will find the body of St Andrew which someone carted here from Constantinople in the thirteenth century. Poor bloke, why couldn't they leave him be?

"But best of all are the cloisters with their delicate arches. There is something a little Moorish about them. I think them quite lovely." He smiles and sits down.

The stern voice of Fenella is heard, bidding them be back on the coach at twelve.

Caroline lingers a little, hoping they will perhaps ask her to join them. She hopes in vain, time is running out and Fenella does not wish to share these precious last hours with a third party. She smiles brightly, including the dilatory Colin in her greeting.

"What are you two going to do first?" she asks. "Hang on," she calls after Gerouin, "you've dropped something." She retrieves a biro. It seems as if Jane is becoming less vigilant.

Miss Aitchinson stops before descending the coach steps and looks at Fenella. There is appeal in her eyes.

"Will he be all right?" she asks uncertainly. Even she seems to realise that it is not a question to which she can expect an easy answer.

"I think you'll find," says Michael, "that he's as right now as ever he will be."

Gino has heard something of the night's events from heaven knows what sources. He asks Michael a question.

"No, Gino," says Fenella, "*Lui non vuole parlarne.*"

But Gino, who is without Anna, is loath to be put off.

Fenella's Italian is good, but it is not as good as Michael's. It pours from him; Fenella is not able to follow all of it. A number of words are unfamiliar to her. But it seems that Gino too does not want to hear any more. He makes various gestures of rebuttal, shakes his head and puts the radio on, as if to expunge from his mind what he has heard.

"Do you want to do the cathedral?" asks Fenella of Michael.

"No," says Michael, "I want to drink five cappuccinos in quick succession and sit opposite your coral sweater in a tourist cafe."

"Tell me about the Duchess," says Fenella when Michael has downed three of his five cappuccinos.

"Well," says Michael, lighting up and indicating to the waiter that he would like more coffee, "I imagine her looking rather like you when you put your hair up; and like you she had a lot to put up with - trouble, I mean, not hair - even more than you. I wish you still smoked, Fen. It's horrid smoking on my own."

"Go on," says Fen.

"Well, the duchess was a widow, and when she married her steward secretly, her brother Ferdinand didn't like that at all because he was in love with her himself. So basically he decided to drive her mad: he let out all the inhabitants of the local asylum to come and disport themselves about her, he sent his creature Bosola in to torment her. Finally he killed her husband and her children, and got someone to strangle her."

"Is he sorry afterwards?" asks Fenella.

"Well yes, he is, but then he goes mad himself and someone kills him. But it didn't go on for twenty years."

"What didn't?"

"Her being tortured like you." He is on his fifth cup now.

"I haven't been tortured," says Fenella carefully. "I've just been very sad when you're withdrawn from my life." She looks at him and smiles her sweet smile.

"Fen," says Michael, "there's something... oh god, there's the Brownes... Let's go and look at the cloisters."

Echoes reverberate around Fenella's brain. "My lovely Fen, I wouldn't ask you to forgive me if I didn't know you to be better and kinder than other people... I have something to tell you, Fen..."

"Michael..."

"Not now, Fen. It was nothing anyway."

He puts down a note of large denomination.

"Come on. We'll give St Andrew a miss."

"I suppose," says Fenella, "the crypt is a bit like the Underworld."

"Yes," he says, "I'd hate to meet St Andrew in my dreams. I've always loathed golf." She knows there's absolutely no point in pursuing his earlier comment. He takes her hand and they walk towards the cloisters.

"Look, Fen," he says as they enter, "it's all white and wimpled like a nun, like a row of nuns. You know in Flemish painting when the women have long high foreheads." He is talking of the cloisters; he cannot believe how ethereal and slender they are.

"*Chiostro del Paradiso*," says Fenella. "Is it your idea of paradise, Michael?" He takes a minute to consider.

"I have always been very rooted in the earth, Fen, worldly, fleshly. I find the thought of relinquishing these earthy, earthly things very hard – even after last night, even after Box; there is something very compelling about the body and the satisfying of its needs – but if, Fen, one could get beyond that, become pure spirit spiralling upwards with the arches of the cloister, perhaps that would be paradise. I don't know."

"If you reduced everything to spirit," says Fenella, "there would be no need to fear the Underworld."

He puts his arm round her shoulders.

"The trouble is, Fen," he has been serious for long enough, "I can't at this moment imagine a paradise that didn't contain your body in it – especially with the coral sweater on."

She longs to ask him about the future, but dare not. They stand for some time, he with his arm around her shoulder, gazing at the delicately sweeping Saracen arches and the wild green grasses that grow in the cloister garth.

"You know the beatitudes, Fen: blessed are the pure in heart and so on?"

"Mm."

"Well, I think of you like that, pure in heart. I think you'll see God."

"What are you saying, Michael?"

"I don't know. I hate woolly thinking and now I am guilty of it myself. I suppose I am trying to say that words in this century have become debased. You, I think, would be comforted if I could express my feelings for you in conventional terms – if I could speak of 'devotion' or 'love', but to me such words are meaningless – they are like advertisements you see on every hoarding, or on every magazine page, they are like freebies found in every hotel bedroom. They are too glib and facile. I cannot use them..."

Fenella stands totally still; he has never made a declaration of love to her before. And this is surely what it is.

"I can speak only in metaphor, Fen." He takes her by the shoulders and impatiently pushes back the loose hairs that are escaping from the great plait at her neck.

"To me you are the soaring arch, the wimpled nun, the woman in the Arnolfini wedding, Ariadne, the Duchess of Amalfi, the very stones of the temple of Apollo at Cumae. And..." he looks tired and strained, "whatever, that is the truth, Fenella."

She puts her head down into his chest. She can no longer look at the nakedness in his eyes.

A passing priest taps them angrily on the shoulders. It seems you do not embrace in the *Chiostro del Paradiso*.

Chapter XXXIV

Paestum

"Paestum," says Michael, "the city of Neptune, being originally Possidonia and Latinised by the Lucanians to Paestum in the fourth century BC. It was a Greek Colony, founded by the Sybarites in the sixth century. So I want you to think of it as very ancient and very Greek. Famous for roses – why do I think of Adonis? – roses blooming twice, once in spring and once in the autumn..." He looks at his audience: Roy Small, with a somewhat cynical look upon his leonine face, Miriam applying lipstick with the aid of a tiny mirror, Gerouin looking vacuous, Caroline horribly attentive and Fenella soft in coral, to whom he has spoken such words as a man speaks to his mistress. He smiles and the lock of hair falls over his forehead.

"'While the Rose blows along the River Brink, With old Khayyam the Ruby Vintage drink: And when the Angel with his darker Draught, Draws up to Thee – take that, and do not shrink' Which of us is strong enough to do that?" he asks.

Fenella longs to pluck him from the Underworld, and always it seems as if she can, and always he slips back into it.

Miriam, who has snapped her mirror shut, thinks how silly he has become. Then she yawns. She is feeling very sleepy.

"And violets," he says, "it was famous for violets. What a lovely verdant place full of roses and violets. Imagine it in late spring.

"Gradually it fell into decay, not falling into the sea like Amalfi, but falling to malaria and the Saracens. The years crept over it and it wasn't until the eighteenth century that it was discovered amidst a tangle of vegetation while they were building a coach road, for the Grand Tour, I suppose. Think of finding Paestum!"

Jane thinks he is waffling; she wants some facts. As if he reads her mind, he says,

"We enter the city by the Porto della Giustia and follow the Via Sacra, and on the right we shall see what the eighteenth century Crusaders thought was a basilica; actually it is the Temple of Hera. I have some handouts for you on the Temple of Hera and also the Temple of Neptune. The Temple of Hera is sixth century. There is something..." he pauses; he looks solemnly at them, "something so majestic, so primitive, so ancient about the two temples, that you will never forget them. They will become part of you. You must also, of course, see the rest of the site, nor must you forget the museum, most especially the paintings from the Tomb of the Diver."

Fenella suggests they may like to lunch in the restaurant at the museum. Gino is certainly going to do so.

"Then I shall sleep," he says. Fenella does not altogether like to think of a tired Gino driving back along the tortuous coastal road. They must be back at four, she says.

There is a presence, a majesty in the old, the *really* old that demands respect, that has no time for the trivial and the petty. The mighty temples at Paestum, built twenty-five centuries ago, look on unblinking, unmoved by life or death or birth. They have seen too many aeons of men and beasts to account them of any worth.

The course members, intent as they are on getting their last Italian lunch, cannot hasten away as they intended, with the Temple of Poseidon looming down on them. Even Miriam hesitates uneasily before the massive Doric columns.

"That prat Percival Jeavons would have plenty to measure with that tape of his," says Joe to Penny.

"Where is he?" she asks.

"Well, I did hear..."

"Overhear?" asks Penny, laughing.

"Well, yes, if you like. Michael was talking to Gino. Well, as you know, I've got a bit of Italian – it struck me that he was somewhere not very nice last night."

"What happened then?" asks Penny.

"I dunno," responds Joe, "I think Michael got him out. He looks knackered, doesn't he?"

"Yes," says Penny, "but he's got those sort of looks, hasn't he? Sort of world-weary."

"I suppose you think him very good-looking?" he asks irritably.

"Well, looks aren't everything," says Penny and takes his arm (the one without the tripod).

Kate and Roy stand looking at the Temple of Hera. It has fifteen massive fluted Doric columns.

"It is wonderful," says Roy, "to see something built on the same scale as ourselves."

"Let's have lunch," says Kate. "I remember having a particularly succulent *maiale al latte* last time we were here."

They do not hurry because, when you are the size of Kate and Roy, you move heavily and surely towards your lunch.

Although Miss Aitchinson has been happy without her stick for some days, she has, of course, had Percival in its stead. Now she has neither. She has a feeling that she will not have Percival's company again. She misses the stick as she walks around the ruined temples. She is less interested in the temples, however, than in joining the Brown(e)s.

Sally thinks that Doric must always be the finest of the three orders of columns; Alice prefers the slender Ionic. Jennifer thinks Corinthian a happy compromise.

Margaret catches up with them by the temple precinct.

"I did know your brother," she says, sternly addressing Alice.

"I know," says Alice triumphantly, "Maggie, he used to call you."

All three Brown(e)s stare at her.

"Did you know my husband?" asks Sally.

"I expect they met at a Classics conference," says Jennifer, "perhaps the SMCA."

The columns of the temple stand imposing before them. The four ladies look very small beneath them.

"No," says Margaret, "I knew him at university. I might have married him once." She stares fixedly at the columns.

"I don't think so," says Sally, the wife. "There was nobody before me."

"Oh yes there was," says Alice. She has very small eyes, but they dart fire. "He liked *her* much more than you. That's why," she extends a scrawny hand to indicate Sally, "that's why I let him marry you, because you were nothing to him." Sally remains silent. Perhaps there is nothing in Alice's comments that she does not already know.

There is great quietness. The steps to the temple are massive grey slabs. There is nothing thc women can say that will move them. It is perhaps the impassivity of the temple that encourages Jennifer to speak.

"But he liked none of you," she says, "as well as me."

The three of them stare at her in amazement.

"What can you mean?" asks Sally, the wife, at last. She is tall and dark. She knows a great deal apparently, about fourth century Athens.

"She means," says the sister, "she has been carrying on with Stuart right under your nose." She is a plain woman, Alice. The pink blouse and anorak give her an insipid air. She is the most insignificant of women.

The four women stand on the steps of the Temple of Poseidon. It is one of the three best-preserved temples in Europe. They do not stand out against it. What might have proved a mighty issue to all four of them seems strangely inconsequential here.

"Jennifer and I teach at the same school," says Sally, turning to Margaret Aitchinson, "it's not very likely, is it?" She speaks without interest.

"Why don't you ask me?" says Jennifer.

They look at her with unease.

"Oh yes," she says. "Stuart and I fixed to come on this course." She turns to Margaret. "He's my Head of Department, but," she still looks in the direction of Alice, "*She* had to put her oar in."

"Do you live together then?" asks Miss Aitchinson, "the three of you. Does he live with his wife and sister?"

"Of course," says Alice, "he would never have left me."

"So that is why," says Sally the wife, "you suggested we went as well?"

"Only then," says Jennifer bitterly, "he decided he wouldn't come after all."

"He has always been weak," says his wife. "He's always done what she says."

Alice smiles triumphantly.

"How odd," says Margaret slowly, "that all four of us have wanted to have him to ourselves, and not one of us has succeeded."

She walks up the temple steps. She has discovered what she wanted to know. It would not have worked, then, being married to him. It was better, Percival had said, to be on your own. She was very well as she was. Michael's handout tells her that the temple is hexastyle peripteron with thirty-six fluted columns. What a pity Percival isn't here to count them.

"I don't know how you can have been so treacherous, Jennifer," says Sally. Her dark eyes are troubled. It is the perfidy of the friend she minds rather than her husband's infidelity. This latter is of little interest to her.

"She didn't get very far," says the sister, "I saw to that." She is pinched-looking and unpleasant. She works in the county library. She is very good at chasing up lost books.

"But there might have been," says Jennifer, looking through the mighty columns at the mountains beyond, "there might have been something wonderful."

As the two sisters-in-law look at her, they see a flicker in her eye and a flush on her cheek; for a moment they see an attractive woman, almost a *femme fatale*. But the moment passes, and they see only the heavy features of a rather uninteresting woman. They cannot stand on the steps of the temple forever, and really no great harm has been done.

"Look," says Sally after they have stood awkwardly together, "the pediments are quite intact."

"No," says Alice, "there is one in ruins over there."
Jennifer hesitates a moment, only a moment, and then comments, "The entablature is so well-preserved, what a pity the roof has gone."

****

Fenella has not succeeded in having Michael to herself at lunch. Perhaps it does not matter now that he has told her - what has he told her? That she is like a Byzantine arch or a woman in a painting by Van Eyck. It will do. She hesitates only a little in joining Gino, sitting glumly by himself over lunch.

"Where is Anna?" she asks him.

"Le ho già detto," says Gino. *"Non le piacciono le vecche pietre."*

"E la caffettiera?" says Fenella, *"è la sua rersponsibilità, no?"*

Gino shrugs. He is not bothered. It is almost the last day.

"Will you marry her - *la sposerà Lei?*" asks Michael wickedly.

"Una donna che non sa fare il caffè in una caffettiera?" asks Gino. *"Come cucinerà in una cucina?"*

"Il matrimonio non è sottanto la cucina," says Fenella, *"c'è altro."*

"Per esempio i bambini, il letto matrimoniale," says Michael.

But Gino is out of sorts today. Perhaps he drank too much strega the night before. He says that two such experts should marry each other - *forse due tali esperti sono degni di sposari.* Fenella looks at the table; Michael tosses his hair back.

"Come on," he says, "I want to go and look at the diver in the Museum."

"He's all wrong, Fen," he explains as they stand gazing at the ancient Greek painting, "his arms and legs and the angle of his head, but it's still absolutely fucking marvellous."

"He's vibrant with life," says Fenella, "even in his tomb. I think that's what you like, Michael." She wants to know what will happen. She is so near, nearer than she has been for twenty years.

"Have to go to the loo," he says, "it's a long way to sit crossing your legs in the coach." He has an unread letter in his pocket. He cannot put off opening it any longer. "Go and buy me a postcard of the diver," he says. "I'll meet you at the coach."

The theme of marriage, mentioned jokingly by Fenella to Gino and sourly by Gino to Michael and Fenella, is to reassert itself.

They come from miles around, the bridal parties, the bride to glide between the columns and pillars of the antique temples, whether through hope of fertility, a yearning for some half-remembered tradition, (the white of the bridal dress contrasting delicately with the stonework), or simply a desire for pretty photos.

There have been at least three bridal parties this afternoon, and this is the last of the three, a very pretty dark girl, her groom and three page boys.

The members of Classic Tours (Southern Italy 1994), standing around waiting for Gino to unlock the coach, regard the wedding party with mixed feelings.

The Brown(e)s make a determined effort not to look. The theme of marriage does not seem a particularly appealing one today.

"Well, it's a good thing I'm not going to be guyed up in all that tulle," says Jane to Gerouin. "I should look a perfect fright." But there is a touch of yearning in her voice. Even in Jane is the little girl who dreams of her wedding dress. Gerouin detects the note of yearning and wishes he could think of something constructive to say, but the truth is, the whole thing is an enormous relief to him. He has had in his mind a picture of his wedding day and Jane going up the aisle in her tracksuit. He can also picture his mother's face. Now all this burden is lifted from his shoulders. He would be a happy man had he not lost his fifty-thousand lire note in the coach the day before yesterday. He imagines (correctly) that he will not see it again.

Mrs Small smiles benignly; she can remember a time some thirty years ago when Roy led her down the aisle. She had never been slim, but she had not been so enormous then, and Roy had been a fine figure of a man in his wedding suit, with his massive leonine head. She thinks how well he has worn; and taking everything into consideration, what a happy and successful marriage it has been: there are six grown-up Small children, all engaged in employment of an academic nature, and Roy himself is perhaps the best-known archaeologist of the century. She herself still does a little teaching. Much of this success can be attributed to her calm and prescient character.

"We shall be celebrating our silver wedding anniversary next year," says Penny. "I'll send you both an invitation."

"That'll be nice, Penny," says Joe. "Cheryl likes a party."

Penny thinks how right that occasion will be. She feels she can meet her husband on equal terms now. For, if he has been unfaithful, so has she. And yet he never need know; and the silver wedding will celebrate the many happy years of their marriage, and some secrets.

Miriam thinks how pretty she looked on her wedding day, and makes a mental note to look through her photos again with Martin when she gets back. Timmy and Joey will like seeing how pretty Mummy looked too.

William reflects on his own marriage with some satisfaction. He is looking forward to getting back now, and sharing a double bed with a woman rather than an empty space. It's been a pretty dull course really. He was well shot of that Miriam. The Brown(e)s too are really very boring women and seem exceedingly frosty this afternoon.

Caroline looks dreamily at the bride as she flits between the columns. She looks too at Fenella and imagines her in such a dress, walking up the aisle with Michael. It is a bitter-sweet thought because, realising that he is far beyond her reach (even though she has been in his arms), she feels that a little of the glory accruing from this aisle-walking may be hers. She identifies with Fenella, she almost *is* Fenella – and, if not, if this thesis isn't entirely convincing, she knows them, she has witnessed their courtship. At the very least, she may be a guest at the wedding – or, if not that, perhaps when viewing a photograph of it, she would be able to say, "I knew them. Once I danced with him. Once I even talked with him in his bedroom. He said he liked my hair."

Gino is unlocking the coach and people are climbing in. It is the last time they will be returning full of knowledge and culture. There is a sense of satisfaction, as well as a wad of handouts, but it is good to have finished with it all. There is something wearisome about too much visiting the past. It makes you uncomfortably aware of your own insignificance.

And now only Michael and Fenella are left outside to regard the temples and the flitting bride. Suddenly he turns to her. He does not toss his hair back or smile his golden smile at her. He looks old and angry.

"No white weddings for you, Fenella," he says coldly. Fenella looks up, surprised and uncomprehending.

"I did have a white wedding," she said. "You told me you came and sat at the back next to..."

"That wasn't your wedding," he says, lighting a cigarette, "and well you know it. Your wedding was on Ithaca."

Fenella touches his arm; she feels fear at his cold tone.

"I think..."

"It wasn't my wedding, though," he continues inexorably, "I was just a seducer, even a rapist, a wandering male seeking..."

"Michael..." Fenella, who is naturally pale-skinned, has gone very white.

"Get into the coach, Fenella," he says, "it is time to go. They are all waiting." He throws his cigarette away and pushes past her into the coach. He is seldom discourteous.

Fenella holds on to the rail while she helps herself into the coach. Gino looks concerned. He imagines they have had a row. He is also fond of Fenella. He thinks her very beautiful and womanly. If she wasn't so loose he would marry her himself.

"*Tutto va bene*?"

"*Va bene*," says Fenella, trying to smile.

Fenella hopes they have all enjoyed Paestum, that it has made a memorable end to the course. The journey back to the hotel will be along the beautiful coastal road, and now the weather is clearer, they will, she hopes, get an even better view than in the morning.

As they know, the flight is at midday tomorrow. The coach will leave the hotel for Naples at nine to allow plenty of time for checking in. She herself will be available until eight o'clock tonight, if there are any last minute problems. She smiles again and sits down next to Michael who is looking out of the window.

"Michael, what are you talking about, what are you...?"

Fenella's plait is coming undone; little stray hairs fall over her face.

"How untidy your hair is," he says.

"I don't understand," says Fenella. Automatically her hand goes to her hair.

"I was talking about marriage," he says, looking at her expressionlessly as she sits next to him, a pile of handouts in her lap.

"Say cheese," says a merry voice. "I must have a little snap of you two for my album." It is Miriam who is poised camera to eye.

"Smile!" says the chirpy voice.

"Oh Miriam, not now," says Fenella.

"Sorry," says Miriam, in a tone that suggests she is not sorry at all.

"Take one of Gino," says Michael, "he's a happy man." And suddenly everyone wants to take a photo of Gino. Michael continues.

"Your marriage, I mean your marriage to Mark, not the event that took place on Ithaca, your marriage to Mark was not successful for various reasons, mainly your inability to be sexually responsive. Is that correct?"

"Yes," whispers Fenella. She looks at the handouts on her lap. She sees that the Temple of Neptune is a hexastyle peripteros with thirty-six fluted columns (fourteen at the side, six at the ends). It keeps running through her head, 'fourteen at the side, six at the end'.

"Unlike your marriage," he continues, "my marriage, my first marriage that is, my second isn't even worth discussing any more than yours is – my first marriage was reasonably successful. My wife Jemima liked to fuck. In fact I fucked her most nights when I was at home, which wasn't that often, if I'm honest. She slept better, she said, after a fuck..."

Gino looks round. His English is very limited, but this is a word he recognises as an interesting one.

"... and if I wasn't there to fuck her, I expect she found it in other places. The MOF used to give her a funny look and there was a nice-looking stable lad. I expect she took a few rolls in the hay with him..."

Fenella looks at the back of Gino's head, 'fourteen at the sides, six at the end'.

"And in case you are wondering, no, I didn't mind. It wasn't of any importance to me. She always presented a good facade; and after all, I didn't live like a monk myself in London. You yourself can vouch for the comfort of the double bed in the flat, and there were others, too whose favours I enjoyed, as no doubt you are aware. Why don't you look at me?"

"I don't know what you're trying to do to me."

"I'm trying to explain to you why my first marriage was successful. Stop fiddling with those handouts and listen to me." He takes them brusquely from her lap and throws them under the seat.

"I am listening."

"It was successful because I was unshackled. Jemima wanted no more of me than I gave her. She wasn't very interested in me. She had absolutely no need of Classics or any interest in my books. She started to read one once and left it out in the garden. One of the children found it months later all sodden and pulpy.

"I provided a little glamour in her life and in that of my daughters. I was an adjunct at a dinner party - an exotic bird.

"But, above all, I was unburdened. I provided a certain amount of money - but I didn't even have to worry about that, Jemima's father provided, I was simply a father figure for the girls, a sort of glamorous preserver of respectability. I didn't know how lucky I was. She told me I'd find out when I married Tabitha, and she was absolutely right."

"Why did you marry Tabitha, then?" Why does he talk on and on about Jemima?

"Because I was vain and greedy. I've told you. I wanted to see myself on television and read about myself in colour supplements."

"No."

"No, you're right. As so often. It was partly that, and partly that I wanted to bring Classics to the masses and stupidly thought I could. Tabitha was the price to pay. Anyway, I'm not talking about her - she's of no interest."

"Jemima is though?"

"Yes. You see, when I'd fucked Jemima she'd turn over and go to sleep. She didn't love me like you." He looks at her blankly. "She wouldn't hold me in her arms all night. She didn't spend her whole life loving me and expecting nothing in return, like you."

"Is that a fault then?" She can no longer remember how many columns.

"Yeah. I can't cope with it, Fenella." He calls her by name for the first time. "It burdens me, it weighs me down. I'm going back to Jemima. Find yourself another man, Fenella. Someone who will appreciate your love."

Her head hangs right down. She remembers it is sixteen at the side.

He looks at her bowed shoulders and speaks harshly.

"It shouldn't be too difficult for you. Look at you." He raises her face with his hand. "You are a beautiful woman, Fenella. There must be many men already..."

"Why did you say those things to me at Amalfi?" She doesn't cry. She feels quite, quite empty. A sort of spasm crosses his face.

"I spoke out of turn, Fenella," he repeats, "I spoke out of turn." He takes his eyes off her and looks out down the cliffs at the sea below. The scenery is unbelievably beautiful.

"You are very good at telling me you do not want me any more, in public places," says Fenella, "but even when you told me..."

"Gesù Christo," says Gino; a car narrowly misses them on the bend of the road.

"... but even when you told me in that restaurant in Soho..." and even now she can see the crème caramel all messed about with her spoon, "... you were getting married, you did not speak to me so harshly, so cruelly as now. I don't understand." She is vaguely aware of sea below the cliffs.

"I received a letter some days ago from her. I have been carrying it about unopened. I have now opened it. I am telling you the consequences of its contents."

"There will be no more courses," says Fenella blankly.

"No."

"Please," says Fenella, "take your things from my room when we get back."

"Of course," he says. There is nothing further to say. Fenella never makes scenes.

Chapter XXXV

The Maenad

Michael has been lying on his bed in his room, smoking incessantly. He has filled the ashtray and is now using an ornamental vase. Eventually he gets up, puts a new packet of cigarettes in his pocket and goes to room 341, which is Fenella's. It isn't locked and he walks in.

He has not known what to expect. He has believed she will not try to harm herself because she has not done so before, but he is nevertheless shocked by what he sees.

Much of Fenella's beauty lies in a sweetness and a serenity of expression. She is the sort of woman you can imagine leading a child by the hand. You feel she will be bothered if you are unhappy. But put beside this a mass of (more or less) natural curly gold hair and huge blue eyes, there is something of Boticelli's Venus. But there is an even stronger appeal; whether it is her large breasts or something pouting about the lips, Fenella is potently sexually attractive; an effect that is enhanced by the impression that this attractiveness is not at all contrived, but is some integral part of her. It is as if it is something over which she has no control, as if she is innocent of it. Men have looked at Fenella and wished they might possess this sexuality. All, except Michael, have been disappointed.

Now Fenella has done something horrible to herself. The innocence that is so much part of the pure Fenella that Michael loves, is gone. She would command a high price in Soho.

Her hair, there seems masses of it, is half up and half down, piled above the forehead and hanging down about her ears and the nape of her neck, and has a wild and sticky quality to it. Fenella, who seldom wears much make-up, is painted. Her eyes are outlined heavily in black; her lashes are long and lustrous; there is a high colour on her cheeks. Her lips, the pouting lips, are large and scarlet. She wears earrings that dangle, and round her neck are many necklaces. But there is worse. She has been surprised in the midst of her body painting. Kohl has outlined not only her eyes, but also the breasts with the shell-pink nipples that Gerouin once glimpsed. Her belly button, too, is featured. She has not ended there. She has moved lower down to highlight her other attractions.

"Come in," she says. "I knew you wouldn't be able to keep away." Her eyes, which are usually so soft and large appear narrow and slitty. Her smile is not the sweet one he knows. Only her hands clench and unclench.

"Christ almighty," he says. His fingers move to his mouth and he bites the left hand nail of his first finger. He stares at her, appalled. She smiles again, perhaps a little less certainly.

"You didn't want my love," she says, "the love of twenty years; you didn't care that I nursed you when you were sick, that I held your head while you vomited over me. You didn't care that I soothed and caressed you when you were tormented. You didn't want that. You threw it back at me."

"Fenella..."

"Listen. You wanted none of that; even though you said you did, you didn't. You wanted the darkness, you wanted what Robin Box wanted, you wanted what Percival wanted; you wanted that darkness you see in your dreams."

"Fenella..."

"So I have laid aside my love; I cannot rid myself of it, I have told you; but I have laid it aside, I have stripped myself of it. I too wish to experience the darkness. I too will seek for pleasure myself. Come. You need fear no love. I want to experience what the maenads experienced in the mountains..." Her hands unclench and move downwards.

"If you do not wish to join me, you may watch, like Pentheus before he was torn apart by his mother Agape. I..."

But before she can continue he has her by the waist and is half carrying, half dragging her into the shower. With one hand he turns it on full and holds her by the neck underneath. The jet of water, as she struggles, drenches him. He takes no notice, but continues holding her underneath.

"Let go of me," she says, but his hand is at her neck, clutching.

"Listen," he says, "I have listened to you."

The water spurts downwards at full speed; they are both wet, he clothed and she naked.

"I am not going back to my wife," he says, releasing the pressure on her neck, "even supposing she would have me. I am no longer so desirable."

"What do you mean?" she says. The water is cold. She is gasping and trembling. He adjusts the switch.

"Stand still," he says. He takes the sponge and soap in his hand and begins to soap her.

"I lied to you," he says. "Shut your eyes. I want to get the black off. All right, you can open them now. There. That's better. More like my Fen." She stands unresisting. "I've had lots of tests, Fenella. No, it's not AIDS, not even I am as irresponsible as that. I'm going to die."

"Michael, you're..."

"Hush. I don't know too much about it yet. The letter. It wasn't from Jemima; it was from the consultant. I should have gone back. I haven't."

"But what..."

He smiles at her; there is a touch of the golden still in the smile. "I didn't want you to know." He switches off the shower. Her arms go round him making him still wetter.

"Darling."

He picks up a towel and drapes it round her.

"Tell me," she murmurs.

"I didn't want you to know," he says, rubbing her dry. "Come and lie down."

"Take your wet things off," she says.

"Mm," he says obediently.

****

"It started with the dreams," he says.

They are lying beneath the duvet, holding each other for warmth and comfort.

"They couldn't find anything; but they have now."

"But you don't know..." says Fen. "It may be curable." Her curls, lost in the wetness, straggle over the pillow; there are still smudges of black on her pale face.

"Ask Kate," he says.

"What do you mean?"

"At Cumae. I could tell. She couldn't see anything for me."

"Oh," says Fenella, "that's nothing."

"Blackness," he says with a shudder. "I didn't want to tell you," he says. "I thought I'd be nasty and send you away. I didn't want..." he sighs deeply, "I didn't want to bother you any more."

"Oh, darling," says Fenella, "you've bothered me for twenty years. I'm not going to let you stop me now."

He buries his head in her breasts. She strokes his wet hair. They lie for a long time in silence.

She has a strange mixture of emotions. She cannot believe that he is ill, nor that he will die. He has looked older, tireder, but he *is* older. It is two years since they were last together. If he is tireder, it is no surprise. He has been going through an unpleasant divorce. He has been sick, but that is due to drinking too much. He has bad dreams; but that is part of him and his imagination. Anyway, what do consultants know?

So there is an unreality to this; but what she does know is that he is not returning to his wife; he is lying naked and shivering between her breasts and has great need of her. So out of it all is a great feeling of overpowering happiness. The future is as unimportant as the past. It is only now that has any reality.

"Make love to me," she says, "Michael, darling, please."

He raises his face from her breasts and she sees for a moment emotion that she has not seen before: his hair hangs wetly over his forehead and in his eyes is fear, vulnerability, love even? The look is transitory. The old

Michael reasserts himself, "'With', Fenny," he says, "you prefer to say 'with'."

She pulls him down on her and stops his mouth with kisses; but he has more yet to say.

"You are very polite," he says, "in asking me to give you what I once snatched so roughly from you."

"You have never," she says, caressing him, "taken anything I have not wanted to give, and I'll never," she opens her legs and guides him within, "stop giving, whatever."

As he takes her breasts in his hands and moves within her, he is no longer capable of conscious thought, but the guilt, fear and despair of the last day are subsumed within the strength of this primordial act. As she draws him and draws him with the intensity of her passion, this woman who he had taken as virgin twenty years ago, his mind empties of thought and the words that he speaks are not formed within his consciousness: "I love you, Fenella." And she cries aloud like a woman giving birth, but whether from pain or pleasure she cannot tell.

Chapter XXXVI

Gatwick

"I think she should have accompanied us back," says Miss Aitchinson to Penny and Joe as they stand waiting for their luggage to come round on the carousel at Gatwick.

"I don't see why," says Joe. "She got us to Naples. There wasn't much she could do if the plane went down. After all, it says in the Cambridge Latin..."

"I see you're using your stick again," says Penny, interrupting impatiently. She has been waiting for ages, and she wants to see Patrick.

"Yes, I fear the beneficial effect of the Italian climate has worn off," says Margaret.

"So soon?" asks Penny; but Miss Aitchinson has seen her one small case coming round. The stick is useful for getting to it. She does not bother saying goodbye to anyone. The others, anyway, are lost in the throng. She does not suppose that she will see any of them again. She hopes Miss Fielding next door has remembered to order her a pint of milk.

"Thanks for everything, Penny," says Joe as Penny gathers up her cases (he is still waiting for the tripod to come round), "don't forget that invitation to your silver wedding party." She smiles vaguely. He can tell that she has already moved on.

****

Percival stands by himself. He has retrieved one case, the one that contains his clothes; he is still waiting for the important one, the one that holds his papers and the hundred handouts on Baiae (ninety-nine, he has given one to Fenella – he regretted that now). She and Thorpe-Smith had been most unpleasant over a small incident of no importance. He is tempted to write and complain about both of them, but he will be too busy writing papers based on the measurements he has taken in Italy. There will be a job application to be written too; he has seen an advertisement for a private tutoring job. It sounds ideal, the boy is eight years old. A disciplinarian is needed. Ah! There is the case with its precious load.

****

"Can I carry anything, Caroline?" asks Colin. He feels much bolder now he knows he won't be seeing her again. Caroline smiles. She feels well-disposed to him for the same reason.

"It looks as if you've got plenty to carry of your own," she says. "I suppose your box is empty now?"

"Yes," he says.

"What did you do in the end about the Boxes' cups?"

"I gave them to Gino and Anna. Anna asked me."

"What on earth do they want with them?"

He smiles and Caroline asks herself why she has never noticed before what a nice smile he has.

"I expect they'll sell them," he says, "or perhaps they want a memory of the course too. Quite a lot of things happened really, didn't they?"

It is one of the longest speeches he has made over the course of the week. It is, after all, surprisingly easy. A lot has happened! Caroline considers this as she gathers her bags and cases. Had it? A lot of things might have happened. She might have had a mad affair with Michael ("you're bound to have a nice passionate time with hair your colour"). She might even have struck up some sort of relationship with Colin. But in the event, nothing had happened. Nothing much ever did with her. No, that wasn't true; she'd met some nice people and she had lots of useful slides and handouts for school. And she had her memories; it wasn't every girl who had been in the arms of Michael Thorpe-Smith.

Colin hasn't finished yet. "You know that photo Joe took of us all in Capri? Well, he's going to get lots of copies made and I'm going to get my father to make some pewter frames, and send everyone a copy."

It is so much easier to give people things than to talk to them.

"Everyone? You mean including the Boxes?" They both have their cases; they make towards the Customs together.

"Well, they were part of it, weren't they?"

"I suppose they were."

For a moment he toys with the idea of asking her to the dinner dance again; but he decides against it. It would involve him in an awful lot of explanation to people.

"Well, goodbye, Caroline."

"Goodbye, Colin. Have a good term."

Soon she is swallowed up by the crowd. For a while he can see her straggly red hair, but soon that too disappears as she makes her lonely way towards the rest of her life.

****

It's really typical isn't it, that out of all those men on the course there isn't a single one to give her a hand with her smart little suitcases (and matching vanity case)? She can see William bustling after the Brownes. What a silly little man he is! How could she ever... Well, all that's in the past now. Timmy and Joey will like their presents, so will Martin. Perhaps she'll just pop into the Ladies' and do her face. She wants to be looking her best when they see her again. Well no, perhaps she won't go to the Ladies' after all. There is Kate Small lumbering towards it. She is best avoided. You never know what she might say. It's good to be back in England, and she won't have to march round any more boring sites. Still, it's not all bad, Italy. She might go back one day, not on a course though. On her own perhaps.

****

"Now, is there anything else I can take?" asks William of the Brown(e) trio. He reflects there is going to be a lot of fetching and carrying from now on. He realises now what a respite there has been from it in Italy. The days of liberty are over. In his household is the pushchair, and the pram, a baby bath too, with an angular stand that snaps tight on the finger and once, he remembers, on the groin. There is a machine for disposing of paper nappies and another for warming tins of baby food. There is a folding cot and a bottle-washing machine, an apparatus for carrying the baby on the back, and another for clamping it to the front. All have straps to be adjusted. It is a life's work. It is easier to be teaching at school. The tedium of the sites is a small price to pay for the avoidance of the everlasting coping.

He is free of the Brownes at least. They are all three in a hurry to get through Customs to be met by a small bespectacled man in a sports jacket.

"A very good course," says Sally.

"Rather overshadowed, I should say," says Alice in her whining voice, "by some unsavoury events."

"It's nice to be home," says Jennifer.

But whether or not she is right lies in the ineffectual hands of the little man in the sports jacket, who has come to meet all of the three women in his life. The fourth he had not noticed; he had even been busy avoiding an aggressive-looking person with a stick.

****

"Do you want the ring back then?" asks Jane. She has her luggage. Only Gerouin's seems not to have appeared.

"Oh no, Jane. You keep it," says Gerouin, looking anxiously at the suitcases as they pass him by.

"Well, I'll be getting on then," says Jane, "I've a long drive back."

"Oh yes," says Gerouin. Not only have the suitcases not appeared, but he can't seem to find his passport.

"We've had a nice time," says Jane. There is something a little wistful in her tone. It occurs to him that she is perhaps waiting for him to say or do something, but he cannot think what because of the suitcases and the passport. So he says, "Goodbye, Jane. Have a good term."

"And you," says Jane. She hesitates for a few seconds more and then makes up her mind. She gives him a great smacking kiss and is gone. There will not perhaps be much more kissing in Jane's life, nor in Gerouin's either.

****

The Smalls, veterans of air travel, as much of their lives has been spent in flying to faraway digs, gaze unconcerned at the carousel. Kate has found a ledge on which to lean her bulk.

"How long are they staying in Italy?" asks Roy.

"Until Fenella persuades him to go back, I suppose," says Kate. "He's an awful coward really. He's even scared of the dark. Don't you remember in Turkey when he always had to sleep with the light on?"

"That's only because he's got more of a vivid imagination than most people," says Roy. "We'd all be scared if we saw what he saw."

"There's my case," explains Kate.

"Is he really ill?" asks Roy, returning with Kate's case, which is surprisingly small considering the size of the clothes it must hold.

"I don't know," says Kate. "All I know is that at Cumae I couldn't see anything for him except blackness."

"Well," says Roy, "not even you are always right, Kate. Look, there's my case too."

"Oh good," says Kate, "now we can go and eat something before we go home."

Epilogue

"You see," says Fenella brightly, "there are masses of birds, even the name Avernus is not right."

The scholar in Michael asserts itself.

"Avernus doesn't mean 'birdless'; people misunderstand the Greek 'aomos'. Anyway," he adds grumpily, "it's still the gate to the Underworld, and the birds are on my left. Any Roman worth his salt knows that's a sign of impending disaster."

"Rubbish," says Fenella, "there's loads over to the right as well! Look!"

They gaze over the lake. It is a lovely day; sunlight glints on the low surface of the water and catches the leaves of the holm oaks that surround it, making great pools of light.

"I think it was a sort of joke on Virgil's part," says Fenella, "making Avernus the entry to the Underworld. Everybody would have known it wasn't scary at all; it was just the sort of place to come and have a picnic. So eat up your *panino* and have some more wine. Come on, darling."

They are sitting on the wall at the lakeside, the picnic basket between them. The sun is hot upon them. Fenella has bought Michael a big shady hat to protect his head, as there is no longer a lock of hair to pull over his forehead.

"Perhaps," he says, not eating his *panino*, "it is at Lake Nemi that the entrance to the Underworld lies."

But Fenella thinks they have spoken enough about the Underworld. She says, "By the way, I had a letter from Kate today. Nigel has got his scholarship. Apparently he was lucky. He got a Latin unseen that he had done before with Kate. A bit of Pliny."

"Boring old fart," remarks Michael. "Which bit was it?"

"I've got the Latin paper here," says Fenella, "Kate thought you might like to see it. I don't know which bit it was." She rummages in her bag in which she keeps Michael's medicines. She is as efficient in her role as nurse as she was as courier with Classic Tours.

"Let me have a look," he says.

Fenella is pleased to see he is no longer thinking of the Underworld and hands him a paper; in taking it he knocks over his stick which has been balanced against the wall.

"You're worse than Miss Aitchinson," says Fenella fondly.

"Yes," he says, "at least she managed to hold on to hers."

"And trip a few people up along the way," says Fenella brightly. "Poor old thing," she adds.

He puts his arm round her. "How sweet you always are, Fenella," he says, "how good."

"Balls," says Fenella, changing the conversation, "let's see if I can translate the Pliny as well as Nigel."

She leans her head on his shoulder gently, knowing he cannot bear too much weight. Once, many many years ago, before she went to university, before she went to Ithaca, she had done A level Latin. She had been good at it, as she is good at most things. There are one or two words she doesn't remember, but she understands the gist of it well enough.

"What do you think of it, Fenella?" he asks, looking at her intently.

"Well," says Fenella lightly, "I'm never very good with subjunctives." She wishes they had never chosen to read this particular piece.

"It's very easy really," he says gently, "look, there's only one tricky subjunctive, *morerentur... simul morerentur*. You know what it means, I think. Will you translate it for me, Fenella?"

But she cannot or will not speak. She can only shake her head. So he does it for her, speaking slowly,

"'She begged her husband that they might die together.'" He takes her hand where the new wedding ring lies. "She was a brave woman, wasn't she, Fenella?" he says.

Fenella looks out over the lake where the sunlight glints. She remembers words spoken in a bedroom at Gaeta, a bedroom that was as green as a pistachio nut:

"It would be terribly lonely, the Underworld, wouldn't it, Fen? Black and lonely." And she had replied, oh so stoutly, "Not if I was there with you."

As she continues to look at the lake she sees on the surface of its glistening sunlit waters the faces of her two dear children who love her so much, and whom she has brought up so carefully. She knows she cannot do the thing that he asks and turns to tell him so. She does not, however, see the tired worn face she has become used to since her marriage, but another face superimposed upon it, the face of a young man with azure eyes and shoulder length sun-bleached hair. Michael, ill as he is, is smiling his golden smile. They both know she has never resisted him in all the years that have passed since he made her so irrevocably his, in the torchlight outside the Cave of the Nymphs on the island of Ithaca.